MYS

THE BREAKFAST CLUB MURDER

CAMILLA T. CRESPI

FIVE STAR
A part of Gale, Cengage Learning

GALE
CENGAGE Learning®

Detroit • New York • San Francisco • New Haven, Conn • Waterville, Maine • London

GALE
CENGAGE Learning®

LIBRARY OF CONGRESS CATALOGING-IN-PUBLICATION DATA

Crespi, Camilla T.
    The breakfast club murder / Camilla T. Crespi. — First edition.
        pages cm
    ISBN 978-1-4328-2805-9 (hardcover) — ISBN 1-4328-2805-3 (hardcover)
      1. Wives—Crimes against—Fiction. 2. Divorced mothers—Fiction. 3. Caterers and catering—Fiction. I. Title.
PS3553.R435B74 2014
813'.54—dc23   2013038374

First Edition. First Printing: February 2014
Find us on Facebook— https://www.facebook.com/FiveStarCengage
Visit our website— http://www.gale.cengage.com/fivestar/
Contact Five Star™ Publishing at FiveStar@cengage.com

Printed in Mexico
1 2 3 4 5 6 7 18 17 16 15 14

ACKNOWLEDGMENTS

I thank Denise Dailey and Augusta Gross for their excellent advice; Judy Moskowitz for listening and encouraging me; Annette Meyers for introducing me to Five Star; Stuart, my husband, for his patience; and Diane M. Piron-Gelman for her meticulous editing.

CHAPTER 1

The Park Avenue doorman stepped out into the windswept rain and blew his whistle while the tall couple waited in the comfort of the wood-paneled lobby.

Tomorrow, Saturday, Robert Staunton—the new owner of apartment 7J and a partner in the law firm of Bellows, Stein, Jeffreys, and Berne—was going to be married to thin, beautiful, and successful Valerie Fenwick, DDS, a woman he had met while she drilled holes in his teeth. Many hundreds of dollars and dental sessions later, Rob had emerged from her care with healthy teeth and a great desire to sleep with her, which he succeeded in doing, as he succeeded in most things he set his sights on. The idea of marrying her only came up a year and half later, when he got careless and his wife of twenty years, Lori Corvino Staunton, found out.

"You should get the car," Valerie said as they left the lobby, tossing her slithery blond mane for emphasis. They were late for the dinner Rob's partners were throwing for them at Nobu57. "We'll never get a cab in this weather."

"The garage is four blocks away," Rob said. Sitting through dinner with wet feet would probably give him a cold. "And I'll never find a place to park."

Valerie gave Rob's chest a soft punch. "I can't believe I'm marrying such a wuss." She waved to the doorman, whose name she hadn't bothered to learn. "Forget the cab." She wrapped her black silk raincoat around her and started sprinting to the corner in her high-heeled sandals.

"Val, what are you doing?" Rob shouted, suddenly feeling abandoned.

The doorman joined him under the protection of the building's canopy. "I believe she's getting the car, sir."

"Oh, for God's sake!" Rob ran after Valerie, who was now crossing the dark side street, dodging between a steady stream of cars. Despite the heavy rain, no one was stopping to let her by.

"Come back, Val," Rob shouted as a gust of drenched wind slapped his face. He plunged into the street toward his fiancée. "Wait up!"

Valerie turned, saw Rob coming, and slipped under the shallow roof of the open phone booth on the corner to wait for him.

Rob, halfway across the street, turned his head toward two glowing headlights speeding through the rain toward him. He stopped to stare, his brain suddenly empty of all thought.

"Watch out!" Valerie shouted, running toward Rob. He felt the front of his raincoat being yanked. The air behind him whooshed. Tires splashed. As he fell on the curb, a wave of filthy water washed over him.

"You almost killed him!" Valerie shouted at the red taillights as the car turned and sped down Park Avenue. Still holding on to the lapel of Rob's raincoat, she contemplated her soon-to-be-husband for a moment. Anyone looking at her would have supposed she was having second thoughts. "Honey," she said finally as she bent over Rob and helped him to his feet. "You've got to watch where you're going."

Safely on the sidewalk, Rob tried to wipe his face with his handkerchief. More rain wet it. One knee throbbed. The palms of his hands burned. He felt anger grip his bones, make them brittle. Anger and fear. When he had crossed the street, there had been a wide gap between cars. The car that hit him—well, would have hit him if Valerie hadn't been so quick to pull him away—the driver had come down on him on purpose, he was sure of it. Was it a warning?

"Did you get the license plate?" he asked Valerie.

She shook her head and pulled at his arm. "Come on, honey. I'm getting soaked to the skin."

Inside the lobby of the apartment building Mike O'Connor, the head doorman, watched the scene with his second in command. He was well aware that duty dictated he run out with a sturdy umbrella and help the new tenants, but Mike considered himself a shrewd judge of people after years in the business. He had this couple pegged. No matter how much he and his colleagues put themselves out, the Christmas envelope of Mr. Staunton Esquire and his toothpick dentist wife would be meager. Besides, he'd had enough of getting wet for one night.

CHAPTER 2

Lori took a bite. There was nothing more sensual than good food. Sensual. Reassuring. Uplifting. Utterly redeeming. Her tongue pressed the tiny pillows of dough against the roof of her mouth. Butter, Parmesan, creamy tomato slid across her taste buds. Tomorrow it was back to the States and a future punctured with question marks, but now, sitting under a canopy of stars and wisteria in an elegant Roman restaurant, with a breeze lifting the ruffles of the silk dress she had splurged on that afternoon and the best gnocchi she'd ever tasted warming her mouth, Lori thought she was doing just fine.

"That looks good," the craggy-faced, bespectacled American at the next table said, just as she swallowed. Up to now, she had welcomed the Italian restaurant habit of bunching Americans together, but this evening, for her last meal here, she wasn't in the mood to compare travel notes and make chitchat with a stranger, even if he was American.

"What's the Italian name for it?" the stranger asked. Lori shook her head, pretending her mouth was still full of gnocchi. What it was full of was a luscious aftertaste that should have made her nice enough to answer. She took another bite instead, and this time didn't swallow right away.

"I'm sorry, I should have introduced myself. Alec Winters." The man smiled.

Lori pointed to her mouth, truly full this time, and went back to basking in the taste of the yummy gnocchi, trying to memorize it. Whisking from her purse the small leather-bound notebook she'd bought on her first day in Venice, Lori started writing. Fresh tomatoes, a little onion, butter, a hint of nutmeg, basil, lemon zest. What else? There was an extra richness she couldn't decipher. Some kind of cheese.

"Are you a restaurant critic?" the man asked.

He has a kind face, Lori thought. "I'm not," she said. Her husband's face had looked kind when he announced he was turning her in for a newer model. She waved to the waiter, who sauntered over. "This dish is fabulous," she announced.

He bowed, taking credit. "*Gnocchi della regina*. Gnocchi fit for a queen. A house specialty."

"I'm a food journalist for the *Greenwich Dish*," Lori said, handing him her business card. Real name, real address. Fake job. "I would love to write about the restaurant and give my readers this recipe."

It was a ruse her friend Beth had suggested during their last lunch together on Beth's deck. Lori had made tuna and fennel sandwiches on focaccia and brought a bottle of an expensive Chardonnay.

"I don't like dishonesty," she had protested as she crunched into her sandwich.

"Here, drink up and get over it. You'll come home with fabulous recipes to start off your catering career."

"Not a start, a re-launch," Lori corrected. After sixteen years it wasn't going to be easy, but she was determined to prove to herself and to her daughter, Jessica, that she could stand on her own. "I know you mean well, Beth, but I've had enough of lies."

For revenge, Beth drank most of the wine and then offered instant coffee.

Lori found the business cards tucked in her satchel after she boarded the flight. She had no intention of using them, but while eating a superb crabmeat risotto in Venice she could never duplicate on her own, accompanied by half a carafe of sparkling Prosecco, Lori decided she deserved a few lies of her own. White, innocent ones, nothing like the ones Rob had told her.

Lori tried smiling at the Roman waiter, but didn't bring it off. Either she'd forgotten how, which was entirely possible, or she didn't want to be that hypocritical. She hoped it was the latter. "Can you please ask the chef for the recipe?"

Out came the charming, full-of-regret smile she'd discovered was an Italian specialty whenever she asked for something they had no intention of giving you. "*Mi dispiace, signora.* It is a family secret."

Before Lori could start to plead, Alec Winters stood up and pushed himself through the small space between the two tables. Suddenly Lori saw her table tilt, watched helplessly as the plate of hot, sauce-laden gnocchi slid down and overturned on her lap. With a cry, she shot up from her chair. The plate crashed to the floor and every diner in the place turned to gape at her. Her mind flashed back to another evening in a fancy restaurant in Greenwich. She'd thrown a glass of red wine in her husband's face. A roomful of diners had gaped at her then, too. Lori held back a scream of rage as the American leaned into her and put a hand on her elbow. She heard a mumble of words, saw his other hand wave a napkin in front of her. She shrank back. He pushed forward. The carafe fell over, splashing red wine all over both of them. Lori stayed rooted to the spot, fighting the humiliation of tears as the waiter offered more napkins, as the man, Alec Winters, offered to pay for the cleaning, offered to pay for the meal, offered to buy her a new dress.

"I don't want your money," Lori cried out. She threw the napkins back at the waiter, fumbled in her bag for euros, dropped them on the table and ran out of there.

Alec followed. "Please let me help. I can't tell you how sorry I am. Please. It was all my fault. Let me make it up to you."

Lori whipped around. "I've gotten really good at taking care of myself." He was unexpectedly tall. She had to crane her neck to look him in the eye. "I don't need your help. I don't need anybody's help. Got that?"

He took off his glasses and nodded.

"Great!" Lori walked away at as fast a clip as her high heels could manage on the cobblestones, her chest throbbing with anger, shame, hurt. She was a good person. She had given up work to be Rob's wife, had cooked countless meals for the law firm's partners, for his clients. When Jessica came along, she divided herself, her time, between the two of them. Everything had gone wrong anyway. She didn't deserve this last humiliation. She didn't deserve any of it.

The *pensione* was a twenty-minute walk away through meandering narrow streets. Lori slipped off her heels and walked on the cobblestones still hot from the June sun. In the dark no one saw the mess her dress was in, the mess she was in. In the dark, Lori let herself cry for the first time since she and Rob divorced eight months ago.

The *pensione* owner handed over Lori's room key without giving her a glance. On the one hand, she was grateful. On the other, she resented being invisible. It was a familiar see-saw. Since she had found out about Valerie, her moods had gone from one day raging to be the center of the whole universe's attention, the next shutting down and hiding from everyone.

In the hotel room, Lori took off her new dress. She wiped off as much of the sauce and wine as she could with a towel. There was no chance it was going to come clean; the silk was too thin and fragile, but she wrapped the dress in the tissue from the store, making sure to fold over the front so that it wouldn't stain her other clothes. She was going to keep the dress as a reminder of her past—irretrievably stained, but with its beauty still showing. Lori felt better after that good cry. Not everything had gone wrong with her life. She had Jessica, her independent, willful, and wonderful daughter, who was thirteen but vacillated between thirty-five and two. She had her home. Her friends, Beth, Margot, Janet. Her impossible mother. And soon, she hoped, she'd have herself back.

Getting ready for bed, Lori avoided the mirror over the dresser. She knew only too well what she'd see: an oval face, large hooded brown eyes, and a long nose that showed her Italian heritage. Full lips she had to stop biting. A forehead ruled with frown lines. A parenthesis of folded skin edged down from her nose to her mouth. She was ready to blame all her aging on Rob. After all, she'd lost her husband and her dentist.

Lori brushed her teeth. Who in his right mind fell in love with a dentist? Sure, dental costs were very high, but Rob's insurance included dental. To add insult to injury, Valerie was a year older than she was. Weren't men supposed to leave their wives for young, sexy babes? All right, some people might consider Valerie beautiful in an anorexic, flat-chested way, but Rob always claimed, while they were grabbing at each other, that he loved Lori's big breasts, her full ass. God, why was she going over this again? Lori stood up. "Don't forget you're great!" a self-help guru had decreed in one of dozens of How-to-Survive-Divorce books she'd devoured. She couldn't remember the last time she felt she was great, if ever, but she had only herself to work with, so she'd have to do.

As Lori moved, the bathroom light caught the prominent streak of gray cutting across one side of her thick, dark hair. She'd had it since her early twenties, a legacy from her now-dead father. That streak had made Rob give her a second glance when he'd spotted her at the party she was catering, and during the early years Rob would nuzzle against her, run his hands through her hair and call her his sweet-smelling skunk. She'd get all squishy inside, knowing he wanted to make love to her. The day the divorce was final she'd gotten a pixie cut, dyed the streak black. Jessica had burst into tears when she came home. "You don't look you!" Now the gray was growing out, her hair covered her ears, and she was gaining back the weight she'd lost in the last eight months, which pleased both her and Jessica. They were both used to a rounder woman.

Jessica was with her father now. Today. His wedding day. Well, it was over by now, and Valerie was officially Rob's wife and Jessica's stepmother. Jessica had pleaded to be allowed to go to the wedding. The thought of it still made Lori tremble with hurt and anger. She'd wanted to forbid it, wanted to yell to her daughter, "I know you hurt, but I do, too. I need you. Stay on my side." Instead she had told Jessica she was free to go if that was what she wanted, then picked up the phone and booked a flight to Italy. Lori felt betrayed, even though part of her understood Jessica's need to be included in her father's new life, her fear of being pushed aside by her father's new woman. But Lori's feelings were so raw she had no control over them.

After a long shower, Lori finished packing, checked her airline ticket for the umpteenth time, asked the concierge to wake her at eight a.m. so she would have plenty of time to get to the airport and go through security. Once in bed, she tried to read the mystery she'd brought with her, but the bedside light was too dim, she was too tired. She turned the lamp off and found herself thinking about the tall American standing in the small restaurant piazza, taking off his glasses as if to show her how sincere he was, nodding to her. A cluster of wisteria dangling over his head had given him a comic look. Craggy face with sharp cheekbones, dust-colored hair limp across his forehead. A studious face. A kind face. A harmless man who tried to help. She regretted treating him badly, regretted even more showing her own vulnerability. Her list of regrets was so long she started counting them and fell asleep.

Lori stands in her bedroom of the Connecticut house she's lived in with Rob since she was pregnant with Jessica, all dressed up in her new silk dress and impossibly high stilettos. "Isn't it beautiful?" she asks Jessica, who is looking at her from the doorway. "You could never be beautiful," Jessica answers and disappears. As Lori runs out of the room to find her, one of her heels catches on the edge of the carpet and she falls. When she picks herself up, her chin is bleeding down her dress and she is standing on an unpaved country road lined with poplars. In the distance she can see Jessica's long legs scissoring the air. Lori kicks off her heels and runs after her. "Wait for me!" Jessica turns, waves and keeps running. A car speeds past Lori, covering her with dust. She starts to cough and recognizes Rob's new Mercedes. The car overtakes Jessica and brakes to a stop. The passenger door flings open. Jessica jumps, the door closes, and the road is suddenly empty.

Lori woke up, snapped on the lamp. One twenty-three a.m., seven twenty-three a.m. in New York, a Sunday. Jessica would still be asleep in Rob's new apartment in Manhattan, but if she waited any longer, Jessica might be having breakfast with her dad and the new Mrs. Robert Staunton. It was now or never. Lori reached for the phone and dialed Jessica's cell number.

Jessica answered after the first ring. "Who is it?"

"Jessica, sweetie."

"Mom! What are you doing?"

"I know I wasn't supposed to call, but I love you and I've missed you so much and I wanted to apologize for being angry at you. Can you forgive me?"

"I can't talk! I don't even know why I answered this stupid phone. God, Mom, how could you?" Her words sounded like the hiss of a cornered cat.

Lori felt them like a jab in her stomach. "Did I wake you? Is that it?"

"Wake me? Do you know what time it is? Seven thirty p.m. Valerie's about to walk down the aisle!"

Lori groaned. She'd gotten it all wrong. New York was six hours back, not forward. Why was she so dumb? Why couldn't she get her act together? Why? Why? Why? "Oh sweetie, I'm so sorry. I got confused."

"I don't believe you." Jessica started to cry. "Oh shit, now I'm going to look terrible."

Listening to Jessica's sobs, a boulder dropped on Lori's chest. "Jessica, you can never look terrible, you hear me? You're beautiful even when you cry and please don't use that word. I'm going to hang up now and you're going to wipe your face with a tissue. You will always look beautiful and you're going to be fine. I love you, honey."

Lori hung up and lay back on the bed. *My poor sweet daughter. She's scared about the future, just like I am. Except Jessica's thirteen. In a couple of years she'll be clamoring to get away from her parents, to throw her beautiful self at what life has to offer on her own. I'm forty-one, look sixty, feel eighty.*

Lori snapped off the light and closed her eyes. Her mother's voice pierced the darkness. "Lori Corvino, stop feeling sorry for yourself this minute!"

For once she was right. And yet . . . Lori breathed deeply and tried to release the tension in her body, something that she was learning in Pilates class. And yet . . . she had to help Jessica and also help herself. How?

CHAPTER 3

Lori walked through the double doors of the customs area at Kennedy into the crowded arrival area. A line of darkly dressed men held up signs with names on them. It brought back the memory of the only other time she came home from abroad—a summer trip to Europe with Beth right after graduating from college. She'd been dating Rob for about a year and he was furious that she preferred ten days in foreign lands with Beth to his company in steamy New York State. Lori was flattered by Rob's need for her, mistook it for devotion. She invited him to come along, out of loyalty more than desire, as she knew he would require all her attention and she wanted a last girl fling with Beth before they both plunged into new jobs—Beth as a social worker at the public high school in Hawthorne Park, and Lori as the owner of a company of one, Corvino Catering. Rob saw no reason to travel that far. "Not even for you." Only later did Lori learn that he was terrified of flying.

As Beth and Lori walked out of customs, Lori had seen Rob in the front row of men, dressed in a dark suit, with a chauffeur's hat on his head. When he saw Beth and Lori coming, he held up his sign, which read: *Mrs. Robert Staunton?* It had been such an exhilarating moment, the surprise of it had left Lori dumbstruck. Beth had to push her forward into Rob's arms. Lori and Rob were married three years later, a week after Rob graduated from law school. Beth was her only bridesmaid.

Now Lori was standing alone, in a line for the van that would take her back home to Hawthorne Park, willing the memory away. The Connecticut van eased in front of her and stopped. The driver got out, swung the back door open, and began to stow luggage. As Lori moved up the line, she felt a tap on her shoulder.

"Let me give you lift." Rob, without a sign this time, looking even more handsome, more tanned, nineteen years later.

Lori turned cold. "Is Jessica all right?"

"Yes, she's fine. I just dropped her home." His smile was re-assuring, believable. Why was he here then—a day after he married someone else? And why hadn't she put on makeup, combed her hair before getting off the plane? So many times she had fantasized about looking drop-dead gorgeous when she ran into Rob for the first time after their divorce. Well, not drop dead, but at least really good, and instead she looked like something the dog had slept on. If they had a dog, which they didn't because Rob was allergic. Good, she would get a dog. A golden retriever that shed a lot of hair. That way Rob could never come back to the house. Great idea.

"Go away, Rob." She reached down to pick up her suitcase. Rob grabbed the handle before Lori had a chance to. Bent close to his head, she smelled a new musky scent on him. Of course, that's how it should be. He or Valerie had probably thrown out that last bottle of Armani she'd bought him just days before she found Valerie's love note in his coat pocket.

"I'm taking the van, Rob. Suitcase or no suitcase."

"We need to talk. The car isn't far." He walked away with Lori's suitcase. Everything always on his terms. Even after the divorce. She meant to stand up to him. She had the strength for it finally—fury had poured concrete into her backbone—but she guessed that his need to talk had to do with Jessica. They had joint custody over her. Lori could divorce Valerie's lover, but not Jessica's father. Lori followed him, curious and a little anxious.

The day was cloudy and humid, but the silver Mercedes sparkled, it was so new. It still had that leather smell. Rob had waited until after the divorce was granted to buy the Mercedes and a two-bedroom apartment on Park Avenue. Lori had accepted a generous monthly payment for the upkeep of the house and Jessica's needs, but only a lump sum for herself, enough to give her a year's respite while she got Corvino Catering back on its feet. Still, she couldn't help wondering how much money he had managed to hide from her and her lawyer. Maybe he had come to give her the monthly check he owed her. He was two weeks late.

"What do you need to talk about?" Lori asked after Rob paid the attendant and swung out of the parking lot.

"You look good," Rob said. The compliment caught Lori unawares. To her shame later, she felt flattered instead of warned. "Trip okay?" He smiled. His teeth were now so white, they looked blue. Compliments of Valerie Fenwick, DDS, for sure. They made him look ridiculous.

"Fabulous. So what is this about?"

"You remember that according to our agreement, I get Jessica for a month during the summer."

"Every other weekend and a month in the summer with the father to be mutually agreed upon," Lori recited. "For the Thanksgiving and Christmas holidays the parents agree to rotate. And also according to our agreement you are supposed to give me a check on the first of each month."

"You'll get it next week. I've had a lot of expenses lately."

Sure, Lori thought, *a big fat engagement ring, a new car, a new apartment, a wedding. Who knows what else.*

"Look, the firm is very busy right now." Rob was a labor lawyer, representing management. While he was still in law school, his goal had been the defense of the downtrodden worker, but with student loans to pay, marriage on the horizon, and a stubborn Irish pride that compelled him to be the sole breadwinner, he turned his back on the downtrodden and joined a four-name New York law firm that specialized in defending big companies. His name was now the fifth one on the masthead. In the months after Lori discovered his infidelity she tried to blame the wrong turn in his career, the giving up of his ideals, for what had happened. It was easier than to think she bored him.

"My whole summer is booked," Rob said.

"Don't worry. I'll see Jessica has fun. For that we'll need a timely monthly check." Lori found herself smiling. She would have almost three months to try to convince her daughter that Dad leaving home was not all Mom's fault.

"By the way, I got you a catering job," he said. "Mrs. Charles Saddler of Bedford, not more than a ten-minute drive from the house, is giving a dinner for twenty-four on July twenty-eighth. She's desperate for a caterer no one in her circle has used before. Saddler's a client of mine."

"No thanks, I'll get my own jobs."

"For Chrissakes, it's a foot in the door of very rich people who entertain every weekend. Once you're back at work, you'll feel better."

"Don't patronize me, Rob!"

"Don't yell at me."

Lori stared at the hands on her lap, waiting for her heartbeat to settle down to cruising. She counted fingers; there were still ten. Then she noticed her wedding ring was still on her finger. She'd forgotten all about slipping it back on during the flight to Rome to ward off the possibility of any male attention in the land of Latin lovers. Lori slipped her handbag over her left hand, hoping Rob hadn't noticed. Twenty-four hours was the length of time his ring had stayed on his finger after their wedding. Lori stole a glance at his hand, relaxed over the bottom of the steering wheel. Long-fingered hands she'd always loved stroking. Yep, there it was, a fat gold wedding band with some kind of scratches on it. Something picked by Valerie for sure. Unless Rob's minimalist tastes had changed suddenly. Well, the twenty-four-hour wedding ring limit hadn't passed yet. Valerie was in for a surprise. That thought made her feel generous.

"Thanks, Rob. I know you mean well," Lori said, "but since Jessica is staying with me all summer I don't want to take on any jobs. Not until she goes back to school. I don't know if you've noticed or not, but she needs a lot of TLC."

Rob took the exit to the New England Thruway before saying, "I didn't say she was staying with you all summer." His voice sounded as flat as roadkill.

"What did you say, then?"

"Look, the only vacation I can take this summer is two weeks starting next week. Valerie and I would love Jessica to come with us."

Lori's mouth went dry. "You want Jessica to come on your honeymoon?"

"It's a vacation, not a honeymoon. It would be a great way for Jessica and Valerie to get to know each other. Valerie's part of Jessica's life now. I realize that's tough on you, but that's the way it is. Whatever you may think, I didn't plan for all this to happen."

What didn't he plan for, Lori wondered. Fucking Valerie on his lunch hour, after work, on supposed business trips? Leaving Valerie's love letter where she was sure to find it? Not giving her up after Lori confronted him? Choosing Valerie when she threatened divorce? It was useless to say anything now. They'd hashed this out over and over again. He would always need to feel the victim.

"If you have your daughter's interests at heart, you'll let her go," Rob said. " 'She needs lots of TLC.' Your words. She doesn't need a hostile mother."

"I see, it's my fault." Using her handbag as cover, Lori slipped the ring off her finger.

"I didn't say that."

"What did you say?"

"I'm asking you to let her go. Two weeks and then you have her for the rest of the summer."

"She's not an object we trade back and forth."

"Exactly. Let her go."

Her thirteen-year-old daughter in a strange hotel room for the first time, while next door her father made love to his new wife? No way. "Where are you going?" They'd honeymooned in off-season Nantucket—three days only thanks to little money. "Arizona? Wyoming? You always wanted to go out West, remember?"

Rob didn't answer right away. Lori thought it was because of the large truck that was bearing down on them. Rob picked up speed, then turned into the slow lane. The truck zoomed past.

"Where?"

"Paris and Provence."

Lori pressed her wedding ring into her palm, resisting the urge to throw it in Rob's face. "Jess stays here."

"She's not going to like that. She'll turn against you."

Lori stared at the ceaseless traffic flowing ahead of her. "Don't threaten me with Jessica's feelings," she said quietly. "My relationship with my daughter is now my affair, not yours. Butt out."

"I'll send you the check next week."

"Jess stays here."

Rob slowed the car down. The car behind them honked in protest. Lori sensed Rob watching her. In the old days, she'd found the sensation sexy. Now it scared her.

"What, Rob?"

He turned to look at the road, his expression hard. "I nearly got killed two nights ago."

She had to laugh. There he was, playing victim again. "Cut the melodrama, Rob. It won't work. Jess is staying in the good old U.S. of A. with me."

"I'm serious. I was running across the street and a car aimed straight for me. If it hadn't been for Valerie—"

"Why are you telling me this?"

"You have motive."

"How about some of the poor people who lost their pensions or their health because of some of the companies you so successfully defended?" Lori thought she caught a flash of fear on his face. "You don't really believe someone's trying to kill you, do you?"

Rob didn't answer.

Not fear. Guilt was what she'd seen on his face, Lori decided. Rob finally understood what an awful thing he'd done to his family. He felt he needed punishment. That's what the therapist had told Lori when she'd thought that Rob leaving her was all her fault, for not rushing to put on makeup before he came home, for not dieting, for not paying enough attention to his needs, for not having picked up on the warning signs before it was too late. Her feelings of guilt had lasted only a couple of months thanks to the therapist and her girlfriends. Now it was Rob's turn. That he had a conscience didn't make her feel any more kindly toward him.

"I was in Rome, Italy, as you might remember," she said. "I will admit I wanted you dead on many occasions, but I love my daughter too much to kill her father." She pressed the window button. The glass slid down.

"You could have hired someone," Rob said.

"You're right, I could have, but you wouldn't be here if I had." Lori pushed her hand out the window. She thought she heard a "ping" when her wedding ring hit the asphalt.

CHAPTER 4

Rob drove away before Lori reached the front steps of the house they'd shared since Jessica was born—a small, two-story, whitewashed brick colonial in one of the few modest sections of Hawthorne Park, Connecticut. On the flight over, Lori had dreaded this moment: coming back to a house that was half-empty but still full of memories that hurt. She looked at her house with its dark blue shutters. It was the home she had dreamed of while growing up in an aluminum-sided four-family home with one plaster Madonna and all seven dwarves in the front yard. Here blooming yellow cabbage roses covered one side of the entrance. The living room windows boasted the crewel-embroidered curtains that she and Jessica had found at a crafts fair. Dandelions shot out between the bricks of the walkway no matter what weed killer she used.

Lori was suddenly filled with love for the place. And hope.

Before she could turn the key, Jessica opened the front door. Her tall daughter stood above her, wearing cutoff jeans low on her hips and a lime-green sports bra. A limp ponytail of hay-colored hair hung over one side of her head and made her look lopsided. Her beautiful, soon-to-be very upset daughter looked at her warily, her whole body tensed, as if ready to leap over her.

Without a word Lori dropped her suitcase and hugged Jessica. "I missed you so much," Lori said.

Jessica pulled away. "Me, too, Mom. I made fudge!"

Her weakness. "Great!"

"I figured we needed a sugar high." Jessica let out a small embarrassed laugh and picked up Lori's suitcase.

"Thanks, honey." Lori's heart quickened. She had to make Jessica understand that going on her father's honeymoon was not appropriate. Not to Paris. Not to Cape Cod. Not anywhere. She had to hold firm.

The low afternoon light poured in from the open door, cheering up the normally dark narrow hallway. On the hall table a Coke bottle held a single yellow rose. "How sweet, Jessica. And the whole place smells deliciously of chocolate. After you, that's the best homecoming present ever. Thanks." Lori looked at her daughter. *Let there be a truce. Let there be only love.*

Jessica shrugged her shoulders, still holding on to the suitcase. "I couldn't find any vases."

"We need to buy some." Lori had thrown all their vases against the pantry wall the night Rob accused her of being immature and provincial for not understanding his generosity in wanting to stay in the marriage for Jessica's sake, even though he had no intention of giving Valerie up. Jessica had thankfully been sleeping over at a friend's house. "But I like the Coke bottle. Let me go upstairs to wash up and change. Are you coming? You can unpack your present."

"I better check on the fudge. It's still in the oven. I'll wait for you in the kitchen."

Lori's heart slowed down. She welcomed the delay in facing Jessica's disappointment. "I'll be down in a sec."

When Lori walked into the kitchen twenty minutes later, Jessica was bent over the kitchen table cutting the fudge into squares. Her hair was down over her shoulders, the ends combed neatly into a flip and she had exchanged her sports bra for an oversized Yankees T-shirt. *She's trying to please*, Lori noted as she held out a tissue-wrapped package. *So am I.*

"For you from Florence," she said.

Jessica unwrapped the present and gasped when she saw the brown leather jacket. "Oh my God! Mom!" Her words came out in a squeal. "It's drop-dead gorgeous!" She held a sleeve against her cheek. "It's so soft."

Jessica slipped the jacket on, zipped it up, and ran to the hallway mirror. Lori watched her from the kitchen as Jessica threw her arms in the air, shook her hips, laughed. "It's perfect. Yummy fudge brown. Much cooler than black." She squinted at her own reflection. "Angie is just going to die." She leaped back into the kitchen and planted two kisses on Lori's cheeks with such abandon Lori's backside hit the kitchen table. "Thanks, Mom, you're the best."

Lori's throat tightened. She looked at her daughter, steeled herself for what she would say next. "Sweetie—" The serious expression that replaced the joy on Jessica's face stopped her.

"I know," Jessica said, the disappointment in her voice clear. "No Paris. It was a crazy idea of Dad's. I don't think Valerie was that into it, either. I mean, who wants a kid along on your honeymoon? It's all right, Mom. Really." Jessica reached over and dug out two fudge squares from the tray on the table. "I should have gone to camp."

"How about a trip, just the two of us?" Lori said, relieved and surprised by Jessica's understanding. "Something grand." She'd pay for it from the lump sum Rob had given her. Throw caution to the winds. "You pick the place, the country."

Jessica offered a square to Lori, who bit into it. "Angie's invited me to her dad's place in Cape Cod for two weeks if that's okay with you. Margot's going to call you."

"Of course, it's okay," Lori said with her mouth full, something she always nagged Jessica about. "Of course it is," she repeated once she'd swallowed.

"We're going next week. Monday, July first, okay?"

Lori nodded. It would be the first time she'd be alone for the Fourth of July weekend in more years than she had the energy to count, but it was going to be fine. Beth and Janet might stick around and she had lots of recipes to test, phone calls to make about lining up some waitressing help. She had to think of strategy, logo design, ad copy. Oh God, she wouldn't have a second to feel lonely. If she got desperate she could always go to her mother's. Really desperate. Lori picked chocolate crumbs from Jessica chin. "I'm sure you'll have a great time."

Jessica flipped her hair from her face with a toss of her head, a sign she was nervous. "Mom?"

"What is it, sweetie?"

"When you called during the wedding and I thought you'd done it on purpose? Daddy was standing right next to me. I'm really sorry." Jessica had tears in her eyes.

Lori blinked back some of her own. "It's okay, honey. You can tell me things even if you think it'll hurt me."

Jessica jiggled her head. "Can I show you the dress I wore? It's smashing."

"Sure." Lori smiled at her daughter's shift from woman to teenager. "I'm sure you looked gorgeous in it. How was the wedding? Did you have fun? Were there kids your age to dance with?"

Jessica had the good taste to turn red. "Mom!"

"You don't have to answer," Lori said, "but I can ask." It killed her to admit it, but she was curious. How fancy a wedding was it? Did they have a band? What food was served? Oysters, caviar, rare filet mignon covered in a cream-laced shiitake and shallot sauce—foods Rob loved—or half a chicken breast and no carbs, a dish she imagined skinny Valerie would favor. Who was the caterer? How much money did they spend? Did Rob make Valerie sign a prenuptial agreement? Well, she would never know, which maybe was for the best. Lori linked her arm with her daughter's. "Come on, let's go see this smashing dress."

Outside, someone honked. Jessica pulled back. "Later." She maneuvered Lori into a chair by the table. "Stay here, in your favorite room."

It had been her favorite. The best, biggest room in the house, where, as a family, the Stauntons had spent countless hours eating and talking at the old round oak table in the center of the room, reading or watching television from the denim-covered sofa at one end. The tapping of Rob's laptop, Jessica's sighs and mutterings as she worked on her homework had kept Lori company on many a night while she cooked, ironed, sewed, did her old-fashioned wifely, motherly duties, enjoying almost every minute of it. Before Jessica reached puberty and preferred her cell phone and the privacy of her room. Before Rob got bored and preferred his dentist. She was going to be spending days in this room, testing out recipes. Lori looked forward to the hard work, the sense of achievement a successful dish was going to give her. Maybe then she wouldn't miss what had been.

Jessica pushed the tray of fudge in front of her mother. "Eat more," she said. "You're going to need the boost."

"Why?" Lori asked, puzzled, although the spark in Jessica's eyes told her nothing terrible was about to happen.

"Grammy is descending on us."

Not terrible. Not good, either. Not that Lori didn't love her mother, but distance certainly made the heart grow fonder when it came to Ellie Corvino, the only grandparent Jessica had. "Now?"

"She's bringing dinner!" Jessica rolled her eyes as she crammed two fudge squares in her mouth. One of Jessica's traits Lori was most grateful for was her appetite. She ate like a sumo wrestler and looked like a gazelle—a gene gift from her father. The Corvino women ate a carrot and another lump mushroomed on their hips. While Lori exercised four days a week and used portion control to stay a size twelve, her mother, a sixty-seven-year-old widow who owned and still ran the Bella Vista Travel Agency in Mamaroneck, New York, had become a vegan and let weight come and go as it pleased.

Jessica picked up the tray. "I'm hiding the fudge in my room."

"Good move. It'll spare us a lecture." The front door opened.

"Hi, Mom," Lori said as her mother tried to balance a large pan while extracting the key from the front door. It seemed to have gotten stuck. Lori went over to help. "How's everything?" She removed the key and gave her mother pecks on both cheeks.

Ellie Corvino, red-dyed short hair in a bristle brush cut, wearing a blue Hawaiian shirt to which she'd added shoulder pads, purple Bermudas, and clunky sandals on her feet, placed the plastic-wrapped roasting pan on the floor and eyed her daughter. "You look terrible. You need some good face cream. Face cream and lots of makeup will make you feel like a million dollars. A billion, I guess. A million dates me. I'll get you some cream tomorrow." She held out her hand. "The key."

"I don't remember giving you a key to my house."

Ellie took the key from Lori's hand, dropped it in the handbag dangling from her shoulder. "The hardware store did a lousy copying job." She picked up the pan with a loud moan and limped past Lori into the kitchen.

Lori was well aware that her mother was not beyond faking things to divert attention from her misdeeds, a trait she shared with Rob. She didn't want to ask, wasn't going to ask, but when she saw Ellie grab the table with both hands to lower herself into a chair, she couldn't stop herself. "Are you in pain?"

"My sciatica is killing me. Where's Jess?"

"Upstairs, taking a shower." Eating the rest of the fudge, more likely. "What are you taking for it?"

"Aspirin colors me black and blue. Ibuprofen eats out my

stomach. I take nothing. 'Grin and bear it' is my motto."

So it wasn't too bad, Lori decided. "About the key?"

Ellie waved at the tray. "Heat up the oven to four hundred degrees, wait ten minutes, pop this in, *without* the plastic, mind you, for twenty minutes."

"Look, Mom, I just got home from a nine-hour flight. In Italy's it's one o'clock in the morning and I'm beat."

"Lasagna direct from the Corvino kitchen. Delish. Figured you need some healthy cooking after all those restaurant meals. Which reminds me," Ellie slapped her hand on the table. "I don't know why I'm speaking to you, Loretta Corvino, going off to Italy without using the Bella Vista agency. What kind of daughter are you, you don't support the family business?"

Lori sat down with a defeated sigh. "I didn't want you on my back."

Ellie shrugged her padded shoulders. "Suit yourself. I could have got you a big discount at the best hotels. I bet you stayed in rat holes."

"I was having a tough time. I wasn't thinking clearly. What's in the lasagna?"

"You're the caterer. You figure it out."

She didn't want to figure it out, much less taste the stuff. Her mother had always been a bad cook, but since she'd gone vegan—"Pasta, tomatoes, and gobs of tofu."

"And broccoli rabe plus a secret ingredient. You'll have to guess after you taste it."

"I love a mystery." Lori got up to turn on the oven and set the table. "Now tell me how you got a key to my house."

Ellie looked over her shoulder at the back door, then at the stairs in the hall. "Is Jess going to be a while?"

"She'll come down when I call her."

"The wedding was lousy."

Lori's throat tightened. "What wedding?"

"Your husband's."

"My ex, Mom. Ex! I can't believe you went. Talk about family support!"

"Who else is going to tell you what it was like? Jess wasn't going to snitch on her dad. And don't tell me you aren't ready to eat all of my tofu lasagna, lousy as you think it is, to find out all about how Mr. Robert Staunton and Valerie Fenwick DDS got hitched. They made the *Times* today. I cut out the clipping. It's here in my purse." Ellie swung a large cotton satchel onto the table and started rummaging.

"I don't want to hear about it, Mom, and I don't want to read anything. I can't believe he invited you." Rob had thought Ellie was fun the first years of their marriage. He couldn't understand why Lori complained about her unwanted intrusions into their life. But once the law firm made him partner, he'd distanced himself, disappearing whenever she showed up, making sure they were never seen together. Lori guessed Ellie had become too low-class for Rob's newly acquired status in a white-shoe firm. Maybe that's what he'd ended up thinking about his wife—not polished enough. Valerie's parents had both been surgeons; Valerie had gone to Harvard; Valerie was skinny and as smooth as a capped tooth. Rumor had it she was also very rich.

"I crashed," Ellie said. "Got a great kick out of the look on his face when I waltzed in. You'd have thought he was looking at a backpack full of explosives. But what could he do with all his fancy Park Avenue friends there, throw me out? I'm getting thirsty. Do I deserve a beer or what?"

"No, you don't, but I'll get you one out of the goodness of my heart."

"Now, mind you," Ellie said, after ignoring the glass Lori had put on the table and swigging directly from the beer bottle. "I did dress great, didn't want to shame Jess. I wore a Loehman's designer room outfit. Green, with sequins. Pricey, but I can always wear it when you get married again."

"Never!"

Ellie tapped her watch. "Oven time. Don't drop the lasagna, okay? And make sure the oven door is shut tight or else it doesn't heat good. Got the plastic bags off?"

Lori slipped the lasagna into the oven. Ellie needed to hear the sound of her own voice to make sure she was still going strong.

"Twenty minutes now, no more." Ellie twisted around to watch Lori. "So I'll wear the outfit at Jessica's wedding. Anyway, Jess said I looked like a queen."

Lori threw the oven mitts on the kitchen counter. She turned to face her mother. "Go on."

Ellie filled her in with great gusto. "The wedding and reception were at the Central Park Boathouse. Flowers to make a funeral home proud. And they had the gall to serve the bloated livers of I don't know how many poor tortured geese and so much bloody meat I thought I'd walked onto the set of *Pulp Fiction*. There was enough champagne to fill the lake. They're all going to get cancer or end up in AA. I was too disgusted to stay for dinner. Valerie wore a strapless Vera Wang and her shoulder blades stuck out like chicken wings and you'll be happy to know her French twist collapsed in the middle of the ceremony. A hairpin got stuck to her veil. Now, our Jessie," Ellie lifted her hefty chest with pride. "She looked like a movie star in her Vera Wang. Just gorgeous. You're going to have to peel the boys off her in a year or two. Rob looked like he hadn't slept in weeks. I'm telling you, Loretta, he's regretting it. I know he's going to come crawling back in six months."

"You don't expect me to take him back?"

"He's Jessica's father. He's a good provider and you're not getting any younger. In my day, just one of those would be enough to make a wife swallow her pride and let the man into her bed again."

"A hell of a lot more than my pride is involved here."

Ellie shrugged. "Maybe."

"Rob thinks someone tried to kill him two nights ago." Lori didn't know why she was telling her mother this.

"Did you?"

"Mom!"

"You could have hired someone." Ellie thought for a moment, then shook her head. "Naw, never believe a lawyer. He's coming back. Mark my words."

When Lori saw Rob at the airport, there had been a fleeting moment when she thought: *he's back, he didn't marry the dentist.* She had denied that thought until now. Could she take him back for Jessica's sake? Love him? It had to be too late for that. No, if she still dreamed of getting him back, it was probably for the satisfaction of turning him away.

"Mom, I've heard enough. Thanks. Now tell me about the house key."

Ellie looked at her wristwatch, a man's Timex that had miraculously stayed intact when her husband fell off the roof of their house while replacing some shingles, dying on impact. Lori had been eight at the time. "Ten more minutes for the lasagna." She looked up at her daughter. "Yes, I have a key to your house. I snitched Rob's when you told me he was divorcing you. They were lying on the front table for anybody to take. I said I had to go to the drugstore and quick as a wink I got a copy made. What if you fall down the stairs or slip in the bathtub and lie there comatose? Jess is a teenager, she's going to be off with her friends. You want some stranger to break down the door, smash the windows? You call me and I come help you."

"I'll call if I'm comatose?"

Ellie shook her hands in Lori's direction. "If you're comatose,

I'll know. I'm your mother. Now get Jess down here and let's eat."

CHAPTER 5

Lori opened one eye and looked at the window. It was pitch black outside. Her stomach growled. It was probably somewhere between three and four in the morning—if she turned on the light to find out, goodbye sleep. She turned over and let her mind travel back to Italy. It was breakfast time there now. She always sat at an outside table, overlooking a canal or a sun-drenched piazza. The *International Herald Tribune*—which she dutifully bought to keep up with the world and which she never read—was folded in her lap. Every morning she ordered a chocolate-sprinkled cappuccino with foam that tasted of coffee and milk, instead of the air you got at Starbucks. After scraping the last of the foam from her cup with a spoon, she ate a toasted slice of focaccia with prosciutto.

She could do that at home. Buy an espresso machine, prosciutto, maybe bake her own focaccia. She could even subscribe to the *Herald Tribune*. There was nothing to stop her. And she'd get that golden retriever she'd always wanted. Why not? She was a free woman.

Lori groaned and reached for Rob's pillow, which she had washed countless times to rid it of his scent. The clean smell of soap reached her nostrils. It made her want to cry. Lori was used to spooning herself against Rob's back in order to fall asleep again. The warmth of his body against hers had made her feel safe. Now she buried her face in the pillow she still thought of as his and rocked herself. *Toss out the empty king-size*

37

bed, she told herself. *Get a queen.* Maybe she'd feel like one.

Lori threw the pillow on the floor and turned on the light. Food. Food solved all problems. She slid out of bed, threw on her bathrobe, and tiptoed to the hallway. To her surprise, Jessica's door was open. Lori peeked into the room to listen for the steady rhythm of her daughter's sleeping breath, a sound that always filled her with the sense that all was right in the world.

"Mom?"

"Oh, Jess, I'm sorry." Lori stepped into the room. "Did I wake you?"

"If you're going downstairs to eat, there's nothing in the fridge. You made me dump Grammy's leftovers and the fudge is gone. I was awake already."

"Dumping was your idea, sweetie." Lori sat down on Jessica's bed and stroked her daughter's hair. "Why aren't you sleeping? Did you have a bad dream?"

"I'm not six, Mom!" Jessica protested, referring to the time her father had gone away for two weeks to argue a case in San Francisco. Every night that he was away she had woken up howling from the same bad dream. Daddy wasn't going to come back.

"I worry about you, honey. You've been through a lot."

Jessica lifted herself up on her elbow and clicked on the light at the other side of the bed. She turned to her mother. One cheek was creased with pillow wrinkles. *At her age they'll disappear in wink,* Lori thought.

"What's with Grammy, Mom? Unprocessed wheat germ?"

Lori laughed. "She's proud of her secret ingredient. It's very healthy."

"It's very awful." Jessica jumped out of bed and grabbed the empty fudge pan that was lying on the floor. "Come on, Mom, let's go scrounge for food."

Jessica, in her oversized Yankees T-shirt and bare feet, stood at the sink washing the fudge pan while Lori, in one of a dozen pajama sets she had bought after the breakup, surveyed the offerings in the refrigerator. A carton of 2 percent milk gone bad, a bottle of ketchup, half a stick of butter, a jar of anchovies, a chunk of Parmesan cheese wrapped in a damp cloth to keep it fresh, and one apple. She tossed the milk and tried the freezer. One shelf was stuffed with red boxes she recognized from the supermarket. Weight Watchers Smart Ones. Lori took one box out—Swedish meatballs—five points. "Jess, did you buy these?"

"No." Jessica turned both faucets to maximum flow and scrubbed harder.

Lori was familiar with the make-enough-noise-to-discourage-conversation ploy. "Please turn off the water—that pan is clean enough—all I want to know is how did diet Swedish meatballs, broccoli and roasted potatoes and I don't know what else get into our freezer?"

Jessica tossed the sponge in the sink and turned off the water. "A present."

"For me? Are you trying to tell me to go on a diet? I'm too fat?"

Jessica threw herself in a chair. "It's not always about you." She kept her head low, her hair covering her face.

Lori wasn't in the least bit relieved to hear that. She pulled out a chair and sat down next to her daughter. "Sweetie, you're five foot seven and a size eight. You're perfect the way you are." She lifted her daughter's hair off her face. Jessica shook it back. "Is Angie on a diet?"

No answer.

"Did you meet a boy you like?"

Jessica shook her head.

"Talk to me, Jess. Please."

"Valerie thinks I'm fat. She said in Paris all the women are real thin like her and I'd feel ugly so she bought me that stuff."

"Ugly!" Rage rose in Lori's throat. How dare that bitch undermine Jessica. "That woman is preposterous! You're beautiful. Don't pay any attention to her."

Jessica looked at Lori with a doleful expression on her face. "I have to. Daddy married her."

"Sweetie, I'm sorry." Lori hugged Jessica's head against her chest. "You are intelligent, thin, beautiful, and the best daughter anyone could have." She stood up and walked over to the refrigerator. She jerked open the freezer door and stuck her head in. "I'm throwing this stuff out."

Jessica got a garbage bag from underneath the sink. "Don't tell Daddy. Please."

"Not a word." Lori started tossing the boxes in the bag Jessica held out. "Given our meager resources, how about spaghetti with butter and Parmesan?"

"Yum. That's almost better than fudge."

Lori held a box of chicken and broccoli in midair, struck by an awful thought. "You did eat the fudge?"

"Yes and then I stuck my finger down my throat and threw it up."

Lori gasped.

"Come on, Mom, give me some credit. I wasn't going to Paris so why would I throw up my fudge? Anyway, that's so gross."

"I give you lots of credit, Jess." Lori threw the rest of the boxes in the garbage bag, opened the back door of the kitchen, and stuffed the bag with the rest of the garbage that would be collected in the morning. Beyond the maple in the backyard she could see light seeping into the bottom edge of the sky.

When Lori walked back into the kitchen, Jessica was filling the spaghetti pot with hot water. "What do you say if we make this meal a celebration?" Lori asked. "Dining room, candles, good china, the whole nine yards."

"Mom? It's four thirty in the morning?"

Lori smiled and took the pot from Jessica's hands. "I'm sure it's an elegant dinner hour in some part of the world. Why don't you put on your new dress and look at yourself in the mirror before you come down. You'll see how skinny you are."

After dinner last night, Jessica had modeled the bridesmaid dress for her mother and grandmother—a steel-blue satin gown that offset Jessica's pale hair. The pleated bodice, modestly low-cut, emphasized her small waist and made her look even taller than she already was.

"Doesn't she look like Cinderella going to the ball?" Grammy had said, using her new cell phone to take a photo of Jessica.

Jessica looked like a woman. The thought had filled Lori with a mixture of pride and sadness. Too soon her daughter would fly away.

Lori turned one of the burners on. "The cook, if you don't mind, will stay in her bathrobe and pajamas." Jessica was halfway up the stairs.

Valerie was jealous, Lori decided. She might be skinny, rich, and good-looking, but Jessica was thin, gorgeous, and *young*. And her father loved her enough to want to take her on his honeymoon. That's what the put-down was about. Valerie was a mean woman.

Lori put the pot of water on the burner, covering it with a bowl into which she cut three tablespoons of butter and a mashed anchovy. The heat from the pot would melt the butter. When the water boiled she would add kosher salt, enough to make the water taste as salty as the sea. Next she grated the cheese and added it to the bowl. As the sky lightened outside her window, Lori thought of the day in front of her. She was going to make the most of it: an hour of Pilates, then coffee with Callie's gals, a run to the supermarket to restock refrigerator and pantry. She had planned to sort her new recipes and begin inputting them in her computer. But now the pasta was ready.

CHAPTER 6

Lori peeked in the glass window of Callie's Place, the old Greek coffee shop just off Elm Street. She caught sight of her best friend's short salt-and-pepper hair; Beth was sitting at their corner booth in a pale yellow tennis outfit. Handsome, loving Beth had a wide sculpted face, light brown eyes, a blink-inducing smile, and a serene way about her that had immediately attracted Lori to her during freshman week at Swarthmore.

Beth saw her and waved. Margot and Janet were sitting on either side of her. Lori waved back. Monday morning at Callie's Place with her friends like almost every Monday of the year. It was great to be back.

Callie, the owner, opened the door. "I know my place doesn't match up to those fancy Italian cafés, but welcome back." She was as short as she was wide and made it her business to know everyone's business. She also baked the best apple pie Lori had ever tasted.

Lori gave Callie a hug. "No place matches this one." She meant it, too. This was her second home, where she, Beth, Margot, and Janet had eaten countless meals, shared laughs, tears. It was here that, seven years ago, Beth had whispered that her husband was dying of leukemia. It was here that childless Janet announced she was adopting a Chinese baby girl; here that she admitted she was pregnant a year later. Here that, only two years ago, Margot let out that she was divorcing her husband

43

because she'd fallen in love with someone else.

Margot air-kissed Lori so as not to smudge her signature red lipstick. It was Margot's daughter, Angie, who was helping Jessica maneuver her way through her own family breakup.

"Angie's a great kid," Lori said. "Cape Cod will do wonders for Jess."

Margot moved her Chanel bag to make room next to her. "Warren loves having her. That way he doesn't have to worry about Angie getting bored."

Janet leaned forward. "Was Italy absolutely fabulous? We want every detail."

"The men first," Margot said.

"Let her sit down first," Beth said.

Lori kissed Janet and blew a kiss to Beth, who was too far away. "Why do I feel as though I've just walked into an episode of *Sex and the Burbs*?"

"Given our age, *Desperate Housewives* is more like it," Beth said. "Welcome back. I've missed you."

"We're not desperate," Janet piped in. At thirty-eight she was the youngest of the group and still pretty in an old-fashioned American Roses way with her natural blond ponytail, snub nose, and perfect teeth. Margot liked to call her Barbie, which Janet found flattering. "We're not desperate!" she repeated.

The other women looked at each other quickly. They all knew that Janet and a jobless Seth were having serious money difficulties.

The only response that popped into Lori's head to break the moment was the old cliché, *hope springs eternal*. She sat down and, inhaling loudly, said instead, "Can you smell? Margot's coffee, Beth's cheese Danish, Janet's orange juice, Callie's apple pies. It's enough to make me happy again."

"How are you?" Janet asked, clasping Lori's hand. "It must be so hard."

"Apart from my stomach muscles screaming after an hour of Pilates this morning, I'm fine. Really." Major or minor problems, Janet always cared. "Thanks." Janet's kids were lucky. So was Seth, who had been a classmate of Rob's at Dartmouth. Janet was all sweetness. Sometimes it got on Lori's nerves, which then made her feel guilty.

"The kids?" Lori asked

"Great. Desiree has announced she wants to be a novelist like Amy Tan and Taylor is going to be seven in two weeks. I've got tons of new pictures I want you to see, but as usual I left them home."

Lori ordered decaf coffee. "Bring them next time." The day before she had left for Italy, Janet had come over with forty new prints.

"I've experienced the same problem with my muscles when I come back from one of my vacations," Margot said. "My personal trainer keeps going on about doing the ab series every morning, but our muscles have a right to a vacation." She waved the milk jug at the waitress. "Are you sure this is skim?"

"Yes, ma'am," Callie shouted from the other end of the room.

"She doesn't like me," Margot said.

"That's the most perceptive statement you've made all morning," Beth said. Margot laughed.

It was easy not to like Margot when you first met her. She was vain, self-involved, always beautifully turned out in the latest, most expensive fashion, but she was kind, fun, and always generous with the fortune her father had left her.

"Let's all hush now and hear from Lori," Beth said.

Three faces turned her way. In the back she could see that Callie was waiting, too. Lori wished she could make up some fantastic love affair: how she and her lover had lain next to each other as they floated in a gondola down the Grand Canal, how he had kissed her in front of Michelangelo's *David*, how she had rubbed herself against him in the Colosseum.

"I saw lots of incredible art, walked my feet to the bone, ate like a goddess, got lots of good recipes thanks to Beth's fake business cards, and even managed to stop thinking about Rob and Valerie every minute. That's my story."

"How much did you gain?" Margot said.

"Don't know and don't care."

Margot's fingers combed her smooth dark cap of hair. "I'm green with envy."

"It was good for you?" Janet asked.

"It was great," Lori said.

"Do you feel up to catering a small dinner party this Saturday for twelve?" Beth said. "It's for Mrs. Evelyn Ashe's eighty-fifth birthday."

"Yikes, so soon?"

"I told her you were very good and very expensive."

Why not plunge in, Lori thought. "I have to ask Jess what she's up to on Saturday."

"She's going to a party with Angie," Margot said.

"If that's the case, I'll say yes, but let me check with Jess first?"

"Tonight's the deadline."

"Thanks." Beth was always coming through for her. She wouldn't have survived the divorce without her, without all three of her friends. They had hovered around her, warming her like a blanket, muffling the awful noise her head and heart were making. "Starting off with a small dinner party would be perfect." She had cooked enough of them for Rob, his partners, his clients. She wasn't ready to cook for a crowd.

Margot tapped Lori's shoulder. "Now don't tell me you didn't meet a breathtakingly handsome Italian man who was dying to ravish you." Her eyes betrayed a mixture of envy, wishful thinking, and intense curiosity.

"I did meet a man on my last night in Rome."

"Your last night?" Janet said. "How sad."

"Not sad at all. He was American, far from breathtakingly handsome as I remember, and as for wanting to ravish me, he spilled steaming hot gnocchi on a brand-new very expensive dress, and then doused the burn with most of a carafe of red wine."

Janet looked startled. Margot wanted to know if Lori had made him pay for the dress. Beth started laughing. Lori laughed, too. What else could she do? "He gave me two thousand dollars in cash," she said to shut Margot up.

Callie came over with her undulating gait and dropped a plate in front of Lori. "Eat." She handed Lori a fork. Lori stopped laughing. In front of her was a slice of apple pie, Callie's cure-all.

Lori took a bite. The apples were warm, firm, bathed in a dark coat of caramelized sugar. "You wouldn't give a desperately unhappy woman the recipe, would you?" she asked Callie.

Callie snorted and walked away.

"Anyone want to share?" Lori asked.

"She'd kill us," Beth said.

Janet sat up. "Is it true that someone tried to kill Rob Friday night?"

Lori took another bite of the pie. She was getting tired of this story. Next she would hear that she was seen trying to run him over.

"Only tried to kill him?" Margot said. "That's too bad."

Beth grabbed the check. "Of course it's not true! Why would anyone want to kill Rob?"

Margot waved fingers at Beth from across the table. "Hello, E.T.? Time to get off your bicycle and come down to earth." She jerked her chin toward Lori.

Lori waited to swallow her food before asking Janet, "Where

47

did you hear that?"

Janet's face turned red. "I don't know. Did you tell me, Margot?"

Margot's voice was indignant. "How would I know anything about that horrible man and that ungrateful woman I introduced you to." Valerie had been an old boarding school friend of Margot's.

"I guess she didn't invite you to the wedding," Beth said. "That is ungrateful, after all the business you sent her way."

Margot squeezed Lori's arm. "Darling, you don't know how sorry I am about her. And I would never have gone to the wedding."

"I know. You're a pal."

"I'm sorry," Janet said, still blushing. "Seth must have told me." She twisted her paper napkin, then smoothed it out with the palm of her hand.

Had Janet and Seth gone to Rob's wedding? Is that why Janet was so nervous? She felt disloyal? Lori squeezed Janet's hand and said, "I'm glad they've made up." Seth and Rob had been good friends until two years ago. If Janet had gone to the wedding, Lori knew it was only because Seth had dragged her there. "You can be Rob's friend, too, you know. That takes nothing away from our friendship." Well, it did take something away, but Lori wasn't going to show that it did. To feel that way was petty and ungenerous.

Margot leaned her head toward Lori and asked in a throaty whisper. "So did someone try to kill him?"

Lori put her fork down. "He was probably jaywalking and the car got within two feet of him. Rob tends to exaggerate." Someone trying to kill him was too preposterous.

"He knows he's been a rat," Margot said, "and now he's begging for sympathy."

Lori thought back to the look she had caught on Rob's face

in the car. That he was feeling guilty was something she had wanted to believe. What if her first instinct had been right? That Rob was scared?

"The whole thing is ridiculous," Beth said, as she took money out of her wallet. "Janet and Margot, you each owe me four and a quarter. Callie's treating Lori."

Lori walked down to the end of the counter and reached over to give Callie a hug. "Thanks. You're a sweetheart."

"Trust me." Callie said. "You'll get over him."

When Lori joined the other women outside the coffee shop, Beth was telling Margot and Janet about the time Lori had called her because Rob thought he'd been poisoned. "He insisted she take him to the emergency room in the middle of the night. All he had was the twenty-four hour stomach flu. You remember, Lori?"

"God, yes," she said, even though she was too tired to remember that she'd called Beth about it. Rob was always sounding the alarm for every little cold or indigestion. A self-absorbed wimp, terrified of dying, that's who she had married. Not a man whose life was in danger.

CHAPTER 7

Jessica was staring at her mother from the bathroom door with disbelief clinging to her face.

Lori's stomach turned over, as it always did whenever Jessica looked unhappy or angry. Well, really anything potentially painful. An unhappy Jessica, any good memory of Rob, her empty king-size bed, the remembered sight of Valerie with a drill in her hand, smiling down at her gaping mouth. The list was endless. Maybe she should ask her doctor for tranquilizers. Lori turned off the hair dryer. "What is it, honey? What's wrong?"

"Flowers," Jessica sputtered. She pointed to the stairway behind her. "There's got to be at least a thousand flowers downstairs."

"Flowers, how nice," Lori said, registering only the fact that a tragedy had not occurred. She smiled at Jessica and turned the hair dryer back on. Her mind went back to rehearsing what she was going to say once she got to Valerie's office. "Ruth"—that was Valerie's office manager—"Ruth, my teeth are bleeding." Or "I left my umbrella last time I was here. I know, eighteen months ago, but it's going to rain any day now. I'll just check all the rooms." Ruth, big, slow, and stuck behind a desk, would never catch her.

And then the big moment—Valerie standing in front of her. Without the drill, Lori hoped. Calmly, she would tell her husband's new wife, her ex-husband's new wife—

"Mom! Someone sent you flowers!"

50

Lori spun around to face her daughter. "Flowers? Why?"

"How should I know?" Jessica's expression was belligerent.

"I'm sorry, Jess. I'm running late for an important meeting in New York this afternoon and I was distracted. Flowers are always wonderful, unless it's a funeral. Let's see them." Halfway down the stairs she could smell them.

"You're not going to see Dad, are you?" Jessica asked in a wary voice.

"No, sweetie, I'm meeting with the accountant over taxes." Little white lies to your child were necessary sometimes. Lori stopped short at the sight of the enormous bouquet of white roses, Casablanca lilies, and pink peonies that now crowded the entrance table. "Holy sky!" Lori said, an expression her mother used for the unexpected. At least fifty flowers bulged out of a round, blue-patterned ceramic pot. They took her breath away.

"This has Margot's signature on it, for sure," she said, picking up the note pinned to the satin bow.

Dear Ms. Corvino,

Again I apologize for ruining your evening in Rome. I could not help but overhear you asking Maurizio, the waiter, for the recipe of gnocchi della regina. *I have sent it along. If you have not received it yet, it should arrive shortly. Flowers and a recipe cannot replace the beautiful dress you were wearing and which I'm afraid I have ruined, but I did want you to know how sorry I am.*

With best wishes,
Alec Winters

P.S. I have many mended bones to prove how hopelessly clumsy I have always been.

"Who sent them?" Jessica asked, leaning sideways to read the note.

Lori slipped the note in her bathrobe before Jessica could

read it. "A man," she said and dropped down on a stair. This was too much. Even patronizing. Did she care about his mended bones? Really! And why hadn't he left a return address? Was she expected to accept and forget?

"Mom, do you have a boyfriend?" Jessica asked.

Lori looked at the flowers again and breathed in their perfume. God, they were so beautiful, and if she didn't watch it she would shrivel into a complaining bitter woman. How sweet Mr. Alec Winters was. How sincerely sorry. And the recipe. How had he gotten the recipe? For that matter, how had he gotten her name and address?

"Mom, if you have a boyfriend I think I should know about it. No more surprises, okay?" Jessica shook her mother's shoulder. "Mom?"

Lori looked up. "Oh, honey, how could I possibly have a boyfriend? No, this is just a man I met in Rome." From where she sat, Lori could see the kitchen wall clock. One forty p.m. The train to Grand Central left at two twenty. She started running up the stairs. "I'll tell you what happened when I come back, okay?"

"Whatever. I'm always the last to know anything," Jessica yelled up at her mother.

"Jess, be fair," Lori yelled back. "We'll talk tonight. Okay?" There was silence from downstairs. A boyfriend. How could Jess even think that? Lori stepped into a pair of beige cotton slacks, topped them with a white short-sleeved jersey. She'd show Jess the ruined dress. That should erase any doubts. The gray linen jacket she'd bought in Florence was wrinkled, but the saleswoman had insisted that linen wrinkles were chic. Lori slipped on the jacket. The wrinkles matched her face. She put on another layer of foundation, a pale lipstick, and let thoughts of Alec Winters float back into her mind. How did he know her name and her address? And how did he get that recipe? She tried to remember what he looked like and couldn't. She'd been terribly rude to him, that she knew. She fluffed up her hair and smiled at her reflection. Damn! Those flowers were softening her resolve to face Valerie. That would never do. She straightened her spine and frowned in the mirror. No jewelry. She wanted to appear severe, strong.

Lori grabbed her handbag.

The front door slammed.

Lori peered down from the upstairs landing. "Jess?" No answer. She skipped down the stairs and checked the kitchen. Jessica had left a note on the kitchen table, held down by the now-empty Coke bottle. "I'm staying over at Angie's tonight. I only told you three times!!!" The yellow rose, Lori noticed, was sticking out of the garbage where she was sure to notice it.

Lori walked back to the hallway and pushed her nose against a Casablanca lily. She inhaled deeply and told herself—*we'll be fine. One day. Soon.*

"The doctor's with a patient. You can't see her," Ruth said.

Lori strode past the desk.

Ruth half-sat up. "Wait, Mrs. Staunton, I mean, Lori! Stop!"

Valerie, in a white coat, three-inch heels, and swaying blond hair, sashayed down the corridor. She stopped at the sight of Lori and smiled, showing off her perfect caps, blue-white to match her husband's. "There's no point to this," she said in a soft voice only Lori could hear. "I'm Rob's wife now. You can't get him back."

Valerie's words were hot lava pouring down Lori's throat. For a moment she couldn't speak. She looked at Valerie's skinny frame and remembered why she was here. "Stop undermining my daughter. There's nothing wrong with her weight."

Valerie's eyes traveled down Lori's body, the smile still hovering on her lips. "Jess has some bad genes to contend with. She needs to watch it. One thing you have to remember now is that Jess may be your daughter, but she's also Rob's daughter. And now mine. I can tell her whatever—"

Lori stepped closer. "She'll never be your daughter," she said quietly, then slapped Valerie hard across her smirk.

CHAPTER 8

"You didn't."

"I did. And she almost toppled over on her three-inch heels." Lori had called Beth on the train coming home and now they were sitting in her kitchen, half a bottle of Falanghina sloshing in their empty stomachs. "Who can stand all day in three-inch heels?"

"What did she do after you slapped her?" Beth asked.

"She said, 'You're pitiful.' "

"Nasty."

"I wanted to hit her again but the bulldog nurse was heading straight for me and I got out before I got hauled out." Lori refilled the wine glasses, took another fortifying gulp, and leaned back in her chair. "Now I'm furious at myself for losing control, for giving her so much power over me."

What Lori really wanted to do was sleep and forget the whole episode. She was ashamed of what she'd done. "It felt great for about three seconds."

"Let's think happy thoughts," Beth said.

"Great idea." Valerie was Jessica's stepmother now. Both she and Jess would have to learn to live with that. "How about food as a happy thought? You hungry? Let me try out one of my new recipes on you. Risotto with baby peas and shrimp. That would be nice for the dinner party on Saturday. Thanks again for that job, by the way. I can do it. Jess is going to a party that night. I'm thrilled to have the distraction. How did you get me the job on such short notice?"

"Her regular caterer had to cancel. I know her son, who's a client of mine. He asked me if I knew of anyone. Hey, you might know him. Jonathan Ashe. You probably fed him at one of Rob's business dinners. He was on the fast track in Rob's law firm. Curly blond hair, blue eyes, six feet or so, with a great dimple on one cheek? Once you saw him you wouldn't forget him. He's cute."

Lori shook her head. "I was so busy worrying that the dinner went perfectly I barely looked up at the guests."

"He's on his own now, doing real estate and handling Mama's money. Over the years Jonathan's managed to convince her that buying art is a good investment." When Beth's husband, Larry, died, she had stopped being a social worker to run his art gallery.

"What about veal *rollatini* with a pancetta and porcini mushroom stuffing, or scaloppine with lemon and capers?"

"Stop, I'm gaining weight just listening to you." Beth turned her chair so that she was facing the hallway. "When I said 'let's think happy thoughts' I was referring to that humongous mass of flowers from Mr. Alec Winters. It's a great mood enhancer. Does he live near here?"

"There was no address."

"Call the florist and tell them you've got something of his you need to return. If they still won't give you his address, mail them your thank-you note and ask them to forward it."

"If he wanted to let me know how to find him, he would have, right?"

"Stop being passive. You're divorced now. Life's in your hands."

"Well, he's supposedly sending me a recipe. Maybe it will come with a return address."

Beth got out of her chair. "Where's your laptop?"

"Next to the microwave. Why?"

Beth walked over to the kitchen counter and opened up the laptop. "I'm going to Google Mr. Alec Winters. You don't give up on someone who sends you that kind of bouquet. Not only can he afford those flowers, he's sensitive, sweet, romantic, and he knows recipes. He's ideal, Lori. Get it? Ideal!"

"I don't even remember what he looks like."

"Ugly you'd remember."

"He probably lives in Alaska. And anyway, I'm not interested in men right now."

"You don't have to marry him, Lori. Just think of him as another great distraction. If he's in Alaska you can e-mail each other, talk about food, Italy, anything. Communicate." Beth turned around and looked fiercely at Lori. "Living alone sucks, so whatever you can do—"

"I've got Jessica."

"And I've had the twins all these years, but children don't replace a man. It's not just sex. It's having an adult companion, someone to share adult thoughts with, someone who can take over if you lose it. You and Janet and Margot have been great, but it's not enough. I don't mean to scare you, Lori, but it's been godawful since Larry died." Beth burst into tears. "Just hell."

Lori was taken aback. She'd always thought of Beth as a pillar of strength. Margot even called her Concrete Beth, both because she was the realist among the three friends and because of her strength. Beth had faced her husband's slow death from leukemia without a tear or complaint. At Larry's funeral and in the months afterward she had concentrated on helping her children and Larry's friends deal with their grief. Now here was Concrete Beth crying like a child. Lori hugged her. "I'm so sorry. I had no idea. You never said anything."

"I tried dating, but no one measured up to Larry, and when

it came to having sex, I just couldn't. I felt like meat for sale. I guess I just want him back."

Why hadn't Beth shared her unhappiness with her friends? Was it pride? Shame? Had she, Margot and Janet stopped paying attention because they were each too busy with their own lives? She considered Beth her oldest, her best friend, and yet here she was suddenly discovering she didn't truly know her, as she had discovered she didn't truly know her husband. As she might not know Jessica. Maybe Donne was wrong. *We are all islands, destined to be lonely.* No! The thought was too awful.

Lori tightened her hug. "I'm so sorry."

Beth sniffed, wiped her nose with the back of her hands. "It's envy, that's all. I'd like to have a man send me flowers without having to put out first."

"You wouldn't like what he did to my dress."

Beth wiped her tears and laughed. "Next year Tommy and Mike are off to boarding school. They wanted to go so badly, I couldn't say no."

"We'll keep each other company." The phone rang. Lori was tempted to let it ring, but Jessica could be calling. "I better get this."

Beth pushed her toward the phone. "Yes, of course." She waved an arm just as Lori got to the wall phone. "Please don't tell Margot or Janet. I'm doing great, really. It's just the flowers—"

"I won't say a word." Lori picked up the cordless receiver, hoping it was Jessica telling her, "You're my mom. I don't even like Valerie. I love *you.*"

It was raspy-voiced Margot. "I want to take you out to dinner with Janet and me. I know you're jet-lagged, but it will be fabulous, I promise. Janet's just dropped the kids with Seth's mother for the night. Seth has a meeting in the city for a possible job and yours truly managed to snatch a last-minute reservation for four at *Jeffrey's,* which you know is impossible to get into even on a Monday night. I'm trying to find Beth to get her to join us. Do you know where she is?"

Lori took advantage of the short pause in Margot's waterfall of words to ask, "What are Jessica and Angie doing?"

Silence. Then a quiet "You don't know?"

"I don't know," Lori repeated as her stomach got ready to do its hundredth flip of the day. She really needed to get a grip. "Did they go to the movies?" Pizza afterward, probably.

"He lied," Margot said.

"Who lied?" She knew the answer right away. That's what she got for slapping the new wife. Now Rob was going to kidnap Jessica, take her to Paris and Provence. Lori dragged herself over to the kitchen table, dropped down heavily on one of the chairs. She'd turned into a sack of potatoes. Rotting ones. Beth, watching her, stopped swirling the mouse button.

"Darling, please, don't be mad at me," Margot pleaded. Her voice was loud enough for Beth to hear. "Rob took the girls to Manhattan. He said he had reservations at Pastis in the Meatpacking District and he thought they'd get a kick out of it. Angie and Jessica started screaming with excitement. I said I'd have to check with you first, but he said he'd called you already and you were fine with it."

"And you believed him?"

"Why wouldn't I? There's no harm in it, is there? God, I'm awfully sorry, but they'll have so much fun and he promised to bring them back no later than ten thirty. Now forgive me and come to dinner."

It was turning out to be a big night for regrets. Lori sighed. "It's okay, Margot, but I don't feel like dinner. Call me when Jess is back." Beth tapped Lori on her shoulder and mouthed, "I'm not here."

"I don't know where Beth is," Lori added.

Margot went on urging her to come to dinner at Jeffrey's, the most expensive restaurant in Hawthorne Park. "I want to welcome you back."

"Thank you, but I'm very tired," Lori said. "But I'll take a rain check. Don't forget to call when Jess is back, no matter what the time."

"I won't forget," Margot promised. "I'll get you another night. Love you and do forgive me for believing that handsome rotter you married."

"Divorced." Lori hung up. Handsome and rotter was right on. She was furious at Margot for letting Jessica go, for not checking with her first. Her heart was fluttering and her mouth was dry. She was having a panic attack. Nothing was in her control anymore.

After one look at Lori, Beth went to the refrigerator, jerked open the door, and rummaged inside until she found a plastic container. Inside was the leftover butter and Parmesan spaghetti Lori had cooked for Jessica early that morning. Beth popped the container in the microwave. "Rob won't let any harm come to his daughter, you know that, right?"

Lori nodded and looked at the flowers in the hall. "Look at something pretty," her father used to tell her whenever she was about to cry. "It lifts the soul. That's why I look at you all the time." The memory helped. Maybe even the sight of the flowers.

She was going to call Rob on his cell, tell him what she thought of his lie right in the middle of his dinner. Jessica would never forgive her. God, what if he told her Lori'd slapped Valerie. She could just hear Jessica wailing, "Mom, that's just so embarrassing!" Or Jessica might give her the cold shoulder for a week. *Please, Rob, don't tell her.*

Beth brought over the reheated pasta and a fork. "You need to eat."

"You sound like my mother."

"Your food's edible." Beth had suffered through several Ellie meals in the name of friendship.

Lori slipped the fork into the spaghetti and twirled the strands into a neat roll, one of the first tricks Papa had taught her. She'd wait until tomorrow to have it out with Rob.

Beth was back sitting on the stool, fiddling with the laptop. "Alec Winters restores houses," she announced. "He lives in Pleasant Gap, Pennsylvania, which is a little far, but long-distance relationships can be more exciting. And *House and Garden* did an article on him. That means he's successful. Too bad there's no photo." She scrolled down. "Ooh, this is getting better and better. Listen, he's involved with not-for-profit and volunteer organizations in New York City. Let's see, he's with the Children's Help Line, DonorsChoose, and, oh—"

"What?" Lori slipped the rolled spaghetti into her mouth.

"He's chairman of the board of Ban-AIDS and a big donor to Broadway Cares."

Lori looked up with a smile. "That explains the gorgeous extravagant flowers. The sweet note."

"You're male bashing." Beth tried to wipe away the frown that had formed on her forehead with a sweep of her hand. "And let's not jump to conclusions. Maybe he's just compassionate."

Lori shook her head. "A gay man is just what a gal needs in bad times. Support, compassion, no sex. We'll share him. Tomorrow I'll call information and get his number. How's that for passive?"

Beth closed the laptop lid. "Come to think of it, Jonathan Ashe would make a great date for you. Cute. Never married. He is a couple of years younger, maybe as much as five, but, hey, younger is the latest trend."

Lori wasn't listening. She took two more bites, then pushed

the plate away. "God, why did he have to take Jessica?"

Beth slipped down from the stool. "Why are you so worried? Okay, Rob lied and you'll have to work that out with him, but Pastis is a hot restaurant for young people. Tommy and Mike raved about it. Jessica will have a ball."

"What if someone *is* trying to kill Rob? What if that person tries tonight while he's with Jessica and Angie? I don't know, a bomb in the trunk, driving him off the road, shooting at the car."

Beth walked over, leaned over Lori, and rubbed her back. "Honey, I think you need to take an Ambien and go to sleep."

Lori's eyes filled with tears. "Oh, Beth."

Beth lifted Lori out of her chair, turned her toward the hallway. "You're jet-lagged and we've both had a lot of wine on empty stomachs."

Lori pushed herself away from Beth. "Why did he leave Jess and show her that love can break her heart. Why didn't he love me enough to give Valerie up? I'm not drunk. Just slowly falling to pieces. I'll go to bed now, but no sleeping pill. I want to hear the phone when Margot calls." Lori headed to the hallway table, lifted the large bouquet of lilies, roses, and peonies out of its blue ceramic pot, separated it into more or less equal parts, and held out a dripping part to Beth. "Friends share the good and the bad."

Beth started to protest, but Lori pushed the dripping flowers against her best friend's chest. There was no saying no, not with Lori as vulnerable as she was. "Thank you. You're the best," Beth said and kissed her friend on both cheeks. Then she whispered, "Rob's not worth killing."

CHAPTER 9

Margot's luxurious home, paid for by her dead father's Wall Street fortune, sat at the end of Tree Haven, a cul-de-sac facing the Long Island Sound. It was a sprawling modern house designed by a Danish architect who, much to Margot's disappointment, had died before becoming world-famous. A nest of smooth granite boxes spread across an emerald green lawn. On the Sound side, the granite was replaced by enormous plate glass windows open to the sky and the vast lawn that dipped down to the water. From the street, all an onlooker could see, between the four copper beeches, were small square windows that echoed the shape of the boxes. The other homes in the cul-de-sac were traditional five- to seven-bedroom colonials and Tudors. Each was meticulously landscaped and enhanced by the century-old maples, oaks, and beeches that had given this exclusive section of Hawthorne Park its name.

The cul-de-sac was in deep shadow thanks to the many tree branches that extended into the street and covered the street lamps. At eleven fifteen at night, the late June sky was finally dark, the moon hidden behind dense, rain-filled clouds. In the red den, Margot, in a purple silk pant outfit, sprawled on the leopard-skin patterned sofa and made a phone call. "Angie and Jess are going to be late. They had to wait a long time for their table. Valerie's bringing them home. Yes, Valerie. Rob is sick or something." After she hung up, she settled back to watch *Charlie Rose*. She'd already told Lori, waking her up.

63

At eleven thirty, Margot switched off the television and went to her bedroom at the back of the house. At eleven-forty, Rob's new BMW slid smoothly into the circular driveway. Angie got out first from the back. "Thanks a bunch," she said, bending down as the passenger side door opened and Jessica got out.

"Bye," Jessica said, with a quick wave. The two girls headed for the front door. Once they were safely inside, the BMW slipped quietly down the dark street. Just as it was leaving the cul-de-sac to turn into winding, unlit Caldwell Street, a car came up from behind and swiftly passed the BMW. The drivers did not glance at each other.

At eleven forty-seven, Lori's cell phone rang.

"I had the best time, Mom. I ate mussels and the best French fries I've ever tasted and you won't believe who I saw!"

A wave of relief engulfed Lori. Jessica was safe, happy, bursting with excitement, and Rob had kept his mouth shut about slapping Valerie. "Who did you see?"

"Sarah Jessica Parker! She's so gorgeous and she gave me her autograph on a Pastis matchbook. Angie too. She's really tiny." Jessica went on about all the cool downtown people she had eaten with. She now felt part of the Manhattan "in" crowd. The mysterious man who had sent the flowers and her mother's bad memory seemed forgotten. Lori simply listened. Finally Jessica said, "Bye now. I'll be home around ten tomorrow morning. Margot's giving me a ride."

"Thank her. I'll be with Mrs. Ashe catering her birthday."

"Cool. Love you, Mom."

"Love you back." Jessica hung up. Lori listened to the steady dial tone as her head sank back into the pillow. She closed her eyes. Life was going okay after all.

It had started to rain. The BMW turned into the first leg of a sharp S-curve at the end of Caldwell Street. Valerie slammed on the brakes, the rear of the car fishtailing. Thank God the road was barely wet or she would have ended up like the car that was now blocking the lane, its trunk hanging over the dividing line, the front fender against a tree. What to do? Her headlights, aimed at the driver's side of the car, shone through the open window onto the driver, who was hunched over the steering wheel, face out of sight. Valerie reached for her cell phone, punched 911. Nothing happened. She tried again. Again nothing. She turned on the overhead light and checked her phone. "Shit!" She lowered her window and called out, "I'll have to drive to get the paramedics. We're in a no-service zone here."

In her bedroom, Angie, dressed for the night in a torn soccer shirt, slipped the DVD of an old episode of *Grey's Anatomy* into the player. Jessica was brushing her teeth in the bathroom. "I just can't get enough of Patrick Dempsey. He sends shivers up my spine."

Jessica rinsed out her mouth and walked back into the bedroom to get undressed. "He's too old."

"That's what Margot said." Angie sat crossed-legged on the bed, waiting for Jessica to join her. "But that's just because she goes for him, too."

"Where is she? Did you tell her we're home?"

"Her bedroom door is closed. She's probably fast asleep."

"Maybe she's watching TV and didn't hear us. I think you should tell her."

"Okay, I'll go tell her." Angie scrambled off the bed. "You want a Coke, or chocolate, or whatever?"

"No, thanks." Jessica put on a short cotton nightgown and climbed into bed.

"I'll be right back," Angie said. "Mom is just at the end of the corridor."

Angie's house was huge. The end of the corridor could be a mile away. Jessica lay back on a stack of embroidered pillows. Angie might take forever getting back. Jessica closed her eyes. She was tired from the excitement of the dinner, the amount of food she'd eaten.

A door slammed. Jessica forced her eyes open and sat up. How long had she slept? Where was Angie? She looked at the heart-shaped clock on the bed stand. Only a few minutes had gone by since Angie left the room. Jessica shook her head to wake herself up. A show about sick people wasn't her idea of fun, but if Angie wanted to watch it, she'd watch too.

Angie strode in, two Snickers bars in her hand. "Okay, I'm ready for show time." She climbed into bed.

Jessica moved over to make room for her. "I heard a door slam."

"That was the wind. The window was open in the kitchen. It's raining now."

"Was Margot asleep?"

"She's out. I looked everywhere." Angie unwrapped a Snickers bar.

"She leaves you alone in this big house?"

"You're here." Angie took a bite of her candy bar. "You're not scared, are you?"

"No way!" Jessica hugged a pillow tight against her chest and inched closer to Angie.

Valerie thought she heard the driver moan. She wasn't sure because of the wind. Then she thought she heard mumbled words. Was the driver asking for help? God, she'd better check. Valerie got out of the car. Her hair, which had been wet from the shower when Rob called from the restaurant to say he wasn't feeling well and would she take the girls home, was tucked inside his Giants baseball cap. She had put on tan slacks, a starched white shirt, loafers.

The rain was coming down steadily now. Just her luck. Her Tod loafers would get soaked. Valerie climbed out of the driver's seat and slowly approached the other car. The driver stayed slumped over the steering wheel. He or she, whatever, better still be alive. Bodies gave her the creeps. That's why she'd chosen teeth instead of organs. "Hello there?"

She heard another moan. The driver wasn't moving, but there wasn't any blood that she could see. "You'll be all right." She walked closer to the car. She mustn't touch this person. She could get sued. "Just hold on. Okay? I'm going back to Hawthorne Park. I'll get help. Hold on now."

Before she turned, she heard a deafening brief burst of noise. She looked at the car in surprise. Something dark had splashed against the door. The driver was sitting up, facing her. An "oh" of recognition escaped her lips just as another burst of noise rang out. Valerie fell on her knees, and her body eased onto the blacktop. She clutched her stomach. It was wet and sticky. "Why?" she asked herself, and then her mind went blank.

CHAPTER 10

"What the hell did you do with Valerie?" Rob yelled into the phone.

Lori glanced at the clock. It was five twenty-three on the morning of her first job interview in sixteen years and from the sound of Rob's voice, he seemed hell-bent on ruining it for her. So what if she'd slapped Valerie. The woman deserved it and Rob deserved a lot worse.

Rob started yelling again. She lowered the cell phone against her chest to muffle his words and listened instead to the wind making a racket in the trees, the rain pelting against the window. A rip-roaring summer storm—thunder and all—to accompany the tirade Rob was screaming into her chest. How fitting and ugly. Lori cut him off and buried her head in her pillow.

Seconds later, Beethoven's Fifth chimed again. Lori reached for the cell to turn it off. She opened an eye. What if it was Jess? Lori sat up, both eyes open. Nope, a 212 number. Rob again. She pressed the talk button, quietly said, "Valerie deserved it," and turned the phone off before Rob could answer. She was shaking now with that awful feeling of loss, of not knowing who she was, that had first come to her when Rob announced he was leaving her. Lori curled herself into a ball. She felt as if the bones of her legs had melted and her spine had turned to sponge. When was she going to find herself again? What had Beth said yesterday? Something about nice thoughts. Think them. That was it.

Lori shot out of bed, threw on her bathrobe, and hurried downstairs to look at Alec Winters's bouquet. She let her eyes feast on the lusciousness of the flowers. She inhaled their perfume. *What a sweet gesture,* she thought. It deserved a thank you. Maybe he could become a friend, and they could go out together to a movie, maybe even get to the point where they would end up having heart-to-heart chats while gulping down cheeseburgers and fries at Callie's.

Lori left the flowers and walked into the kitchen. The answering machine was flashing. One message. When Lori pressed the play button, she heard Rob's voice, "It's three o'clo—" She pushed erase and switched on the small TV, pressed the TiVo button to the Food Channel. Lori cut two slices of semolina bread, covered them with Dijon mustard, added imported Fontina cheese, slipped the slices into toaster oven, and settled down to forget Rob and watch skinny, grinning Giada De Laurentiis take her back to Italy's glorious food.

The elevator of one of the new luxurious apartment towers in White Plains whisked shut. Lori checked herself in mirrored walls, reapplied lipstick, and took several deep breaths before pressing the penthouse button.

At the top floor, the elevator opened to reveal a large, stocky woman with a protruding chest, a jutting jaw, and a stern look on her face. "Hello, Mrs. Ashe." Lori extended her hand and introduced herself. Mrs. Ashe nodded and moved aside to let her in. She was wearing a gray suit with matching pearls, and as Lori looked around the living room, she noticed that Mrs. Ashe also matched the decor. The walls, the furniture, the carpet were all done in varying tones of gray. Even the art—prints and oils—were black and white. Only the plants on the terrace that flanked one side of the vast living room displayed another color, green. No flowers that Lori could see. Maybe the family was color-blind, Lori thought as she sat down on the velvet armchair Mrs. Ashe indicated. Or maybe it had something to do with the name. She was glad she'd picked a white skirt and matching top instead of the turquoise dress she first tried on. She might have lost the job right off.

Lori reached into her straw tote. "I've brought four menus for to you to choose from." What if she had to come up with gray food? Gray sole? Overcooked veal? She held out the sheets she had typed at six this morning. Mrs. Ashe was still standing, the sun from the terrace streaming on her back. It was awkward, having to crane her neck to meet her client's eyes.

Mrs. Ashe took the menus with twisted fingers. "Forgive me for standing, but to add to my mishaps, my body has decided to humiliate me. If I sit for more than two minutes, I have difficulty getting up."

Lori jumped up. "Then I'll stand, too."

One side of Mrs. Ashe's mouth rose in what Lori assumed was a smile. Lori smiled back.

"Do you want to see the kitchen or shall we walk the terrace? Movement is good even for the young. And it calms me down."

"Movement." It would help steady her nerves, too. "The kitchen can wait."

Mrs. Ashe donned a large white hat, offered one to Lori. The night's storm had swept the sky clean of any clouds to temper the sun's heat. Lori took the hat and thanked her, at the same time wondering why Mrs. Ashe's nerves needed calming.

The east-facing terrace was long and narrow, with a part of White Plains spreading below it. Lori could see all the way to Bloomingdale's on her right, in the center the hilly park of the New York Presbyterian Hospital, to the left the Stop and Shop, the gas stations, the car wash where Rob took his car every Saturday. White Plains was only twenty minutes from Hawthorne Park.

"It's not a view that compares to the one I had in Manhattan," Mrs Ashe said, as she and Lori walked down the length of the terrace and then back. "At last, I have found an apartment that is ideal, small, only one bedroom, but not far from my old one. Jonathan is vehemently opposed. I would have thought he'd be more than happy to get rid of his mother, wouldn't you?" Mrs. Ashe stopped walking and turned to Lori for confirmation, a mixture of disappointment and frustration on her face.

Lori felt sorry for her. "I'm sure he's only looking out for your best interests." She hadn't expected intimacies.

"I've embarrassed you. Please excuse me," Mrs. Ashe said, resuming her walk at a faster pace. Lori kept up. "Do you have children, Mrs. Corvino?"

"A thirteen year-old daughter."

"Children can be difficult."

"And wonderful."

"That, too," Mrs. Ashe conceded with what Lori thought was some reluctance. So mother and son did not get along. It was none of her business.

"I would like to tell you about the menu I had in mind for the dinner," Lori said.

"Please do."

She went down the list of hors d'oeuvres. Cheese puffs, artichoke toasts, prosciutto rolled on breadsticks, cherry tomatoes stuffed with bacon bits, varied French and Italian cheese platters and fresh vegetables and low-fat dips for those on a diet.

Mrs. Ashe stopped in her tracks.

God, she hates my menu already, Lori thought.

"Before you go on, Mrs. Corvino—"

"Please call me Lori."

"There is something I need to know." Mrs. Ashe looked at her sternly.

"I brought recommendations with me," Lori said. Okay, so they were written by friends. Margot, Janet, her next-door neighbor for whom she had actually cooked a Thanksgiving meal the year the neighbor was undergoing chemo.

"Those won't be necessary," Mrs. Ashe said. "It has to do with your husband."

"Ex-husband," Lori corrected.

"That is what my son said, but I wanted to make sure. The divorce is final?"

"He remarried last Saturday."

Mrs. Ashe linked her arm through Lori's and started walking again. "I'm relieved. You see, I'm not a fan of Mr. Staunton's and had you still been married to him, I couldn't bring myself to hire you. I hope you will forgive me for my prejudice."

What's Rob done to you? Lori was dying to ask, but, for her job's sake, it was better not to.

"I do hope I can work with you, Mrs. Ashe. I've been divorced eight months and I need this job to start getting back on my feet financially and mentally."

"Being a widow is not the same as being divorced, and my husband left me well off, but I do understand the hurt, dear. Above all the disorientation of being suddenly and irrevocably alone, despite children." She squeezed Lori's hand. "It's dizzying, but you'll manage. Women always do."

Lori squeezed back, happy to discover Mrs. Ashe had a soft side to her. "Let me tell you more about the menu. Since the weather has been so warm, I thought you could start with a chilled tomato soup dotted with crabmeat and cilantro, followed by a veal loin poached in broth and white wine, thinly sliced and then bathed with a tuna sauce and served cold. For side dishes, steamed asparagus and orzo pasta with tiny diced yellow and red peppers sprinkled over it. For dessert, roasted peaches cradling a dollop of crème fraîche. And an ice cream birthday cake. How does that sound?"

"You are making me hungry, Lori. I have some good croissants in the kitchen we will both enjoy. At my age, a birthday cake is embarrassing. Let's limit dessert to the peaches with a dollop of ice cream. I do fancy ice cream."

Lori's heart lifted. "Done!" Her first job was in her pocket. This was the beginning of good things; she could feel it.

Once out on the street Lori took out her cell phone. There were six messages. They were probably all from Rob, and she was in too good a mood to listen to his angry sputtering. Lori called Jessica's cell. There was no answer. She called home and got the answering machine. Jess had said she'd be home by ten, but maybe something more fun had come up. She'd call Margot in a minute to find out what the girls were up to. First she needed to talk to Janet.

At Sally's Blooms, they told her Janet was delivering flowers. She called her cell. No answer. This wasn't her day for phone calls. Lori got in her car and decided she might as well take advantage of the Stop and Shop and buy some groceries. Then she was going to swing by Whole Foods and see what they offered for Saturday's dinner. She might have to go to Little Italy in Manhattan to get the imported buffalo milk mozzarella and the Parma prosciutto, but that wouldn't be until Saturday morning. Maybe Jess would go with her. Everything had to be as fresh as possible.

As Lori turned to enter the Stop and Shop garage she saw Janet standing at the car wash talking to a man in tennis shorts. She parked the car and walked over. She had seen the man before—blond, medium height, with smooth good looks and great legs—but she couldn't place him.

"Hi, Janet, I just called you at the shop."

Janet looked startled for a moment. "Oh, I had to wash the car." She swung her arm toward the man. "You two know each other, I think."

The man turned to Lori with a smile and extended his hand. "Of course we know each other. Twice I've had the pleasure of her company and her superb cooking. How did it go with my mother?"

So this was Jonathan Ashe, who had been at Rob's law firm. How could she not remember him? His smile was so genuine and heart-warming. Maybe it was because her heart didn't need warming back then.

"I have the job."

"Good. Mother can be difficult at times. She's taken her widowhood very hard."

Janet waved her hand at them. "Listen, I better get back to work. The car is ready."

"Excuse me," Lori said to Jonathan, and hurried after her friend. "Janet, can you do the flowers for Mrs. Ashe on Saturday night? She wants me to take care of everything. I can barely get the food together at such short notice, and your arrangements are always great."

"Okay." There was no enthusiasm in Janet's voice. Without looking at Lori, she slipped into the driver's seat. "Give me the details tonight when I get home from work." She started the car and slammed the door. A bad mood day. Lori decided she'd better wait until tonight to ask if Janet would help her serve. With what Mrs. Ashe was paying for the dinner, she could afford to pay her well. Janet and Seth did need the money. At forty-six, it was impossible for Seth, a computer programmer, to compete with kids barely out of their acne-spotted teens, and Janet's mother's small inheritance wasn't going to last forever.

"Is Janet a good friend?" Jonathan asked as he sauntered over, hands in pockets, to where Lori was standing watching

Janet's car speed away.

"Yes. Seth and Rob were college roommates at Brown. How do you know her?"

"Rob introduced me. I forget where or how. Quite a while ago. And I see her a lot at Sally's Blooms."

Flowers probably sent to a girlfriend or girlfriends. There hadn't been any flowers in his apartment that she could see. She really had to get going. Find out where Jess was, do some food shopping, plan out her time. Instead she stood still and let the sun and Jonathan's presence warm her.

"I knew my mother would take to you," he said.

"She wouldn't have hired me if I was still married. What does she have against Rob?"

"She's convinced he was responsible for my leaving the law firm. It's not true, of course. In fact, Rob was my stalwart supporter. I left because I wasn't cut out to write the fine print. Mother can't accept that. You see, my father was a famous trial lawyer, the kind people 'oh' and 'ah' about. Impossible shoes to fill. Besides, law is abstract. I prefer playing with real estate, which is something I can put my foot on. Pun intended."

Lori laughed politely. So his humor wasn't great. How much younger did Beth say he was? God, what was she thinking? It had to be the heat, which always made her feel languid and sexual. The heat and the fact that a male hand hadn't touched her body in over ten months.

A Honda Accord slid into view behind Jonathan. Gunmetal gray, with droplets of water gleaming in sun. A car wash attendant quickly wiped it dry. "Ready, sir."

Jonathan beamed a smile at Lori and opened the car door. "It's time I left, too, but it was great seeing you again." He shook Lori's hand. She was surprised at how cool his touch was. "Thanks for taking on the job at such short notice."

"Thank you."

He waved. She waved back and he was off. *Too bad,* Lori thought as she walked back to her car. She slid into the driver's seat and leaned her head back. Too bad for what? Too bad Jonathan Ashe left so quickly? Too bad he wasn't going to run his hands over her naked body? Too bad she even had to think about another man? What did it matter? It was a glorious day and she was on her way to a great new career.

CHAPTER 11

Ellie Corvino was sitting on the front steps when Lori came home, her cotton satchel draped over her head to keep out the sun. She was wearing her favorite work outfit—pink Juicy Couture sweats that held her in a death grip, shoulder pads to minimize her large breasts, and silver sneakers she'd bought on her last trip to Florida.

"Hi, Mom, what brings you here?" Lori was relieved to see Ellie's lap wasn't holding a pan of tofu lasagna. "Is the travel business slow today?" She lowered the grocery bags to the steps and unlocked the door, briefly wondering where Jessica was. She hadn't been able to get hold of Margot. Angie's cell number was what she needed. "Do you want lunch? I have salad, carrots, radishes. Even hummus, which I know you love."

"I didn't come here for food." Ellie lifted herself up cautiously, refusing Lori's help with a shrug of her shoulder. Another woman in a bad mood.

"Isn't it a glorious day?" Lori nudged the door open with her knee. "I just got my first catering job." She was about to pick up the groceries when her cell phone rang. She checked the number in case it was Rob again. It was Janet.

"Don't tell Seth you saw me with Jonathan this morning."

"Okay," Lori said. "You all right?" Janet sounded rattled.

"It's just that Seth doesn't like him. I don't know why, but he just doesn't."

"I'm not going to say a word, Janet." Lori had never thought

77

of Seth as the possessive, authoritarian type. He came across as mild-mannered, even weak, but you never knew what went on behind the closed doors of a marriage. "By the way, can you help me Saturday night?" Lori told Janet about flowers for the dinner party, asked her to be her wait staff.

"I'll have to check with Seth. I'll let you know tonight." Janet hung up.

"She say anything to you?" Ellie asked.

"Nothing of importance, why?"

"If you'd let me keep the house key, I could have gone inside instead of frying out here." Ellie never did like to answer questions.

"You could have sat in the car with the air-conditioning on."

"Not with the price of gas gone to Mars. You should answer your phone and listen to the radio."

Lori picked up the groceries and stepped aside to let her mother enter the house first. "I was at a job interview, which I got, so you should be proud of me and you know I prefer tapes. James Taylor. Phil Collins. Remember 'You Can't Hurry Love'? I used to listen to it over and over again." The perfume of Alec Winters's flowers engulfed Lori the minute she stepped into the front hall. She wondered if Jonathan Ashe sent such wonderful bouquets to his girlfriend. Maybe they were even more beautiful. Then Lori realized her mother, who never missed a detail—and the flowers were a detail that hit you smack in the eyes and nose—was trudging up the stairs without paying the blooms the slightest attention.

"Where are you going?"

"The bathroom."

"There's one down here."

Ellie stopped on the last step to catch her breath. "I'm not a guest. I'm your mother."

A small knot of worry slid into its usual place in the middle of Lori's chest. Ellie had used the downstairs bathroom countless times. She debated following her mother upstairs, but decided against it. Ellie would only resent it. Lori hurried into the kitchen, put the groceries away, and waited.

When Ellie walked into the kitchen, her face was red and she looked twenty years older. The knot in Lori's chest swelled into a fist. "Has something happened to Jessica?"

"Jess is okay. She's with her father."

"Again? Why?"

"Lori, sit, listen, and don't interrupt."

Lori sensed that what she was about to hear was going to be unpleasant at best, and after many years of not obeying her mother's commands, did as she was told.

"Sometime last night, during the storm, an oak tree fell across Caldwell Street where it intersects with Foster Lane and blocked all traffic, so no one noticed the car at the bottom of the ravine until the road was cleared. That was around ten o'clock this morning. When the police finally pulled the car up, the trunk popped open." Ellie wiped her mouth with her hand. "Valerie was inside. Shot to death. The car was Rob's BMW."

Lori sat without moving. Her brain couldn't grasp her mother's words, make sense of them. She didn't immediately know what to think or feel except that she was cold. "Dead?"

"Murdered."

Slowly Rob's enraged words came back to Lori: "What have you done with Valerie?"

She had only slapped her. Nothing more. Just one slap. Oh Lord, how she had hated her, even wished her dead. And now. "It makes no sense," she said. "Who would want to kill her? Why?"

"Jessica told me this morning that Rob got sick and Valerie ended up driving them back in Rob's car."

Lori jumped up. "I have to call Jess. Rob. I'll go into the city.

They need me."

"Wait." Ellie grabbed Lori's arm and pulled her back down into the chair. The phone rang. "Don't answer that. It's just going to be friends or the newspapers. It can wait. Now take a deep breath." Ellie rummaged in her satchel and brought out a tarnished silver flask the family called *la Croce Rossa,* the Red Cross. It had first belonged to Lori's Abruzzesi grandfather. "Here. Take some grappa. It gets the brain cells going again."

"My brain cells are fine." Lori took a swig anyway.

"You're not going into the city."

"Yes, I am."

"He doesn't want to see you."

"What do you know about it?"

"The first time he called me was at six this morning. I was in the middle of my calisthenics. I nearly spit out my heart when I heard the phone. Thought something had happened to you or Jessica. After six or seven phone calls with the man, I know what I know. I hear you gave her a good whack."

"She was still standing when I left." Lori tilted the flask into her mouth, hoping the grappa would burn her back to normal, with Valerie alive and Jess having a great time upstairs on her cell or computer.

"Standing is good. You got an alibi for last night?"

Lori stared at the wall. She was sure her breath could set the house on fire. "An alibi? What for?"

"Rob thinks you killed Valerie. He's telling the police right now, so I think you should stay right here and get your story straight."

Lori walked to the wall phone by the refrigerator and dialed. Jessica answered after the first ring.

"Honey, are you okay? I'm coming into the city to be with you and Dad. I'll leave right now and bring clothes, toiletries. Food, too."

"You can't come, Mom. Dad just wants me."

"But this is so awful. I want to help, be with you." *Don't you want to be with me? Wouldn't any other thirteen-year-old want their mother at a time like this?*

"Mom, please! Don't come."

"I didn't hurt her, Jess."

"You slapped her."

"I didn't kill her."

"I know that, but you shouldn't have hit her. The police know."

"I was trying to protect you. Where are you?"

"At the police station. I gotta go now. I'll call you later. Love you."

"Which police sta—" Too late. Jessica had hung up. Lori spun around to face her mother with a little laugh to cover up the sting of the rejection. "She couldn't talk. Someone walked into the room. She's calling me later."

Ellie sat back in her chair. "She's going to keep choosing sides for a while. Better get used to it. It's part of the Divorce Reality Show."

Lori shook her head. What was Jessica thinking now? Was she hurting? Scared? Had she liked Valerie? Loved her, even? Poor, sweet girl. The divorce had been bad enough for her. Now this. "Rob doesn't really think I killed her, does he?"

"It's what the police are going to think that I'm worried about. I called up Joey Pellegrino. He's going to look into this for me."

"Mom! I can deal with this myself!" Even if she couldn't, Lori didn't want her mother taking over with her worries, with her need to always be central in any situation. "And who the heck is Joey Pellegrino?"

"A retired police captain in Mamaroneck, that's who, and he owes me because I get him real good prices to Naples for his really big family—six kids, four grandkids, brothers, sisters, enough to make me go bankrupt, but you never know when you're going to need the police on your side."

The phone rang. Lori let the machine upstairs pick up. She wanted time, space to herself. If only her mother would leave. She felt guilty for having slapped Valerie just hours before the woman died, for having hated her. The worst feeling of guilt and shame came from the tiny spark of satisfaction she had felt when Ellie gave her the news. Valerie and Rob both punished. *Good,* had been her first thought before the enormity of what had happened hit her. "The police are always supposed to be on your side."

"Not if they think you killed Valerie. Do you have an alibi?"

"I was here by myself. Jessica called me when she got to Margot's." Beethoven's Fifth rang out from the depths of Lori's handbag. She reached in and turned her cell off. A vague memory stirred but stayed hidden.

"Valerie was killed after she dropped off Jessica," Ellie said.

"But I would have had to know Valerie was bringing the girls home."

"What if the police think Jessica told you. What if they—"

"Stop it with the cop stuff. I'm getting a headache." Woozy from the grappa, Lori pulled open the refrigerator door, unwrapped the chunk of Parmesan cheese, and broke off the tip. She leaned against the freezer door. Ellie's "Go Vegan" magnet fell to the floor. "I don't have a gun." Lori bit into the Parmesan. It was way past her lunchtime.

"Guns you can buy off the street for two hundred bucks. And eating cheese is going to give you gas and maybe stomach cancer. And please pick up my magnet from the floor. I'd do it myself, but I'd stay bent for life."

Lori picked up the magnet and put it back on the freezer door. She would have preferred dumping it into the trash, but accepting "Go Vegan" on her refrigerator had been Lori's peacekeeping gesture.

"By the way, this was in your mailbox." Ellie dropped an envelope on the table.

Lori picked it up and squinted to read the return address. "Taking mail from a mailbox that is not your own is illegal. I might tell Joey Pellegrino on you."

Ellie let out a snort, her way of laughing. "I got bored waiting and was hoping for a magazine. Who's this Alec Winters who lives in Bedford and writes on expensive stationery? He addressed it to Mrs. Lori Corvino. Not telling him about the divorce is good strategy, Loretta. Doesn't scare him off. Is he the guy who sent the flowers?"

Lori slipped the envelope into her pocket. "I'd rather talk about murder. Here's the truth. I didn't kill Valerie and once the police hear me out, they'll move on to someone else. I'm a good mother, an upright citizen. I have no terrorist ties. I give money to charities. And now, dear mother, you'll have to excuse me." Lori stood up and went back to the refrigerator to take out eggs, carrots, celery, an onion, parsley, the paper bag with the Parmesan, a tube of tomato paste, a package of ground chuck, and a head of escarole. From the cupboard she took out four cans of chicken broth and a package of orzo, then stuffed everything in a large cloth shopping bag to which she added a loaf of Italian bread. Valerie had struck Lori as a woman who ate out or ordered in, if she ate at all. On second thought, she had better bring along an unopened bottle of olive oil just in case.

As Ellie helped herself to grappa from the Red Cross flask, she watched her daughter bent on her mission to erase all misery with food. "You're going to New York whether those two want you or not and you're going to feed them."

"Right on. Papa's cure-all. Escarole soup with meatballs."
The doorbell rang.

CHAPTER 12

"Is there anything I can do?" Jonathan Ashe said when Lori opened the door. He held out a bouquet of yellow cabbage roses. "I thought these might cheer you up. Thirteen, one extra for good luck. I hope you're not superstitious. I heard the news on the radio."

"That's very thoughtful," Lori said, burying her face in the flowers. She felt suddenly awkward, embarrassed by Jonathan's kindness. "We hardly know each other," she said quietly. She could hear her mother's halting footsteps coming nearer.

Jonathan leaned in closer. The perfume of roses mixed with the lemony scent of his aftershave. "You cooked for me, remember? Twice. And on Saturday you're cooking for my mother. That makes us fast friends in my book."

"Aren't you going to invite the man in?"

Lori jumped back at Ellie's words. "Of course. I'm sorry. I—"

As Jonathan stepped in the front hall, Ellie gave Jonathan the once-over. She was obviously pleased by the sight of his well-cut navy blue suit, the yellow silk tie, the smile that could melt chocolate. "Who are you?"

With a quick glance toward Alec Winters's large display of flowers on the corner table, Jonathan introduced himself with a handshake. "I used to work with Rob at the law firm."

Ellie folded her arms across her vast chest. "If it's a reference you're giving me, that one doesn't get you the job."

Jonathan laughed and turned to Lori, who was still holding the roses to her face. She was sure she was blushing. Because of Ellie. Because of his good looks. Because her breath smelled of grappa for sure.

"Listen, Lori. I didn't mean to interrupt anything," Jonathan said. "I just wanted to make sure you were all right. I called Rob and I know your daughter's with him. I didn't want you to be alone."

"Thanks," Lori said. He was too good to be true. "That's very nice of you. Actually I'm about to leave. Jessica wants me in the city and I think Rob can use my help, too." Why was she lying? What was she trying to prove? That she hadn't been shut out, that she was needed? If her mother said anything to the contrary, Lori was going to make her swallow that magnet.

Jonathan looked at his watch. "I have a three o'clock meeting in midtown. I'll drive you in."

"Oh, no, thank you. I'll take the train. Really."

"She'd love to go with you," Ellie said. "Just give her a minute to get her stuff." Ellie took Lori by the shoulders, turned her around in the direction of the stairs and whispered, "Jessica could handle this better than you."

During the ride into Manhattan, Jonathan kept up a monologue. How he had to work not to be taken in by the thrill of the deal just for the deal's sake. How he worked at being honest, although the temptation to cut corners in the real estate business was like trying to resist the sirens of the Odyssey. How there had been many times when he wished he had a mast available to tie himself to as Ulysses had done. After a few minutes he would stop and give Lori a questioning look. She would nod and say, "Go on," relieved she did not have to keep up her end of the conversation. She was furious at Ellie, but happy to be riding next to a nice, handsome man. He distracted her from thinking of what lay ahead.

She listened to Jonathan telling her how difficult it was to have his mother stay with him, how she was finally coming out of the worst part of her grief and thinking of finding a new home of her own. How strict and distant his father had been with him. His biggest regret was that resentment had stopped him from telling his father how much he loved him before he died. He spoke of his meeting that afternoon to discuss a possible partnership in a new venture with an old school friend coming in from Pennsylvania. They were going to buy grand old dilapidated homes across the country, restore them to their former glory, and then resell them.

When they reached the West Side Highway, Jonathan said, "I always shut up when I get to this point. The view is so great."

Lori looked out of the car window. The Hudson River glittered under the sun. The sailboats glided like so many swans. The George Washington Bridge was majestic in its breadth. A sight that had always made her feel good. But now . . . if what Ellie had said was true, which was never a given, Rob thought she was the murderer. How could he think that? And what was he going to do when he saw her. Kick her out? Call the police? Hug her and say how wrong he'd been all along? Was Jessica going to forgive her for barging in even if she brought food? God, she had inherited her mother's worry genes. Why couldn't she be more like Papa, who was quiet and kind and fell off the roof he was fixing without even a peep?

They left the highway at 96th Street. "I'm sorry I ran on like that," Jonathan said in a warm voice, glancing at Lori hugging herself. "Is the air-conditioning too high?"

Lori shook her head and released her arms. "Don't be sorry. It helped."

"Good, that was the intention. Next time it will be your turn. I don't mean Saturday night. You'll have enough to do without telling me your life story. But I do want to hear it."

"About Saturday night—"

Jonathan stopped Lori with a squeeze of her hand. "Please don't back out."

"I might be a suspect." Even if they didn't arrest her, she would be worried enough to burn everything. "I don't think your mother would approve."

Jonathan started laughing.

He made her want to laugh, too. The idea of being a suspect was so ridiculous. She tapped his thigh. "Stop. It's not funny."

With one hand, Jonathan pulled his mouth down into a grimace. "Better?"

"Much."

"My mother will be delighted to show off a murder suspect to her friends along with excellent food. It's so original it just might send them over the edge with envy. I think I'll have an ambulance on call, just in case."

"You're being mean."

"No. I'm playing the clown. I want to see you smile." He swung the car onto Park Avenue and stopped in front of Rob's building.

"You know the address," Lori said, surprised. She hadn't told him.

"Yes, but I've never been in the apartment. And I never met Valerie. Does that clear me?"

"But you're Rob's friend?"

"Not a social one. Purely business."

Jonathan leaned over to open the door for her. His arm almost brushed her breasts. Almost. She needed to get out of the car fast. "Promise me only jail will keep you away on Saturday."

Lori didn't move. "It depends on how Jessica is doing."

"Okay. That I can understand. Let me know as soon as you can." He kissed her cheek lightly after she thanked him for the ride. She wanted to kiss him back, on the lips. Instead she swung her legs out of the car, stood up with as much grace as she could muster, and walked away. When Mike O'Connor, the head doorman, opened the door for Lori, she turned around. Seeing Jonathan still there, Lori felt a rush of warmth envelop her body. She had to watch out for this man. He was sure to go down as smooth and sweet as crème caramel.

CHAPTER 13

There was no need for Rob to call the police. They opened the door to his apartment. Two of them. No mistaking who they were. Over six feet. Between two hundred and three hundred pounds each, was Lori's guess. Ex-football players for sure. The ones who did the tackling. "Who are you?" the white one asked her.

Lori raised her L.L.Bean bag full of food. "The cook," she said. *Get to the kitchen. Start cooking,* she told herself. *Everything will be fine.* Lori edged her way in between them. Barely. How did they fit in the same car? That's what she'd seen on TV, two detectives always riding together, eating doughnuts, hotdogs, holding a cup of coffee, sometimes a gun. They'd probably like her soup. "Where's the kitchen?" Lori asked. And where was Jessica? "Have you seen a young girl?" she asked the smaller of the two, a black man with a rumpled face and startling blue eyes.

"Your name?" he asked. He didn't sound mean. Merely curious.

She thought of lying, but that would really get her into trouble. "Lori Corvino. Where's Jessica?"

"The ex-wife," the white detective said.

Lori stayed with the black policeman. He looked kinder, and he had a button dangling from his jacket that under different circumstances she would have offered to fix. "What's your name?" she asked.

"Detective Mitchell. Your daughter's taking a nap."

My daughter is clever was Lori's thought. "And where's my ex-husband?"

"At the funeral home," Detective Mitchell said.

Of course, the grim details of death needed taking care of. Lori couldn't help feeling pity for Rob. His bid for a new life, selfish as it was, had been too quickly, too horribly interrupted.

"It'll be a while before we release the body." The white policeman introduced himself. "Detective Scardini." He had an incongruous snub nose and a head too small for his size. His eyes were so deeply set Lori couldn't tell what color they were. "We're with the Hawthorne Park Homicide Squad, investigating the death of Valerie Fenwick."

"If Rob's gone and Jessica is asleep, what are you doing here?" Lori asked. "Babysitting?"

Scardini shook his melon ball of a head slowly. "Lady, you have attitude."

"I'm just a little upset about my ex's new wife getting shot. This bag weighs a ton and I really would like to go to the kitchen and get started on my father's famous escarole soup and meatballs. My daughter loves it. My ex loves it and if you have some, you'll clear up the murder in no time at all. Now where's the kitchen?"

A crack of a smile showed on Mitchell's face. "Sounds good to me." He held up a hand. "Back, past the dining room, to the left." The detectives followed her. On the way, Lori's eyes took in the furniture—sleek, shiny, lots of glass, black leather. Bare walls. Everything ultramodern. Cold, uninviting. The dining-room table was oblong white and gray marble. The lamps on the wall looked like white porcelain bats. What had happened to Rob's love of the old, comfortable lived-in look? Well, he'd dumped her, so obviously his tastes had changed. *And not for the better*, she told herself for courage. Being here was awful enough. She didn't need two detectives on her tail.

Lori set the food bag down on one counter and turned to examine the kitchen, always the best room in a home in her opinion. She was glad to see it was smaller than her own. Mottled brown marble tiles. Granite counters. Granite back-splash. Pale wood glass-fronted cabinets. A gleaming Sub-Zero refrigerator that held no magnets. A Garland stove with a grill. Were they ever used? There wasn't a speck of dirt or grease anywhere. Nothing on the countertops. A granite-covered island sat in the middle of the space, one side jutting out to accom-modate two tall steel stools. The kitchen looked more like a lab to dissect frogs than a place to cook a meal. But then she couldn't picture Valerie in an apron bending over a hot stove, and Rob could barely assemble a peanut butter and jelly sand-wich.

"We'd like to ask you some questions," Scardini said.

Lori held up her hand. "First let me peek in on my daughter to make sure she's all right."

Mitchell nodded. "We're not going anywhere." Scardini blessed him with a dirty look.

So Scardini was the bad cop to Mitchell's good cop. She liked that. There was some justice to it. "Do you know which room she's in?"

Mitchell started to move, but Scardini blocked him. "I'll take her."

Lori followed him through another kitchen door to a corridor carpeted by long, narrow Oriental rugs. They passed three doors. Scardini kept going until he got to the last door. Lori waited until he stepped aside before slowly turning the doorknob. She opened the door only wide enough to stick her head in. She didn't want the detective to see Jessica awake, counting the minutes until they left.

"Jess?" she whispered, then closed the door quickly. "Out

cold," Lori said to the detective. Which was the truth. Jessica was curled up under a white duvet, the air conditioning going full blast, hugging the needlepoint pillow Lori had stitched for her twelfth birthday, which read, "You Are My Sweetheart." It was enough to make Lori blubber again. Something she wasn't about to do in front of these detectives.

"I'll answer questions while I get the soup started," Lori said when they reached the kitchen. She opened cabinets until she found a brand new All-Clad pot and sauté pan, placed them on the stove, poured a little olive oil in both. She then dug out the onion from her bag and began peeling it. "Cooking helps me concentrate." Gave her confidence was more the truth.

"We were waiting for you," Scardini said.

Lori stared, wide-eyed. "How did you know I was coming?"

Mitchell grinned, his eyes scrunching up. "Your mother called. She said to warn Jessica you were coming over. She didn't ask who I was."

Lori's knife slashed into an onion and quickly reduced it to paper thin slices.

Mitchell stepped back from the counter. "Aren't those going to make you cry?"

"You bet," Lori said. And her mother was going to make her scream.

Scardini took the lead in the interrogation. Why did she hit Dr. Fenwick just hours before she was killed? Because Valerie had hurt her daughter, Lori explained, as she turned on one burner and dropped the onions in the pot.

Where was she last night between the hours of ten thirty and midnight? Lori grated two carrots, added them to the sautéing onions along with a spoonful of tomato paste, and repeated what she had told her mother.

Scardini picked up the wooden spoon Lori had brought and stirred the contents of the pot.

"He's Italian," Mitchell said as an excuse.

"It was about to burn," Detective Scardini said in his defense. "Anyone to verify that fact?"

"That it was about to burn?" Lori asked. She was annoyed at him for taking over. And just a little bit scared. "My daughter called me when she got to Margot Dixon's house."

"She made no mention of a phone call to you."

"Why should she?" Lori stopped rolling a meatball to look up at Mitchell's nice face. "You don't really think I shot Valerie? I don't want my husband back and he doesn't want me back, so what would be the point?"

" 'Hell hath no fury,' " Mitchell quoted.

Lori cut him off. "If that's true I would have shot Rob." She caught the two detectives exchanging glances. "Listen, I didn't shoot anyone."

"No one is saying you did," Mitchell said. "We have to ask."

"Okay," Scardini said. "You just made an interesting statement. 'I would have shot Rob.' Now this is one possible scenario. Operative word is 'possible,' so you don't have to get all hot under the collar. Here goes." He settled back against the counter while Lori rolled meatball after meatball. She was making far too many, but the motion soothed her.

"Husband of sixteen years leaves you and your kid for another woman," Scardini continued. "A very rich woman. He lets you keep the house and throws in child support, but no alimony. None of the above is going to sit well with most wives."

"I didn't want any alimony." She turned on the flame under the sauté pan. "And I'm not most wives."

Scardini raised a skeptical eyebrow. "Do you own a gun?" He took the meatballs she had rolled and settled them gently in the pan.

"No and stop interfering!"

"You sound like my wife. How about your ex, while you were

still married to him, did he own a gun?"

"No!"

"That's settled, then. Last night your ex takes his daughter and her friend to a fancy restaurant in Manhattan without getting your permission first, which could only add to your bad feelings. You know that he's going to drive them back to the Dixon lady. You say your daughter called when she got back, but if she did, I bet she didn't tell you the new wife drove her back instead of her father because she's a sweet girl and didn't want to upset you."

Those were two details Scardini got right. Jess was sweet and Lori would have been upset if she had known Valerie was driving them back. Maybe not upset, more like jealous. She'd lost a husband to that woman. She didn't want to lose a daughter. Now, of course, there was no danger of that. Maybe Scardini would think that was an added motive. Lori slipped the spoon out of Scardini's hand and stirred the washed and chopped escarole into the pot. She and Mitchell watched it wilt.

Scardini kept talking. "You know your daughter's back. You get in your car, drive fast to Caldwell Road, park the car in the middle of the road, hide in the trees. Dr. Fenwick comes along a few minutes later. You hail her down or your car blocks her way. She gets out of her husband's new BMW—a car you know, because he picked you up at the airport when you came back from Italy."

"I see my ex has been very talkative."

"From your vantage point all you can see is the car and a tall person—Dr. Fenwick was only two inches shorter than Mr. Staunton—dressed in chinos, a man's shirt, wearing your ex's baseball cap. You're blinded by fury, by the darkness in the trees. You aim, shoot, and kill the dentist instead of the ex."

Lori added the chicken broth to the escarole, turned the meatballs to brown evenly. "I would say that's an impossible scenario. First of all, Valerie would have had to stay put at Margot's for at least ten minutes in order for me to reach Caldwell Road in time to stop her, and secondly, even blinded by fury and the dark, I would still recognize my husband just by the sound of his footsteps. Sixteen years of marriage does that. Besides, I love my daughter too much to kill the father she adores."

"That's a good point," Mitchell said.

Scardini didn't let up. "So maybe you knew who you were killing. Three-day-old wife, bang, bang, dead. Like you saying to the ex: 'So much for your new life, buster.' "

"Did you find tire tracks on the road to match to my car?"

Scardini pushed a finger in the air. "Now that's a good point. We'll need to take your car."

Lori dropped the wooden spoon and stared at him. "You're kidding, right? How am I going to get around? Public transportation stinks where I live."

Scardini shrugged. "Rent."

While Lori glared at Scardini, Mitchell bent down to pick up the spoon and handed it to her.

"Thank you," she said and pointed to the dangling button. "Be careful with that. You'll lose it." He gave her a smile that almost made up for the other guy. "The car's at home."

"Okay, tomorrow," Scardini said. "And don't try cleaning anything because we'll spot whatever was in there."

Lori washed the spoon, dried it. "I thought that worked only on TV." Renting a car was not in her budget and she was about to ask how long they'd keep the car, but she was afraid the answer would only make her feel worse. Maybe Margot would lend her one of her cars—the least fancy one. She had three.

Mitchell took a deep breath. "The soup sure smells good." He had a baritone voice, the kind that wraps itself around you like a blanket on a cold day.

Lori gave him a smile. He was trying to make her feel better. "What about the gun?" she asked. Being under suspicion did not stop her from being curious. "Did you find it?"

The look on Scardini's face stopped Mitchell from saying anything.

"I can answer that myself," Lori said. "You found nothing."

"How's that?" Scardini wanted to know.

"You asked me if I or Rob owned a gun. If you'd found it you'd know already who it belonged to."

Scardini shook his head. "It's that fast only on TV."

Lori lifted the pot lid and stirred the soup. Neither of the men moved. "Any more questions?" she asked after a few minutes of silence. She couldn't think of anything else to ask.

"If we do, we'll let you know," Mitchell said. 'We're only at the beginning of our investigation."

"Are you waiting for Rob?"

"No." Scardini glanced at his watch. "Soup's been simmering for twelve minutes."

"I know."

Scardini looked at her, looked at the meatballs. Mitchell took another deep breath. Lori looked at the crystal wall clock. It was five minutes to five. Snack time. Feed your enemy, make a friend, her father had taught her as she sat on a stool to watch him cook. By the time she was seven he had taught her Bolognese, pesto, and carbonara sauces. More lessons were going to follow, but suddenly he was gone.

Maybe Scardini was teaching his kids how to cook. If he was, she could forgive him his stupid "possible" scenario. And Mitchell was a sweet man. Lori dropped the meatballs into the soup, gave the soup a stir. "Three more minutes and it's done." She unearthed two soup bowls, two spoons, grated cheese into the bowls, ladled out the soup and fed the two homicide detectives.

After Mitchell and Scardini left, Lori washed out the bowls and the spoons, dried them, and set them in front of the two stools on the other side of the island for Rob and Jessica, and then walked down the corridor.

"Are they still here?" Jessica asked as soon as Lori opened the door. She was still under the duvet.

"Fed and gone." Lori picked up the needlepoint pillow from the floor, set it against the back of a white leather armchair. The entire room was white. "Hi, honey." She bent over to kiss Jessica. "You don't seem surprised to see me."

"You're like Grandma. Once you get something in your head, that's it."

"You mean, I'm just like you."

Jessica started crying. Lori sat down on the bed and held her, stroking her back, kissing her head. "I'm so sorry you're going through this, Jess."

"Is Dad here?" Jess finally asked, letting go of her mother to reach for the tissue box.

"Not yet."

"I'm so worried about him, Mom." Jessica blew her nose. "It's just so mean for this to happen to him."

"I know."

"I can't go to Cape Cod with Angie on Monday. He needs me here."

"We'll see." Lori said. Staying with Rob with the police hanging around and making life miserable for everyone was the last thing her daughter needed. "I'll talk to Dad about it."

"I'll talk to him," Jessica said with the annoyed voice she used whenever she thought she was being treated like a little girl. "I think you should go before Dad comes back. He doesn't want to see you, Mom. I'm sorry."

Lori didn't care if Rob wanted to see her or not. After listening to Scardini's "possible scenario," she needed to find out why Rob was going around saying he was the intended victim.

"Please, Mom?" Jessica's lower lip trembled. Tears were about to start again.

"Okay, hon." Scardini wasn't going to arrest her tonight, not without more solid evidence, and Jess needed to be coddled. With Valerie gone, Lori suspected Jess felt responsible for her beloved Daddy and didn't want rejected Mom to run interference. "I just came to make sure you were all right." Lori got up from the bed, smoothed the duvet over Jessica's body. She would talk to Rob tomorrow. He was probably too upset to make much sense tonight. "I hope those two detectives were nice to you?"

"They asked me a lot of questions about the divorce, how angry you were at Dad, did you hate Valerie, dumb stuff like that. It was like they thought you'd killed her so I didn't tell them I called you when I got to Margot's house."

"Why not? Your phone call tells them I was home when Valerie dropped you off."

"But you didn't answer the phone! I let it ring and ring. I hung up and called you on your cell. That means you could have been anywhere."

"That can't be." Lori felt her stomach hollow out.

"Mom! I'm not lying."

Now she had no alibi. "I know you're not, but I was home, Jess. In bed. Right next to the phone. Even if I was asleep, I would have heard the phone. You must have dialed the wrong number."

"I tried three times! I know my own home number. I'm not stupid."

"Of course you're not." Would Jessica's cell phone records show a dialed wrong number? Of course not, no one had answered. "Wait a minute! The answering machine should have picked up."

"It didn't, Mom. You always forget to turn it on."

No, she had turned it on, Lori was sure of it. Had she somehow unplugged the phone without being aware of it?

Lori planted a kiss on the top of Jessica's head and gave her a reassuring mother smile, the kind that was supposed to communicate *Be brave, we'll get through this somehow*. It was meant to help her as much as Jess. "I've made escarole and meatball soup for you and Daddy. There's some grated Parmesan in the fridge. I'll be home if you need me. Okay?"

Jessica clutched her pillow to her chest. "I told them you didn't kill her." To Lori's relief, there was no doubt in Jessica's eyes.

"Thank you, sweetie, you're the best." They hugged. Jessica scrambled out of bed and, linking her arm through Lori's, walked her to the front door. Whether out of love or the need to make sure her mother was leaving, Lori didn't want to know.

The train was jammed with commuters. Lori was lucky to find a middle seat in the last car. Once the train emerged out of the Grand Central tunnel, she reached into the pocket of her skirt for a tissue. Scrunched at the bottom she found Alec Winters's letter and stared at it for a few minutes, not remembering why it was in her hand, why the man had written to her. She thought of slipping it back into her pocket—she still needed to find a tissue—but was momentarily distracted by the strips of sun-burnt clouds flashing in between the buildings as she tried to let go of the hard ball of tension in her chest.

The train stopped at the 125th Street Station. More commuters streamed in, looking for seats, walking past to the next cars. People-watching was one of Ellie Corvino's favorite occupations, always ready to make snap judgments on what they did for a living, how happy or unhappy they were, from where they or their parents or grandparents had come. Right after Rob's betrayal Lori had picked up the habit, counting on the great variety of faces and expressions to confirm her hope that life would be bearable again. Well, it had become more than bearable. Until now. *Put that thought aside,* Lori told herself, *and read Alec Winters's letter.* She tore one end of the envelope open.

"Happy news, huh?" a man's voice said from the aisle.

Lori looked up to her right. Janet's husband was grinning at her, a welcome change from the beaten-dog look he'd been carrying around for the last couple of years. Seth still had the tight compact body from when he'd been a star of his college ski team, but now his dark brown hair was thinning and deep lines ran across a face Lori had thought handsome for many years.

"Hi, Seth. You're looking good." He was dressed in a gray suit, white shirt, blue tie—the perfect interview outfit—but from the relaxed look on his face, Lori guessed he had finally landed a job. She smiled back at him. Seeing satisfaction light Seth's eyes again took the edge off this horrible day.

"Getting out of the hole, finally." He raked fingers across what hair he had left. "Tough about Valerie, huh? No skin off your back, though."

Seth had never scored high on sensitivity. Janet was always trying to find excuses for his blunders. "It's terrible for Rob and for Jessica," Lori reminded him.

"Sorry. I didn't mean . . . any chance now the two of you—"

Lori cut him off. "No."

"Rob's going to be one filthy rich mister, but I guess there's too much water under the bridge for the two of you—"

"A tsunami's worth. And they'd only been married three days. I doubt Valerie had time to change her will."

Seth leaned into the seat. "Right. Didn't think of that."

The man on the aisle seat next to Lori rustled his newspaper loudly, gave Seth a nasty look, and left his seat.

"Thank you, sir," Seth said, and slipped in. "Now we can get personal. Isn't it funny she should get it when Rob thought somebody was after him."

Lori gave him a questioning look.

"He was telling everyone at the wedding."

Lori played nonchalant. "That explains how Janet knew, before I told anyone." She must have been too embarrassed to say they'd gone to the wedding. "Did you believe him?"

Seth shrugged. "Not really. You know how Rob likes to make a big deal out of nothing, but still . . . you never know these days. With all the bad news we keep getting, people are going crazy. What's your take on it?"

"He was looking for sympathy," Lori said. What if Rob was the intended victim? Was it possible? The killer would have to be blind not to spot the difference between Rob and Valerie, even with her wearing chinos and his baseball cap. Rob was thin but he had a paunch, his shoulders were wide, and his gait was heavy. Valerie moved with the lightness of a breeze. And why would anyone want to kill Rob? Or Valerie, for that matter? Lori hated the uncertainty of being lost in unanswered questions, in "what if" scenarios. She'd already had a year of it.

She changed the subject. "I'm glad you and Rob have made up your differences. Rob missed you." Rob and Seth had been best friends since college, and they'd often gone out as a foursome, but about two years ago, Rob and Seth stopped speaking to each other. According to Rob, Seth had turned his back on the friendship because he was too ashamed he couldn't pay back the five thousand dollars he had borrowed a few weeks before he lost his job. According to Janet, she had asked Seth to stop seeing Rob because she was tired of Rob rubbing his own success in Seth's face. Rob did like to brag. Maybe Janet was right, maybe Rob was right. Or maybe the truth was somewhere in between.

"I don't even remember what got us off," Seth said with a laugh, "but we're old buddies again."

"He's going to need your help. Now tell me what good things are happening to you."

"I'd like to keep it for Janet, if you don't mind."

"Of course. I'm sorry." Lori was embarrassed. She had forgotten what it was like to have a partner come first.

Seth stood up. "I really think I should give that man his seat back. See you around, and Janet said she's going to be helping you with your dinner Saturday night. Soon she won't have to do any of that stuff. Don't forget to read your letter."

Lori looked down at her hand, still clutching Alec Winters's letter addressed to Mrs. Lori Corvino. She'd worn her wedding ring to Italy, that's why he thought she was married. Her mother had it all wrong. She'd worn the ring to keep men at bay, not to bring them on. Lori slit open the envelope with her finger.

Dear Mrs. Corvino,

I enclose the gnocchi della regina *recipe you were interested in. I hope your readers enjoy it. I have tried to make it and failed miserably, but I am sure you will be successful. The trick is interpreting the meager Italian directions. They always assume everyone is a natural cook, which I'm sure you are. My talent resides in pushing buttons on the microwave. I wish you well.*

> *Sincerely,*
> *Alec Winters*

For a moment Lori wondered what he meant by readers; then she remembered Beth's calling cards, her own lie to the Roman waiter about being a writer for the *Greenwich Dish.* She read the recipe, written out in a neat, almost childlike handwriting. The waiter had claimed the recipe was a family secret. How had Alec Winters managed get hold of it? It didn't look daunting. Maybe on her way home she should buy some potatoes and the other ingredients and try making the gnocchi and their sauce tonight. It would keep her mind off Valerie's death. *Alec Winters, you're a sweet man, and a lifesaver,* Lori said silently, putting the letter and recipe in her handbag. The ruined dress was forgiven.

Chapter 14

"You holding up?" Callie asked as she refilled Lori's mug with freshly brewed coffee.

Lori was sitting at her usual booth, her back to the wide window that revealed a morning with the perfect blue sunny sheen that always reminded her of the September morning when the idea of a safe world burned to nothing. She was reading "dogs for sale" ads in the *Hawthorne Park Post*. "If I don't end up in jail, I'll be fine." She had hastily put on a jeans skirt and a white T-shirt, run fingers through her hair, and forgotten makeup. Whatever she looked like, Lori knew Callie would always welcome her. Ten years ago, she had stopped one of Callie's seven grandsons from chasing a ball into the street just as a car whisked past, and a friendship was sealed. "Thanks, Callie."

"You sound hoarse," Callie said.

"Too many phone calls." Once she had gotten home from Manhattan last night, she had answered calls from various newspapers, from people who had dropped her after her divorce but now wanted in on the latest murder news, and, of course, her mother, Janet, Margot and Beth. Only to her three friends did she give honest answers. Then she'd unplugged the phone and gone to bed, feeling grouchy, exhausted, and excluded—a woman exiled from her family. Making *gnocchi della regina* might have helped, but the thought of botching it up stopped her. She couldn't deal with failure right now. She'd left the cell phone on, but Jessica didn't call.

"The others coming?" Callie asked.

Lori sipped her coffee and nodded. It wasn't their usual breakfast morning—that only happened on Mondays when Beth's gallery stayed closed and Sally's Blooms opened at eleven—but these were extraordinary times and she needed help. After a sleepless night, she'd come to the conclusion that she'd better be proactive in this investigation if she didn't want to end up at the Bedford Correctional Facility.

"I'll get you some fresh lemon juice and honey," Callie said, "and from the looks of you, you need to take home a couple of apple pies. When the going gets tough, eat. Which reminds me." Callie squeezed herself into the booth next to Lori and brought her thick black eyebrows together in a formidable frown. She smelled of browned butter and caramel.

Lori looked at her in surprise. Callie sitting anywhere in her coffee shop was a first. "What's up, Callie?"

"Take a piece of advice from an old Greek woman." Callie leaned closer. Powder or flour sat in the deep groves of her face. "Bearing gifts or no gifts, be careful of friends."

"What do you mean?"

Callie looked up behind Lori. "I mean you should take care of yourself." She edged herself to the end of the booth. "If you don't watch it, you'll come down with a bad cold." She pulled herself up just as Margot walked up. "And I'd get a mutt, if I were you. Fancy dogs are like fancy cars. They always need fixing."

"Good morning, Callie," Margot said, then leaned down to peck Lori's cheek.

"Glad it's good for you," Callie said. "I'll get that lemonade with honey."

"She's such an old grouch," Margot said, sliding into the booth and spraying the smell of Opium in the air with a toss of her hair. She was wearing the same pink Juicy Couture sweat pants and top as Ellie, except this one looked great on Margot's size-six body.

Lori watched Callie walk toward the back of the coffee shop with the characteristic sway that made her look as if she's just hit land after six months at sea. What had she meant by "be careful of friends"? Surely she wasn't talking about Callie's Gals, as she'd dubbed the breakfast group in one of her more generous moods. And no, Lori wasn't planning to get a dog, fancy or mutt. She'd just been trying to keep herself from staring at a stunning close-up of Valerie splattered on the front page next to a two-column article on the murder. At least she had learned the murder weapon was a nine-millimeter revolver. Useful information if you knew what to do with it. "Callie's upset about the murder," she told Margot.

"Aren't we all. To think the killer could have been lurking outside my house waiting to follow Valerie. It gives me the shivers. How can I help?"

"I'm going to need a car. The police are taking mine sometime today."

"Ooh, that bad?"

"That bad."

"Silver Mercedes SLK55 or white Lexus LS 430? I got rid of the Jag, a real lemon."

"I'd be too scared to drive either. Got a battered Ford in your stable?" Her Ford was eight years old.

"You're driving the Mercedes. You'll love it. It's like slipping into a lacy thong."

Lori grimaced. "Ouch."

"When's the last time you had sex?" Margot asked in a voice full of concern. "Not alone, I mean."

Jonathan's lean body dressed in tennis whites flashed before Lori's eyes. She lifted the coffee mug to her face in an attempt to hide the blush she was sure was there.

"I get it," Margot said with a dismissive shrug of one shoulder. "None of my business. Get the police to drive you over to pick it up. That's the least they can do."

Lori thanked Margot for the fancy loaner. "When you called me the night before last to tell me Jess and Angie were going to be late, did you call my home phone or my cell?"

Margot widened her eyes. "You expect me to remember? I sure could use some coffee to get the brain cells working." She jangled her bracelets at Cy, the counter man, one of Callie's countless relatives. He grinned back with a nod.

"It's important," Lori said.

Margot stood up and walked over to the counter, her pink mules flipping against her bare heels. Cy held out a mug full of coffee. She blew him a kiss and drank half of it on the way back to the booth. "I remember now," Margot said, sliding back in. "Your cell. You didn't answer your home phone. Why is it important?"

"Now I've got no alibi for that night. I must have unplugged the phone in my sleep. The funny thing is, I don't remember plugging it back in either."

"You're turning into a sleepwalker? Stress can do that to you. You better lock your front door. You don't want to wander through the streets at night in your nightgown."

"I wear pajamas."

Margot smoothed Lori's forehead with a finger. "Please stop worrying. Alibi or no alibi, the police can't possibly think you killed anyone. They're taking your car because they have to show they're on the case. Have to keep the boss happy."

"I hope you're right, but just in case you're not, did you see anyone lurking around your house when Valerie drove the girls home?"

"No, I was in my bedroom, which you know faces the water."

"Can you ask your neighbors?"

"They won't have seen anything. I'll walk into a hornet's nest if I start asking around. The cul-de-sac is dark because of all the trees, and just two weeks ago, some of the old biddies insisted on calling a meeting to discuss safety issues. I invited them all to my house for cocktails, thinking that getting them drunk would make it all go away. I couldn't have been more wrong. They want to cut down most of the old trees, can you believe that? Those trees are legendary!"

Lori put her hand over Margot's. "Please? If some of them are so worried about safety, they might have looked out of their window when Valerie drove by. They could have seen another car, taken down a license number. Start with the older owners."

"Oh, all right. Maybe I'll invite them over again and make it a game. Like Clue. Whoever saw something gets a bottle of Kettle One for a prize."

"Margot, this is serious."

"Of course it is. I just hate it, that's all. Valerie might have been a bitch, but I knew her from forever, and to think she got shot down like a deer and stuffed into the trunk of a car." Her eyes showed a mixture of fear and genuine sorrow. "How do you cope with that?"

"By trying to find out who killed her," Lori said.

"Sure," Margot said. "I'll work on one of those gorgeous CSI guys, and while he's in mid-moan, I'll clamp my legs together and get him to tell me all about the incriminating fibers he found on Valerie's body. Come on, Lori, we can't compete with the police."

"I know we can't, but we can try to make sense of it. I can't just sit back and let the police stick their noses in my life and in Jessica's. I want some control. I need it."

"And I bet you're itching with curiosity, just like I am."

Lori found herself smiling. "It's given me a rash."

"Where do we start?"

"Tell me everything you know about Valerie."

Margot pursed her lips to indicate she was thinking. "Well, what is there to say? She wasn't popular at boarding school. You know, one of those all-A students who liked to rub it in how clever, rich, skinny, and gorgeous she was. And very ambitious, which is more than I can say for myself. No one could believe she wanted to become a dentist. We all thought it was grubby work, staring at decayed teeth and wet tongues all day long, but she said holding a drill to someone's mouth was sexy and empowering."

"Why didn't she marry before?" The *New York Times* wedding announcement that Ellie had left lying on the kitchen table hadn't mentioned a previous husband.

"I know she had some serious relationships along the way. I remember Dad once asking Valerie why she'd broken up with some perfectly nice guy who'd proposed to her, and she said that since she had money of her own and she didn't want to have kids, she saw no point to locking her door."

Lori wondered which of Rob's qualities had bowled over marriage-phobic Valerie. Was it the droop of his ass? The mushrooming paunch? His snoring? His lying tongue? God, what if Valerie had wanted a child? "Do you have any idea why she changed her mind?"

"I stopped talking to her when you told me she'd snared Rob. Look, I was as surprised as you were, you know that."

Callie's insidious words, "Be careful of friends," curled themselves in Lori's ear. "Yes, I do know that," she said finally, believing it. Margot was too straightforward, too self-centered, to lie. She wouldn't understand the point of it.

"Look, I didn't like her a lot," Margot said, "but she'd been in and out of my life since I was a kid, and she could be fun when she felt like it. You have to admit she was a great dentist.

Warren had extensive work done and was very pleased, and you know my ex-husband and still dear friend is very stingy with compliments—one of the many reasons I left him. He used to date her, you know. Before me. In fact, I met Warren through Valerie. Stole him right from under her upturned nose."

"Sorry I'm late," Beth said, suddenly appearing dressed in a gray linen pantsuit. "Janet will be here in a sec. I saw her parking the car. Hi, Margot." Margot waved fingers. Beth leaned over to hug Lori. "How are you? God, what an awful thing to happen. Are you okay? Have you heard from Rob? Do the police have any idea yet?"

"I'm a little shaky and no word from Jessica or Rob."

Beth slipped into the booth next to Lori. "Call now," she suggested, always ready for instant action.

"Later." During the night, Lori had also realized that she was scared of facing Rob. How would she feel seeing him suffering over Valerie's death? Would she start hoping again? Out of loneliness? The need for sex? Or simply because she wanted to make Jessica happy? "I didn't know Warren dated Valerie," she said, to stop the questions whirling in her head.

"Not for long, but she wasn't a bit pleased when I stole him, which I confess gave me no end of pleasure. What about you, Lori? Aren't you just a little bit glad she's dead?"

"Margot!" Beth said, in the command voice she used to rein in the twins.

Margot tossed her hair. "Come on, girls, let's get real here. That woman was bad news and it's only natural—"

Beth interrupted her. "Could you please swallow the exquisitely pedicured foot that's in your mouth, sweetheart?"

Margot looked at Lori's tired face. "I'm sorry. I was being bitchy. I didn't mean anything by it. Look, I did one good thing. I called Warren before coming here and told him he had to do something about the police annoying you. He wants you to call him."

Callie slid a mug of hot lemonade and honey toward Lori, then swayed away on her slippered feet before Lori finished her thank you and Beth said hello.

"Could we please order?" Margot called out after her.

"She'll be back," Beth said and turned to Lori. "Are you sick?"

"Callie thinks so. I'm just beat." She took a sip. And scared. Maybe depressed. She had to get herself together for Saturday's dinner. In a fit of early morning optimism, which had lasted about ten minutes, she'd called Jonathan and told him her arrest was not imminent, her daughter didn't want her around, and she was going to go ahead with the dinner.

"Thanks, Margot," Lori said. "I will call Warren. I don't mind having a lawyer on my side even if he isn't into criminal law." Warren had negotiated her divorce. He'd been kind in his gruff way, and told her she was a horse's ass not to ask for alimony. Maybe he knew something useful. Warren and Rob had been friendly until Rob dumped her. Warren had taken their divorce very badly, saying it brought back the time Margot left him. He claimed he was still in love with her.

"What's the plan for us?" Beth asked.

"To find out as much as we can about Valerie." Lori filled her in about the phone being off the hook, then turned back to Margot. "Do you know any of Valerie's friends? People I could talk to?"

"I don't think she had any, but let me think about it, go through my old address book. Her office manager, Ruth what's-her-name. She was a friend from way back. High school, I think. Valerie dragged her over to my house a couple of times. A sad girl. Never opened her mouth."

Lori's hand flew to her mouth. "Oh, Lord, I forgot about

Ruth. She must be devastated, poor woman. I have to write her a note."

"You should grill her on Valerie," Margot said. "I bet she knows a few unsavory things about our dearly departed."

"God, Margot," Beth said. "You are heartless."

"Maybe, but also realistic."

"I doubt she'll talk to me after my physical outburst in Valerie's office," Lori said.

"Let me, then," Margot offered.

"Thanks, but be kind, tactful, compassionate. Promise?"

Margot crossed her heart with a finger. Beth chortled.

"Hi everyone, sorry, but the camp bus was late." Janet, in a lace-edged white blouse and jeans, slipped into the booth just as Callie came back with a tray holding a slice of apple pie for Lori, a toasted whole wheat unbuttered English muffin and no jam for Margot, a large orange juice and a fruit salad for Janet, and English Breakfast tea and a cheese Danish for Beth. Lori and Beth thanked her.

Callie fixed Margot with her Greek warrior look while Janet gave Lori a hug. "Why waste your breath and my time with an order when all of you have the same stuff every morning you're in here?"

"One day we might surprise you," Margot said, managing a tiny frown on her smoothed forehead.

Callie grunted and left.

"It's such a terrible thing to happen," Janet said in a whisper. Her face was craggy with worry. "I'm so sorry for you and Jess and Rob."

"Thanks," Lori said, kissing her cheek. "Jess thinks she now has to give up having fun and take care of her dad."

"I know," Margot said. "She told Angie she can't go to Cape Cod and now Angie told Warren she won't go, either, which means he's upset and I'm stuck with a moping daughter and twelve bottles of Skin So Smooth."

"I hope Rob will convince Jess otherwise," Lori said.

"Hey, gals," Beth said, ready to fit the conversation into a brighter groove. "Our Lori here made quite an impression on Mama Ashe, and from what Jonathan tells me, that's like getting an abortionist to win over the pope. Good for you." She gave Lori a high five, which Lori returned half-heartedly. "All right," Beth sighed. "Here's what I can do for the cause. Jonathan Ashe knows half of Manhattan, probably the same half that Valerie knew. If you want, I'll ask him to see what information he can ferret out about her. Unless you want to ask him yourself?"

Lori noticed a hint of a smile in Beth's eyes. The woman was relentless. "Jonathan is all yours." She had enough on her plate without having sex take over her thoughts.

"What can I do?" Janet asked.

Margot leaned over her coffee mug before Lori could answer. "How well do you know Jonathan?" she asked Beth.

"He's bought a lot of art from me."

"You know him?" Lori asked.

"His father and mine were best friends." Margot leaned closer to the group and almost purred, she was so pleased with her piece of gossip. "I hope he's paid you for all that art because I heard he just got burned in some real estate deal."

"How do you know that?"

"Warren told me," Margot said. "Which reminds me, thanks to my dear ex, I lost out on a lot of money with a real estate deal. I was going to invest in Waterside Properties, which is in the Bronx of all places. Lots of land and abandoned buildings along the water. Now it's been sold for oodles of money to some big German developer. There was a big article about it in the *Times* yesterday. Rob's in on it, lucky bastard."

Lori put her fork down. "Rob? Are you sure?"

"Well, he's the one who asked me to go in on the deal with him a couple of months ago," Margot said, "but Warren advised me not to, so I didn't. Whatever other faults he has, my ex has never made a mistake about money." Margot jangled a bracelet. "I guess there's always a first time."

Janet shook her head, as if ridding herself of a bad thought, and speared a pineapple chunk. "I don't understand why you left Warren." She looked at Margot with wide, questioning eyes. "You're such good friends. Isn't that enough to keep a marriage together?"

"Maybe." Margot retreated into a crunchy silence by nibbling her toasted English muffin.

Janet turned her attention to Lori and asked once again, "How can I help?"

Lori hesitated. She was reluctant to involve her. Janet had been through enough with her mother's death and Seth being out of a job for so long. Which reminded Lori. Had Seth given Janet his good news? She didn't look in the least relieved.

"I'll ask Seth to talk to Rob," Janet offered, a smile coming to her face at last. "Rob must know everything there is to know about Valerie. Maybe he even has some suspicions as to who did it."

Aside from me, Lori thought. "Great idea," she said. She planned to pigeonhole Rob herself, but there was no guarantee that his answers to her, if any, would be honest. "Okay, we're set. Margot, you're going to talk to the neighbors about whether anyone saw a strange car that night and you'll talk to Ruth. Beth, you're going to convince Jonathan to go snooping among his Manhattan friends, and Janet is going to ask Seth to help with Rob. And I, to start with, am going to talk to my mother whose friend, Joey Pellegrino, a retired police captain, supposedly can get the scoop on what the Hawthorne Park detectives are up to. Then I'll call Warren and see what he says. Okay, girls, thanks for coming. What would I do without you?" Lori stood up. She had to get back home to deliver her car to the police.

"If you don't eat your pie," Beth said, getting her wallet out, "Callie will never give you another one."

"No one knows what Callie will do," Callie said, appearing behind Beth. "Not even Callie." She handed Lori a plastic bag holding two apple pies. "If you want to share with your girlfriends, that's your business, but don't microwave. Turns the dough into a wet towel." She started gathering the half-eaten plates and mugs and putting them on a tray. "Out, gals, people are waiting." A line had formed outside. "You'll pay next time."

"Thanks for the pies." Lori planted a kiss on the back of Callie's neck. "I'm going to eat one all by myself and save the other one for Jess." Then she whispered so the women wouldn't hear. "I want to talk to you about what you said." Lori trusted her girlfriends completely, but she did want to understand why Callie had made that comment.

"Can't." Callie fussed with the plates and flatware and did not turn around. "Too busy."

"I'll come back after the lunch hour, then."

"This is a bad day. Forget what I said." Callie, her face averted, waved her hand behind her. "Go. Go. Please."

Lori stepped back. "See you next Monday." Outside, the women were waiting. Lori joined them. Margot slipped her the car keys to the Mercedes. They all kissed goodbye and went their ways.

As Lori reached her car, a man popped out of a store doorway, pen and notebook in hand. He blocked her way. "Mrs. Staunton, is it true you socked your ex-husband's wife in the face hours before she was murdered and you have no alibi for that night?"

Lori took a quick look at him. Young, eager, trying to do his job for some paper. But not on her back.

"Your fly is open," she said, pointing.

He looked down long enough for her to slip past him and get in her car.

"Hey, wait a minute!" he yelled as she drove away.

CHAPTER 15

Lori was staring out the kitchen window at the dandelions growing in the cracks of the walkway. She could always get on her
knees and start weeding. The police had come and driven her to
Margot's where she'd picked up the Mercedes. Back home she
changed into shorts and a T-shirt and made her phone calls. Ellie was too busy booking a group tour of Britain's Lake District
for forty-two retired English high school teachers to talk for
more than two minutes, and her police captain, Joey Pellegrino,
hadn't called. Warren was out of the office. Jessica's cell phone
was off and no one answered at Rob's apartment. When she
called his office, Katie, Rob's secretary, informed her that he
had taken the week off.

It was too hot for weeding.

Across the street, Nancy Fisher waved at her. Nancy had
probably seen the police take her car away, Lori decided, and
was dying to find out more. Nancy had once been a casual
friend, coming over for coffee and harmless gossip a couple of
times a month. Once Rob left, she suddenly claimed she was
too busy to stop over. Lori had noticed that other married
women she had been friendly with avoided her now. "Do they
think divorce is catching?" she had asked Beth. "More likely,
they see you as potential bed fodder for their husbands" had
been Beth's answer. Lori walked away from the window now,
without waving back.

She had let the police have her car without a warrant, happy to know the judge had refused to issue one, which meant the police didn't really have a case against her. Lori felt she had relinquished the car with great flair, hoping the policeman who came to pick it up would refer back to Scardini how cooperative she'd been, how innocent she obviously was. Besides, she liked the idea of driving Margot's obscenely expensive and beautiful Mercedes sports car for a few days. Let the mean-spirited of Hawthorne Park—Nancy Fisher included—think she'd splurged on a new car to celebrate Valerie's death; she didn't care.

She glanced at Alec Winters's flowers. They needed a change of water. And a thank-you note was due. That would keep her distracted for another twenty minutes. Then, Jonathan's cabbage roses needed a makeshift vase. Ellie had insisted on floating them in a bathtub full of cold water to stop them from drooping. The narrow asparagus steamer would be perfect, a wedding gift she'd never used but couldn't bring herself to throw out because it seemed so elegant and posh to own one. Lori ran upstairs, gathered the roses, dripped water all the way down the stairs, cut the ends of the stems on a bias, filled the poacher with warm water, and arranged the flowers inside. She changed the water in Alec's vase, removed a few yellowing petals, and placed both bouquets on the kitchen table. She stepped back to survey the effect. So many flowers together was overkill, maybe, but why not feel like a star on opening night, surrounded by gestures of devotion from two admirers? Lori waited for the flowers to work their magic. They didn't. She felt more like a corpse in a funeral parlor waiting to get the burial over with. Why wasn't anyone getting back to her? Why was Valerie dead? Why was she alone?

Time to stop feeling sorry for herself and write that thank-you note. Lori extracted a box of note cards from under the pile of cut out recipes sitting on top of the small desk at one end of the kitchen. Each card depicted a vase of flowers painted by a different painter—Manet, Redon, Matisse, Van Gogh.

Dear Alec, Lori wrote in her mind as she crossed over to the table. *Your flowers are*—No, Alec was too informal. He'd called her Mrs. Corvino. Lori dropped down in a chair, picked Van Gogh's irises, and began to write.

Dear Mr. Winters,

Your flowers are incredibly beautiful. Thank you. You'll be happy to know the cleaners were able to remove all the stains on my dress.

The little white lie would make him feel better.

There was no need for you to send anything, although I'm glad you did. I do appreciate the recipe, even though I wonder how you were able to get it. I thought it was a family secret. Are you part of the family?

Lori crossed out the last sentence. He might feel compelled to answer her, maybe even think she was flirting with him. She should have remembered Ellie's childhood warning and written a draft copy first. Those cards had cost two dollars each. Lori took out another card—*Pansies on a Table,* by Henri Matisse.

Dear Mr. Winters,

Your flowers—

God, what was she doing, sending pansies to a gay man?

A swoop of Lori's arm threw the cards and her pen on the floor. She strode over to the phone and called her mother again. "Has Pellegrino gotten back to you yet?"

"He'll call when he knows something. I gotta go. By the way, Jess called."

Lori felt a punch in her stomach. "She called you?"

"That's what I just said. She was helping Rob pick coffins, can you believe he'd put her through that? And she was upset and didn't want to call you because she knew she'd start crying the minute she heard your voice and want to come home and she can't break down because her father needs her. She wants you to know she's okay."

"Why didn't you call me? I've been worried about her."

"And how should I know that? Do you ever tell me anything?"

"You're a mother, damn it, you should know," Lori wanted to yell into the phone. Instead she walked to one of the cabinets, phone to her ear, and took out the canister of flour, then reached down in the lower cabinet for the bag of red boiling potatoes she'd bought last night.

Ellie kept talking. "Now I'll tell you what I'm thinking. Right now I'm booking a trip to Australia and New Zealand with a stop in Hong Kong for a family of five that just might pay for a week's worth of Jessica's college tuition, but after that I'm done, and I'm thinking I've got those face creams I promised you, which I know you can use right now. So what are you doing for dinner?"

"I'm going out with Warren," Lori said. She was getting good at lies.

"What use is a divorce lawyer in a murder case?"

"He'll pick up the bill. Good night, Mom. Let me know if Jess calls again."

Picking coffins. Lori shuddered. Ellie was quick to blame Rob, forgetting who had picked Papa's coffin, a plain oak one with a blue velvet lining that cost too much. She'd insisted on going, wanting her mother to know how strong her daughter was, how she would take care of her now that Papa was gone. Lori was sure that Jessica too had offered to help Rob with that horrible task. A strong Jessica. Devoted. Ready to prove to her beloved Daddy he needed no other women. "Please call me," she said out loud, unfolding Alec's recipe.

Two kilos of big farinaceous potatoes cut in pieces, 400 grams of sifted flour. How many ounces in a kilo? In a gram? And the recipe said nothing about servings. Four people, six, eight? She'd bought two pounds of potatoes. She had lots of flour. Hell, she'd wing it.

Lori was up to her elbows in flour, kneading the mashed potatoes and flour together when a thought popped into her head. The killer had to know Valerie was going to drive the girls back that night. According to Jess it was a last-minute decision. Rob ate something that didn't agree with him and had called Valerie to take over. Maybe Rob was right; someone wanted him dead.

Lori rolled the dough out into a long sausage shape. Could the killer have mistaken Valerie for Rob? Unlikely, but possible. If the killer was nervous and pulled the trigger the minute she got out of the car, not giving himself time to really see her.

The recipe called for a one-inch thickness, but Lori kept rolling, the dough sausage getting longer and as thin as a cigarette. Was Rob still in danger? Lori smashed the potato dough with the palms of her hands. God, Jessica was with him!

The doorbell rang. Now what? Lori lifted her hands, caked in flour. She heard the front door open. Ellie! No, she no longer had keys. Jess wouldn't ring the doorbell. Who was it? Lori picked up the paring knife she had used to peel the potatoes and tiptoed to the kitchen door. She wasn't panicking, she told herself, just being cautious.

A stooped Rob stood in the hallway, Jessica's panda bear key chain dangling from his hand.

"Hi," he said in a forlorn voice.

Lori slipped the knife into her pocket and leaned against the doorjamb. "Where's Jess?"

"With Angie."

"You should have brought her home."

"Margot's bringing her." He shuffled his feet. He was wearing loafers without socks, chinos, a baggy sweatshirt even though it was eighty-nine degrees outside. He was always worried about catching a cold. She stared at her husband of sixteen years. To her surprise Rob's presence inspired no feelings, either of pity or anger. There was no need for revenge. Rob hadn't been in their house, her house, since the day he had packed and walked out. Now he looked odd, incongruous, like an old piece of furniture that didn't fit in with the new decor.

"Jess was all over me," Rob said. "I know she meant well, but I need some space right now."

Lori nodded, walked back into the kitchen, assuming he would follow. She no longer had to fear wanting him back and the relief made her want to be kind. At the sink, she turned on the water faucets. "Have you had lunch?" She could whip up an omelet, slice some tomatoes.

"I can't eat a thing."

Wifely duties died hard. "I have an apple pie from Callie's."

Rob hesitated, then shook his head and sat at the kitchen table without being asked. Lori felt a twinge of annoyance, but rinsed it off along with layers of flour and mashed potatoes.

"Have some orange juice, at least." She poured out a glass, then remembered that she'd bought the kind with pulp, which Rob disliked. She poured the orange juice back into the carton and gave him tomato juice.

He drank it in one gulp, his eyes fixed on the flowers. "Celebrating the event?"

Lori faced him with a level-headed gaze. "Don't go there, Rob."

"Aren't you happy she's dead? Don't you want to gloat? I would."

"I'm not you."

"You're better, I know."

"Valerie's death has made you humble."

"I can't begin to tell you how I feel."

Don't, she wanted to say, but she had opted for kindness. "I am sorry she died." She dried her hands and sat in the chair opposite him. She pushed the flowers aside to see him better. "Rob, you said someone tried to kill you."

"No, no, I exaggerated." He dismissed the idea with a shake of his hand. "I blew the whole Friday night thing out of proportion. I guess I was nervous. I've been stressed with too much work and then getting married again. Anyway, I was wrong. Nobody was trying to kill me. It was a crazy idea of mine. Believe me, no one wants to kill me."

Was he telling the truth? Lori wasn't sure. If he stuck his neck out with an opinion he usually held on to it, afraid to lose face. In a few days he'd gone from telling everyone who would listen that someone wanted to kill him to acting as if the idea was preposterous. "Valerie was the intended victim?"

"No!" Rob protested in a loud voice. "Who would want to kill her? It was a random thing. It could have been me, you, anybody."

"What do you mean?"

"A carjacking. Robbery. Some drugged-out kid. Maybe even a sex maniac, although the police assured me she wasn't molested. Who knows?"

"Scardini and Mitchell didn't say a word about any of that."

"Why would they tell you?" Rob ran his hands across his scalp. He looked desolate.

"Do you want a drink?"

He perked up. "What have you got?"

"White wine."

"What happened to the twenty-year-old Napoleon cognac Warren gave us two years ago?"

"Part of your spoils."

Regret made a rare appearance on his face. "Oh." A moment of silence, then he gave Lori the conceding smile he might offer an opponent in court who had just scored a point with the judge. "Let's have white wine, then."

Lori went to the refrigerator and got out the last bottle of Falanghina Beth had brought over Monday afternoon.

"Why are you here?" she asked as she poured a full glass and offered it to him.

Rob took the glass. "I don't know." He took two long sips. "I'm feeling a little disoriented."

Had he never said thank you before when she offered him something? Wouldn't she have noticed? "I want Jess to go to Cape Cod with Angie and Warren," she said.

Rob finished the glass. "She's going. I have enough to handle without worrying about my daughter."

"Good."

"Good?" Rob's expression was accusing.

"That she's going away," she explained. "Murder is not something she needs to deal with."

Rob narrowed his eyes at her. "You didn't kill Valerie, did you?"

Lori stayed calm. "No, I didn't, Rob. What purpose would it have served?"

"Well, I mean, she stole me away. You might have thought with her gone—"

"I don't love you anymore, Rob, so there was no reason to kill her."

Disbelief flashed across Rob's eyes, then was gone. With his conceding smile, he lifted an imaginary hat off his head. "Touché, my dear."

Lori leaned toward him. "What happened Monday night? You got sick?"

Rob sat up, always happy to get back to the subject of himself. "My blood pressure must have taken a sudden drop. I felt dizzy and started sweating. I'd only had a beer because I had to drive the girls back. By morning I was fine, except Valerie hadn't come home." He ran his fingers through his hair again, a favored gesture to show off the thick, brown waves that were the envy of his balding friends.

Lori wondered why she'd never noticed these quirks before, or if she had, why they hadn't bothered her.

"God, I can't forgive myself," Rob said, his voice torn with emotion. "Valerie would still be alive if I hadn't asked her to drive the girls. How will I live with that?" He eyed the empty wine glass.

Lori patted his arm. She wasn't going to refill it. He had to drive back to Manhattan. "The bottle's empty," she said gently.

He met her eyes. An old understanding passed between them: *You fool me, I'll fool you.* "I didn't want any more."

"Who knew Valerie was driving Jess and Angie back?" Lori asked, moving on after that brief moment of connection.

"The girls. No one else that I know of."

"You didn't mention it to anyone, see anyone afterward?"

"I went straight home. Angie might have called Margot. I know she called while we were waiting for a table to say she was going to be late getting back, but that was before I got sick. Did Jess tell you?"

"No. She wouldn't want me to know Valerie was driving her back."

Narrowed eyes again. "So you didn't know?"

"Rob, you were married to me for sixteen years. Do you really think I could kill someone?"

"I think we all can, given enough provocation. The police have you high on their suspect list."

"They're clutching at straws. They don't suspect you? The husband is always on top of the list."

"God, no!" Rob stood up. "I'd better go. I've got an appointment with my accountant."

Lori walked him to the front door. "You were so sure someone was trying to kill you when you picked me up at the airport Sunday. You even accused me. What made you change your mind?"

"I guess I sobered up to real danger with Valerie's death."

"If you're in any danger, you'd tell me? We have to think about Jessica. If someone wants to hurt you, they might hurt her."

"No one is going to reach Jess in Cape Cod."

"Then there is something!"

"No! There's nothing. Stop worrying." Rob opened the front door to hot, humid air. In the hemlock at the end of the pathway, a mockingbird was trilling a stolen song. "Listen, the police don't know when they're going to release Valerie's body, and I'm going to wait until Jess gets back in two weeks to hold the memorial service. I was wondering if you could—" Rob looked up as the bird stopped singing and flew to the Fishers' weathervane. "I was wondering if you could help?" He turned back to face Lori, looking for a moment like a lost four-year-old. "I know it's a lot to ask."

Lori took her eyes off Rob to glance at the blue Toyota in her driveway. "The police still have your car?" The murderer had stuffed Valerie in the trunk.

"I'm selling the BMW the minute they give it back," Rob said. "This is a rental."

Lori let her mind wander to the expensive car he'd bought only months after their divorce, from there to Rob's new three-bedroom apartment on Park Avenue, to his monthly child support payments, to the mortgage he was still paying on this house. A lot of money was involved. Valerie, afraid men wanted to marry her only for her money, wouldn't have helped pick up the tab. She turned to Rob. "I hear you made out well on a real estate deal."

Rob looked irritated. "What are you talking about?"

"Some land in the Bronx that a European developer bought for a lot of money. Margot said you were involved."

"I had nothing to do with it."

If he was telling the truth, where had all his money come from? "You don't owe any money, do you?"

"Don't be ridiculous." His face was flushed with anger, which made her suspicious. She still hadn't received her child support check for last month. Up to now, Rob had always been prompt. "If you were in some kind of trouble, you'd tell me, wouldn't you? For Jessica's sake?"

"Thank you for your concern, but the only trouble I'm in now is trying to come to grips with Valerie's death and planning a memorial service." Rob dropped Jessica's panda bear key chain in Lori's hands.

She pictured loan sharks coming after him, ready to beat him to a pulp, even kill him as a lesson to others. "Please tell me the truth, Rob."

"May I remind you that you have never been very good at spotting the difference between my lies and my telling the truth."

Lori could have burst into tears at that cruel reminder. Instead she said, "Ask Valerie's office manager. I'm sure Ruth will help you with the memorial service. Goodbye, Rob." He nodded and walked away.

Lori went back to her kitchen and threw the potato dough into the garbage pail. Making gnocchi was for another day, a day when she would get it right.

CHAPTER 16

Lori opened the gate to Margot's garden and took off her sandals. Walking barefoot across the vast velvety lawn always made her feel graceful and somehow special. On each side of the garden, thick white bands of oak-leaf hydrangeas, Asiatic lilies, and roses slid down to the end. Beyond it, Long Island Sound glistened in the sun like a gray-blue swath of rippling silk. Jessica and Angie were sitting by the pool at one end, sharing the earbuds to an iPod, heads bobbing in rhythm. "Hi, girls," Lori called out with a big wave. Jessica gave a reluctant baby wave back.

As Lori got near enough to catch her daughter's scowl, she slowed her stride. Angie removed her earbud and stood up as Lori approached. She was a short girl with her father's broad face and stocky body, and Margot's confidence and beautiful hazel eyes. The girls were both wearing shorts. Angie had on a halter top with a wide band of chubby midriff showing a gold navel ring. Jessica, to Lori's great relief, had so far only insisted on getting her ears pierced.

"Hi, Jess." Lori leaned over Jessica's chair and felt her stiffen. She turned to Angie and gave her the hug her daughter didn't want. "What are you two up to? Have you had lunch yet?"

"All Mom can think about is food," Jessica said, staying put in her chair, her expression changing from shattered to sullen. She was wearing a too large T-shirt that Angie must have lent her. It made her look frail.

"All I can think about is food and you." Lori laughed. She didn't know how else to handle Jessica's hostility. "Food helps smooth out the wrinkles of the soul, and you make me happy."

Jessica looked down at the bottom of the pool. Angie offered an enthusiastic smile. "I'm starved," she declared.

Lori lifted her arm to show the plastic bag she was carrying. "Well, I brought one of Callie's apple pies for Margot. I'm sure she won't mind sharing."

"Great," Angie said, taking the bag.

"Does Margot have anything in that truck-wide Sub-Zero of hers?" More than anything Lori wanted to reach her daughter, hold her tight, but she knew how important it was for Jessica not to break down, to come across as strong and in control. Once she came home, after a good cry, a heart-to-heart talk, Jessica might slowly go back to being a teenager, thinking of herself, her friends, about inconsequential details, such as what to pack for the trip to Cape Cod. At least, Lori hoped so.

Angie held up her thumb. "Our fridge holds skim milk." She moved on to the other fingers as she went down the list. "Orange juice, Mr. and Mrs. T. mix, caffeine-free Diet Coke, low-fat yogurt, celery, and a jar of caviar we're not allowed to touch." Angie wrinkled her nose. "As if. And a bottle of vodka in the freezer, also forbidden."

"How about coming home with me and I'll make lunch?"

"Can't," Angie said. "Mom's getting her hair done and the carpet cleaner is supposed to come any minute." She looked at Jessica, then at Lori, looking like she needed to assess what to do next. "We've got cans of tuna," she said finally, "and I make a mean tuna salad, right, Jess?"

Jessica nodded, the pool with its black and white checkered pattern like a giant unsolved crossword puzzle still holding her attention.

"I should make the salad," Lori said. "You girls are sunbathing."

"No." Angie's voice was firm, adult. "You stay here with Jess. I'll be right back." She sprinted across the black flagstone path toward the house before Lori could protest.

"Yell if you need help," Lori called out.

"I think we even have some crackers," Angie yelled back.

Lori sat down on the white metal lounge chair Angie had vacated. "Daddy came to the house this morning," she said. "He said you've been wonderful to him. You've helped him a lot. He's very grateful."

Jessica's lower lip trembled. "Then why is he sending me away?"

"He's not sending you away. He wants you to have a good time with Angie. And he also needs to be alone. It's hard for him to grieve when he's worried about you. Right now, he has too much to think about. He has to say goodbye to Valerie, he has to digest what happened. You can understand that."

Jessica nodded, her jaw tight to fight the tears now running down her cheeks.

Lori leaned forward, elbows on her knees, her expression intense in her need to explain, to make things better. "Remember when Daddy left home, how you shut yourself up in your room for days on end? You didn't even want to see Angie."

Jessica stood up and squeezed herself into Lori's chair. Lori leaned back and let her daughter settle against her chest, as little Jessica had done whenever she'd felt overwhelmed. They both closed their eyes.

"He needs looking after, Mom," Jessica said.

"Daddy has many friends."

"Not like us. We're family."

Lori said nothing.

"He feels guilty for getting sick and making her take us

home," Jessica said. "She didn't want to. He argued with her."

"She was probably undressed, ready for bed."

"It must make him feel worse, though."

"Tell me what happened at Pastis." Maybe it was too soon to ask for details. "If you want to, hon."

Jessica snuggled closer, the top of her head brushing Lori's chin. "The food was great and we were having a really good time. Then Daddy's cell went off." Jessica stopped to watch a chipmunk scurry from one flowerbed to the next. Lori waited.

"Whoever it was sounded pretty mad. I could hear him yell over all the voices and the music in the restaurant. I think it was a guy, but it could have been a woman, I guess. Someone with a real low voice. Daddy got up and went outside to talk, and when he came back he was different, you know?" Jessica jiggled a leg. The lounge chair trembled in rhythm. "Everything was annoying him. He complained to the waiter about the noise, about how long it took them to bring us dessert, about our water glasses not being filled fast enough. He embarrassed Angie."

Which meant Jess had been embarrassed, too, Lori thought as she slid her hand over Jessica's knee to stop the jiggling.

Jessica sat up with an accusatory look at Lori. "You haven't said anything. Do you care at all what happened to Daddy?"

Lori covered her chest with her hands, suddenly cold without Jessica. "Of course I do! I'm the one who asked, remember? I didn't want to interrupt, that's all." She'd been afraid Jessica would stop talking or spin off into another direction. "Did Daddy tell you he wasn't feeling well right after the phone call?"

"No. Maybe fifteen, twenty minutes later." Jessica wriggled herself down to the end of the lounge chair and crossed her legs. "After Angie and I finished our lemon tarts. They had all these great-sounding desserts—upside down apple cake and chocolate mousse and pistachio something and something else called panache and lots of other goodies, but Daddy—you know he has the biggest sweet tooth of all of us—only had coffee. I asked him what was wrong, and that's when he told us he had a stomachache and he was going to ask Valerie to take us home. He went out on the street to call her. I could see him argue with her through the window. It really annoyed me. Now I feel bad about it."

"Maybe they were discussing something else. After all, you couldn't hear him."

Jessica shook her head in her deliberate nothing-will-sway-me way. "She didn't like me."

"I'm sure she did, sweetie. Maybe she was a little bit jealous of how much Daddy loves you."

Jessica smiled. "You should get a job in advertising, Mom. You're getting to be a really good spin doctor."

"I am not! Where did you learn that expression?"

"Mom! Hello?" Jessica waved a hand in front of her face. "I don't live on the moon, you know."

"Sorry, I forgot. You've been gone so long. Will you come home after lunch? We can start going through your clothes to see if there's anything you need to buy for Cape Cod."

Angie walked down the pathway with lunch.

"There you go again." Jessica got up to help Angie with the tray. "Bribing me with shopping."

Lori stood up, too. "Is it going to work?" She strolled over to the round white marble table near one corner of the pool, an area semicircled by tall white delphiniums, to help Angie.

"You're on, Mom. I need a new pair of jeans."

They quickly set the table with black plastic plates and glasses, white napkins, Coke cans. Angie placed the large platter of tuna fish and the bowl of rice crackers in the middle and sat down. The apple pie stayed on the tray. "Hysteric Glamour, that's the best brand," she said. "Mom has a pair. They're cool and really expensive."

Jessica sat down next to her. "Knowing my mother, I'll get Levi's or Gap."

"Right you are, sweetie." Lori mounded tuna fish on each plate and then sat down. After the first few bites, she complimented Angie on the tuna salad. It was good, but what made it special was Angie's thoughtfulness. She had understood Lori's need to be with Jessica alone for a few minutes.

They ate silently after that, the need to satisfy hunger taking over. When Jessica put her fork down, her plate was clean. "You know what I've been wondering, Mom?"

"What?" Lori asked, the fear she'd been carrying with her since Valerie's death momentarily appeased by the food and the girls' sweetness.

"If Daddy's stomach was hurting, why did he drink coffee? He always said caffeine was bad for stomachaches." She cut a slice of pie and loaded it on a paper plate Angie had brought.

"Maybe he thought the hot liquid would do him good."

Jessica swirled her fork between her fingers. "I'm not sure." She raised her head to look at Angie.

Angie took the prompt and a slice of pie. "What we've been thinking is that Mr. Staunton didn't really have a stomachache. It was just an excuse. We think the phone call was a diversion."

"What do you mean?" Lori suppressed a smile. Both of them had been avid Nancy Drew fans a few years ago.

"Valerie's killer, maybe that's who called," Jessica said, leaning forward on her elbows, her face flushed with excitement. "He or she—we couldn't hear the voice—told Daddy he had to see him right away. Daddy made up the excuse he was sick so he could convince Valerie to drive us home. Daddy went to the appointment and no one showed because the killer was following Valerie so he could kill her once she dropped us off."

"Did your father tell you this?"

"No," Jessica said. "I didn't think I should ask him. I mean, if it's true, it would make him feel even worse."

"That's very thoughtful of you," Lori said. A rush of love filled her heart for a moment as Jessica blushed at the compliment. Thoughtful and clever, both girls. They had overabundant imaginations, but what they proposed wasn't that crazy a theory. But why didn't the killer keep things simple and call Valerie directly, ask to see her? If not that night, another night? Was it because Valerie would refuse to meet with her killer? Was time a factor in the killing? And how could the killer be so sure Rob would meet him right away? If it was a he. If Valerie was the intended victim.

Lori leaned back in her chair and felt her stomach hollow out, her skin turn clammy. How was this horrible story going to end for Jess? For herself?

"Mom? Are you okay?"

Lori opened her eyes to smile at Jessica. "Just a little headache." She sat up and started putting the empty plates on the tray. "Good job." The pie was half gone. "The next time I see Detective Mitchell I will tell him your theory. And now let's clean up and go shopping." She picked up the tray and started to walk toward the house.

Jessica jumped up from her chair. "I want to tell him. No, I'll tell Detective Scardini. He looks like he's straight out of *The Sopranos.*"

Lori turned sharply. "You watched *The Sopranos*?"

"No!" both girls said in unison. Which meant they had, or still did, in reruns. As Lori was sure they avidly followed the raunchy reruns of *Sex and the City.* And now they were enmeshed in a real murder. Whatever had happened to clean, innocent adolescence?

★ ★ ★ ★ ★

Warren called in the late afternoon just as Jessica was throwing her new purchases and all her old summer clothes on Lori's big bed in order to decide what to take to Cape Cod. Lori took the phone call downstairs, out of earshot.

"Are the police still harassing you?" Warren had a soft rumbling voice that Lori had found comforting during the months leading to the divorce. It still had the power to calm her.

"Well, they asked a lot of questions, and today they took my car. I guess they were just doing their job."

"They had a warrant for the car?" He sounded surprised. A warrant meant there was probable cause, which would have been bad news. She'd learned that much from *Law and Order*.

"No, they didn't. I know I should have insisted on one, but—"

"I know, you wanted to show them you're innocent, just like you wanted to show Rob your independence by not asking for alimony." Warren let out a loud breath; he was probably smoking a cigar. "What am I going to do with you, Lori? Why don't you learn from your friend Margot? She can get blood from a diamond. Come over for a drink, and we'll strategize in case the problem escalates."

"The problem is not going to escalate, and I need to stay home with Jessica."

"I hear you don't have an alibi."

"Where did you hear that?"

"Margot."

"I was right here, in bed. I must have unplugged my phone somehow. For a divorced couple you two communicate a lot. That's nice." Maybe with time she and Rob—

"We even bed each other off and on."

"I don't need to know that."

"You're right," Warren said. "Sorry. Look, I've got a great

criminal lawyer lined up just in case, so you can sleep tight and I would love to check on how you're doing in person. How about lunch tomorrow? That way you can also fill me in on how Jessica's doing with all this. I want to make sure she has a good time with us in Cape Cod."

"Mom!" Jessica yelled from upstairs. "Grammy just drove up. Cook something quick."

Great, Lori thought. Just when she was looking forward to an evening alone with Jess. "Lunch tomorrow would be great, Warren." But then maybe Ellie came bearing news from her policeman friend. "Where and when?"

"My golf club." The doorbell rang once. "The Maples. You know where it is." The bell rang again. "One o'clock all right with you?"

"Mooom!" came from upstairs. "Grammy's at the door!"

Why Jessica couldn't run down the stairs on her young, agile legs and get the door herself was something Lori would never understand or change. "One o'clock is perfect, Warren. You're sweet to worry about me. Thanks." Now the doorbell ring was one persistent wail. "See you tomorrow."

Lori hung up and hurried across the front hall. She jerked open the door. "What's wrong, Mom? Arthritis got your finger?" Here she was sounding like Ellie again. Hostile. It had taken Lori many years to understand that her mother's sharp remarks were her oddball way to show affection, and Lori, to defend herself, had learned to give as good as she got, both in sharpness and affection.

"I thought you guys had gone deaf," Ellie answered.

"We have now. I was on the phone and Jess was in the bathroom." One day soon she had to stop making excuses for her daughter. "Come on in, Mom."

Ellie stepped inside and lifted both her arms. Her satchel hung limp from the crook of her elbow. "You can stop worrying. The only food I've got on me is mints. I'm counting on being able to eat your stuff. If not, I'll starve." Ellie offered one cheek, then the other, the Italian way she insisted on.

Lori kissed her and smelled Chanel No. 5. Her mother's only perfume ever since Marilyn Monroe told a radio interviewer that was all she wore to bed. "Do you have news from Joey Pellegrino?"

Ellie slipped off her shoes, short-heeled navy pumps. "Is Jess coming down?" She was whispering.

"Of course she is. She wants to say hello to you." Lori found herself whispering, too. "Did Pellegrino call?"

Instead of answering, Ellie headed for the kitchen in her bare feet, the pumps abandoned on the front hall floor. Lori followed, noticing the blue cotton suit her mother was wearing, the stockings on her legs. Perfume she only wore on Easter Sunday and Christmas Day. "You look good, Mom. What's the occasion?" She was even wearing makeup. Only her hair retained its helter-skelter look.

Ellie lowered herself into her usual ladder-backed chair by the kitchen table. "I had meetings." She fingered one of Jonathan's roses. "Did you put in a drop of bleach? That'll keep them for days. Kills the bacteria."

"I thought the trick was half an aspirin."

"Flowers don't get headaches. Use bleach."

Lori walked over to a kitchen cabinet and took down a box of De Cecco spaghetti. "Was one of your meetings with Pellegrino?"

"Holy sky, Loretta! The murder can wait. Now I want to be with my family, all that's left of it, have some supper, *and*"—she swung her satchel onto the table, where it landed with a thud— "fix up your face." Ellie rummaged inside, took out five jars of cream. "This is top of the line, costs a fortune, but it's worth it for my baby."

Lori smiled. She hadn't been Ellie's baby in years. Her mother must have good news. Of what kind, Lori couldn't guess.

Ellie held up one jar. "Morning regime. You exfoliate with this"—she held up another cream—"then you smear on this antioxidant cream." The last two she pointed at. "Next, moisturizer, eye-lifting cream, then sunblock. At night you skip the exfoliant and the sunblock. In a month you'll be as good as new. Keep them in the fridge."

"I didn't think I looked that bad, but thanks. I'll give it a try." Lori gathered up the jars, still in their cellophane wrappers, and released them into the refrigerator's vegetable bin. She was never going to put all that stuff on her face, she told herself as she took out a pint of tomatoes and some basil and walked back to the counter. "Now for supper, I'm making Jess's favorite summer pasta. Spaghetti with a sauce of fresh cherry tomatoes, basil, ricotta, and olive oil." She'd made the ricotta this morning after throwing out the gnocchi dough. A welcome-back-home present for Jessica. "I'll leave out the ricotta for you, okay?"

"Yes, but remember your father's lessons. The spaghetti has to be *al dente* and put in enough salt in the water, *after* it boils, so it tastes like the Mediterranean."

"Hi, Grammy." Jessica walked in. She was wearing her new Gap jeans and a striped blue and white shirt she had snitched from her father. Lori thought she looked lovely and brave. "Why can't you put in the salt before?"

"The water takes longer to boil. Hi, gorgeous. Come and kiss your Grammy." Jessica kissed Ellie on both cheeks. "So. Sit down next to me and tell me all about yourself."

Jessica talked about her upcoming trip with Angie, about the shopping she and Lori had done that afternoon. Lori prepared dinner. Jessica helped set the table. They ate. Ellie approved of the food with a nod of her head and a second helping. They talked about the latest fun movies, about the boredom of the summer reruns on TV, about Ellie's passion for Sudoku. Valerie's murder was carefully avoided. After a dessert of vanilla sorbet and warm berry sauce, Jessica loaded the dishwasher and excused herself. "I've got stuff to do."

"Sure, hon. Thanks for the help."

"I'm working Saturday," Ellie said. "You come visit. And when you get back from Cape Cod I'm going to put you to work. It's time you learned how to earn some money."

"I'll come with Angie." Jessica kissed her grandmother and loped away to the inner sanctum of her room upstairs.

"Mom, I haven't seen you look so elegant in ages," Lori said, quickly washing the spaghetti pot and the pasta bowl. "Tell me about these meetings."

Ellie shrugged and ran her fingers through her hair. Lori left the pot and bowl to dry on their own and sat down facing her mother. "Was one of those meetings with Joey Pellegrino?"

Ellie raised her chin to the door. "I don't want Jess to hear."

That didn't sound good, Lori thought, as she got up to close the door. "What's up?" she asked, sitting back down.

"Joey treated me to a drink in Greenwich." That explained the fancy clothes, the perfume, the makeup. "He's very happy to help me." The dreamy look in Ellie's eyes squeezed Lori's heart. She had never stopped to think how lonely her mother must have been all these years, raising her daughter alone, working six days a week. Never a date with another man while Lori still lived with her. And now here she was with a crush on a married police captain. It was sweet, senseless, and sad all at the same time. "He sounds like a very nice man," Lori said.

"Too nice. His wife doesn't know how good she's got it."

"Mom, be careful. I don't want you to get hurt."

"What are you talking about? I just had a drink with the guy. To help you."

"I know. I really appreciate it. Thanks."

"The police lab isn't through with your car yet, but those two detectives went to talk to Valerie's lawyer." Ellie crossed her arms under her chest and leaned back on the chair with a smug look on her face.

"What, Mom?"

"Both Rob and Valerie rewrote their wills the morning she was killed, and it's manna from heaven for our little Jess." The grin on Ellie's face could have put the Cheshire Cat out of business.

"She left Jess money?"

"She left the whole pot of gold to Rob, with just a few thousand to her office manager."

"Seth was right, then."

"What about Seth?" Ellie had been Seth and Janet's travel agent when they still had money to go places.

"I met him on the train yesterday. He assumed Valerie's will had already been changed in Rob's favor."

"That's Seth for you, always guessing at things. How's he doing? Got a job yet?"

"I think so. He looked pretty happy yesterday, although Janet didn't say anything this morning so I could be wrong. What else did Pellegrino tell you?"

Heat rose up Ellie's face like pasta water roiling to a boil. "Lots, but it had nothing to do with the murder." She pushed herself up from the table with both hands. "I'm going home. It's been a big day for me."

"Thanks for your help, Mom." Lori gave Ellie a rare strong hug. "And the creams."

Ellie pushed herself away. She'd never been one for physical shows of affection, except for the regimented double kiss. "Just because your husband left you is no reason to stop looking your best." She walked to the front hall. Lori followed. "And who knows what's around the corner." She tried to slip back into her pumps, found she couldn't, and brought them up close to her nose to examine them. "Why did they shrink?"

"The air-conditioning," Lori said. She picked up the shoes and handed them to her mother, who could never admit to swollen feet. "I'll get you a pair of open-back slippers." Ellie had size nine feet, Lori and Jessica size seven and a half.

"Forget it. These stockings have a run in them anyway. Has that handsome young man come calling again?"

"Men don't come calling anymore, Mom. If anything they e-mail. And no, I haven't heard from Jonathan." Although she had caught herself thinking about him a few times.

"I bet you think men don't open car doors for women anymore either." Ellie smiled and waved a finger in the air. "But they do. They do. I wish that for you. A man who comes calling with flowers and opens doors for you. Good night and make sure Jess comes over Saturday."

Lori wished her mother good night and watched as she padded down the walkway to her car.

From across the street a camera flashed. A woman came running across the street, a camera man following her. Ellie veered from the path and pushed all her weight right into the woman, who fell backward with a yelp.

Lori had time to hear her mother apologize loudly before shutting the door. She did not answer the doorbell.

Jessica walked into her parents' bedroom in her pajamas and settled herself on Rob's side of the bed.

Lori, who was already in bed, put her book down and smiled at her daughter.

"Mom?" Jessica took in a big breath as if getting ready to lift something heavy.

"Hi sweetie, what's up?"

"All those flowers you got? You'd tell me if you had a boyfriend, right?"

"You'd be the first to know." Lori explained why Alec Winters had sent her flowers. She also brought up Jonathan's yellow roses. "They were both just being nice, honey. What about you? You'd tell me if you had a boyfriend, right?"

Jessica rolled over on her hip, her head propped up by her arm. She looked at her mother for a few seconds, her expression intent. "I don't know, Mom," she said in a hesitant voice. "I mean, if I got serious with someone I'd feel funny about telling you."

"Whatever for?"

"Wouldn't it make you feel bad? Being alone and all?"

Lori reached over and gently lifted a strand of hair from Jessica's face. How lucky she was to have this generous child. "If he treated you nicely, I'd be happy for you. And I'm not alone. I have you, my friends, my work. That's more than enough. Life isn't just about having a man in your life. It really isn't."

"Well, maybe, but there's this guy in school, kinda nerdy? Skinny? Wears glasses? But I think he's cute. He's a year ahead of me and he hasn't noticed I exist so I can't call him a boyfriend." Jessica giggled. "Yet."

"What's his name?"

"Ha!" Jessica sat up. "I'm not going to tell you. You'll call up his mother and arrange something totally obnoxious."

"That sounds more like Grammy."

"Yeah, it does, but you're her daughter."

"And you're mine. So then how about giving him an alias? That way you can refer to him whenever you want and I'll know he's your special guy."

"Okay. Deuce."

Shake It Up had been Jessica's favorite program before she moved on to more adult fare. "Can you tell me why you like

Deuce so much?"

"I don't know. I'd just like to go up to him and say hi. He looks so lost."

"Why don't you?"

"Because if I do, I might kiss him. That's what I really want. That would be way too embarrassing."

"Say hi from a safe distance."

"Then what if he comes close?"

"You smile that smile of yours and he's a goner."

Jessica blushed. "You're just saying that."

"If he isn't, he doesn't deserve you."

"Oh, Mom." Jessica flung herself at Lori, hugged her, and with the hug, the sobs came. Lori cried with her. Each hid her face, but held on tight to the other.

"It's going to be okay again, honey," Lori said, after Jessica quieted down. She handed her the tissue box and dried her own tears with the palms of her hands. "I promise." She was completely beat from too much emotion. "What have you got planned for tomorrow?"

"Angie, me, and a group of kids from school are going to Playland."

"Is Deuce going to be there?"

Jessica nodded, the blush rising on her cheeks like a fever.

Grammy and Jess were both harboring crushes, Lori thought. In Jess's case it was lovely. "You should go."

"It's okay? I mean, with Valerie dead?"

Maybe it wasn't okay, but Jessica needed to have fun. "Why don't you ask your father?"

Jessica scrambled over Lori to get off the bed. "I'm going to call Dad now."

"It's past eleven thirty."

"He never goes to sleep before two. Don't you remember?"

"I guess I didn't. I'm sure he'll say it's okay." She sat up and blew Jess a kiss. "Good night, sweetie. Sleep tight."

Hours later a weight fell on Lori, waking her up. With only the light of a half moon to help her, Lori turned her head slowly to see Jessica lying next to her, fast asleep. Lori leaned over, planted a light kiss on Jessica's forehead, and cradling the arm her daughter had flung across her chest, closed her eyes. With a great sense of peace, she fell back asleep.

CHAPTER 17

The day was gleaming as Lori drove onto the grounds of the exclusive, two-hundred-thousand-dollars-initiation-fee Maples Country Club. The clubhouse, a low stone building barely visible through the trees, spread itself on top of a hill of wild grasses sprinkled with black-eyed Susans. As Lori reached the roundabout, she stole a quick glance at the rearview mirror. In a burst of foolishness she had layered all of Ellie's creams on her skin before leaving the house. She was surprised oil wasn't oozing out of her pores, although her skin actually didn't look half bad.

"Hey, Lori," Warren said, coming out of the club as soon as she stepped out of Margot's Mercedes. He was wearing green slacks, a yellow linen shirt, and tasseled loafers without socks. Short, stocky, with a sizable paunch and a large flattened nose, it was the power he exuded that attracted both men and women to him, a power he wore as lightly as the shirt on his back.

Warren kissed Lori's cheek while taking the car keys from her and handing them to a waiting valet, who drove the Mercedes to some hidden region of the club. "Margot's car looks good with you in it. I'll tell her to give it to you. I paid for the damn thing."

Lori smiled. "I can't afford the upkeep."

Warren wagged a finger at her. "Your fault, not mine. Kidding aside, I'm glad you're here." He squeezed her arm.

"Thanks for inviting me. I can use a strong shoulder to lean on right now."

"You got it."

Warren, hand on her elbow, steered her through the open door into the club. As they walked by the round table in the center of the front hall, Lori said, "What a lovely scent."

"The smell of money is always refreshing."

Lori laughed. "I meant the flowers." In the center of the table, a green ceramic pot held a tall grouping of yellow daylilies and lavender.

"They cost money, too." Warren turned to her. "You look great, by the way. Divorce suits you."

Lori had dressed up for the club in an off-white linen pantsuit she had taken pains to iron this morning. She was even wearing heels. She had only been here once before, for a Saturday dinner with Rob, Margot, and Warren. She remembered how shabbily dressed she had felt compared to the designer outfits the other women were wearing. And fat.

"I made a few phone calls." Warren knew a lot of the power brokers of the city, was on chatting terms with the mayor. Born on a chicken farm in New Jersey, he had made his wealth from hard work and sound investments. Still holding on to Lori's elbow, he walked her through the main room of the club, which was decorated in an array of green, tan, and pink stripes and plaids and a large quantity of mismatched throw pillows. "Your car is clean. They'll probably bring it back tomorrow. If not, you'll get it Monday." As Warren walked, he nodded at the various members who crossed their paths on the way to the patio in the back. The women were in tennis shorts, khakis, Bermudas. Even jeans. So this time Lori was overdressed. Well, she wasn't going to let it get to her. "Turn it around," Ellie used to tell her when she'd come home from school moping about some embarrassment. She wasn't overdressed. Those women were underdressed. Besides, she had all that cream on her, which was bound to turn her into a thirty-year-old beauty any minute.

The patio was covered in flagstone and overlooked a vast lawn edged by flower beds filled with hothouse dahlias of every color possible. Warren chose a table far to one side, under a blue striped awning. Lori would have preferred to sit in the sun, but said nothing. Her face might start oozing.

"Let's have a drink and then order." Warren held out a chair for her.

How nice, Lori thought as she sat down. It was a habit Rob had dropped once they'd married.

Warren sat next to her. "You're not in a hurry, are you?"

"No. Jessica is happily at Playland with Angie for the day."

"Angie is trying to take good care of her."

"I know. She's been wonderful. You're lucky."

"So are you. With our children, that is. Our mates a little less so. By the way, I'd like to take the girls up to Cape Cod tomorrow afternoon. I have some business I need to look into early Saturday. Would that be all right with you?"

Warren's request flustered Lori. "I don't know. I'll have to ask Jess. And with what Rob's going through, she might not want to leave so quickly." She was the one who didn't want Jess to go.

"It's the best thing for her."

"Yes, I know it is." But still.

"If you prefer, she can fly to Boston on Monday and we'll pick her up."

"I'll let you know tonight." She had been counting on a Sunday with Jess. Mrs. Ashe's dinner over with, she would be free to take Jess to the beach, to the city, to anywhere she wanted to go. A chance to indulge in her daughter's company before the void of the next two weeks.

A Filipino waiter with a round face and a wide smile asked, "Mr. Dixon, the usual?"

"Yes, Arnold. What will you have, Lori?"

"A Virgin Mary, thank you."

"After what you've been through, make it a bloody."

She'd fall asleep after lunch. "Sure. Why not?"

Warren held out his hand once the waiter left. "Give me a dollar."

Lori opened her handbag and looked into her wallet. She wasn't sure why Warren wanted money from her. "I only have a fiver." She dropped the bill onto Warren's open palm.

"Five will do. This is payment. Not a loan."

"Cheap drink," Lori said, still having no idea what this was about.

The waiter brought the drinks and two menus over to their table. Warren's usual turned out to be beer on the rocks. "You have just hired me as your lawyer. I can now claim lawyer-client privilege, which means whatever you say to me stays with me. You understand?"

Lori stirred the carrot stick around in her glass, took a sip. She didn't know whether to be annoyed or grateful. Annoyed that Warren thought she had something incriminating to say. Grateful that he wanted to help. Lori took a bigger sip. The spices and Tabasco zinged in her mouth, gave her courage. "I didn't kill her, Warren," she said in a low voice, "and if you don't believe me I'm going to leave and never speak to you again."

Warren brought his chair closer. "I would mind that very much but, dear Lori, believing innocence or guilt is not my job. And it won't be your defense lawyer's job either, should you need one. What I'm trying to find out from you is if the DA can come after you or not. For instance, why didn't you answer your phone the night of the murder? Margot had to call you on your cell phone to get you."

"I was home, in and out of sleep, waiting for Jess to call. I called the phone company this morning. They insisted there was no disruption of service. I can't explain it." She raised her glass and drank, hoping the alcohol would relax her. "Even if I'd inadvertently unplugged the phone, I would have had to re-plug it because I used it the next morning. I don't remember doing that. Warren, I don't know what happened."

"Could someone else have unplugged and re-plugged it?"

"No one was at the house that night." Lori tried to remember back to Monday afternoon. She'd been drinking wine with Beth, telling her about slapping Valerie. Margot called to invite her and Beth to dinner. She was pretty sure that had been on the home phone. She remembered not wanting to answer it because Beth was upset. Could Beth have unplugged the phone? What for? She had left shortly after that. And if Beth had unplugged it for some strange reason, who had re-plugged it? The next day the phone was working. "The phone company has got to be wrong," Lori said. "There's no other explanation."

"It doesn't look good, but I think you'll be okay. Let's order and then I'll tell you why. I always have the same thing, but you choose what you want. The chef here is great."

Lori picked up the menu. There was nothing like food to distract. A basket of toasted and buttered pita bread appeared as she glanced at the choices. Too many. She was tempted by the hamburger with mozzarella and bacon, the apple pancake with sour cream, the chicken quesadilla with cheddar cheese, avocado, and salsa, but after hearing the handsome slim woman two tables away ordering a junior Cobb salad without the blue cheese and house dressing on the side, Lori ordered the same. When in a foreign country do as the natives do, Ellie always told her clients. The waiter had no need to ask Warren what he wanted.

"You're a creature of habit," Lori said.

"I don't do well with change. Comes from having a shaky

150

childhood. My parents were drunks."

This personal revelation surprised Lori. Warren came across as such a confident, well-balanced man that she had pictured him coming from a strong, supportive family. "I'm so sorry. It must have been very difficult, but look how well you've done."

"It's not information I share easily."

To lighten the moment, she said, "Maybe you should pay me a dollar, then."

Warren set his dark hooded eyes on her, his expression carved in stone. She suddenly felt like a deer being met by headlights, and for a fleeting moment Lori wondered if he were capable of physically hurting someone. She shook the thought away when he said, "You're Margot's friend, which makes you my friend. I trust you."

Lori smiled at him. She was in a sorry state to have such an awful thought.

"Not liking change," Warren said, after a long swallow of beer, "is one of the reasons I still pine for my wife. I also like having my way. I'll get her back one day. Maybe not till she's old, but I'll get her back. And now for the interesting news. Rob—"

The waiter interrupted them by bringing Lori's Cobb salad and Warren's club sandwich.

Warren waited until the waiter was out of earshot to continue. "Rob is now in the hot seat." He kept his voice low. "He's being looked at very carefully by the Hawthorne Park Homicide Squad."

"Because of Valerie's will?"

Warren raised an eyebrow. "You know about that?" He didn't seem pleased.

"My mother has connections."

Warren bit into his club sandwich. It was huge, but so was his mouth. "Of course she has connections, she's Italian," he said, after he'd swallowed.

"Not nice, Warren."

"You're right. I apologize. I wanted the kick of surprising you with the news. Forgive me?"

"Of course." She had heard many worse slurs against Italians in her lifetime. So many she was almost turning a deaf ear. Almost.

"Who's your mother's connection?" Warren asked.

"A friend of a friend."

"You're sounding vague."

"That's all I know." Lori didn't want to mention Joey Pellegrino's name. She wasn't sure why. Maybe because of Warren's curiosity. Maybe because Ellie had a crush on Joey. For all she knew, they might even be having an affair. "Is it important who the connection is?"

Warren sat back and sipped his beer. "No. One thing I bet you don't know is how much Rob is getting."

"Please don't tell me, Warren. I find it painful."

Warren reached over and took her hand. "God, Lori, I don't know what's the matter with me. Of course it hurts."

Lori slipped her hand back onto her lap. She wasn't hungry anymore. Because of Jessica, she was worried about Rob. "They can't really think Rob would be so stupid as to kill his wife on the same day that she changed her will, can they?"

"Sure they can. He had opportunity—that excuse about feeling sick wouldn't convince an addled sheep. He had means—"

Lori started to object. He waved his hand to stop her. "Yes, I know, anyone can pick up a gun without making a dent in their wallet, but motive is the clincher. By signing over her money to him on her death, Valerie gave Rob the number one motive for murder. Greed."

"You looked into his money situation for my divorce. Did you see anything that spelled trouble? Did Rob have debts?

Were there risky investments? Anything that might show he was in desperate need of money?"

"His accounts looked okay to me. He had some real estate investments that had done very well for him. Some high tech stuff I would have stayed away from, but he didn't put in a lot of money, so even if the tech stuff went south, it wouldn't hurt him. Of course, in divorce cases you get shown what they want to show you. For all we know, Rob could have made investments offshore. You didn't want me to investigate that, remember?"

"I remember." Lori had wanted to keep the divorce as dignified as possible.

Because Warren was eyeing her untouched plate, Lori took a bite, chewed slowly, swallowed. She eyed the woman two tables away, who was eating her Cobb salad with relish. To Lori it tasted of straw. "Rob didn't kill her," she said. That much she did know about her ex.

"That's not the point. The point is he's being investigated big-time, which means you are probably off the hook and that's good news. Yes, I know you're thinking about Jessica. All the more reason to let me take her to Cape Cod tomorrow. Get her away from here before she sniffs out that her sweet daddy might get indicted for murder. Has the media been hounding you?"

"A couple of reporters showed up at the house and I screen my calls." Lori pushed the plate away. "What if Valerie was not the intended victim? What if the killer thought he was shooting at Rob?"

Warren looked up from his sandwich, eyes alert. "Have you got a motive besides jealousy?"

"No, I don't."

"Then let's not go there. Because if Rob was the intended victim, you're going to start looking good again to those two idiots on the case." Warren leaned forward his chair, beer mug and plate empty. "How about some ice cream? Guaranteed to slide down your throat no matter how upset you are." He patted her arm. "Give it a try."

He looked worried for her, so Lori said yes. Warren called Arnold over to order two chocolate ice creams and two coffees. While they waited, Warren said, "There's a new man in Margot's life."

"I don't think so," she said in a soft voice to counter the bitterness of his.

"I want to know who it is. Can you do that for me?"

"If it was anyone important to her, Margot would tell me," Lori said. "Women friends usually share that kind of information." Even if she did know anything, which she didn't, she wouldn't rat to Warren. Margot was her friend first. "What makes you think she's dating someone?"

"She looks more beautiful. She's more relaxed. I've been through this before, of course. I get jealous each time, but I've never been worried. As you know, Margot has short-lived crushes—a month, two at the most, then she moves on like a bee to the next flower. She's always told me about them if I asked. This time when I ask she gets angry, which tells me whoever it is, he's important to her." Warren took a cigar from his breast pocket, unwrapped it, snipped off the end with a gadget that looked like a mini guillotine. He contemplated the cigar for a moment—a cigar he was not allowed to smoke on the premises—with a rueful look, which he then shifted to Lori. "I'm a fool and I'm embarrassing you."

It was true that he'd embarrassed her, but instead of thinking him a fool, Lori felt sorry for him. "Loving her so much must be very painful."

"I don't wish that kind of obsession on anyone." Warren tucked his unlit cigar back in his breast pocket. "For you to tell me anything about Margot's love life would be an egregious breach of loyalty on your part. I am the first to appreciate that. Can you forget I asked?"

"Of course," Lori said just as the ice cream came. As they ate, Warren asked about her trip to Italy, about her plans to be a caterer, wanted her business cards as soon as they were ready to give out to friends at the club. He was caring and gentle, and Lori forgot the moment when his gaze had frightened her.

CHAPTER 18

Lori's cell phone rang as she was leaving the Port Chester Costco parking lot.

"The neighbors saw and heard *nada* Monday night." Margot's whiskey voice sounded disappointed. "And I couldn't come up with any real friends of Valerie's except Ruth. I took her out to lunch in the city today at Le Colonial. Have you been? Fabulous. It's like going back in time and dining in a lush French plantation in Vietnam."

"Sounds great, but tell me what Ruth said." Lori turned the air-conditioner to high to keep the food she'd bought for Saturday night's dinner cool.

"She ate, mostly. Coconut shrimp, chicken ravioli, beef *briolle* with sticky rice, eggplant, and chocolate mousse. And drank most of a bottle of 1999 Pouilly-Fuissé. She kept crying between bites and sips and my heart went out to her. She's taking Valerie's death very badly."

Lori veered left onto Main Street. "They were that close?"

"Ruth, as it turns out, is Valerie's cousin. Her only living relative."

That explained why she was the only one of Valerie's employees mentioned in the will. "Does she have any idea why anyone would want to kill Valerie?"

"Well, she mentioned you, and said she didn't really think you'd go that far. She leans toward the carjacking theory."

"That's what Rob thinks, and I wish the police did, too."

"By the way," Margot said, "Ruth loved your condolence note. She claims she doesn't know much, but she's more than happy to talk to you. She seemed eager to help. I don't think she's had too many people pay much attention to her."

"Did she say anything about inheriting money from Valerie?"

"Oooh." Margot exhaled into the phone. "Did she?"

"Yes, according to Warren."

"Well, I hope it's a lot. So what did my ex have to say?"

"Are you seeing anyone?"

There was a moment of silence. Lori thought she could hear Margot stewing. "I'm seeing several ones," Margot finally said.

"Well, he's convinced you're in love."

"Warren likes to own people and things and Warren doesn't like to be crossed. One of the many reasons I left him."

"But you still see him."

"Let's not talk about him. Tell me more about Valerie's will."

"Another time. I need to stop by Sally's Blooms"—Janet wanted to show her some flower arrangements for Mrs. Ashe's dinner party—"and I've just spotted a parking place large enough to accommodate your gorgeous car. By the way, are you in love?"

"I'm not ready to go public, but if and when, you'll be the first to know."

"Good luck." Lori clicked off the phone, pushed the stick shift into reverse, and silently prayed for a smooth, silent maneuver.

"You're looking good," Janet said when Lori walked into the flower shop.

"I had lunch with Warren at his club. How are you?" Lori asked. Her friend looked tired and out of sorts.

Janet stopped fiddling with a pot of startling blue hydrangeas and tried on a smile. "I was going to ask you, you know, about that other business." She glanced backward at Shirley, the owner, who was with a customer in the rear.

Lori leaned into the counter. "The plot thickens, but I'll tell you later."

"Seth has left Rob lots of messages." Janet's role in the sleuthing was to have Seth pump Rob for information about Valerie to try to come up with a possible suspect other than Lori. "He doesn't call back."

Of course Rob didn't call back. He was suspect *numero uno* now. At least according to Warren. "I might be off the hook," Lori said.

"That's nice," Janet said with surprisingly little enthusiasm. "Let me show you what I've thought of."

Janet had to be really down to respond that way. "I'm sure whatever you've planned is going to be beautiful."

Janet walked over to the refrigerator section and removed four small cream-colored ceramic bowls with different combinations of flowers. "I followed your suggestion and called Mrs. Ashe and asked her what she was going to be wearing Saturday night."

"Gray?"

"Mauve, so I thought we could go for purple, white, and pink flowers, or just pink and white or pale orange and white. Which do you prefer?"

"Why don't I bring them over to Mrs. Ashe and have her pick?"

"She said you should decide."

"All three are gorgeous. If I have to pick one, I go for the orange and white arrangement, but it's really your choice. You're my flower expert." Lori lowered her voice. "Hon, are you okay?"

Janet did not meet Lori's eyes. "Shirley thinks the purple, pink, and white arrangement is the prettiest, and she's the real expert, so I'll go with that, if you don't mind."

Lori raised her hands. "You're the boss. See you Saturday at the Ashe apartment. I'll be there from three o'clock on, so come any time after that. Guests are arriving at seven p.m., and I'm home tonight if you have any questions." Lori waved and walked to the door.

"Wait!" Janet called out.

Lori turned around.

Janet came close. "I'm fine. So is Seth," she said in a whisper. "Our problems are over. We're going to be fine."

Why was she whispering? What was there to hide? "Oh, great!" Lori hugged her. "He has a job?"

Janet shook her head. "We're going to be fine," she repeated. "An investment came through."

"That's the best news I've heard in ages," Lori said, her eyes fixed on Janet's face. "I'm really happy for you both."

"Thanks," Janet said. "What should I wear? I've never been a waitress before."

The arrangement they had made for Janet to help Lori serve the food had been made on Monday, when Janet still needed money. "You're still okay with helping out?" Lori asked.

Janet looked hurt. "I'm not going to back out on you at the last minute."

"Thanks. I really appreciate it. Black slacks or a black skirt and a white shirt is the usual uniform. And you're a food server, not a waitress. As for never having done it before, I guess Seth's been eating out every night."

Janet nodded. The smile Lori was hoping for didn't come. They kissed each other's cheeks, said goodbye. As Lori walked to Margot's car, she wondered. If Janet and Seth's money problems were finally over, if they were "going to be fine," why didn't Janet look happy?

★　★　★　★　★

At home, Lori put the food in the refrigerator, changed into her usual shorts and T-shirt, washed makeup and layers of cream off her face, then called Jess on her cell phone. She explained about Warren needing to leave tomorrow. Angie had already told Jessica.

"I don't know, Mom. Dad said it's okay but . . . I don't know."

Rob hadn't told her about Valerie's will. It would have been the first thing she would have blurted out. "Jess, whatever you decide is fine with me, but I'm going to be too busy preparing for the dinner party to drive you anywhere tomorrow or Saturday."

"What about Grammy? She wanted me to come over on Saturday."

"I'll drive you over tomorrow morning early."

"Then it's okay to go?"

"Of course it is. What do you want for dinner?"

"Pizza. It's lousy where we're going. And Mom, oh, Mom, I've got lots to tell you except I can't talk now."

"Deuce?"

"Uh huh."

"Can't wait to hear all about it. Come home soon."

"Forty-five minutes max."

Lori went downstairs to the kitchen. Now she needed to call Rob. She was still scared. It was nice to think the police might not suspect her anymore, but she had Jess to worry about. First her mother a murder suspect, and now her father. What if the police arrested Rob? What kind of scar would that leave on her daughter? Rob had to have an alibi. The doorman must have seen him come home that night. And if he was meeting someone as Angie and Jess thought, that person could vouch for him and he'd be fine.

Lori changed the water for the flowers. They were still holding up. Lord, she hadn't sent Alec Winters a thank-you note. What was she waiting for? Such a small task, why couldn't she handle it? Lori walked over to her desk with determination. On a plain card, she wrote a fast thank you, addressed the envelope, sealed it, put a stamp on it, and went to leave the note on the hall table to put in the mailbox later.

Back in the kitchen, she glanced at the wall phone by the refrigerator. She had no desire to get involved in Rob's problems. Thanks to him, she had enough of her own. Concentrate on pizza. She had tried making it countless times. She'd even bought a baking stone in order to get a crisp crust, but she never could match Gino's Pizza, three miles down the road. She'd stopped trying. Lori walked to phone. First the pizza. Then Rob.

She called Gino's and ordered a large pizza with pepperoni, mushrooms, and extra mozzarella that she would pick up in an hour. Now it was Rob's turn.

"How was lunch with the bear?" Beth asked when she answered the phone at the gallery.

"Fine." Lori walked the receiver over to a chair by the table and sat down. Somehow her fingers had dialed the wrong number, which Lori took to mean that she needed comfort first. She told Beth about Rob's visit, about Valerie's will, and the police shifting their suspicions to Rob.

"That's good for you and tough on Jess, which I guess ends up making it even tougher on you," Beth said.

"Jess doesn't know anything yet, and I'd like to keep it that way for as long as possible."

"How much is Rob inheriting?" Beth asked.

"I don't know the dollar amount, but according to my mother, except for a few thousand for Ruth, the office manager, he gets the lot."

Beth whistled.

Lori told her about Janet. "She said her money worries are over, that an investment came through for them, which is great, but she didn't look in the least bit happy."

"Maybe it's not that easy to shrug off the worry weight. Maybe she's afraid to believe that they are finally going to be okay. People can react to good news in funny ways. Give her time."

"You're right," Lori said. "When you made dean's list, you had to write it down on an index card that you carried with you for a week before you allowed yourself a smile."

Beth laughed. "Ah, the good old days. No worries, no fears. And now . . . Lori, I can't believe how well you're holding up. You're a mountain of strength. I'd be blubbering in a closet."

"I can't fall apart with Jess around, but believe me, inside I can't stop shaking."

"Want me to come over with a case of wine?"

The thought made Lori smile. The last time they had gotten drunk together was the night before Beth's wedding. They'd ended up dancing in their underwear in Beth's backyard with all the sprinklers turned on. The next morning Beth's wonderful mother had wondered why they hadn't stripped everything off.

"Thanks, Beth, I'd love it, but it's my last night with Jess for a couple of weeks." They made a brunch date for Sunday at Beth's place in Bedford. Before hanging up, Lori asked, "You didn't by any chance unplug my phone when you were here on Monday?"

"Why the hell would I do that?"

"I don't know. Maybe you tripped on the cord?"

"What did you have to drink for lunch?"

"Bloody Murder. It can make you a little crazy." Lori took a deep breath. "Sorry. I'm being silly."

"No, you're not. You're trying to get a grip."

After hanging up, Lori reached into the fridge for a slice of salami, which she rolled and popped into her mouth. A little fat always helped.

Lori got Rob on his cell phone. "I'm glad you're letting Jess go to Cape Cod tomorrow."

"I can say the same for you."

"It's the best thing for her."

"Ditto."

"You do have an alibi?"

"As a matter of fact I don't."

"Didn't you go straight home from the restaurant?"

Rob answered with a big sigh, then, "Lori, I know you mean well. You always do. I know you're worried about what Jessica will suffer if I should . . . Look, I've been answering questions at the police station for hours today, and a bunch of reporters are panting outside my building, which means that right now all I want is to sit down and drink myself through a bottle of Scotch, so if you don't mind I'm going to hang up and do just that."

"Jessica doesn't believe you were sick. If you were sick, you would have gone straight home. You were meeting someone. A man, a woman, whoever it was, that's your alibi. And if he or she didn't show up, then maybe he or she is the murderer. Did you tell the police that?"

"Listen, I don't need your help anymore."

A bubble of hot anger burst inside Lori. "Now you listen to me, Rob. For all I care you can rot in some hole for the rest of your life, but you happen to have a daughter who you've hurt more than you'll ever know, and I'm not going to let you end up in jail for murder and ruin her life." Lori stopped to breathe.

"Where were you Monday night?"

His answer was a dial tone.

"Deuce gave me his e-mail address and his phone number AND, Mom, you won't believe this." Jessica paused to add drama, her eyes glittering. The pepperoni and mushroom pizza had been polished off. They were now indulging in Callie's apple pie.

"What won't I believe?" Lori asked.

"He's going to be fifteen miles from us up in Cape Cod!" Jessica beamed enough happiness to light up the Empire State Building. "And he's got a bike up there and he's going to come over."

"That's great, sweetie," Lori said. She had better call Warren in the morning to let him know there was a potential boyfriend within necking distance, and tonight she had better talk to Jess about cherishing her own body, about restraint. She had heard horror stories about twelve year-old girls going down on boys to be popular. But for now, let Jessica fly with her happiness.

"Tell me step by step how you two got to talking to each other."

Lori woke up in the middle of the night, her chest tight. Spreading herself out on a bed that had become too vast, she wanted to scream out the feeling of helplessness that had come over her after Rob hung up. She wanted to scream out her loneliness. Sleep came hours later.

CHAPTER 19

At eight o'clock the next morning, Lori was already showered and dressed, sitting at the kitchen table with a mug of coffee at her elbow. She was working out a game plan for tomorrow's dinner party. She still needed to buy local vegetables and fruits. That could wait until tomorrow morning. Today, after Jessica left, she was going to go into the city to shop. First to Little Italy, then Greenwich Village. It was a long haul from Hawthorne Park but worth it.

The doorbell rang as Lori got up to refill her coffee mug. She tiptoed to the hallway. It could be Rob at the door, early to pick up Jess who was upstairs taking one of her never-ending showers. Last night Lori had reluctantly agreed to let Rob take Jess out to breakfast, then over to Ellie's for a quick goodbye before delivering her over to Margot's house where Warren would be waiting.

Rob or another reporter. Lori peered through the peephole. A distorted freckled face stared back at her. "I'm with Hawthorne Park—"

Lori opened the door wide to stop the word *police* from being shouted out for the whole neighborhood to hear. "We're returning your car, ma'am," he said softly, now that she was standing in front of him. Lori leaned her head to one side and saw her Ford Taurus parked behind a black Chevy with a sun-glassed driver facing her way. The car looked the same. Dented, in need of a wash. Hers, a home away from home. She felt a rush of warmth envelop her body. She would never have to worry about scratching Margot's Mercedes again.

Lori turned back to the policeman on her doorstep. He handed over the keys. He had a nice square face—a red crew cut, freckles spattered on his face like cinnamon on a roll, and a nose peeling from too much sun. The name tag on his chest read *John O'Dowd.*

"Thank you, Sergeant O'Dowd," Lori said.

"She's clean as a whistle," Officer O'Dowd said.

"You cleaned out all the junk from the backseat. And washed it, too? That's great. Thanks."

"No, ma'am," John O'Dowd said with a deadpan face. He was cute but he had no sense of humor. Maybe that's why he was a policeman.

"I was kidding," Lori said. She signed for the car, thanked him again, and watched him climb into the unmarked Chevy at the end of her driveway. As the two policemen drove away, a sparkling forest green Jaguar that had been parked a few doors down the street eased its way toward Lori's house. Rob got out, raised his hand to say hello. Lori nodded and went into the darkness of the house, leaving the door open.

Once inside the house, Lori sensed Rob looking her over. He always did that to women. Even if they weren't available. Even if he wasn't at all interested, which Lori was sure was the case with her. He just needed to assess what was out there. She had dressed for it. White slacks that hugged her slimmed-down butt, a white T-shirt with her best uplifting bra, Ellie's regimen of creams on her face, blotted down with a light brush stroke of powder, makeup. Not her usual breakfast attire. Lori wanted to look good, to look sexy, not to get him back but to show him she was fine without him, that in the end he had done her a favor by leaving. Lori wasn't sure she believed that, at least not yet, but she wanted Rob to think it. It would give her the upper hand and make their relationship easier for her.

"I see you got your car back," he said, following Lori into the kitchen.

"And that's quite a car you've got. Another rental?" She offered him coffee. "It's decaf."

"Thanks for the warning. No, thanks. The car is mine. Picked her up last night."

"I thought you were going to stay home and go through a bottle of Scotch."

"I did."

"I guess that explains the car."

"I can afford it."

"If you can afford it, why haven't you sent me a check yet?"

Rob studied his black Prada sneakers. "I've had a lot of expenses lately. I'm waiting for a check myself."

Lori folded her arms across her chest and waited for Rob to raise his head and look at her again. When he didn't, she said, "But you bought a new car?"

"I didn't pay for it yet."

"I guess that makes it all right, then. In your book."

"You'll get your check on Monday."

"Good. Look, Rob, as far as I'm concerned you're free to spend as much as you want as long as you take care of Jessica, but I'm not sure that buying such an expensive car three days after your wife gets murdered and leaves you pots of money is going to look good before a jury. If it should come to that."

"It won't. I didn't kill her."

"I know you didn't, but there are an awful lot of people in jail despite the truth." She poured him a cup of decaf anyway, which she knew he wouldn't drink, but she needed to keep busy. "I'm sorry I flew off the handle yesterday," she said.

"Your apology is accepted."

Your apology is accepted? Had he always sounded so stuffy?

"Do the police have any suspects?" Lori asked as she handed him a blueberry muffin on a plate.

"Yes, me." Rob accepted the muffin without a thank you. "Is Jess ready?"

"Besides you, I meant." She didn't want to call Jess just yet. She had questions to ask.

He started eating standing up. "I'm it."

"You can sit."

"I'm not staying that long."

"Jessica is showering. Sit down. It won't ruin the crease in your slacks." He was wearing a bright striped shirt with cuffs rolled up and perfectly ironed tan slacks. He'd always been a natty dresser. Lori sat down at the kitchen table, waited for Rob to join her.

"Those flowers have had it," he said, coming closer, towering over her.

He was right, but she didn't want to throw them out yet. "I just need to clean out the droopy ones."

"They're dead." Rob held out the empty plate for Lori to take. Her hand indicated the sink.

"I'm glad you and Seth have made up," she said.

"No, we haven't."

"He went to your wedding."

"Why would I invite him? Seth's a loser."

"Please don't call him that." Something wasn't making sense. Why would Seth lie? "You used to be good friends."

"You used to be my wife."

He's getting back at me for looking good, Lori told herself. *He's getting back at me because men have sent me flowers. He's getting back at me because he owes me money. He's getting back at me because he's the murder suspect now and not me.* She had to stay calm, not let him see he was getting to her. "True enough," she said finally. She stood up and took Alec's vase of flowers to the sink.

Rob walked out into the hall and called up. "Hey, Jess, let's get going! I'm hungry."

Jess yelled back. "I'll be right down."

"Right down" in Jess's language usually meant another ten or fifteen minutes. Lori started to remove the dead flowers and re-arrange the half-dead ones. When Rob walked back into the kitchen, she said, "What made you change your wills so quickly, Rob? You were barely married. Was it Valerie's idea, yours? What was the rush?"

"That's none of your business."

"Maybe not mine, but the police must be very interested in the reason. Did you tell them that you thought someone tried to run you over Friday night? It would explain changing your will two days after you got married."

"No one tried to kill me Friday or any other time. I had the wedding jitters. I was being paranoid."

"You're not that paranoid, and the only time you ever had the jitters was when you thought you were getting sick. Look, you did tell a lot of people that someone was after you. Why are you now backtracking? What are you afraid of? That someone might start asking why anyone would want to kill you? Come on, Rob, what kind of trouble are you in?"

Rob's jaw muscles twitched, a gesture Lori had repeatedly witnessed when he was angry with her, when he wanted her to shut her mouth. Usually those confrontations ended with Rob leaving the room without an added word. This time he said, "She was my wife. I was her husband. That's why we changed our wills. There was no hidden agenda. We'd prepared the changes the week before. On Monday we signed. Tell Jess I'll wait for her in the car and get rid of those flowers. They stink of rot."

★ ★ ★ ★ ★

Ten minutes later, Lori was still in the hallway, stewing, when Jess, in cutoff jeans and a Camp Trip Lake T-shirt, came down the stairs, her duffle bag thumping behind her. "Where's Dad?"

"He's waiting for you outside."

"What did you do to him?"

"I fed him," Lori said, taking the duffle bag from Jessica's hands. "Now he's communing with his new toy."

"What?" Jessica ran to the glass panel on one side of the front door. "Oh gosh, did he buy that?"

Lori joined her. "Last night."

Jessica tossed her ponytail. "That's so out of control!"

"Grief shows itself in many forms," Lori said.

"Yeah." Jessica frowned, thinking thoughts Lori wished she could divine. Her daughter continued to gaze at her father's new car—the sun gave it a bling-like shine—then shrugged her shoulders. "I guess it's kinda cool. Wait 'til Angie sees it. A Jaguar's much groovier than a Mercedes."

Rob honked. "You'd better go now." Lori hugged Jess tightly. "Remember what we talked about last night."

Jessica hugged her back. "Stop worrying. I'm not going to do anything yucky like that. Besides, Deuce would never ask." She looked at her mother with serious eyes. "You're going to be okay, right?"

Lori nodded.

Rob honked again. Lori opened the front door, grabbed the handles of the duffle bag. "I'll walk you down."

"Mom! I'm not going to the moon."

Lori stepped back, tears stinging her eyes. She knew she was being ridiculous, but she couldn't help it. "Have fun and call me every day."

"Every day," Jessica called out as Lori's eyes followed her walk down the path, ponytail wagging, body leaning to one side to counter the weight of the duffle bag. Halfway down the path, Jessica dropped the bag and came running back to her mother.

"Did you forget something?"

Jessica gave her mother a quick kiss and whispered, "Don't tell Dad about Deuce, okay? He might get jealous."

"Our secret, sweetie."

Lori waved as Rob drove their daughter away, her tears coming freely now.

Bordered by a spreading Chinatown, Little Italy was turning into Tiny Italy, Lori thought as she walked the few remaining streets under a blistering sun with a growing sense of sadness. How had she not noticed the change before? Its Italian authenticity was gone. It was just a tourist hub. Lori wove her way through mounds of people dressed in shorts and tank tops, who were checking the menus posted outside the countless restaurants on Mulberry Street. It was almost lunchtime, and waiters tried to flag her down with promises of better, cheaper food than the place next door. She passed souvenir stores stuffed with the usual soccer shirts, flags, T-shirts, and CDs, as Dean Martin's honeyed voice poured onto the street, singing "Bella Mia." Eight-by-eleven glossies of Sinatra, Al Pacino, Stallone stared back at her as she rushed by. The corner of her eye caught something that stopped her. Lori backed up a few paces and looked at the photo of the cast of *The Godfather*. Above the photo, James Gandolfini smiled from a hanging T-shirt. Another T-shirt boasted THE MAFIA in big red letters. Yet another read THE SOPRANOS. Her eyes dropped down to the photo of Al Pacino as Scarface. A group picture of the cast of *Jersey Shore* leaned next to it.

Lori felt her cheeks burn, as if she'd just been slapped. How could anyone with Italian blood in them sell the Mafia as something to be proud of? And why was anyone buying the stuff? "We are so much more than this!" she wanted to shout out, but she felt diminished and powerless in front of this onslaught of cheap commercialism, this reverence for violence and vulgarity.

"Keep moving," Lori told herself and walked briskly to Grand Street. More changes greeted her. The Food Center, a large corner store that once did a bustling business, was now defunct, its wide windows boarded up. A block away, a Malaysian restaurant had dared to intrude. Poor Papa, he'd be roaring *"tradimento,"* in his grave.

Lori rushed into Alleva. This had been Papa's store—a corner of the old country, a pilgrimage of sorts. Once or twice a month, on Saturdays, she and Papa would take the train to the city, then the subway to Little Italy. Ellie wasn't into food or nostalgia, and anyway she had to work at the travel agency, which she didn't own then. A visit here always brought a grin to Papa's face and sometimes watery eyes.

Thankfully, the place hadn't changed. The smell was as Lori remembered it, sharp from the aged cheeses, sweet from the meats, a smell that softened her mood. Logs of provolone hung from the ceiling. Varying sizes of mozzarella balls floated in white plastic vats, ready to be plucked. Rolls of salami, mortadella, *capocolla, guanciale,* and legs of prosciutto sat lined next to each other atop shelves, cut side out to tempt the customer with their patterns of varying ratios of fat to meat. Lori smiled at the counterman, a large man with thinning strands of dyed black hair swept over his balding head and *Sal* in red letters stamped on his white jacket. Sal balled up his cheeks with a grin that brought her father back. "Dear *signora,* what can I do for you today?"

Lori said nothing for a moment, relishing the memory of her father shaking hands with the owner, checking the thinness of the prosciutto slice, rolling the mozzarella in its milk to make sure it was as fresh as the counterman claimed. Behind her, the door chimed. Another customer walked in and Lori shook herself out of her reverie to order mozzarella, Parmigiano Reggiano, and prosciutto. While Sal filled her order, she picked up four cans of Italian tuna and two packages of marinated white anchovies for herself. In the car she had a cooler to keep the food fresh.

Just as Sal offered her a transparent slice of prosciutto to taste, Lori's cell phone sounded its Beethoven notes. She went out on the street to answer.

"Any chance I can see you today?" Jonathan asked. "I'm in the city now, but I'll be home around five. Maybe I can tempt you from your labors for my mother and take you out for a drink, a quick dinner?"

"Is anything wrong?" Lori asked.

"If wanting to see you is wrong, then yes."

Lori found herself smiling, while at the same time deciding Mr. Jonathan Ashe was not to be taken seriously under any circumstances. "I'm in the city right now. In Little Italy, shopping for tomorrow night."

"We can have lunch. Want me to come down there?"

"I have to go to Bleecker Street next."

"Murray's Cheese?"

Lori laughed. "How did you know?"

"I saw French cheeses on your menu. I can meet you there in thirty minutes."

"Make it forty-five."

"Why bother to go all the way down to Little Italy?" Jonathan asked as he expertly rolled linguine with clam sauce onto his fork. They were sitting at the bar at the Gotham Bar and Grill, one of Manhattan's great restaurants, Lori's shopping over with.

All the tables were taken. "You had everything you needed on Bleecker."

"You're right. Murray's Cheese, Amy's, and Faicco's all on the same block, but I guess I was feeling a little nostalgic." She picked up a goat cheese raviolo in pancetta and shallot sauce, chewed on it slowly. She hadn't been back to Little Italy since Rob left her. She hadn't visited Papa's grave since then, either, always finding an excuse when Ellie asked Lori to accompany her. What had stopped her, she wondered. Was it shame? Did she feel that by getting divorced she had let Papa down? He hadn't been in her life for so many years—Lori was eleven when he died—but he had been the only significant man in her life before Rob. Maybe when she thought of him, she turned into the little girl she had been when he was alive, the same way she had remembered Little Italy as it was when her father took her there. Yes, that was it. Lori, the girl, was ashamed of having been abandoned. Lori, the woman, was trying to deal with it.

"Have you gone on a trip?" Jonathan asked.

Lori gave an apologetic smile, embarrassed by her rudeness. "I'm sorry. I was just thinking how unnecessarily complicated we make our lives."

"Right you are. I've been looking into apartments for my mother, but she turns everything down. She can't stand the idea of having to downsize, but I can't stand the idea of her living with me much longer."

"I thought she had found an apartment she really liked."

"She told you that?" He seemed surprised.

Lori nodded.

"I understand Mother wanting a view of Central Park, but she doesn't need three bedrooms."

What had Margot said about him? Something about losing money in one of his real estate deals. Lori bit into another raviolo and was willingly distracted by the tart taste of the goat cheese contrasted with the sweetness of the pasta and the saltiness of the pancetta. Delicious. She must buy the cookbook. But now to business.

"Jonathan, I need your help."

"I know. Beth asked me if I could dig up some info about Valerie."

"I was thinking more about Rob's business dealings. I know that Rob was trying to get people to invest with him to buy some real estate. Do you know anything about it?"

Jonathan took a long sip of his white wine. For a moment Lori thought he wasn't going to answer. "Sure," he finally said, putting his glass down carefully on the wine coaster. "Rob asked me to invest, but I was short of cash and had to turn him down, and I've been kicking myself ever since. He was trying to put together an investment package to buy into Waterside Properties in the Bronx, part of the city's effort at gentrification. The land is on the water with some abandoned buildings on it. I forget how many acres the city was offering, but to invest you had to raise five million dollars, twenty-five percent of the total cost. Not much by today's standards. The return was projected at doubling your money and now, from what I hear, it's going to triple it if not more. It hurts in the gut to think about it."

"Then Rob didn't lose any money from it?"

"He never went through with it. I'd know if he had. Either changed his mind or couldn't come up with the money."

"If he had the money now, could he still invest?"

"No. The deal closed last week."

Lori polished off her plate with a misplaced sense of relief. With Waterside Properties out of reach, Rob didn't have a motive to kill Valerie, she thought, not focusing on Jonathan's words, *or couldn't come up with the money.*

Jonathan called the waiter over to refill their wine glasses. Lori watched the golden wine slowly being poured into her glass, knowing she had a long drive home and a lot of cooking to do, but she wanted to relax and enjoy herself in this beautiful Greenwich Village restaurant in Jonathan's company. Dressed in a beige linen shirt, with dark tan slacks and smiling eyes to match, he was very handsome company.

With his elbow on the bar counter and chin in his hand, he peered at her with an intense expression.

"What?" she said.

"I'm glad we've met."

"I am, too." She meant it. There was something fun and out of the ordinary about Jonathan, like a glass of champagne you only had on special occasions.

"I like you," he said. "Your face, your hands. I won't embarrass you with the rest, but I like you more than is comfortable." Jonathan sat up and twisted his stool to face the bar again. "What about Portale's inimitable flourless chocolate cake?"

Hoping she wasn't blushing, Lori agreed to take a bite of the cake and asked for a double espresso.

The cake was astoundingly good, so light it felt as if she was swallowing sweet air. "Did you find anything out about Valerie?" she asked.

"Her friends were mostly superficial ones, the kind who meet at parties or dinners and accuse each other of not calling, but only really want to talk about the great vacation they've just had or the fabulous dress they've just bought. I'm sure you know the type."

"Luckily, I don't."

"I should have known." Jonathan smiled and gave her a look that made her feel as if she were being caressed. It was sexy and infuriating at the same time. "She was dating Warren for a while," he said, "but I think Margot already told you that. And Margot told you about Ruth, right?"

"Yes. She's Valerie's cousin." She took a sip of her double

espresso. It was hot and bitter, just what she needed to jolt her out of the wine haze.

"There's more to the Ruth story," Jonathan said, "if my mother is to be believed. Of course, she doesn't remember what. Supposedly something happened when Valerie and Ruth were little. If there was something, I'm sure it had nothing to do with Valerie's death, but my mother is like a terrier with a bone. She's calling around to friends, the few that are left, to jog her memory. If there's anything to it, I'll let you know, but don't count on it."

"I like your mother, Jonathan." Lori didn't like him putting Mrs. Ashe down. It made him small.

"And I like your mother."

Lori finished her coffee in silence.

CHAPTER 20

Lori sat at her bedroom window that overlooked her small garden. Tomorrow she would have to weed, deadhead, fertilize, make her garden shine again, but for now she just wanted to sit, chin in hand, and take in the sights and sounds of a Saturday summer morning. The air was cool, the sky clear except for a few low wisps of white far on the horizon. Sprinklers ticked almost in unison. Sprays of water, looking like so many swirling tutus, glinted in the early sun. A mockingbird went through the different notes of its repertoire. A basketball smacked a backboard and bounced with a dull thud on the asphalt of a driveway. In the distance, a too-diligent husband or son started mowing the lawn.

The rude noise was an unwelcome reminder that it was time to shake off her lethargy and start working on Mrs. Ashe's dinner again. Last night she had poached the veal, made the tuna mayonnaise, and assembled the dish so that the taste of the sauce would have twenty-four hours to penetrate the meat. She had blended and dressed the artichoke hearts and grated the various cheeses for the cheese puffs. Today she still had to buy vegetables, make the tomato soup, roast the peppers, and cook the orzo for the pasta salad. Later, at Jonathan's apartment, she would assemble the hors d'oeuvres; while the guests ate the main course, she would roast the peaches for dessert.

Jonathan. She leaned her head to one side of the window, her thoughts going back to yesterday. He had kissed her outside the restaurant. On the street. In broad daylight. In front of people walking by. Rob had barely touched her if there was a chance someone might catch him at it. Earlier boyfriends had limited their kissing to cars, doorways, fraternity rooms. Jonathan had reached for her, turned her around, and kissed her. She didn't push him away.

The kiss had been gentle, his lips soft on hers, his hands warm and firm against her back, simply holding her, without pressing his chest against her breasts. He held his lips to hers for a long time, broke away only to rest his cheek against hers. She had felt awkward and excited all at the same time, like the young girl she had once been, starting out in a more naive sexual world than the one Jessica had to maneuver through.

"I want to see more of you," he told her, cheek to cheek. "Lots more of you." The sudden twinge she felt between her legs had made her pull away and toss her head to shake off the embarrassment of his kiss, his words, and her reaction.

During the night, Jonathan made love to her. In a dream. How long had it been since she'd had the real thing? A year? A year and a half? She ached for a man to skate his hands down her body, to kiss her breasts, to push himself inside her and rock her with him. But the only man she had ever made love with was Rob. He had known her when her breasts sat up, her stomach was flat, her skin was taut. When he made love to her older, bigger, softer body, she had always assumed that he held on to the sight and the feel of her twenty-year-old self. A new man would have no such memory to enhance her in his eyes. Lori thought of Shirley MacLaine in *Terms of Endearment,* facing a horny Jack Nicholson in her negligee. How embarrassed Lori had been for her, how convinced such a humiliating moment would never happen to her.

Could she do it? Lori wondered. Expose her middle-aged nakedness to strange eyes? Toss off her clothes and jump into bed with a man she barely knew?

Lori left the window. Like Scarlett, she'd think about it tomorrow. Today, she had work to do.

"Need any help?" Beth asked on the phone as Lori was leaving the vegetable market. "I think I can be trusted to chop onions without getting blood all over your kitchen."

Lori was tempted. She wanted to talk about Jonathan, about having casual sex at their age, about Beth feeling like "meat for sale" when she dated. About the murder. "Thanks for the offer." Lori turned onto King Street. Home was only ten minutes away if she didn't hit traffic on the Merritt. "I'd love the company, but with you in the kitchen, I might end up pouring wine in the soup instead of broth. We'll catch up tomorrow."

"Actually I hate chopping," Beth said. "What I was really hoping for was a tasting. And an update on Valerie's murder."

"I haven't heard anything new." She hadn't told Beth about Ruth being Valerie's cousin, but that could wait until tomorrow. "I do want us to put our heads together and see what we know so far, but today's not the day."

"I know it isn't," Beth said. "Listen, Janet called me this morning. She grilled me about what I knew. You told her something about being off the hook, and she wanted to know who was the new suspect. She sounded nervous, upset. I debated telling you because I know she's helping you out with this dinner. I didn't want you to get worried. What I'm trying to say is that if for some reason she doesn't come through at the last minute, I can pitch in. With me tending bar, those ladies would make some mean whoopee."

Lori laughed despite herself. "Again, thanks, but Jonathan is tending bar, not Janet." Lori didn't believe Janet would let her down at the last minute—she was too loyal and generous a person—but, just in case, she was glad she had planned a cold meal. With dessert being the only last-minute preparation, she could manage serving dinner by herself.

"I can help serve," Beth offered.

"That would be a great way to end my catering career before it starts." Beth had, in the first two years of marriage, managed to break almost every plate of her grandmother's Tiffany service. What was left—three bread plates and two soup bowls—she'd hung on the kitchen wall, out of harm's way. "You're sweet to want to help, but I'm sure Janet is going to do a great job. Maybe she had a fight with Seth or the kids are driving her crazy."

"I don't know," Beth answered. "All she talked about was the murder. We all pledged to help you to try to find out more about Valerie, and maybe Janet has gotten too emotionally involved in the outcome. She's had a rough year, but listening to her, I thought she was scared."

"Thanks for telling me. If she's still upset when she comes to work, I can try to make the evening easier for her. I'll talk to her while we're cleaning up and see if there's anything we can do."

"Good. I know your dinner is going to go off without a hitch. See you tomorrow at eleven. Don't bring a thing. I'm picking up two quiches for us, mushroom and leek, from Callie's before she closes tonight."

After saying goodbye, Lori switched off her speaker phone and veered onto the exit for Hawthorne Park. Beth's call had reminded her she had a question begging for an answer. She looked at the car clock. Nine thirty-five. She had time to take a detour.

Saturday morning, half the town came for breakfast at Callie's. Lori had to walk past a long line to get to the coffee shop. It was the worst time to get Callie's attention, but she couldn't just go back to her kitchen and cook tomatoes. She had to find out what Callie meant by her warning to be careful of friends.

Eugenia, Callie's daughter, was standing by a booth in the front, stacking dirty dishes on a tray while her sixteen-year-old daughter, Vicki, wiped the table clean. "I need to ask your mother a quick question," Lori said, not catching sight of Callie.

"She's not here," Eugenia said, "and this is no time to ask any of us questions. If you want to eat, get in line, if not . . ." Eugenia lifted the tray above Lori's head and walked back toward the kitchen without another word.

Vicki leaned toward Lori and whispered, "Grandma's at the cemetery," before waving in the next customers.

Lori thanked Vicki and walked out onto the street, back to her car. Callie at the cemetery, probably visiting Nick, her husband. His picture, showing a handsome burly man with a snazzy moustache and a thick head of wavy black hair, hung in a black frame in the coffee shop, over the cakes display. It was Nick's life insurance money and a bank loan that had allowed Callie to buy the coffee shop and provide for her family.

Lori sat in her car. It smelled funny. The police must have sprayed some chemical on the seats. She opened all the windows and picked up her cell phone. She didn't have time to come back today, and tomorrow, Sunday, the coffee shop would be closed. She would have to wait until Monday, after breakfast with the girls. Lori punched in her mother's phone number. When Ellie answered, she said, "I'd like to go with you to go visit Papa tomorrow."

There was silence at the other end of the line.

"I know, it's been a long time."

"You've still got Margot's Mercedes?"

"Yes." Beth was going to help her return the car tomorrow.

"Come by at nine and honk the horn. I want Mrs. DeRosa to bite her tongue from envy."

Lori laughed to herself. Mrs. DeRosa was Ellie's sworn enemy because Papa had once, under the influence of too much wine at a block party, declared for everyone to hear that there wasn't a finer specimen of womanhood in the entire block than Mrs. Ernestine DeRosa.

Lori pressed the speaker button and started the car toward home. "How's Joey Pellegrino?"

"Lonely. His family's gone to Long Island for a couple of weeks. I was thinking of inviting him over for some food."

Lori didn't like the sound of that. "He's a vegan?"

"Don't go huffy on me. I can still remember how to make a meat sauce that'll put hair on your chest."

"I'll remember that if I should ever need it."

"I didn't raise you to be a sarcastic daughter."

"You're right. I'm sorry. It's just that—"

"Loretta, don't go there. There's nothing wrong in feeding a lonely man."

"Mom, a *married* lonely man."

"All right, Miss High and Mighty, we'll take up this discussion after you've been without a man's company for years, and now I've got this to tell you. This married man is clamming up on me. He's just remembered that he may be retired, but he's still a cop and if he leaks anything out it might compromise the investigation. See you at nine sharp and don't forget to honk real loud."

Lori parked in the garage next to Margot's car and sat back against the seat. She was sorry she'd been patronizing and sarcastic with Ellie. She had no right to interfere, especially since she'd always resented her mother butting in on her life. And who was she to make moral judgments? It was only a dinner. It didn't have to mean anything else. How had Rob's affair with Valerie started? Chit-chat between drillings, then a friendly lunch to keep each other company? Lori knew that her role as betrayed wife made her very sensitive about married men stepping out on their wives, but it was the yearning in Ellie's voice that had gone straight to her heart. The realization of how great her mother's neediness was, the extent of her loneliness, hurt terribly. Ellie had hidden it well behind an in-your-face attitude of independence. Or maybe Lori, smug in her married happiness, had never stopped to read between the lines of Ellie's bluster as she had never spotted Beth's unhappiness. Now she hurt for her mother and her friend. She worried for herself. Was loneliness her only future, too?

While the peppers were blistering in the broiler, the pasta water was reaching a boil for the orzo, and the tomato soup was waiting to be strained, Lori's doorbell rang. She took a quick peek out the kitchen window. A car she didn't recognize sat next to her driveway. Whoever it was, a reporter, a Jehovah's Witness, the Ten Million Dollar Sweepstakes people, she didn't care. Right now she couldn't deal with anything except Mrs. Ashe's dinner. She checked the broiler. The peppers were nicely charred, the peel already curling away. Lori used a pair of tongs to remove the peppers and drop them into a paper bag, which she folded over to let them steam and cool down. The doorbell stopped ringing. The lid on the pasta pot started rattling. Before Lori could reach the stove, the lid lifted and foamy water gushed out of the pot. She ran to lift the lid and cried out. The lid dropped to the floor. Her fingertips throbbed. She went to the windowsill, tore off a leaf from the aloe plant, pierced the stalk open with a fingernail and pressed it against her fingers to let the gooey juice soothe the burn. A tap on the window made Lori look up.

Margot waved fingers at her. "Let me in," she mouthed.

Margot clacked into the kitchen on her high-heeled mules and pecked Lori's cheeks.

"What brings you here?" Lori asked. She was too busy and in too foul a mood to welcome the interruption.

"I was worried about you."

Lori dropped the orzo in the boiling pasta water. "There's no reason to be."

Margot sat on one of the ladder-backed chairs and crossed her legs carefully. She was wearing a skimpy white dress that would have looked great on Jessica or Angie. "The police are looking into phone calls."

Lori turned to look at her friend. Margot's usually alabaster complexion looked flushed and a frown was trying to worm its way through the Botox freeze. Lori set the timer for five minutes, knowing she would need a reminder, and sat facing Margot.

"How do you know?"

"Two big detectives came over. They said they were in charge of the case, that they had my phone records, and they wanted to know why I'd called your cell the night Valerie died instead of calling you on your home phone. I didn't know how to lie. I'm sorry." Tears appeared at the edges of Margot's eyes. "I'm so sorry."

"It's all right. Really. Lying would have only made things worse. Scardini and Mitchell would have found out sooner or later." They couldn't arrest her on such skimpy grounds, could they? No. At the most it meant the two would come visiting, ply her with questions again. She hoped not today. "Come on, Margot, they're not going to arrest me." She stood up and circled Margot's chair to put an arm around her. To Lori's immense surprise, Margot was crying into her hands. Margot crying for her? It was sweet, but out of character. Lori ran a hand across Margot's shoulders and waited for her to calm down. Her ideas of the world around her were being totally upended.

After a couple of minutes, Margot looked up. "I'm so sorry.

It's just that—"

The timer went off. "Give me a sec," Lori said. She fished out a few bits of orzo with a ladle, blew on the pasta to cool it down and tasted. It needed two more minutes. Margot joined her at the stove, her face composed. Lori smiled at her and noticed, in a frivolous second she was instantly ashamed of, that Margot's mascara hadn't run.

"You saw Jonathan yesterday," Margot said lightly.

"Yes, we had lunch together. He wanted to fill me in on what he'd found out about Valerie."

"What?"

"He knew about Ruth, but you'd already told me."

Margot looked down on the boiling pasta pot as if she'd never seen the likes of it before. "Do you like him?" she asked finally, in the same tone of voice she used to ask if anyone wanted a drink.

"Sure." Without checking the orzo, Lori lifted the pot off the stove—with oven mitts this time—and drained the pasta in the fine mesh colander she had placed in the sink. "Jonathan's fun, good-looking, nice. What's not to like?" She ran cold water over the orzo to stop the cooking.

"Be careful," Margot said, narrowing her eyes.

Lori was reminded of a cat eyeing a fishbowl. "Why?"

"He plays the field."

"I wasn't planning to marry him. He hasn't asked me out, either."

Margot kissed her. Lori's nose was overwhelmed by the smell of Opium. "I don't want you to get hurt."

"Thanks for letting me know about the police," Lori said, dropping the orzo into a stainless steel bowl. "You did the right thing and please don't worry. Now I really have to concentrate on the dinner."

Margot offered to help, despite her freshly manicured nails. Lori turned her down with a laugh.

Later, while peeling the peppers and cutting them into thin strips, Lori thought about Margot's warning. That Jonathan played the field didn't come as a surprise. And he was at least five years younger than she was. Did it matter? If he asked her out, would she say yes? She was sure he would make a beautiful, considerate lover. She'd always thought lovers were like the tasty pre-dinner bites fancy restaurants offered, what the French called *amuse-bouche*, something to keep the mouth entertained momentarily. Maybe that could be all right for now, but she wasn't too old to hope for a solid, deeply satisfying relationship with a man. If she was capable of loving a man again.

CHAPTER 21

Lori was in Jonathan Ashe's gray marble kitchen, having just finished setting the dinner table, when Janet arrived with a hand truck that held three boxes filled with flowers in their vases. Janet had put on makeup, unusual for her, and tied her old-fashioned pageboy in a low ponytail. She looked pretty and young, dressed in the catering staff uniform: black loafers, white socks, black trousers, a white button-down shirt, and a black bow tie she had borrowed from Seth. Lori was wearing the same outfit without the bow tie.

"You look good," Lori said, opening up the bread stick boxes. "Thanks for coming so early." It was five o'clock. The guests were expected at seven. "Those flowers are gorgeous."

"It's all Sally's doing."

"I'm sure you helped." Janet was always putting herself down, and after what Beth had said, Lori expected Janet to be upset or nervous. If she was, she was keeping it well hidden, to Lori's great relief. She wanted Mrs. Ashe's birthday party to be as perfect as she could make it. If the guests were impressed, she was counting on them to spread the word or hire her for their own parties. Later, when they were washing up, she and Janet would have a talk.

"Where shall I put them?" Janet asked.

"Anywhere you'd like." Lori knew exactly where she wanted the flowers, but micromanaging was counterproductive. She'd learned that lesson from Ellie. Lori was hoping she and Janet

188

could become a team if and when Corvino Catering took off.

"Hey, Janet," Jonathan called out, striding into the kitchen in bare feet, a white terry cloth bathrobe covering what Lori presumed was his naked body. His hair was still wet from the shower. "Glad you're here to help out," he said.

"Hi," Janet said, and hurried out of the room with her box of flowers.

Jonathan edged himself next to Lori at the island in the center of the room, close enough for her to smell the soap he'd used: sandalwood. She carefully rolled prosciutto slices onto pencil-thin bread sticks and thought of the first time she had seen Jonathan. At the car wash, chatting with Janet as if they were old friends. "Need anything, Lori?"

She wanted to ask him how he and Janet knew each other, but she was afraid of sounding jealous.

"I can help." Jonathan reached for a prosciutto slice and folded it into his mouth.

Lori pushed him away with her hip. The intimacy of the gesture brought instant heat to her cheeks. "No distractions, please, and no picking at the food."

"Anything you say. Until later, then." He planted a kiss on the back of her neck that sent a shiver down her spine. His departure left wet footprints on the floor.

Janet walked back into the kitchen. "The flowers are in place. What do you want me to do now?"

Lori asked her to arrange the cheeses on the ornate, gold-edged Mottahedeh platters Mrs. Ashe had given her, platters that had been wedding gifts. Platters that would need to be hand washed with the rest of the gold-edged Duke of Glouces-ter dinner service. Next time, Lori promised herself, she would ask to see the plates before setting a price.

"How do you know Jonathan?"

"From the shop," Janet said.

"He orders flowers for his girlfriends?" Lori wanted to kick herself for acting like a schoolgirl, but that kiss on the back of her neck had made her go soft in the head.

"He comes in with his mother to pick an orchid, which we make into a corsage for her. It's a weekly ritual."

"I don't like to give up old habits," Mrs. Ashe said from the doorway.

Startled, Lori broke the bread stick in her hand. "I'm sorry, Mrs. Ashe." Lori turned around to face Jonathan's mother, who looked the epitome of old New York elegance in her long mauve chiffon gown, triple string of pearls resting on the shelf of her bosom, a deep purple orchid corsage pinned just below one shoulder. A hair stylist had swept her silvery gray hair high above her forehead. She looked like she was wearing a tiara. "I hope you won't think we were gossiping."

"Women ask all sorts of questions where my son is concerned."

So Margot was right, Lori thought. Jonathan did play the field.

Mrs. Ashe took a few cautious steps into the kitchen. "The flowers are very handsome."

"Thank you," Janet said.

"To answer your curiosity, Lori, my husband used to present me with an orchid corsage every Friday evening after he came home from the office. It was his way to celebrate our weekend. My son helps me keep up the pretense. When you two young ladies get older you may discover that you need little subterfuges to make life palatable. And as for Jonathan, he is a wonderful son, and the day he finds a woman with some backbone to her, he will make an even better husband and father. I'll leave you to your work. I have to take care of the place cards."

"Now I know why he's not married," Janet whispered, after making sure Mrs. Ashe was out of earshot.

"She is a bit formidable," Lori said, "but I feel for her. She's trying to hold on to what's gone and what can be sadder than that?"

"Not knowing what's around the corner is pretty bad, too," Janet said, carefully unwrapping a gooey Camembert on one of the many large zucchini leaves Lori had gotten at the vegetable market. The smell of the cheese was delicious and overpowering. The future *was* scary, Lori thought. For the whole world. She swept a finger over the wrapping paper, caught a streak of the cheese, put the finger in her mouth and sucked, feeling instant comfort. One of the first things she had learned as a caterer years ago was not to eat your own food. She must remember that or she'd end up rolling instead of walking.

"At the shop you said you were off the hook with the police," Janet said. "Do they have another suspect?" She looked up at Lori and tried on a smile. "I mean, it's great for you. Really, but who do they suspect now?"

"I think Rob's on top of the list."

Janet gave what sounded like a nervous giggle. "Rob, of course, who else? The husband is always the first one to be suspected."

"In this case, the ex-wife took precedence until the police found out about Valerie leaving Rob all that money."

"Did Valerie have a lot of money? Does the will say how big her estate is?"

"I don't know, but everyone said she had a lot of money. What makes you think she didn't?"

"No reason, except that we're always making assumptions about people that turn out to be wrong. You, of all people, know what that's like."

"Yes, I do." Lori looked straight at Janet. "Hon, is there something you want to talk about?"

Janet's face clouded over. "No. I just keep thinking that

maybe whoever killed Valerie was someone she knew, someone she trusted."

"Like Rob?"

"Who knows?"

"He may be a louse, but he's not a killer."

"Oh," Janet said, tugging at a zucchini leaf weighted down by a hefty wedge of Roquefort. "Sorry." The leaf broke. There were no more to replace it. Janet looked crestfallen.

Lori turned off the tap. She'd been washing the cherry tomatoes. "It's fine," she said. "Tuck the torn end under the Pont-l'Évêque. No one will notice."

Janet fussed over the cheese plate for what Lori thought was a long time. "That looks great," Lori said, in an attempt to re-assure her.

Janet finally placed the platter on the round glass and steel table at the far end of the kitchen, near the sliding door that led to the terrace where the hors d'oeuvres would be served. "I'm sure Rob didn't kill Valerie," she said, walking back to the island, "but would you have ever thought you couldn't trust him?"

"No," Lori admitted.

They worked silently after that, scooping out the cherry tomatoes, cutting the bottoms so they would sit up, cooking the bacon in the microwave, crushing it into bits to stuff into the tomatoes at the last minute so the bacon wouldn't get soggy. They toasted the pita bread, spread the slices with the artichoke spread, artfully laid out the fresh vegetables around the dips on more gold-edged platters. As they worked, Lori wondered if Janet and Seth's marriage was in trouble.

The doorbell rang just as the peaches were ready to be taken out of the oven. Lori lifted the peaches out and cursed silently. She'd have to answer that. Janet was in the dining room, clearing the entreé plates. Lori was carefully setting the baking pan on the wooden carving board so as not to damage the marble countertop when she heard Jonathan call out, "I'll get it." He waved at her as he rushed past the half-open kitchen door that led to the foyer.

Good, Lori thought, and turned to see Janet come through the swinging door to the dining room with a tray of dirty dishes. They started stacking the plates next to the sink.

"You're a success," Janet said in a tired voice. "They practically licked the plates clean."

"Couldn't have done it without you." Lori raised her hand. Janet gave her a limp high five and a limper smile. Lori hoped that Janet would open up later, tell her what was going on. Now it was time to top the peaches with a scoop of vanilla ice cream. Decaf coffee was percolating in the urn. One silver tray held a doily covered with chocolate lace cookies. Another was filled with dark and white chocolate truffles. Lori felt herself relax. The evening was coming to a successful end.

"How are you, my dear?" Mrs. Ashe's voice slipped through the opening in the kitchen door. She was talking to the late arrival. "I have missed seeing your handsome face." The warmth in Mrs. Ashe's voice made Lori listen.

"I am so happy to see you," Mrs. Ashe said. There was a moment of silence and Lori imagined them hugging. Then Mrs. Ashe said, "It's so sad about Christopher. How difficult it must be. Only a year has gone by, hasn't it? My Edward died three years ago and I still miss him terribly. How are you getting on?"

"Better," Lori heard the man answer, followed by footsteps, then silence. They must have gone into the dining room. She had to finish with the peaches, top them with crushed pistachio nuts. The green looked pretty against the creamy white of the ice cream and the orange of the peach. Should she get another dessert plate ready? Thankfully she had roasted an extra peach. "Janet, please check if the new arrival wants dessert, or dinner for that matter."

"Will do." Janet picked up the platter of roasted peaches and ice cream and swung the door open with her hip. Lori heard glasses clinking. Jonathan was serving more champagne with dessert. A few soft "happy birthdays" came though the door. Mrs. Ashe had made it clear she didn't want anyone bursting into song.

Janet came back and picked up the two silver trays of cookies and truffles. "He says peaches make his mouth pucker up, but he'd love the ice cream."

"Coming up." She scouted around for a small bowl. The Duke of Gloucester service—Mrs. Ashe's wedding service, she'd been told—was stashed in the stainless steel and frosted glass sideboard in the dining room and Lori wasn't about to go in there to rummage around while Mrs. Ashe's guests were toasting her. In the last kitchen cabinet, made of a burled wood stained pearl gray—Jonathan was taking this Ashe-gray thing too far—she found a cornflower blue cereal bowl and matching plate. Sweet and colorful. Lori loved it.

"Mrs. Corvino!"

Lori turned around. The man was standing in front of the swinging door, a white napkin edged in lace in one hand. "What a surprise and a pleasure."

She stared at him. He was tall, wearing khaki pants that needed pressing, heavy Timberlands on his feet, a blue button-down shirt with no tie and a wool tweed jacket he must have been broiling in. His face was craggy, with sharp cheekbones, topped by gray-blond hair with a strand straggling down his forehead. Intense blue eyes stared back at her. She had seen this man before, but couldn't, in this moment of surprise, place him.

He came forward, hand outstretched. The napkin fell to the floor. "Alec Winters. I owe you a dinner and a dress."

"Oh, heavens." Lori wiped her hand on her apron, held it out, and shook his. "I'm sorry, it's been a busy night." She felt foolish for not having recognized him. Hadn't he worn glasses?

"I'm out of context. White Plains is very far from Rome. And laser surgery has fixed my eyesight. No more glasses." He smiled.

Lori thought he looked kind and immediately realized that was what she had remembered about him in Rome, when, in her room in the modest *pensione*, she looked back on their awful meeting. Kind and sad. Or was she imagining the sadness because she knew that Christopher had died? Had Christopher been his partner?

"How did you know I was here?" From the corner of her eye, she saw Janet slip through the door to the foyer.

"Mrs. Ashe was singing your praises and handed me your card, in case I ever gave a dinner party again."

"That's sweet of her." Why was she embarrassed? She'd worked hard on this dinner; she deserved the praise. Or was this man with his intense gaze and the warmest smile the reason? Oh God! She remembered the flowers. Her note.

"Your flowers were the most beautiful ones I've ever received," Lori said, hearing her voice go gushy with overkill. She swallowed and said simply, "Thank you."

"I still owe you."

"No, you don't. I wrote you a thank-you note, but I forgot to mail it." She could see it in her mind, sitting on the hallway table next to the enamel key tray.

Alec nodded. "Mrs. Ashe told me you've been through a lot lately. In fact, when I joined the guests just now, you were the talk of the table, but everyone thinks you're too good a cook to be guilty." He smiled again.

"Suspicions have shifted, but thanks for the tip," she said, playing along. "If worse comes to worst, I'll cook for the jury." What a nice face he had. She changed her tone. "You've been through a lot, too."

He cocked his head, looking puzzled.

"I'm sorry. I overheard Mrs. Ashe in the foyer when you came."

His jaw tightened. She barely knew him. She shouldn't have brought it up.

"Yes, Chris," he said. "I think the ice cream is melting."

Lori turned to look at the blue bowl on the counter. "Oh God, I'm sorry." The ice cream was now syrup. "That was the last of it. Would you like some veal *tonnato* instead?" She wasn't making any sense. Where was Janet when she needed her?

He didn't crack a smile. "I'd prefer gnocchi," he said.

Before Lori could answer, not that she knew what to say, Jonathan stuck his head through the swinging door. "My mother is getting jealous."

"Of course," Alec said with a quick bow of his head. "Sorry." He walked to the counter and picked up the bowl of melted ice cream. "Just the way I like it," he said and walked back into the dining room. Lori wasn't sure, but she thought he'd winked at her.

Jonathan waited for the door to swing shut. "Everything was fabulous. I'm taking you out to dinner tomorrow night to celebrate," he said. "Jeffrey's." Margot's favorite eatery, the most expensive restaurant in Hawthorne Park.

"I think you should ask me first before telling me." She was wondering why Alec Winters had flustered her.

Jonathan got on one knee. "Ms. Corvino, will you do me the honor—"

"Stop that." He'd made her laugh. "Yes, but not Jeffrey's. Someplace more relaxed, less noisy."

"I know just the place." Jonathan jumped up and swept his knee clean. "I'll pick you up at eight."

★ ★ ★ ★ ★

In bed that night, Lori replayed the scene in the restaurant her last night in Rome. When Alec spilled the gnocchi and then the wine on her lap, he had been so apologetic, and she'd lashed out in anger. She was ashamed of that now. That's why his presence in Jonathan's kitchen had flustered her. She was the one who needed to apologize.

CHAPTER 22

Ellie, dressed in dark red spandex slacks and an orangey red ruffled top, was on her knees, wiping clean the red plastic tulips that she kept in a metal vase at the foot of her husband's grave. It was ten o'clock Sunday morning, and Lori and Ellie were in the Catholic section of the Hawthorne Park cemetery, under an elder tree. The sky was a thick cap of gray. The weatherman had predicted rain for the next three days. In contrast to the surrounding elaborate graves, Papa's burial site was marked by a simple granite headstone laid flat on the ground. Ellie had originally dreamed of a small, expensive, red marble pedestal covered in carved garlands of flowers on which an angel wept, but, not knowing what the future had in store for her and Lori, her practical side had won out, and with the passing years she had grown to be proud of the grave's simplicity. She'd decided it was elegant. The headstone read:

ROCCO CORVINO

August 9, 1943–May 15, 1981

He did his best

"It's a waste," Ellie said when Lori stooped down to add the vase of sunflowers she had brought. "Real flowers just rot and Papa doesn't need dead flowers to remind him how he ended up. Plastic lasts forever. Besides, you're not going to be here next Sunday to throw out your flowers. And he never did like yellow. Red was his color." She heaved herself up.

"Sunflowers are cheerful," Lori protested, reaching out to steady her mother. Even at the funeral Ellie had not wanted real flowers. She said their fragility depressed her. Today Lori had picked sunflowers because they looked strong, and perhaps lasted longer. "I might be here next week to clean up."

Ellie dusted off her knees and gave Lori one of her you-wanna-bet looks.

"I mean it, Mom. I finally figured out why I didn't want to come."

"I could have told you that. You were ashamed you didn't keep your man."

Lori looked at her mother in surprise. "How did you know that?"

Ellie aimed a finger at her. "Because we raised you a Catholic even though you don't go to church any more. Because you come from a people who believe that to be without a husband is a punishment from God." The finger kept jabbing the space in front of Lori's chest. "Because you've got pride in your genes. Because I couldn't have faced my father dead or alive if my husband had walked out on me. You think you're so different from me, but you're not, you know, and that's not such a bad thing." The finger rested.

"You're right. It isn't." Lori pushed her mother's hand down and gave her a kiss on the side of her head.

Ellie scowled back. "I'll tell you this. We're both dumb to feel that way. Shame is for whoever killed that woman your ex married. A nasty piece of work she was, but she didn't deserve to die. You and me," Ellie straightened her back—she was five foot one to Lori's five-five—and puffed out her considerable chest, "we should stand tall."

Lori smiled and straightened her back, too. "Done."

Ellie turned back to the grave and made the sign of the cross, her mouth moving silently. Lori blew her father a kiss and mentally asked his forgiveness for not visiting. In the first months after Rob left she had thought of her father a lot, trying to remember his face, his voice. His face came back to her only from photos. She thought his voice had been grainy, but she didn't ask Ellie, not wanting to be wrong. She did remember some of the advice he gave her during his cooking lessons, mixing instructions for food preparations with those for life. "Bitterness is for broccoli rabe, not for you." "Let the natural goodness of a food shine. No fancy sauce to muck it up. That goes for you and those you care about. Whatever they are they are. Adding ketchup isn't going to change that."

Another part of her father that Lori still remembered were his hands, callused and cracked from bricklaying, the nails split, always spotlessly clean, as they chopped, folded, kneaded. If she was heading off somewhere, one hand would cup the back of her neck, scratching her. It had made her feel controlled, held back. Only after he was gone did she realize he was only trying to steer her toward the right way.

"What do you remember of Papa?" she asked when Ellie tucked the rag she had used to clean the plastic tulips back in her satchel, a sign she was ready to leave.

"It was a pretty good marriage. We used to fight, then make up."

Lori was surprised. She didn't remember fights. "That's it? The sum of a married life?"

"It's gone. I don't want to talk about it." Ellie started to walk back to the car park. Lori followed, disappointed. She wanted more.

"I don't visit like I used to," Ellie confessed as they reached the Mercedes. "Sometimes I'm just too tired to face death." She looked at Lori across the expanse of the car. "You think that's terrible?"

"No. He's been gone a long time."

"He sure has. I wish I could say I still miss him, but I'd be lying. I loved him, but that was then. Now, I don't know what I feel. I guess what I don't like is the idea that I'm getting close to joining him. Coming here reminds me. I don't like it one bit."

Ellie's words froze Lori to the ground. "Oh, Mom, you're going to live forever."

Ellie caught sight of Lori's anguished face just before Lori disappeared into the car. Ellie lowered herself into the car seat, strapped herself in, and gave Lori a quick pat on her arm. "Come to think of it, Loretta, I just might."

Driving back to Mamaroneck, Ellie announced, "We're great women, you know that?"

"If you say so." Lori didn't feel very great with Valerie's murder hanging over their heads, but her mother was looking very satisfied with herself. Maybe it was because Mrs. DeRosa, behind lace curtains not sheer enough to hide her, had watched Ellie get into Margot's car. As the car drove away, Ellie had leaned out of the window and waved back at those lace curtains, a wide grin on her face, as if she and Mrs. DeRosa were the best of friends. Or maybe, Lori thought, it was something else.

"Did you invite him?"

Ellie's expression became a mask of seriousness. "Tonight's the night. I got to get back and start cooking. Lots to do. The house is a mess."

"Men don't usually notice," Lori said.

"Maybe not, but he's a good excuse to do some long overdue cleaning." She glanced at Lori. "How about that handsome young man who brought you flowers? Jonathan something. Have him over. Take advantage of Jessica being gone. Get the house cleaned. Last time I was over I saw a lot of dust. How is she, by the way? I got to see all of three seconds of her on Friday with your ex making a big show of being in a hurry." It started to rain lightly. Lori turned on the windshield wipers.

"She called this morning," Lori said. The rain was just what she was in the mood for, an excuse to put off any gardening work for another day. "It's raining up there, too, which she says is fine with her. She's reading *To Kill a Mockingbird* for school and loving it."

"The movie was great. It was about injustice and Daddy love. She's going to think of Rob."

"Mom, let's not talk about that, okay?" Going to visit Papa's grave had made her feel even more vulnerable than before. What she needed now was some food and a long talk with Beth, who was always clear-headed. Then tonight, Jonathan was going to make her laugh. She was counting on it. "I need a day off."

Ellie snapped her satchel open and closed a few times, her way of showing impatience. "If you want I'll make double the meat sauce. Papa proposed to me after I fed him lasagna with that sauce."

"You're making that up."

Ellie chuckled and put her satchel down. "It makes a good story."

"By the way, Mom, last night's dinner went very well. Thanks for asking."

"Of course it did. Only someone who doubts asks."

Lori laughed. Ellie always had to have the last word. She turned into Ellie's street, which was flanked by modest two-family houses that had small front yards filled with flowers and varied statuary: the Madonna, the seven dwarves, deer, bunnies. Lori remembered it as a cheerful street, filled with nosy but loving neighbors exchanging recipes and gossip, bringing food to the sick, raising money for a neighbor when it was needed. Mrs. DeRosa, despite what her mother thought, had always been

kind, filling Lori's pockets with candy while she waited for the
school bus on the corner. "To light up the brain," she said each
time, and Lori had pictured her ideas coming out of her head in
candy colors, lit up like Fourth of July sparklers.

She hit the brakes when she saw them a few yards short of
her mother's front yard. Luckily no car was behind her.

"Hey!" Ellie shouted as the sudden stop flung her forward,
the seat belt stopping her from hitting the dashboard.

With the screech of Lori's brakes, Scardini and Mitchell
straightened up from leaning against their unmarked car. Scardini tossed his cigarette onto the street. Mitchell shrugged his
jacket on. The rain didn't seem to bother them.

"What got into you?" Ellie asked.

Lori lifted her chin in the direction of Scardini and Mitchell
looking like two football players dressed up for church. "Those
two are the detectives on the case."

"That's no reason to get me strangled."

Lori eased the car forward. Damn and double damn. Margot
had warned her they'd be after her again. Now she had to find a
parking spot, not an easy job on a Sunday. The homes didn't
have driveways. She drove slowly past the detectives. Scardini
nodded. Mitchell raised his hand and called out a hello. She
scanned the length of the street. There was a spot at the very
end, probably in front of a hydrant, but these two were
homicide, not traffic, and she was only going to give them a few
minutes. Beth was waiting with quiche and wine. She stopped
to let her mother off. "Tell them I'm not running away."

Ellie closed the car door, started to walk away, turned back,
and knocked on the window. Lori pressed the window button
down. "What?"

"Maybe I should feed them something. Make nice. They look
hungry."

Lori slapped her hands together in prayer mode. "Please,

Mom. Leave it alone." She had visions of Ellie covering veggie burgers with chopped tofu. They'd both get arrested.

"I know what it looks like," Lori said as she reached the detectives. She opened her umbrella, even though the rain was barely wet. It made her feel protected. "But I was home that night."

"Were you?" Scardini said, one eyebrow raised. Mitchell had a look of apology, like a dog who's just gnawed on your favorite shoe.

"Why talk in the rain?" Ellie asked, her eyes shifting back and forth from the detectives to the lace-curtained window next door, her satchel flapping against her hip. "Something to drink, maybe? A soda, a beer, a glass of ice water? I got a nice sofa to rest on. You both got a lot of weight on those feet."

"No, thank you, ma'am," Mitchell said. Ellie gave him her best frown. "We could sit in the car," he suggested.

"No!" Lori didn't care if it started pouring. The thought of being questioned in such close quarters made her shudder. "Mom, it's okay," she said, covering her with the umbrella. "You've got nice neighbors." She turned to Scardini. Already his brown jacket was covered in wet polka dots. Mitchell's jacket was too dark for rain to spot it. "My phone must have been out of order, that's why Margot had to call my cell."

"And your daughter."

"That's right. My daughter, too. What more to do you want to know?"

Ellie pushed herself between Scardini and Lori. "How did you two find us? Did Mrs. DeRosa tell you I was with my daughter?"

"No, ma'am." Mitchell grinned. Maybe he knew all about rivalry between neighbors where he lived. "When we got to Ms. Corvino's home, we saw her driving away, so we followed. When she came here, we started to get out of the car, but you two were pretty quick. We didn't want to butt in at the cemetery."

"That was nice of you," Lori said to Mitchell. "Thanks."

"Your phone wasn't out of order," Scardini said. "We checked with the phone company."

"Then it got unplugged somehow, but the crazy thing," she was talking only to Mitchell, "the crazy thing is that I don't remember plugging it back. I don't know what to tell you."

Ellie stuck her head out at Scardini. She reached his chest. "Now don't go telling me the police can't figure out where a cell phone is when a call is made or answered. Isn't that how they got those kids that killed Michael Jordan's father? They were dumb enough to use his cell phone? Well, isn't it?"

Scardini folded his arms across his chest. Ellie didn't back off. "We can tell within a three-mile radius," he said. "We know from the base station that you were in the area of your home. So was Mrs. Staunton, for a brief moment on her drive to her death. She was killed in a no service zone."

The most awful feeling of fatigue mixed with fear overcame Lori. She leaned against the unmarked police car. "So I'm not off the hook?"

Scardini managed not to look pleased about the news. "Let's just say, not number one, but still in the running."

"No, she's not," Ellie announced with the determined voice she used to address dogs she deemed dangerous. "I have a perfectly good explanation and it's the truth. My daughter got home from Italy the day before. I checked in on her at seven thirty Monday night. I found her in bed, out like a light. She was jet-lagged and her husband just married to someone else. I wanted her to sleep, so I unplugged her two phones. The next day I went back and plugged the phones before Loretta found out. She doesn't like me to interfere even if it's for her own good. In fact, I would say especially if it's for her own good. Do you have children?" she asked Scardini.

He answered with a lopsided smile. "Two."

Mitchell laughed. "I got four girls.

"Then you know what I mean."

Lori lowered her umbrella to cover her face even though the rain seemed to have stopped. She was afraid her skepticism would show on her face. Ellie had given her back the keys to the house on Sunday. There was no way she could have gotten in. But she did want to hug her mother for trying.

When she dared look up again, Scardini's face had turned impassive. "Maybe what you say is true, ma'am, but you taking your daughter's phone off the hook doesn't mean she didn't wake up sometime after you left and go for a drive with her cell phone and murder on her mind."

Anger clenched Lori's chest. "I didn't kill Valerie. I can't even kill a spider. But if you think I did, then arrest me and let's get this over with."

Ellie spun around and grabbed Lori's arm. "Have you gone crazy? Where's your head?" She was hissing.

Lori hissed back. "Mom! I'm tired of this cat and mouse game!"

Mitchell intervened. "We're not going to arrest you. We're not arresting anybody yet, and we didn't come here just to talk about your phone."

"What, then?" Lori felt like a fool.

Scardini leaned his too-small head to one side. "What can you tell us about Warren Dixon's relationship to your ex-husband?"

"Mr. Dixon was my divorce lawyer." What did Warren have to do with anything? "When he was still married, we saw each other as couples a few times." Rob hadn't liked going out with the Dixons, saying that Warren was arrogant. Lori suspected he was envious of Warren's wealth.

"They did business together?"

"Not that I know of, but my ex kept me in the dark about his business dealings." Lori was getting more and more curious. "Why are you asking me about Warren Dixon all of a sudden? Have you discovered some connection between him and Valerie's death?"

"They used to date," Mitchell said, which brought a nasty look from Scardini. Lori had no way of knowing if it was an act or not.

"That was a long time ago," Lori said.

"You lunched with Mr. Dixon last Thursday at his club," Scardini said.

Lori was aghast. "Are you following me?"

"This is outrageous!" Ellie said. "I'm going to call my senator."

"No one's following your daughter, ma'am," Mitchell said. "Mr. Dixon told us about the lunch."

"You questioned him?" Lori asked. What was going on?

Mitchell leaned forward. "Just bear with us."

Ellie raised her hands to the sky, which now showed a small patch of optimistic blue. "Now why in heaven's name would Warren Dixon kill Valerie Fenwick?"

Lori pulled at her mother's sleeve. "Mom."

Ellie pulled her arm away. "Well, there's got to be a reason they suspect him and I want to know why."

Scardini shook his head. "We're just asking questions, lady, and we're not about to tell you anything."

Mitchell stepped forward, blocking his partner from view. "You're both nice women, I'm sure, and we're sorry you got caught in the middle of this, but you got to appreciate that a woman is dead and we got to find the killer."

Lori felt somewhat mollified. "I do appreciate it."

Scardini started jiggling the car keys. "Stick around, will you?"

Lori nodded and closed her umbrella.

"I tried your meatball and escarole soup on my wife and kids," Scardini said, his stony face softening for a moment. "They loved it."

Lori nodded again. She couldn't quite bring herself to be polite to him.

"That's her father's recipe," Ellie said as the two men got in their car.

As Lori and Ellie stood together watching the car drive off, Ellie said, "This is going to keep Mrs. DeRosa happy for a month."

Lori glanced up at the window with the lace curtain. No one was standing behind it. "I don't think she's home, Mom."

Ellie shrugged and ambled up to her front door with Lori. "Well, then I'll just have to tell her all about it. Poor woman, she's got nothing else to keep her going." At the top of the steps, Ellie offered her face to her daughter.

Lori leaned down to kiss both cheeks. "Thanks, Mom. You were super."

"Nothing to it." Ellie slipped inside.

"The only explanation I can think of is that Warren recently made a lot of phone calls to Rob," Beth said. After having left Margot's car in her driveway and polished off Callie's quiches and a salad, she and Lori were now stretched out on lounge chairs on Beth's deck overlooking a mass of boulders a long-ago glacier had left as a memento. Thick stands of pines, oaks, and maples crowned the rocks and fanned out into the distance, hiding the other homes in the area.

"You said the police were looking into who called whom."

"According to Margot and Joey Pellegrino, they are. Let's assume you're right and Warren's been calling Rob and maybe Valerie, what's the connection between them? Warren doesn't even like Rob."

"Knowing Warren, I'd say business." Beth poured herself another glass of white wine. As she raised it to her lips, the sun shone through the wine. In Lori's eyes, the golden glint took on the form of an earring or a bracelet Beth might have dropped in the glass for safekeeping. Lori said no to more wine.

"I need to make sense of Valerie's death." She stood up and dragged her chaise longue into the shade of an elder tree's overhanging branches. Maybe she would be able to think more clearly.

"You must be feeling so vulnerable." Beth's voice was low and caring. "I don't know how to help. We don't have that much information. This isn't something we can Google."

"Let's go over what information we do have. At Pastis, with Angie and Jess as witnesses, Rob gets an angry phone call. The girls think it's a man. We don't know what it was about."

"The caller could have been Warren," Beth said.

"Or it could have been a client, a friend, anyone pissed off at Rob. What's important is that right after that call, Rob says he's not feeling well and gets Valerie to drive the girls home. The killer would have had to know that, and he could have known it in two ways. Rob told him or Valerie did."

"Or the girls."

"Who are they going to call besides me and Margot? Some school friend? No, the killer found out from Rob or Valerie."

"Can't Ellie persuade Joey Pellegrino to cough up some real information?" Beth asked, raising her face to soak up the afternoon sun.

"Ellie is cooking him dinner tonight."

"God, he'll clam up for good."

Lori laughed. Beth was the only person, besides Jessica, who was allowed to diss her mother. "Maybe not. She's making him my father's old signature dish, rigatoni with meat sauce. It's yummy."

"Now we're getting somewhere."

"Then there's Seth, who lied about being at Rob's wedding. Why did he do that?"

"Probably because he wanted to be there badly enough to lie about it to you and maybe even to himself. I saw that with a lot of kids when I was still a high school counselor. Adults are no different."

"He knew or assumed that Rob and Valerie had already changed their wills."

"A good guess." Beth reached over to the bowl of fruit on a low table and picked a tangerine.

"An off-the-wall guess," Lori said. "How many people change their wills the day after they get married?"

Beth sat up. "Rob thought someone wanted to kill him, that's why he changed the will so quickly."

"That's what I thought, but Rob now says no one was trying to kill him. He claims he exaggerated because he had wedding jitters, and that they had already made the appointment with Valerie's lawyer. I called Kate, Rob's secretary, and she only found out about the lawyer appointment that Monday morning. Did someone try to kill him or was it just an accident that almost happened?"

"I can't help you there," Beth said, "but maybe it was Valerie who wanted him to make a will. Rob did go on and on about almost getting killed, and from what Margot says about Valerie, she was a greedy woman."

"That would explain why Rob's secretary didn't know anything about it, but it doesn't get us anywhere."

Beth threw the tangerine peels onto the greenery below the deck. "The Hefferfields love fruit peelings."

Lori leaned over the deck railing, half-expecting to see a

couple munching on tangerine peels. "Who are the Heffer-fields?"

"A family of raccoons that Mike and Tommy discovered. I keep feeding them."

All Lori could see was pachysandra. "What I want to know is if Rob was lying about someone wanting to kill him."

Beth sat back in her chaise longue and started eating her tangerine. "Let's pretend Rob wasn't lying. Someone wants to kill him. We already know someone was very angry with him—"

"Whoever the caller was," Lori interrupted, "he had enough power over Rob to make him change his plans and send the girls off with Valerie, which, according to Jessica, Valerie didn't appreciate one bit, something that Rob must have already known about his bride. That phone call has to be important."

"Do you know if Valerie received or made a phone call to anyone while she was driving the girls home?"

"No. Let me call Jess." Lori dug into her purse for her cell phone and punched in Jessica's number. "She's not picking up." She left a message asking to be called back. "I don't believe for a moment that Rob was the intended victim. The killer would have to be blind to do that."

"It was raining hard. And it was dark."

"Valerie's lights must have been on." Lori took a large, plump apricot and tossed it from hand to hand. Talking about Valerie's murder had wiped out her appetite. So had the quiches. Did the Hefferfields like apricots? "Don't raccoons often have rabies?"

"So do dogs," Beth answered.

Lori let the apricot fall into the pachysandra below. "I can't get rid of the feeling that Rob is somehow mixed up with Valerie's death. That maybe something he did, or didn't do, got her killed."

"What, for instance?" Beth asked.

"He tried to raise five million dollars to buy a share of Westside Properties. He asked Jonathan and Margot. Warren thought it was bad idea so Margot didn't participate and Jonathan didn't have enough money, but I'm sure he asked others. Rob has had a lot of wealthy clients who he has gotten out of a lot of tight corners. And then there was his bride-to-be with all her millions. How come he wasn't able to raise the money? It wasn't an exorbitant sum in today's real estate market."

"Valerie's greed might explain her not participating, and it must have seemed a shaky deal if Warren thought it a bad bet."

"Warren made a big mistake. According to Margot, Jonathan, and the *New York Times,* Westside Properties is raking it in."

"Warren doesn't make mistakes." Beth moved her chair to follow the sun. "Let's talk about Jonathan."

"Everyone makes mistakes."

"Warren didn't get from a New Jersey chicken farm to having his own extremely successful law firm by making mistakes. Where's Jonathan taking you to dinner tonight?"

Lori ignored her. "Then there's Ruth, Valerie's office manager and cousin. She inherits money and Mrs. Ashe claims she was involved in some scandal way back, although she doesn't remember what it was."

"Don't go to bed with him on the first date."

"You sound like my mother, except then it was, 'Don't let him kiss you before the third date.' Tomorrow I'm taking Ruth out for lunch and maybe she'll help with the Valerie enigma."

"Since when is Valerie an enigma? She was rich New York—beautiful, successful, steely, and nasty."

"She may have been all those things, but why did she get killed? And why, after years of being single, did she marry Rob?"

"I had sex on one of my first dates after Larry died. Afterward I felt like I'd had a junk meal, a McDonald's burger and fries, scarfed down just to get rid of the craving. I must have taken five showers that night. I don't advise it, even if you think you're falling in love."

Lori had no plans to jump into bed with Jonathan tonight, even though her body would have liked it very much. "You were used to making love with your husband. It had to be difficult at first, but didn't it get better?" Lori didn't think she would feel cheap afterward, if the sex was both exciting and lovely. For the lovely part she would need to know Jonathan better, to feel him as a friend besides a lover.

"Men wanted sex from me," Beth said. "Not love."

Lori watched Beth as she peeled an apple and fed it to the hidden raccoons below with the determined look of a mother worried about her children's health. Lori understood now the need to adopt the raccoons. The twins were at camp for most of the summer and in the fall they would go off to boarding school.

"Do you miss the boys?" Lori asked.

"Not every minute. I enjoy the quiet. And don't change the subject. I know I'm sounding negative, but I want life to be beautiful for you again."

"Thanks, I appreciate that, but what about you?"

Beth waved the question away. "I had Larry. Anyone else would be second best."

Lori didn't want to argue that a "second best" man could be seen instead as a "different" man with his own special values and endearing tics. She knew she would have lost the argument. Holding on to Larry's memory for dear life was Beth's survival tactic.

To steer the conversation to a different place, Lori started telling Beth about Mrs. Ashe's birthday dinner, how Alec Winters had appeared at the last minute. She told her about the death of a man called Chris, who she thought was his partner. What a nice and at the same time sad face Alec had. How he had flustered her.

Beth wiped her hands on her jeans. The Hefferfield feeding was over. The shadows of the trees had gotten long. "Did you find out why Janet was upset?"

"No, I didn't." Lori got up. It was time to go home. "I asked her if she wanted to talk. Her answer was that the killer had to be someone Valerie trusted. She said that really worried her. Maybe something's going on between Janet and Seth. I meant to talk to her some more after we finished cleaning up, but then with Alec Winters showing up and Jonathan asking me out, I forgot. Maybe she'll open up tomorrow at breakfast."

Beth got up and hugged Lori. "Don't listen to me. I've become the crotchety old spinster of Hawthorne Park. Follow the throb between your legs and have a great time."

CHAPTER 23

Sam's Fish was small, an upscale shack really, with cedar shingles weathered to a warm rusty brown. Next to it was the fish shop, whose success had allowed the owners to open the restaurant. The shop was closed on a Sunday night, and the fish smell was diluted by the tangy smell of salt water and the profusion of herbs growing in wooden vats below the deck. Jonathan and Lori sat outside, at a corner table facing the Long Island Sound awash with orange and pink from the setting sun. Streaky clouds echoed the colors across the sky.

Jonathan raised his wine glass. "To a new friendship."

"I like that," Lori said, clicking her glass against his. They both sipped. She thought Jonathan looked very good in a white and blue wide-striped shirt and white slacks. The fact that he was wearing socks with his loafers gave him extra points. Women's heads had turned as they walked in, which had made her feel awkward rather than proud. She knew she didn't measure up to his looks, although, in front of her closet mirror, she had approved of her outfit: white slacks topped by a matching camisole and a sheer white blouse with billowing sleeves. That's how she wanted to feel on this first date after her divorce. Light and billowing. Now she was nervous, not quite sure how to act or what was expected of her.

"To be friends, we have to know more about each other," she said.

He put his glass down and studied her face intently. She

could almost hear Beth saying, "Watch it, honey. He's one sexy dude."

"You start," she said.

He shook his head slowly, the smile still on his face. "Ladies first."

To get away from his gaze, Lori looked out at the line of sailboats gliding home. Slowly she filled him in on her father, how his parents, expecting him, had come from a small town in the Abruzzi mountains. How he had been a tailor for a fancy cleaner in Old Greenwich, how he had died young. She talked about Ellie, how her teenage wanderlust had turned her into a travel agent, how widowhood and Papa's life insurance had given her the push to open up her own successful agency. She didn't talk about Rob or their marriage. Jonathan knew him, Lori wasn't sure how well, but she didn't want any comment of hers to get back to Rob.

"You have a great group of friends," Jonathan said. "The breakfast club, right? Margot, Beth, Janet. That must have been a great help."

"Yes, they are. You seem to know them all."

"Not well. Janet I know from the flower shop. Margot's dad and my dad did business together so we'd run into each other when we were kids. Now I bump into her at dinners. You know what that's like. 'Hi, what's up? Things good for you? That's great. Yeah, me, too. Couldn't be better.' You gulp down a few hors d'oeuvres and you move on to the next person."

"I thought you know each other better than that."

Jonathan shook his head slowly, a thin smile sliding across his mouth. God, was she sounding jealous? Lori filled her mouth with rosemary-crusted focaccia and chewed. "This is great food," she said, not waiting to swallow.

With his napkin Jonathan wiped a crumb off her chin. "I know Beth better. I've bought a lot of art from her." He was still smiling, damn him!

Their entrées arrived just in time. For Lori, tuna tartare, diced and mounded, crowned by two large ridged potato chips and a chive flower. The seafood salad of calamari, mussels, and shrimp that Jonathan had ordered was also piled in a neat mound, surrounded by a circle of small black *niçoise* olives and halved cherry tomatoes. She watched as Jonathan took a bite.

"Great," he said, "but I'm going to reek of garlic." Jonathan speared a few rings of calamari and offered them to her. "For self-protection."

"Thanks, but I don't need to do that."

"I hope you do."

Lori felt herself blush as she clasped his hand and bit into the morsel on his fork. The salad was delicious, with just the right amount of dressing. And it wasn't that garlicky. "Now it's your turn for story time," she said as soon as she had swallowed.

Jonathan leaned back in his chair. "The Ashe saga is boring. The family's been here long enough to have washed out whatever interesting characteristics they might have had originally back in England and Germany. The women have distinguished themselves, as was the custom, by bearing children, some of them dying in the process along with the children. The men, as far back as I know, have been lawyers."

Lori thought there was a note of disdain in Jonathan's voice. She dipped a forkful of tuna tartare in the creamy wasabi sauce on the side. "There's nothing wrong with being a lawyer." The wasabi sauce was so strong it made her tear.

"That's right, you married one. The law is too rigid for me. Always having to look up precedents. And why does my family have an entire genealogical chart filled with lawyers? The only explanation I can think of is that when the nurse weighed an Ashe male newborn, something in his genes made him instantly relish the power of being able to tip the scales. As for the female babies, maybe listening to all those other sniffling, mewling newborns in the warmth of the nursery left them with a lifelong need to keep coming back to take care of them."

Lori laughed. "You became a lawyer."

"And my mother, who would much rather have been a lawyer, had me. We had no choice. As you know, I rebelled after five years at Rob's firm. Real estate is much more fun."

"Isn't it a risky business?"

"That's the part I like. Real estate allows me to be my own boss, to follow my gut. There's a lot of excitement in not knowing when the next great deal is coming, but striving for it anyway."

Lori thought of Rob not raising the five million for a quarter share of Westside Properties. "And when a deal falls through?"

Jonathan poured himself more wine, topped off Lori's glass. "You lick your wounds and move on to the next possibility."

Lori blurted out, "Why couldn't someone as connected and successful as Rob raise five million?"

Jonathan raised his arms in the air as the waitress cleared the plates and brought their main course. They had both ordered roasted striped bass with chive and sour cream sauce accompanied by spicy potatoes and zucchini. "Why didn't his rich wife help, that's what I wonder." He leaned toward Lori. "Let's not talk about your ex on our first date, okay?"

His eyes were flecked with green, she noticed, and he had a small dent on one side of his mouth, a childhood scar perhaps. Lori fought the urge to smooth it out with her finger. "You're right. The question just slipped out."

Stay in the moment, she told herself. *This handsome young man is interested in you. And you in him.* Lori forked a slice of zucchini. "What was your father like?"

"Rigid, indifferent to me. A man who saw no reason to connect to another human on anything except an intellectual or economic level. Emotions were for the female sex."

"Your mother loved him very much."

"She's very much like him. Their brains loved each other. She didn't like having to produce a child. I couldn't exactly warm my hands at the fire of her love. I read that expression in some book, I think. It hits the spot where my mother is concerned."

Lori didn't quite believe that. She'd seen kindness in Mrs. Ashe. "She told me how your father brought flowers to her every Friday and how you keep up that tradition."

"For him it was a ritual, nothing more."

"You're not anything like him, then."

Jonathan bowed his head in her direction. "Thank you for the compliment."

"Or her, if what you say about her is true." Jonathan was open, warm, fun. Maybe too aware of the power of his charm and his looks, but who was she to judge? Lori couldn't remember the last time she had turned a man's head.

"The only truth I can offer," Jonathan said, "is what is true for me."

The tone of his voice made Lori look up and for the first time she saw regret in his face. "That goes for everyone, I think," she said, curious to know what his regrets might be.

"Of course you're right, but sometimes that truth isn't something you want to share."

"I agree."

Jonathan said nothing. Lori started talking about movies she had seen, wanted to see, a safe conversation starter. Jonathan joined in. His good mood seemed to return and their conversation turned from films, to theater, to past and future trips. When Lori filled Jonathan in on the wonders of her trip to Italy, Alec Winters's face intruded in her thoughts. "Tell me about your friend, Alec," she said.

"No. I don't want anyone breaking into our dance."

He was like a kid, Lori thought, hungry for attention. Well, so was she. "Forget I asked."

They finished the wine bottle, ordered hot brownies with vanilla ice cream for dessert. The dinner had been wonderful, she thought, made richer by that touch of regret that Jonathan had shown. He wasn't just a handsome charmer, then. Regret gave him substance.

Walking to his car, Jonathan held her by the waist. She could feel the warmth of his hand seep through her blouse and camisole to her bare skin. It felt wonderful and yet her need embarrassed her. On the ride home, she made silly chitchat about her catering plans, about her garden.

Jonathan stopped the car in front of her house and before she could reach for the door handle, pulled Lori to him. He kissed her, this time with his hands cupping her breasts. A bolt of heat shot up between Lori's legs. She heard herself moan.

Jonathan let her go. "I'd love some coffee."

Lori nodded, not sure she could find her voice. As she fumbled to insert the key in her front door, Beth's words dropped into her head. Afterward I felt like I'd had a junk meal, a McDonald's burger and fries, scarfed down just to get rid of the craving.

It wouldn't be like that for her. She wouldn't let it be.

Jonathan closed the door behind them and took her face in his hands. "You are so lovely you are edible." He started to munch on her ears. She pulled back and kissed his lower lip, his upper lip, his nose. She was so hungry for him that she could have flung herself on the rug and let him have her, but she wanted this first lovemaking with a man she barely knew to be slow, gentle, something to savor for days.

"You're teasing me," he whispered into her neck, slipping his hand inside the back of her slacks, pushing her against his chest.

"Uh-huh."

With his lips sealed on hers, Jonathan led her toward the stairs.

Lori clasped her arms around him, to keep herself from falling backward. Oh, this was great, lovely, wonderful. She wanted to eat him up, too, but when had she last changed the sheets? Yesterday? A week ago? Should she steer him toward the sofa in the living room? Too late! Jonathan was lifting her up the first step. *Give into this, Lori, dirty sheets and all. Men never notice anyway.*

Beethoven's Fifth rang out when they hit the fourth step.

"Don't answer," Jonathan ordered.

Lori gasped for air, noticed her purse was still dangling from her arm. "It'll only take a sec." She reached in for her cell phone, flicked it open. "Hello?"

"Are you all right?"

Sweet Jess! What terrible timing. "Yes, yes, just a little out of breath. Look, hon, can I call you back later? I'm rushing out."

"It's eleven o'clock at night! Mom, is someone with you?"

Why couldn't she have said she was taking a shower? "No one is with me, honey." If she weren't so horny, this would be funny. "Can I call you back?"

"Deuce kissed me," Jessica said.

Lori sank down on the stairs and smiled apologetically at Jonathan. "I'm all ears, honey."

Jonathan backed away. Lori motioned him to wait. He slowly shook his head, blew her a kiss, and gently closed the front door behind him.

Lori leaned against the banister and listened. Jess was in seventh heaven. That's what mattered now.

"Oh, Mom, I'm having the best time," Jessica said, summing up. "I love Cape Cod and Deuce is the coolest guy in the world."

"I'm happy for you."

'Night, Mom. Angie and I have to get up at five tomorrow. Deuce and his friend Tom are taking us on a hike."

"Good night, sweetie."

"Oh, Mom. Have the police found the murderer yet?"

"Not yet, but please don't worry, Jess. I want you to have fun."

"I wish I could help, Mom."

"Maybe you can. When Valerie was taking you and Angie home, do you remember if she made or received a phone call?"

Jessica was silent.

"Yes? No? Hon, are you not free to talk?"

"I'm alone. Angie is playing gin rummy with Warren. She always wins."

"Did Valerie make a call or receive one?"

"I slept most of the way back."

"Ask Angie and let me know. Good night, sweetie. Please don't worry. I'm so happy for you and, one day, I hope you'll introduce me to Deuce."

"Is it real important?"

"Yes. I want to meet 'the coolest guy in the world.' "

"I mean the phone call. Is it important?"

"It could be."

Jessica breathed loudly. "She did get a phone call, but you have to promise not to tell anyone."

"Tell who? If anyone called, the police will already know about it."

"Then why do you want to know?"

"Because I'm trying to make sense of what happened. It makes me feel better."

"I promised not to tell."

"That's okay. Don't break your promise. Good night. I'll call you tomorrow. I love you."

After Jessica hung up, Lori sat on the stairs thinking. Who

did Jessica promise not to tell? Angie was the only other person with her in the car with Valerie. Who would Angie want to protect? Her mother? But if Margot had called, she was probably only wondering what time the kids were coming home. Warren? Why would he call Valerie?

Was Jessica trying to protect Rob?

Oh, to hell with this, Lori thought, running up the stairs to the bathroom. She turned on the shower. Couldn't Jonathan have waited? Why were men always in a rush? All right, she really only knew about one man. Rob had always been in a rush, wanting her to drop everything whenever he got a hard-on, assuming she was in the mood if he was. Well, she was in the mood tonight and going solo now would be too much of a letdown.

Lori undressed and looked at her naked body in the mirror. Could she still pass muster? Jonathan probably made love to twenty-year-olds, but tonight he'd wanted her. And then she had hurt his pride.

What had possessed her to answer the phone? Her worry about the sheets on the bed? His ordering her not to answer the phone? Or was she scared to take the plunge?

Once settled in bed, she called Jonathan. "I didn't expect you to leave."

"I didn't expect you to answer the phone."

"I'm sorry. It's a compulsion of mine." Why was she lying to him? "Look, my daughter has fallen in love for the first time. I couldn't cut her off."

"I understand perfectly." He didn't sound as if he did. Then he laughed. "Okay, I was pretty pissed and I had to go jogging around several blocks before I could make it home to Mother."

"I took a cold shower."

"What are you doing for the Fourth of July?" His voice was suddenly close to the phone.

Next Saturday? Something in her stomach fluttered. "Jess will still be in Cape Cod."

"Good. Let's go off somewhere for the weekend. Okay?"

"Aren't all places booked by now?"

"If we can't book a room anywhere, there's always the Lori Corvino Inn."

Lori hesitated. Two days and two nights to make love. Enticing. But what if it didn't work out? How would she feel then? She'd never know if she didn't try. "All right," she said finally. This time she would make sure her sheets sparkled.

"Great. And now I have some news for you."

"What is it?"

"Remember Ruth, Valerie's cousin and office manager? The scandal Mother couldn't remember?"

"Yes, of course, I remember."

"Mrs. Sheridan, who was at the dinner last night, made a few phone calls to old friends and told my mother this evening."

Lori sat up. "Told her what?"

CHAPTER 24

The next morning, Lori got to Callie's late for the Monday Breakfast Meeting. Her friends had already been served.

"Hi, everyone. I'm sorry." She slipped into the corner booth next to Beth, who was wearing her jogging clothes. Lori had changed into jeans and Jess's high school T-shirt at the gym. "My Pilates instructor was late, which meant we went over the hour and then I had to get gas and then I got a phone call from Alec Winters." She'd had to put off calling Ellie to find out how her meal with Joey Pellegrino had gone.

"Ooh!" Margot pursed her lips. "Do you have a date?"

"He's the chairman of Ban-Aids," Beth said, "and a big contributor to Broadway Cares, so Lori thinks he's gay."

"Pretty good supposition, I'd say," Margot said. She was looking beautiful in a purple spandex jumpsuit tight enough to show up a mole if she'd had one. "They make wonderful dates if you need a sex break."

"Good," Lori said, although she'd been on a break far too long. "He's taking me out to dinner tonight to make up for spilling gnocchi in my lap and wine over the rest of me."

"How was last night?" Beth asked.

Margot looked first at Beth, then at Lori. If she'd been a cat, her whiskers would have been curling. "What happened last night?"

"I went out to dinner with Jonathan Ashe," Lori said dismissively. She was afraid her cheeks would heat up if she talked about him. "Guys, I have stuff to tell you about Ruth."

Margot shook her bracelets. "Was it fun?"

Before Lori could answer, Callie presented her with a mug of coffee and an English muffin, her usual breakfast.

"Thanks. You and I need to talk." Callie's "be careful of friends" still needed explanation.

Callie ignored her and stared at Janet's plate. "What's wrong with my food?" Janet hadn't touched any of her scrambled eggs.

"I'm not hungry," Janet said.

"Waste of money," Callie grunted and ambled off.

In Lori's rush to sit down and apologize for being late, she had barely looked at Janet hunched over in the dark corner. Now that the sun had slid between the two buildings across the street, light poured through the window and Lori could see that Janet's eyes were red.

"Jan, are you okay?"

Janet shook her head and moved closer to Beth, away from the light. Tears dropped down her cheeks.

"Oh, honey." Beth hugged her. Janet cried harder. Lori offered a crumpled-up tissue. No one said anything, waiting for her to calm down. At the far end of the coffee shop, Callie watched.

After a minute or two, Janet sat up and wiped her face with her free hand. The other hand was clutching Lori's tissue as she might clutch at something to keep her from falling.

"Has something happened to the kids?" Lori asked.

Janet shook her head.

"Seth?"

Janet tried to smile. "I'm sorry. I don't know what got into me."

"Cut the crap, Janet," Margot snapped. "You know perfectly well what got into you."

Lori kicked Margot under the table.

Beth said, "That was unnecessary," in her coolest tone.

Margot lifted her hands in surrender. "Okay, sorry. All I'm trying to say is if you spit it out you'll feel better. You've been going around like a whipped puppy since last week."

"It's hard," Janet said.

A cup of chamomile tea appeared in front of her. "I don't have a liquor license," Callie said. "How about some apple pie to go with that?"

Again Janet shook her head.

"I could use some apple pie," Margot said.

Callie gave her a look and walked away.

Margot grumbled under her breath.

"I'm afraid," Janet whispered.

Lori leaned closer. "Of what?"

Janet took a sip of the tea and made a face.

"Pretty awful, isn't it?" Lori said to ease the moment. "My mother swears it can cure anything from corns to cancer."

"What are you afraid of?" Beth asked, looking at Janet with a steady gaze. There was something strong and reassuring about Beth that made it easier to answer her.

"The night Valerie was murdered," Janet said, "it was Seth who called Rob at the restaurant. They made a date to see each other afterward. Rob pretended to be sick so he could meet with Seth. Rob told the police."

Lori was taken aback, but quickly said, "There's nothing wrong with that." It had been an angry phone call, the girls had said. Why would Seth be angry? "Why did he call?"

Set on telling her story, Janet ignored Lori's question. "Seth never showed up. He had done something very stupid without telling me and he was desperate. We have no money. The minute my mother's inheritance came through, Seth paid back the five thousand dollars he owed Rob." Janet's words rushed out like water from a burst pipe. "Rob said they were friends again and

Seth trusted him and then Rob cheated him and Seth was afraid I'd find out. He was sure I'd leave him and take the kids. That's why Seth didn't wait for Rob. He was afraid. Of me. Of himself. He was sure Rob was lying. He was mad enough to punch him."

"You're not making any sense," Margot said.

"How did Rob cheat him?" Lori asked.

Janet grabbed Lori's hand. "I'm so sorry. You've been through so much. I didn't want you to know any of this. But now I'm scared the police think Seth killed Valerie. I don't know what to do." She let go of Lori and gulped down all of the tea.

Beth wrapped her arm around Janet's shoulders and said, "Let's take this one step at a time. First, what did Seth do that you weren't supposed to know?"

"He took the money my mother left me, three hundred thousand dollars, and gave it to Rob."

"Why would Seth do that?" Lori asked.

Janet swallowed air. "Rob was raising money to buy a partnership in Waterside Properties. When he found out we had a little bit of money he convinced Seth to participate. He said we'd make it back ten times over once the land got developed, and Seth believed him. After their fight about the five thousand, Seth wanted to get Rob's friendship back so badly. That's why he did this dumb thing. He trusted Rob. Rob was his college buddy, the guy who had made good. And then nothing happened. I mean Rob didn't raise enough money, so Seth asked for the money back, but Rob's been stalling him. Seth is furious."

Lori's mind started racing. Was Rob in debt? Was that the reason he hadn't sent her the child support check for June? He'd tried to match Valerie's life style with a Park Avenue apartment, a fancy car, an expensive honeymoon. She probably wouldn't have him if he hadn't. Was he in trouble now? He had to be. There was no other explanation.

"And now the police won't leave Seth alone," Janet said. "He got so scared, he confessed everything to me." Janet turned her tear-stained face to each of her friends. Lori's heart went out to her, but questions kept popping up in her head.

"You know he didn't kill Valerie," Janet said.

"Of course not!" Beth and Lori said at the same time.

"No way," Margot added in her indolent way.

How angry, how desperate was Seth, Lori wondered, trying to keep an encouraging smile on her face for Janet's sake. *We're all capable of killing*, isn't that what Beth had said? Seth had seemed happy on the train the day after Valerie was killed. He'd mentioned Rob inheriting Valerie's money. That would mean Rob could pay him back. How desperate had Rob been? How much in debt? Who else had he approached for the Waterside property deal? Why didn't Valerie help him out?

"What's Valerie got to do with Seth?" Margot asked.

"Detective Scardini thinks the killer might have mistaken her for Rob," Lori offered as a diversionary tactic.

"But Seth was meeting Rob," Janet said. She wiped her face with her hands. "It's not just his word. Rob confirmed that they were going to meet at a bar on Second Avenue."

Lori avoided Beth's glance, knowing what she was thinking. What if Valerie had been killed so that Rob could inherit? What if that was the reason Seth didn't show up for the meeting? He would have had to know that Valerie had changed her will. "Look, Janet," Lori said. "The police have to ask all sorts of questions. How else are they going to piece things together? That doesn't mean they think Seth killed Valerie." They had to think Rob killed her. If he was in debt. Which he had to be. Why else wouldn't he pay Seth back? And yet he had splurged on a new expensive car. Lori felt the air leave her lungs.

"Those two detectives have been after me and after Rob," Lori said. Janet was following her words with a string of nods.

"Now they're asking questions about Warren."

Margot's eyes went wide. "Warren?"

"They're grasping at straws," Lori said, sorry she had brought up his name.

Margot gave an unconvincing laugh. "Warren will tie them up into knots. He's very good at that." She patted Janet on the arm. "You'll both be okay, I'm sure of it." Her voice turned soft, reassuring. "And you know that any time you need help, I'm here for you." Help for Margot meant money. She had offered money to Janet countless times, but Janet had been too proud to accept.

"Thanks, I know that." Janet let out a big sigh. "Lori, Seth lied about being at Rob's wedding. He lied about it to me, too. He didn't want us to know anything was wrong."

"I understand," Lori said. How sad for Seth. How awful for both of them if he had anything to do with Valerie's death.

"You guys are great." Color came back to Janet's cheeks.

Relieved for her, the women turned their attention to their various breakfasts. Lori chewed her English muffin slowly to try to calm her heart. Janet ate with gusto. Margot played with her fork. Beth crunched into toast, swallowed, and asked, "What's the stuff you have to tell us?"

Lori gladly stopped eating. She had a story that would set Janet's heart at ease, if not her own. "Ruth, Valerie's office manager, remember her?"

The women nodded.

"She is Valerie's cousin, and Mrs. Ashe thought she had been involved in some kind of scandal when she was younger, but she couldn't remember what it was. Last night a friend came through with the story."

Beth and Janet gave Lori their full attention. Margot studied her nails, painted in the latest fashion color—Chanel black.

"Okay, if I got it straight, this is how it goes. Ruth lost her father when she was eight. Her mother remarried quickly but died three years later in a car accident. After the mother's death, the stepfather didn't want to take care of Ruth—it seems they never got along—so the Fenwicks, Valerie's parents, took her in."

"That was generous," Beth said.

"It was their duty," Janet said.

"Get to the point," Margot said.

Beth looked her squarely in the eye. "Stop being so hostile."

"I have to get a manicure and a pedicure."

Beth waved to the door.

Margot tossed her hair back. "I'm just as curious as you are, except I'm in a hurry."

"Stop it, you two," Janet said. "You're friends." She turned back to Lori. "Go on."

"After about two years, when Ruth was thirteen, she was suddenly banished from the Fenwick home. No explanations given, but lots of rumors. She stole money, or jewelry. Or Valerie's mother got rid of her because her husband was taking an unhealthy interest in her. Or she was caught having sex with the gardener and I don't know what else. The stepfather was apparently so scandalized by what she had done, he wouldn't take her back and Ruth ended up living with the Fenwicks' housekeeper and her family."

"That's it?" Margot asked.

"That's it for now. I'm having lunch with Ruth in the city. Maybe she'll tell me more."

"Valerie never even mentioned her to me," Margot said. "I remember the housekeeper. A Filipino. She gave the best massages."

"If Valerie had anything to do with getting rid of Ruth," Janet had a wishful lilt to her voice, "that would give Ruth a very good motive for killing her."

Margot dropped a twenty-dollar bill on the table. "I've got to go. We still owe from the last breakfast. I wouldn't want sweet Callie to think we're shortchanging her." She kissed her palm and blew the kiss their way. "Bye, gals. Keep me posted on the latest."

"Thank you," Janet said, blowing a kiss back. Margot walked out.

"What got into her today?" Beth asked.

"I shouldn't have mentioned that the police were asking about Warren," Lori said.

Janet took money out of her handbag and started sliding across the booth. "What I don't get is why she left him if she's still in love with him."

"I don't think she's in love with him," Beth chimed in. "She's upset because she still thinks he's hers, and she doesn't want what's hers to be tarnished."

Janet frowned.

Beth raised her hands. "I know. She has a heart of gold, but sometimes she gets to me. I can't help it."

Janet leaned over and kissed her. "You're great. And I can't thank you both enough for being such wonderful friends. I feel so much better. I can't wait to go home and reassure Seth." Janet scooted out of the booth, gave Lori her money, and left.

Cy, the counterman, brought over the bill. Callie was the one who always brought the bill. *She's avoiding me,* Lori thought. "Thanks." She handed over everyone's money. "We don't need any change."

"You don't think Seth could have?" Beth asked after Cy walked away.

"I don't know what to think," Lori said, which was the God's honest truth. "Maybe Ruth will clear up some things. If not about herself, about Valerie. You can't work with a woman for years and not know her."

They both got up. "What time is your lunch?" Beth asked. "I have to show a painting in the city later this morning. If you want, I'll give you a ride."

"Great. I'm meeting her at the Boathouse in Central Park at one o'clock."

"I'll pick you up at eleven thirty." Beth walked to the door, then looked back. "Aren't you coming?"

Lori shook her head. "I need to ask Callie something."

Beth smiled. "She'll never give you that apple pie recipe." She waved. "See you later."

"What did you mean by 'be careful of friends'?" Lori cornered Callie with the question just as she was coming out of the bathroom at the far end of the coffee shop.

Callie raised both thick black eyebrows. The women suspected she dyed them because the rest of her hair was gray. "I said that?"

"Yes, advice from an old Greek woman. 'Bearing gifts or no gifts, be careful of friends.' That's exactly what you said."

"I got no time now." Callie squeezed her sizable girth between the wall and Lori and walked over to the counter to wave a hand at Cy, who was now sizzling bacon and eggs on the grill. "Get this gal another toasted English, with butter this time and bacon well-done. She's grumpy."

"I want an answer, not a sandwich," Lori protested. "Come on, Callie. Please."

"A sandwich is what you get." Callie swayed down the narrow aisle between counter and booth, nodding as her customers greeted her.

Lori followed. "Please, Callie, just tell me. I haven't been sleeping nights, wondering."

Callie stopped and turned. "You look like you've had the best night's sleep since you got rid of that man, so don't go making up stuff."

Lori felt herself blushing. Yes, she had slept wonderfully last night, dreaming. "I'm sorry. But how about telling me what you meant?"

Callie didn't move. After a few seconds she called out to Cy, "Take over for five," and walked out to the street. Callie's Place had a bench on each side of the door. Callie sat in one. Lori sat next to her.

"I shouldn't have opened my mouth," Callie said, folding her arms over her aproned belly. "Words can put a snake in your heart. It was a bad day." A pigeon waddled over to Callie and looked at her expectantly.

"Why was it bad?"

Callie reached into her pocket and scattered crumbs at her feet, then threw more crumbs in a widening arc to include the sparrows. "It's the day Nick died, twenty-two years ago." An aneurism had killed her husband in his sleep when he was only thirty-seven. Eugenia had been three at the time. Callie's two boys, eleven and nine. "That's the day I go to the cemetery and it breaks my heart in two because I see him, you know, like he'd be now. A little fat, a little bald, still with the moustache but now it's gray like he's been eating too many powdered sugar doughnuts. He never could get enough. I see him and I miss him so much it's like a wall has dropped on my chest and I can't breathe." Callie squinted at Lori. She was facing the sun. "My kids think I'm nuts."

Lori put her hand over Callie's. "I think you're still in love."

Callie nodded. "Like the day he walked into my parents' home to fix the piano." She lifted her gaze to the blue dome of the sky. The wisps of clouds had disappeared. "I visit Nick every Sunday, but he only shows himself on the day he died, like he's trying to tell me something about it. What do you think he's trying to tell me?"

Lori didn't know, but she felt a mixture of admiration and envy for Callie's strength of feeling. "Maybe Nick is showing you that he didn't die that day," Lori said. "He's still with you."

Callie reached over and opened the coffee shop door. "Hey, Cy, did you have to go kill the pig?" she called out. "Lori's hungry." She let the door go. "Enough about my bad day. And don't go telling anyone I'm seeing my husband's ghost or there'll be a run on the shop, if that Starbucks across the street doesn't do me in first."

"Never," Lori said, but she wasn't so sure. Downtown Hawthorne Park had once been a vibrant mixture of the quaint, the dilapidated, and the fashionable. The thrift shop sat next to the designer boutique, which shared a building with the bookstore. The exquisite little antique shop faced the pawnshop across the street, and the pharmacy with oak wainscoting, a beamed ceiling, and old apothecary jars in the window was next door to the hardware, which had been owned by the same family for over seventy-five years and looked like it hadn't been dusted in over a hundred. Then the overflow of the wealthy from Greenwich had bought up homes in Hawthorne Park only to tear them down and build McMansions. The McStores—Starbucks, The Gap, Barnes and Noble, and CVS—followed.

"If you shut down, I'll move," Lori said, this time with conviction.

Callie grunted. "To where?"

"The Australian Outback. Now about your warning?"

Callie rubbed her eyes, scrunched up her face. "There's nothing worse than a ratter, but sometimes you just have to, you know. So here goes." Callie took a deep breath, then plunged. "When you asked your friends, sitting in my coffee shop, about the night that woman was killed, your friend Margot didn't tell you everything."

Lori leaned forward. "Go on."

"Five minutes after that woman drove—"

"Her name was Valerie."

Callie squared her shoulders. "Five minutes after that woman drove your kid and Margot's kid home, Margot drove off and left those kids alone in that huge house."

"How do you know that?"

"I know from my sixteen-year-old granddaughter Vicki, who babysits the Carltons' ratty little dogs next door to Margot's place. They got four dogs that yap their heads off if Vicki isn't there to keep them company. And they growl whenever a car goes by or when Margot's garage door opens or closes. So Vicki heard that woman drive up to Margot's roundabout, and she saw Margot drive off five minutes later. Make of that what you will, and I'm sorry if this upsets you."

"I'm surprised, that's all." Surprised and confused. *Why didn't Margot tell me?* Lori asked herself. *Was she worried I'd be upset she'd left the girls alone? Did she see something she didn't want to share? Where was she going? And what will happen to our friendship if I confront her?* "Thanks, Callie," Lori said. "You're not a ratter. Ratters are self-serving. You mean well."

"Okay, since I'm so good, I'll add some advice. Lose that real estate guy you've set your eyes on."

Lori's cheeks burned. "Who?"

"Jonathan something. Six-footer, handsome enough to curl your toes. That's who."

"What makes you think I've set my eyes on Jonathan Ashe?"

"Because Ellie came in here on Tuesday and told me he brought you flowers. Because last night I was sitting right here with Vicki and the two of you drove by, and you looked as pretty as a Georgia peach. Because today you look like you've swallowed that peach and liked it."

Lori couldn't believe her mother. Correction: she could

believe, she just didn't want to. "How do you know he's in real estate?"

"Your mother Googled him."

Ellie! What next? "Thanks for the advice, but I haven't set my eyes on him."

"Good. The right guy will come along. I feel it here." Callie pointed to her heart.

"What do you have against Jonathan?"

"The fact that his looks curl my toes. You can take it for a Greek superstition, or Callie going crazy, but trust me on this. Curling my toes is not good."

Cy's hand reached out the door, holding a paper plate on which sat a toasted English muffin bacon sandwich.

Callie took it from him and handed it to Lori. "It's on the house for all those nights you didn't sleep, wondering. Now off with you." Callie heaved herself up from the bench. "I've got to go make a living."

Lori bit into the sandwich. It was delicious, but it didn't stop her from doubting whether Callie had told her the whole truth. She loved Callie, wanted to accept her every word, but a man's looks curling her toes?

CHAPTER 25

In front of the neo-Victorian brick building that housed the Boathouse Restaurant, Ruth greeted Lori like a long-lost friend—kisses on both cheeks and a lung-scrunching hug. Ruth was a big woman with a smooth round face and the rosy cheeks of a kid, although she had to be at least forty according to Mrs. Ashe. She was wearing a beige short-sleeved pantsuit that matched the color of her short hair. An expensive-looking tiny red leather handbag dangled from one hand. On her feet, brand new white Nikes. She clutched Lori's shoulders. "You must be feeling great!"

Lori extracted herself and asked, "Why?"

Ruth was already walking ahead of her through the gate to the terrace where she gave the hostess Lori's name. The hostess, a pretty young blonde with a sexy swing to her walk, accompanied them to a front row table facing the lake and handed them two menus. A gondola that had once escorted the rowboats bobbed gently in front of them. In the distance the tall buildings of Central Park West rose above the canopy of trees.

Ruth looked at the water and shook her head. "Why can't we sit there?" she asked, pointing to a table in front of the restaurant's glass windows. The hostess bowed her head and walked them there. A couple at the next table were talking loudly into their cell phones.

"I bet they're yelling at each other." Ruth gave them an angry look and strode to the other side of the terrace. The hostess and Lori scrambled after her. "You're it," Ruth said to a table near the entrance, dropped her handbag on an empty chair, and sat with her back to the lake. *So much for picking an atmospheric restaurant,* Lori thought, as she gave the hostess an apologetic smile.

"Water gives me the creeps," Ruth announced.

"You should have told me. I would have made a reservation elsewhere."

"I'm good here. Isn't it obvious why you should be feeling great? Valerie Fenwick, DDS, is dead. You know, when you slapped her, I had to pretend I was mad. I didn't want to lose my job, but I could have hugged you."

"You didn't like Valerie?"

"Now I didn't say that. She was my cousin, you know. Next thing you'll think I killed her." She stopped talking to squint at the menu, then started fanning herself with it. "Aren't you hot? It's hot. I'm too young to be flashing."

The temperature was in the low eighties but Lori had to admit it was muggy.

"You're flashing already, right?" Ruth asked.

"Wrong." Lori was beginning to worry about this lunch.

Ruth ignored her answer. "All I'm saying is Valerie needed to be taken down a peg or two and you did it. No one ever had the guts. You have no idea what a spoiled brat she was. I lived with the Fenwicks for a few years when I was a kid, you know."

"I had no idea you were cousins," Lori said. Embarrassing Ruth by revealing that she knew about her falling out with Valerie's parents would not get her the information she wanted.

"I was good for hired help, but she didn't want anyone to know we shared genes."

"Tell me more about her."

The busboy came by to fill their water glasses. Without looking up, Ruth ordered the country pâté appetizer, the Boathouse burger well done, and a side order of the house-made *cavatelli*. The busboy nodded and went to fetch a waiter.

"She could do no wrong in that household," Ruth said. "Her father adored her, her mother was drunk most of the time and didn't know which way was up, and the servants were scared stiff of her."

"Were you?"

"No. I made her cringe. She was rich, gorgeous, and skinny. I was poor, with acne all over my face and thirty extra pounds on my body."

"Are you ready to order?" the waiter asked in a heavy Slavic accent.

"I already did," Ruth said.

"I'm sorry, you have to tell me."

"Why? Didn't the kid understand English? Why do they hire people who don't understand English?"

Lori felt like crawling under the table. "The kid is the busboy, Ruth. He's not supposed to take our order."

Ruth's mistake did not faze her. "Are we going to get a bottle of wine?"

"I don't drink," Lori lied. "You're welcome to have a glass if you want." Lunch was on Lori.

After informing the waiter that red wine made her sweat, Ruth asked for a glass of Chardonnay, then rattled off her food order and picked up where she had left off. "We avoided each other. That way we got along just fine." Lori slipped her order of a house salad and an appetizer portion of lump crab cake between Ruth's sentences. "We worked together for nine years, and we got along because we kept it strictly business."

How could this be the woman who Margot said had shed a lot of tears over Valerie's death? "How long did you live with the Fenwicks?" Lori asked.

"Three or four years. I don't remember. Then my stepfather wanted me back."

Lori didn't blame Ruth for lying, but she did want to know why the Fenwicks had asked her to leave. Maybe Ruth had a long-buried resentment that had come to the fore. Especially if there was money waiting in Valerie's will. "You kept up with the Fenwicks?"

"Why are you asking about me? Who do you think killed Valerie? Rob?"

"Didn't you tell Margot you thought a carjacker killed her?"

"That was a dumb thought. Valerie's car wasn't hijacked. Look, you're here asking questions so I figured you were worried about your ex or for yourself."

"I didn't kill her and neither did Rob. He loved Valerie."

"For her money."

"He has money of his own," Lori said, then quickly added, "Why do you think she married Rob? From what I hear she turned down many men, afraid it was her money they were after."

A smug look appeared on Ruth's face. She took her time answering. "Maybe at thirty-nine she thought she was getting old. And Rob is a charmer, isn't he?"

"Valerie could have wanted children," Lori said, finally voicing a fear she had held inside ever since Rob had announced he was marrying her.

Ruth raised both eyebrows. "Valerie ruin her figure? No way."

Their food arrived and for a few minutes they didn't speak. Ruth scraped her fork against her plate and chewed loudly. The wine glass was empty in two gulps. Lori watched her and decided her childhood must have been very miserable.

"Have the police questioned you?"

"Sure thing," Ruth said. "Two of them came around to the office, which my new boss didn't appreciate."

"A new dentist has already moved in?"

"Three days after Valerie died, there he was, ready to take over her lease and her practice. Read about her death in the paper. That's New Yorkers for you. A bunch of hyenas. You should try him. He's good."

"Have the detectives come around more than once?" Lori was trying to find out if the police suspected Ruth. "They've questioned me three or four times."

"They're buzzing. The minute someone leaves you even a little money in their will, they're going to think it gives you motive. I'm getting a lousy fifty thousand. Rob's the one who's cashing in. He's the one with motive to spare."

Lori wanted to point out that people had been killed for much less than fifty thousand, but instead said, "Were you surprised Valerie left you money?"

"Valerie and I weren't compatible but she was good to me. She hired me when I came back to the city and needed a job." Ruth popped a cornichon into her mouth. "Blood is thicker than water." She grabbed the waiter's arm as he passed by. "Another glass of wine and tell the cook to ease up on the salt." She released the waiter and turned to Lori. "Of course they oversalt the food on purpose so we'll drink more. Liquor is how they make their money."

Lori gazed at the swan gliding by in the distance and wished herself away. A new thought came to her, one that should have come much earlier, but she found detecting hard. You had to be cynical and tough like Scardini. You had to be willing to probe into people's private lives and not care if you hurt them with your questions. Unpleasant as it was, Rob was innocent and she had to help him, for Jessica's sake, if not for his. That had to be her focus. She turned back to Ruth. "Did you know Valerie had changed her will?"

in the guardsmen for a stunned moment and hurried out to the open space of the street. Most visitors gazed up at the beauty of the renovated barrel-vaulted ceiling depicting the sky with all the constellations. Like New Yorkers themselves, they took the guns and the barricaded streets in stride. It was the latest look of a city that was always changing. At three o'clock in the afternoon, the concourse was fairly empty and quiet.

Lori's cell phone rang as she was standing in line to buy a ticket back to Hawthorne Park. "Was Ruth any help?" Beth asked.

"Yes, she was." Lori spoke softly. "But I don't want to talk about it now." The news she had wasn't something she wanted overheard even by strangers.

"You sound down," Beth said.

"I'm tired. I'll call you in the morning."

"I'll be home by six and I may have some information for you. I'm on my way to the county clerk's office on Centre Street to find out who's behind Waterside Properties."

Lori was the first in line now. "Hold on a sec." After she paid for her one-way ticket, she picked up her cell again and walked toward her gate. "Why are you doing that?"

"Because I have time to waste before my next meeting in Soho," Beth said. "Because I'm curious. Because if you don't ask you'll never know. Look, I'll call you the minute I get back."

"Dinner with Alec Winters is early." He was going to pick her up at six.

"Then call me when you get back from dinner."

"All right."

When she got home, Lori found that Jonathan had left a message announcing that they were all set for the weekend. "We're going to rural Pennsylvania, a bed and breakfast near Pleasant Gap. I liked the name."

What if she didn't want to go to Pleasant Gap, Pennsylvania? Pleasant Gap. Lori was sure she'd heard of the place only recently, but she couldn't remember the context. She and Rob had driven through Pennsylvania once, many years ago, and she'd found the farms, the rolling hills, the intense green of the land beautiful. She would enjoy visiting again, but Jonathan could have asked.

Lori kicked off her shoes and padded to the kitchen, switching her thoughts to Valerie and her lover. Valerie calling a 914 number, Valerie taking the train to White Plains. Jonathan driving Lori to New York, straight to Rob and Valerie's just-bought apartment. Had Rob told him where he lived?

Lori ran her hands through her hair, a nervous gesture of hers whenever her mind raced.

She reached into the refrigerator for the milk carton. Of course, Rob had told Jonathan where they lived. Why was she being so suspicious of Jonathan? Because someone had killed Valerie, that's why. Lori poured herself a glass of milk and drank it down in one gulp. She could just hear Beth guffawing, saying, "Dear Lori, you're suspicious of Jonathan because you're dying to go to bed with him and you're scared stiff."

Well, maybe.

Lori reached for the phone and called Margot's cell.

"Talk loudly," Margot said. "I'm at Leonardo's getting my hair blown dry."

She had planned to ask Margot about leaving the girls alone at home the night of Valerie's murder, but Margot would never yell the answer for all in the hairdresser's to hear. "Just a quick question," Lori yelled over the noise. "Do you remember the name of Valerie's housekeeper?"

"Whatever for?"

"I'd like to talk to her."

"What for?"

She wasn't going to shout out the reason. "I want to check something out."

"Ellen. I never knew her last name. Who knows where she is now."

"Thanks. Bye." Lori hung up and welcomed the sudden silence of her home. Slowly she went upstairs to her bedroom to undress. Maybe Mrs. Ashe's friend would know how to get hold of Ellen. Probably Ruth had lied about being reunited with her stepfather to save face, but there was also a chance she had lied to protect herself from suspicion. As Beth had said earlier, if you don't ask, you'll never know. She should call Mrs. Ashe now, call Jonathan back, call Rob to ask where her check was and get him to talk about his money troubles. Call Seth, her mother, Jessica.

Lori lay back on the bed in her underwear and shut her eyes. She didn't want to call anyone, not even Jess, and she wasn't sure she wanted to go anywhere with Jonathan. Whatever sexual heat he'd stirred up was now at a very low ebb. She was depressed. Above all, she wanted out of this murder mess.

Half an hour later, Lori was in the shower, hiding behind a wall of steam as she soaped up for the fourth time and thought about her evening with Alec Winters. What would he spill on her tonight? She should wear something indestructible like jeans. He had said to dress casually. Jeans and an old dark shirt just in case. Pleasant Gap, Pennsylvania. She remembered now. That's where Alec lived.

CHAPTER 26

"This place is perfect," Lori said, turning slowly around to luxuriate in the vista. "Thank you."

When Alec had appeared at her doorstep, in perfectly ironed khakis and a white polo shirt, he had asked if she'd like to go on a picnic.

"Most definitely," she had told him, happy not to have to sit in a noisy restaurant where she might be recognized and stared at as a possible murderer or ex-wife of one.

Now here they were, in an opening among the fir trees in the 144-acre PepsiCo Sculpture Garden in Purchase, stunning grounds filled with every variety of tree imaginable and the best sculpture of the twentieth century from such artists as Henry Moore, Alexander Calder, Giacometti, Claes Oldenburg, and David Smith. Lori had power-walked the grounds with Beth many times, but only in the early morning. The garden was only a twenty-five-minute drive from her home. She had never taken in the late afternoon light, which was now golden green, or had a picnic here.

In front of the picnic area was a small lake with an island on which a lone blue heron reigned. On the opposite side of the lake, a row of willow trees surrendered their boughs to the pull of the water. It had been a scorching day, but the trees made the air bearable. There was even a whisper of a breeze swaying the leaves.

"Let me help," Lori said. Alec was unpacking china plates,

glasses, and silverware from a large wicker basket sitting on the grass. He straightened up, his lanky body towering over her—he had to be at least six-four—and shook his head. His blond-gray hair was dark, still wet from the shower. His face was scrubbed pink. He looked serious, professorial, Lori thought. She wondered how old he was. Somewhere in his mid-forties was her guess.

"Let me do it all," Alec said, leaning close to her as he lifted the picnic basket onto the bench. "You worked hard on Saturday." He tore off a paper towel and started wiping the scoured wood table. "Mrs. Ashe and her ladies wouldn't stop talking about how good your food was. I'm sorry I got there late."

Lori smiled at the compliment and sat down on the bench. She picked up one of the plates he had stacked on one side of the table. It had a homey blue-flowered pattern. "Did you bring this china all the way from Pennsylvania?"

"I wish I always traveled prepared to have a picnic," Alec said, "but everything except the food is courtesy of the kitchen of friends of mine. I'm staying in their house in Bedford for the next two weeks while they're on vacation."

"What brought you up here?" At the near edge of the lake a duck raised her bill in the air and came waddling in their direction. Other ducks untucked their bills from under a wing and followed.

"I'm restoring a horse farm not too far from them. Here." Alec held up a clear plastic bag filled with torn pieces of bread. "You can give them this, if you like."

"You think of everything."

"Chris used to feed the ducks in Central Park." Alec watched the ducks approaching, their necks eagerly extended in front of them. "And he fed the sparrows, and the pigeons, and the squirrels. He loved animals, but thank God he drew the line at rats."

He held the bag toward her, a gentle sadness washing over his face, despite his smile. "Do you want a go?"

Lori wanted to say how sorry she was about Chris dying. She wanted to stand up and press her hand against his cheek. She wanted to hold this man and make it better.

"I'd love to." Lori took the bag and turned toward the ducks. Four adults and two younger ones made a semicircle around her feet and waited. She tossed bread. The ducks scrambled for the pieces. A few sparrows joined them, the birds looking up at her after each swallow with undivided attention. She could see how one could get hooked on this. She kept it up until all the bread was gone, while Alec set the table. Lori thought of Beth and her raccoon family. When Jess left for college, maybe she'd come here every day and adopt a bunch of ducks. She heard the pop of a cork and turned around. Alec was pouring Prosecco into two glass champagne flutes. The blue plates were now resting on white linen placemats, flanked by real silverware and two cloth napkins. Lori looked up at Alec in surprise. "This is a picnic fit for royalty. What are we celebrating?"

Alec smiled. "I'm apologizing for destroying a very beautiful dress and ruining your evening in Rome."

"Oh, you've apologized enough with those beautiful flowers. And there was no reason to. The cleaners got the stains out. The dress is fine."

"As I told you, I restore houses for a living," Alec said. "I've become pretty good at judging what can be saved and what should be razed to the ground." He handed her the flute and his smile widened. "I appreciate the fib, though."

"Your flowers were more than enough apology." Lori's eyes absorbed the warmth radiating from Alec's face, noticed how handsome that warmth made him. Lori took the glass Alec held out to her.

"To a no-spill meal."

Lori laughed and they clicked glasses and drank. Alec then unwrapped a plate of sliced tenderloin of beef. Next he uncovered a small bowl filled with creamy horseradish. A larger bowl held a mozzarella, tomato, and basil salad. "That's it," he said, sitting down on the opposite bench.

"This is fabulous," Lori said. She felt strangely confident in his presence. And serene. "Thank you. Did you make this?"

"I can manage simple things."

"I haven't had a meal home-cooked by someone else in years. All my friends do takeout. This is just what the doctor ordered." She meant that. His generosity moved her. "How did you know?"

"I read the papers. And then Jonathan filled me in. I'm the one who suggested the inn you're going to next weekend."

Why had Jonathan intruded into the conversation? He didn't belong with Alec. She couldn't picture them as friends.

"Have you guys been dating a long time?" Alec asked, dropping a perfect pink slice of tenderloin on her plate, spooning the horseradish sauce next to it.

"No." Now she was embarrassed. Alec was going to think she was the kind of woman that hopped into bed at a moment's notice. "I'm not sure I'm going away." Why was she being so ridiculous? Why did she worry about what Alec thought? And besides, he was gay. He wouldn't care who she slept with or when. And yet she wanted his good opinion. He was a kind, sensitive, warm man. Charming in a quiet way Jonathan would never be.

"Are you and Jonathan good friends?" she asked.

"I met Jonathan through Chris. They were friends in boarding school. Now Jonathan wants to do some business with me. I'm not sure, though. Like you."

They smiled at each other and began to eat and sip their wine. This time Alec didn't spill anything. Lori's embarrassment evaporated in the cooling air. The sun lowered and launched its reddening light through the trees, washing the picnic area in a rosy glow. The birds started their hectic evening chatter. The ducks slept, one or two intermittently waking up and squawking for attention.

"What were you doing in Rome?" Lori asked, while Alec changed their plates for dessert. He still would not accept help. "Business? Vacation?"

Alec reached into the wicker basket and brought out a peach cobbler. "I have to confess I bought this."

Lori clapped her hands like a delighted child. "Good. I was beginning to think you were perfect."

"Far from it, and I know exactly what you mean."

Lori took the knife and spatula from his hands to serve him. It made her feel good that he had let her. She took it as a compliment.

"I've made sure that none of my friends are perfect," Alec said. "That way they can't make me feel inadequate. I do a good enough job of that myself."

Lori slid a generous slice of cobbler on his plate. "Do you?" She was surprised. He seemed so confident.

"At times. I'm hard on myself and I take things too seriously. At work, I'm a perfectionist and drive most people crazy."

Lori gave herself a much smaller slice. "And at home? Aren't you able to relax there?"

"At home I'm alone. That's not much fun. I'm rarely there. I scout for houses all over the eastern states."

"Sometimes I think I'd like to have a job that takes me away," Lori said, "but I am lucky to have my wonderful thirteen-year-old daughter Jessica, who stops me from getting lonely most of the time."

Alec looked chagrined. "I'm sorry. I shouldn't have brought up the subject of loneliness."

"Why not?"

His eyes held hers for a moment. "Mrs. Ashe told me that you had recently divorced."

"Did she?" Lori wondered why. "You can talk about anything you want. How else are we going to know each other?"

"You're right. You asked about Rome. I go there as often as I can. I spent two years there after graduate school. I'm officially an architect, and I got a job with an Italian firm, grunt work really, but it paid just enough to keep me there soaking up the beauty, the food and the crazy, generous, wildly inefficient Romans. Chris joined me after a year, hoping to break into the movie world. He got bit parts there, bit parts in plays here. Never what he deserved. He was damn good. What about you? Did the *Greenwich Dish* send you to Rome for an article?"

Lori was amazed he remembered what she had told the Roman waiter. Now she'd have to confess her lie. Would he think less of her? "It was the first time I'd been back to Italy since a trip I took after college." She explained that she didn't work for any magazine, that the business card had been her friend Beth's idea. "I felt guilty about tricking the restaurants, but the food was just too good and I got greedy. Having those recipes would give me an edge on the competition. I need the work."

"I have to thank your friend, then. Your card was lying on the floor between our two tables. That's how I knew your name and address."

"I was terribly rude to you that night," Lori said. "Even before you knocked the gnocchi in my lap. You wanted to talk and I blew you off." She took a bite of the peach cobbler. It wasn't good, but she would eat the whole slice to please him. He needed pleasing.

Alec pushed his plate aside after one bite. "I'm the one who shouldn't have bothered you, but you looked lovely in that dress."

His words left a glow on her skin. She felt lovely now. Lori leaned on the table and studied his face. *Lucky Chris,* she thought, then instantly regretted it. Chris was dead.

Lori sat up, chewed and swallowed another bite of cobbler. "How did you ever manage to extract the secret gnocchi recipe from the chef?"

Alec's broad smile pulled a smile out of her, too. "Generosa's the cook and the *regina,* the queen, in that family. I rented a room from her for those two years in Rome. She took pity on my poverty and usually fed me for free. I guess I became like a son to her. She had only girls. Four of them. Whenever I go back, I eat my meals at her restaurant, paying this time. When the waiter turned you down, I got up to ask Generosa for the recipe. The girls have taken over the cooking, but she still commands. She wrote out the recipe herself, although I can't guarantee that she didn't leave out an essential ingredient.

"I was too eager to get that recipe for you. I wanted to make you happy and I stood up too quickly. The rest is messy history."

"Did I look that forlorn?" Lori asked.

A rueful expression appeared on Alec's face. "I have the intrusive need to try to read people's state of mind. It can be annoying, I know. I'm sorry."

"Well, you read correctly. I was miserable. My ex was getting married the next day with Jessica attending."

"I'm sorry for that, too." Alec lightly placed his fingers over her wrist, then slowly shifted his gaze from Lori's wrist to her face. She thought he was mulling something over. Something she might not like.

"What is it?" Lori asked.

He let go of her and ran his hand over his head. His hair had dried to a pale gray-blond. A fine, straight lock fell down his forehead like an arrow pointing to his eyes. They looked amused and hesitant at the same time. "Please forgive me if I say that I'm not sorry for spilling gnocchi and wine all over you. How else would we be sitting in this beautiful spot, surrounded by sleeping ducks and great art, and getting to know each other?" He covered Lori's hand with his and an unexpected shiver ran up her arm.

"I hope you agree," Alec said. It took her a moment to realize what he had said.

"Yes, I do," Lori answered simply.

He laughed and there was joy in his face. "Please stop trying to finish that bad cobbler." He stood up. "This time I will need help packing up. The guards are going to kick us out of this Eden in five minutes."

Lori got undressed. It had been a wonderful evening and she hoped there would be others, although Alec hadn't mentioned getting together again. At the door he had only said, "You are a very special woman, don't forget that," and wished her good night with a brotherly kiss on her cheek. If he didn't call, she would. She did feel special. Somehow he had boosted her courage, her morale, even though they hadn't talked about the murder, barely touched upon her divorce. Lori wished she had done the same for him. Next time maybe he would open up to her, talk more about Chris and what must be his tremendous grief at losing him.

In her pajamas, Lori padded down to the kitchen to check her messages. Beth had called saying she had "interesting info," which probably meant something to do with Valerie's death. It was still early—only nine thirty. Lori knew she should call Beth back, but she was reluctant to lose the serene state she was in. Maybe Beth could wait until morning. She would call Ellie and Jessica to check in with them, but first she was going to make herself a *sgroppino*, a Venetian after-dinner drink: lemon sorbet blended with a generous splash of vodka. She would substitute some club soda for the alcohol.

While Lori sipped her drink at the kitchen table, her legs propped up on a chair, she decided that the reason Alec had made her feel special and lovely was his sincerity. There was no come-on involved as there was with Jonathan. Alec wasn't selling himself. He was a good, sincere, sensitive man. A man she could trust.

After Lori finished her *sgroppino,* she walked over to the wall phone and dialed Jonathan's number.

To Lori's disappointment, Mrs. Ashe answered. "My dear, I'm sorry but Jonathan is out this evening. Can I take a message?"

"Just tell him I called. Good—"

"Please don't hang up." Mrs. Ashe sounded breathless.

"Of course not." Lori leaned against the wall.

"Mrs. Stafford is going to call you in the morning, dear. She was quite impressed with your talents and wants you to cater her fiftieth wedding anniversary in September. Fifty guests."

So many! "How wonderful," Lori said, when she found her voice. "Thank you."

"Don't mention it. And may I ask if you are still interested in Ruth?"

"Well, yes, in fact." She might as well ask, now that she had Mrs. Ashe on the phone. "I was wondering if you knew how I could find the Fenwicks' housekeeper."

"I'm afraid I can't help you, but I did find out why poor Ruth was asked to leave their home. I managed to remember that my husband had tried to help her. He kept meticulous notes on his work. He was going to write his memoirs, you see." Mrs Ashe let out a long sigh.

"What did happen?" Lori prompted.

"The poor girl is dead so we can't hear her side of the story, but according to what Ruth told my husband, Valerie accused her of being one of those girls that . . ." Mrs. Ashe hesitated with a fluttery breath. "I don't wish to embarrass you," another flutter of air, "but Valerie said that Ruth was one of the girls, well, like that comedian. Ellen DeGeneres."

"You mean a lesbian?"

"Yes, I suppose that's what they're called. Valerie told her father that Ruth had confessed to being in love with her and was making inappropriate passes at her. If it was true, the parents had a perfect right to distance Ruth from their daughter, but Ruth denied it and my husband believed her. He was a very good judge of character." Mrs. Ashe paused. "It was a terrible thing. You see, when Ruth's stepfather died a few years later, he left the money that should have rightfully gone to Ruth because much of it was her mother's money—well, he left a good deal of it to Valerie. The rest went to charity. Ruth got nothing."

"Is there a direct connection between Valerie's accusation and the stepfather's will?"

"According to my husband's notes, Ruth's stepfather changed his will a few weeks after Valerie's accusation."

"Do the police know about this?"

"They may have discovered it on their own. Jonathan has urged me to tell them, in case they haven't."

"Oh, please do tell them, Mrs. Ashe."

"Well, yes, if you think so, too. I'll call them in the morning, but I don't like the idea of hurting that poor girl. My husband quite liked Ruth, despite her bad manners. He found her very intelligent."

Intelligence was not an attribute Lori would have applied to Ruth. A certain animal cunning yes, but then she was hardly a good judge of character. Rob was proof of that.

"My husband thought Valerie lied," Mrs. Ashe said, "because she was jealous of how her father had taken to Ruth."

"You have important information, Mrs. Ashe. I urge you to call the police as soon as possible."

"They haven't arrested your ex-husband, have they?"

"No. He didn't kill Valerie, Mrs. Ashe."

Mrs. Ashe sniffed. "Perhaps not, although in my experience it is always hard to admit to the failings of people we love. It diminishes our own good opinion of ourselves. Your husband ruined my son's career."

Lori thought of protesting, of telling Mrs. Ashe she was dead wrong, that she should ask her son why he had left Rob's law firm, but instead she said, "Jonathan seems very happy with what he is doing now." There was no reason to defend Rob to a stubborn and grieving woman. Let her hold on to her convictions, wrong as they might be. They were probably what kept her going.

Mrs. Ashe was silent. It was time to hang up, but Lori had one more question. "Did you know Valerie?"

"As a child, then a teenager, yes. We socialized with her parents on occasion, but when my husband took up Ruth's cause, we stopped seeing them. My husband wasn't able to help Ruth and so we never spoke of it again, which is why I forgot. I'll tell Jonathan you called. I'm sure he's already sent you a check for the dinner."

Lori had just sent the bill this morning, and for a moment she felt slighted by Mrs. Ashe's assumption that the only thing she would have to discuss with Jonathan was the money he owed her. Then she shook the slight off her shoulders with a shrug, wished Mrs. Ashe good night, and hung up.

Lori was only halfway across the kitchen when the phone rang.

"I'm sorry to disturb you," Mrs. Ashe said.

"You're not disturbing me." Lori reached over for a chair and sat down.

"Perhaps you can help me," Mrs. Ashe said. "I am having difficulty with the thought that Ruth could be the culprit. You see, if she wanted revenge for what Valerie did to her, wouldn't she have acted years ago? Why kill Valerie now?"

CHAPTER 27

"I told Mrs. Ashe I didn't know," Lori said to Beth the next morning as she pulled an oversized T-shirt and baggy pants over her gym clothes.

"But you do know." Beth had joined Lori in a Pilates mat class, claiming it was the only way to catch her. The previous night Beth had called again after nine thirty, but Lori hadn't answered the phone.

"I don't want Mrs. Ashe to get more involved than she has to."

"But then she won't tell the police about Ruth and Valerie." Beth had taken a shower and was now dressed in a short-sleeved beige linen dress, combing her hair in front of the full length mirror in the dressing room.

"She promised me she would." Lori was going to shower at home. "If she doesn't, I'll ask Detective Mitchell to talk to her." She toweled her hair and face. The class had been harder than usual. "I don't know why Ruth would wait years to kill Valerie, if she did kill her, unless Valerie had left her more money in the original will and Ruth knew it. Maybe there wasn't an earlier will."

"Maybe not, but Ruth was Valerie's only relative, so she could assume some money was coming her way, especially in light of what Valerie had done to her. Once Valerie married, Ruth stood to lose out."

Lori stuffed her gym clothes and towel in her bag and hitched it over her shoulders. "Ruth would have had to know that Valerie was driving the girls back to Margot's that night."

"Valerie might have called her before leaving or from the car. The police must be checking everyone's phone records." Beth applied lipstick to her top lip and then pressed her lips together. She was now ready to face a day in her art gallery.

"I, for one, know they're checking," Lori said. If only Jessica would tell her who had called Valerie while she was driving them back to Margot's, but she had to respect Jess's refusal to break a promise. Lori was frustrated but proud of her daughter's integrity.

Beth glanced at Lori and laughed. "Ah, that's right, you have the mysterious phone that gets unplugged and plugged all by itself."

"Don't tease. It's scary."

Instantly contrite, Beth gave Lori's arm a squeeze and they left the dressing room, both waving goodbye to Dawn, the smiling and beautiful manager of the Pilates floor. At the juice bar downstairs, a glassed-in space facing the street, they ordered two low-calorie strawberry smoothies.

"So what is this interesting info that you're dying to tell me?" Lori asked.

Beth climbed on a stool. "How's Jess?"

"What's this?" Lori sat next to her. "Avoidance tactics?"

Two blenders started whirring loudly. Beth had to raise her voice. "You made me wait. Besides, I'm curious about Jess. Is she having a great time?"

"According to our last conversation, she is, but I didn't get to talk to her last night. Warren's housekeeper said he'd taken the girls to the movies. And if you're thinking of asking me about my mother next, she was out, too." The blenders stopped. The sudden silence caught Lori shouting, "I hope not on a date with Joey Pellegrino."

Beth laughed. "She might just be trying to pump him for information."

"Or she's using that excuse to see more of him." Their smoothies appeared on the counter, each with a straw. Lori thanked the counterman and turned to Beth. "Now that info, please."

Beth took a maddeningly slow sip of her drink before answering. "I went to the county clerk's office yesterday and discovered that one-fourth of Waterside Properties—I assume the fourth that Rob was hoping to buy—is owned by your friend and divorce lawyer, Warren Dixon."

"That can't be true. He told Margot not to give Rob the money, that it was a bad investment."

"Maybe Warren wanted Rob to fail so he could buy the one-fourth share of the partnership for himself. Maybe he just changed his mind."

"Can Warren be that devious?"

"He's a lawyer."

"But how could he lie to Margot if he's still in love with her?"

"I wish it weren't true, but money does trump love for a lot of people."

"How awful!" Lori propped both elbows on the counter, and without touching the glass, sucked down all of her smoothie through the straw. "We can't tell Margot," she said after the glass was empty. "She'd be so hurt."

"I have a feeling she wouldn't be in the least surprised," Beth said. "I never bought the story that Margot left Warren because she was in love with someone else."

"Why else would she divorce him?"

"What if he was the one who wanted out? You know her pride would never let her admit that."

"Oh no, he still loves her." Lori remembered the lunch at

Warren's club, how fiery his eyes became when he talked about Margot.

"Maybe he still wants to possess her," Beth said. "If he loved her, he would have let her invest with him in Waterside Properties. At least by my definition of love."

"How does Warren's investment tie in with Valerie's death?"

"I don't know. I find it interesting, though, and I'm willing to bet that Rob's failed attempt to raise money for Waterside Properties does have something to do with the murder."

"Who, besides Seth, loaned Rob money and got stiffed?" Lori asked rhetorically. "Maybe Rob will tell me. Today's the day I'm driving to New York and confronting him. And I should talk to Seth. We've only heard Jan's version of what happened that night."

"You think she's not telling the truth?" Beth looked skeptical.

"I'm sure she is, but as my mother often reminds me when she doesn't agree with me, our truths don't always match up. Besides, Seth might know who else gave Rob money to invest."

"Be careful." Beth checked her watch and reached for her purse.

"Rob's not going to do anything to me."

Beth lowered her voice. "I meant Seth. If he killed Valerie, he's not going to welcome you with open arms."

"He would have had to know Rob was going to inherit. Otherwise he has no motive."

Beth slipped off her stool and paid the counterman. "This one's on me," she said before Lori could protest. "Look, Seth assumed Rob was going to inherit when you met him on the train. Maybe Rob had told him or he found out some way. Just be careful, okay? With both of them." She started to walk out.

Lori followed her through the glass doors. "I'll walk you to your car."

Beth eyed Lori's outfit. Old black baggy slacks cut off at the ankle, a man's extra-large black T-shirt with Kids in Crisis written on it—a charity event handout—and black flip-flops. She hadn't combed her hair.

Lori shrugged, knowing she looked like a bedraggled crow. "Who cares?"

"Jonathan might. Now quickly tell me about your dinner with Alec."

"It was lovely," Lori said, perfectly aware those were easy, overused words, but she couldn't begin to describe the evening, either quickly or at length. Alec had managed to make her feel good about herself again. This morning she had woken up an optimist, convinced that she was worthy of a good life and that a person unknown to her and Jess would turn out to be the murderer. Alec had also unwittingly shown her what she wanted in a man, but she was hard put to define to herself or anyone else how he had accomplished all this in the few hours they were together. It was like trying to describe falling in love.

Lori knocked on the glass front door of the Bella Vista Travel Agency. From the window, a gorgeous tanned woman in a Band-Aid sized bikini smiled back at her from the beach of Puerto Vallarta. Lori sucked in her stomach and knocked again. The agency wasn't open yet, but she knew Ellie always showed up for work an hour early to check on yesterday's bookings in peace and quiet.

Ellie shuffled to the door, peered at her daughter for a moment before opening up. Lori peered back, taking in her mother's mane of newly dyed hair. Her gray had turned into a dull deep black that wiped the color off her face.

"Mom, you dyed your hair!" Lori blurted out as soon as Ellie opened the door.

"Glad you got eyes."

Lori stooped to give Ellie the required cheek kisses. "You

look good," she lied and went to sit in the chair facing Ellie's desk. Two other desks with their requisite computers crammed the small space, which was wallpapered with posters of more smiling beauties, hunks, and wholesome families tempting the onlooker to all corners of the world.

"At least the creams I gave you are helping." Ellie dropped into her swivel chair and swung herself to face the computer, which was emitting a low hiccuppy groan.

"You should get yourself a new computer, Mom."

"Nothing wrong with this one." Ellie fiddled with the red-rimmed glasses on the end of her nose. "How's my gorgeous granddaughter?"

"She's having a great time. Are you okay?"

"Busy, that's all."

"I called you last night. You weren't home."

"Were you?"

"No, I went on a wonderful picnic at PepsiCo."

"With the real estate guy?"

"No, with a very nice guy who happens to be gay. Alec Winters. You can Google him, too."

"No need to. Gay won't get you anywhere."

"Actually he's already gotten me somewhere, but don't ask me to explain because I can't. How was dinner with Joey Pellegrino?"

Ellie stopped her fiddling, swiveled her chair to peer at Lori above her glasses. "Dinner was just great. Just great." She paused and sadness seeped into her face. "I forgot how a man changes a room, like when you take your curtains down to wash them and for a few days the place takes on a new look, bigger and brighter, and you wonder why you put curtains up in the first place. I cooked for him last night, too. Same recipe, he loved it so much. I just didn't answer the phone because I didn't want to miss out on a second of him."

"Oh, Mom." Lori felt the depth of her mother's yearning as if it were her own. It hurt.

Ellie waved a hand in the air. "Aw, don't worry. I'm not falling in love or anything."

Why else would she color her hair, Lori wondered.

"It was just that Joey reminded me, you know? What it was like with your papa. It was good. I wish that for you again." The sadness was gone from Ellie's face, replaced by concern.

"Thanks, Mom. I'm going to be fine. I found a new friend"—she hoped that's what Alec would be—"and he's already removed the curtains."

Ellie looked doubtful. "The gay guy?"

"His name is Alec, Mom."

"Not the real estate guy?"

"Jonathan's just sexy."

"Nothing wrong with that." Ellie's throat turned a deep red.

"Mom, you didn't!"

"None of your business." Ellie hugged the collar of her shirt to her neck. "Enough with the sentimental stuff. It wasn't all fun and games with Joey, you know. I was also investigating. He wouldn't talk Sunday night, but I got him last night with a double helping of pasta and two bottles of Montepulciano."

"That's all?"

"As I said, none of your business. So this is what I found out for you. First of all, Valerie didn't have a will before the one we know about, so her cousin, Ruth what's-her-name, would have gotten all her money. But it looks like Ruth has some kind of alibi. That's why she hasn't been arrested. They're checking it out. Now wait 'til you hear this." A bell rang and Ellie stopped to look up as Sharee—one of her two assistants—walked in, popped her bubble gum, and waved at them both. Ellie sent her out to get coffee.

Once Sharee was gone, Ellie turned back to Lori. "You'll

never guess who drew up Valerie and Rob's will."

"Someone in Rob's law firm."

"Nope."

"Valerie's lawyer, then."

"Wrong again. It was a real rush job, as if they knew one of them would be dead soon, which doesn't look too good for Rob. So guess who the lawyer was? Two vowels, four consonants."

"You're not going to tell me Warren."

Ellie nodded. "I am."

Lori said nothing at first, not knowing what to think. She knew how she felt, though. Somehow betrayed, disappointed. Warren had been on her side, her divorce lawyer. She had considered him a friend. Obviously she was only a client, someone who would bring him money, nothing more. He had offered lunch at his club saying he was worried about her, wanted to help her with the police, but thinking back on it now, Lori wondered if the real reason for the invitation hadn't been to pump her for information about Margot's love life. "I'm surprised," she said quietly.

"Maybe you should drive up to Cape Cod," Ellie said, "and bring Jessica home."

"Let's not jump to conclusions. Warren goes where the money is, that's now obvious, but that doesn't mean Jessica is in any danger."

"He could be the killer."

"Come on, Mom! He's got no motive."

Ellie half stood up. "Then I'll go. I've got a real busy day coming up and I'm one person short, but I'll go and bring my Jessica back."

"Mom! Stop it. I will drive up there to talk to him, and I promise, if I don't like his answers I'll bring Jess back. I promise." Lori stood up to leave.

Ellie settled back in her chair. "Since for once you're taking my advice, I'll tell you something else."

"What now?"

"What I told those two detectives, you know, about coming into your house that night and unplugging the phone?"

Lori chuckled. "That was fast thinking on your part and they bought it. I can't thank you enough."

"I wasn't lying."

"But you gave back the keys!"

Ellie shrugged. "I got an emergency copy, just in case."

Lori didn't know whether to be angry or grateful. "Oh, Mom. What am I going to do with you?"

"Feed me to the dogs, but I'm keeping that key."

Lori walked behind the desk and planted a kiss on Ellie's head. "I guess I'll just have to keep loving you, but dye your hair brown next time, okay?"

It was a beautiful, clear day, yesterday's humidity having dissipated during the night. Lori chose the West Side Highway to drive into New York even though Rob's office was on the East Side. She took in the view as she drove. A barge eased itself toward the ocean through the sun-speckled ripples of the river. A Circle Line boat filled with tourists motored under the George Washington Bridge. Lori turned off the air-conditioning and opened her window to let the rush of air ruffle her hair off her shoulders. This calmed her even more than the view. She wasn't looking forward to her facedown with Rob, then the long drive to Cape Cod to question Warren. Was Ellie right? Could he be the killer? It was hard to believe, but she could feel a worry knot tighten in her chest. *Think of Jess,* she told herself. *How nice it will be to see her.*

Lori punched in Warren's number. He answered after one ring. He must have been waiting for a call. "I need to talk to you," she said, her anxiety making her forget to say hello.

"They've arrested Rob." There was no question in his voice.

"No, I need information, but I don't want to do this over the phone. I'd like to come up late this afternoon. Is that okay?"

"Sure. Whatever you want to know, I hope I can be of help. You'll spend the night. Even better, why not stay a few days? I've got plenty of room, and I could use the company. The girls are always off at the beach being girls and the few times they're around, their conversation isn't exactly stimulating."

He sounded so nice, so welcoming. The worry knot eased. "I really appreciate that. Thanks." She hadn't thought about the drive back at night. "Expect me around six, traffic permitting. I'll call from the road when I'm close. I'll get directions from Margot."

"Bring her along."

"Warren . . ."

"I know you don't want to get involved, but try. Please. I'd appreciate it."

Here was another person yearning, Lori thought after disconnecting. Everyone she knew was hungering for something or someone, herself included. Beth and Callie for their lost husbands, Alec for his lost partner Chris, Ellie for a new love, Jess for her first boyfriend, Janet for reassurance, Seth for his money, Mrs. Ashe for a new home. Rob must want money to pay his debts, and his new wife back. Jonathan? Lori remembered the moment of regret on his face during their dinner together. She suspected he too was aching for something. More money, more girlfriends? Fame? Or was she being unfair? Maybe all he ached for was the loving father he never had. He hadn't called back. Lori wondered if Mrs. Ashe had given him the message. She needed to talk to him before more time elapsed.

"Jonathan? Hi, it's Lori. Is this a bad time?"

"I'll always have time for you. I'm sorry I didn't return your call, but I've been bogged down with my mother and that apartment she insists on buying against my better judgment. She's accusing me of being cruel, so I'm giving in. It is her money. Look, I'm glad you called. About this weekend—"

"That's why I'm calling. Look, I'm not up to going. I'm sorry. I really am. I was hoping to tell you in person, but I have to drive to Cape Cod this afternoon to see Jess and I'm staying the night." The words were coming out so quickly, Lori felt she was blabbering. "It has nothing to do with you. I had a wonderful time Sunday night. Really. I mean if Jess hadn't called we would—" She stopped, not knowing what to say next.

"But your daughter did call and we didn't and now you've changed your mind." His voice was neutral, and Lori couldn't tell whether he was angry or didn't care.

"You're a very attractive man, Jonathan. It's just that I'm not ready." She was grateful to him for reawakening her sexual desire and for wanting her, but after meeting Alec, she knew she would never fall in love with Jonathan. Making love to him would have been only a trifling thing that would leave her with a hole in her heart waiting to be filled. She understood Beth now. "Please forgive me."

Jonathan laughed. "Nothing to forgive. I was about to cancel on you."

"Oh. How come?" she asked in a small voice.

"I have to close a deal on Saturday."

The Saturday of the Fourth of July weekend? Did he really expect her to believe him? "Then it's all right," she said. "No harm done on either side." Well, she did feel a little insulted, but it proved her point, didn't it? Jonathan was not the dependable type. She thought this over for a second and burst out laughing. "I'm sorry, I'm laughing at myself. It's all right for me to cancel, but I don't like it one bit when you do."

"Does that mean there's a chance for a rain check?" He had

moved his phone closer to his lips. His voice was low, seductive again.

Lori suppressed a giggle. He was really a silly, vain charmer. "A platonic rain check would be great."

"Sorry, but you're much too attractive for that."

"So are you."

"Okay, then. I'll call you in a month or so. Sound good?"

"That sounds fine." And then she remembered what Ruth had told her. "Jonathan," she tried to keep her voice light. "There's something I want to ask you."

There was silence at the other end of the line.

"You knew Valerie, didn't you?"

"Valerie?"

"Yes, Rob's wife," Lori said. "Last week, when I wanted to know more about Valerie, Beth mentioned that you might help as you two traveled in the same circles. Did you know her?"

"When I drove you to Rob's apartment," Jonathan said, "I told you I'd never met her, didn't I?"

"I don't remember that," Lori lied. She'd never get the truth out of Jonathan if she put him on the spot.

"Well, I did know her. In fact, I dated her for a while. I'm sorry I lied to you, but I didn't think you'd see me anymore if you knew about Valerie."

"You're right."

"She was much too aggressive and fixated on money. I walked away."

"She must have been upset," Lori said.

"Look, it was a long time ago. Why did you ask?"

It was her turn to tell the truth. At least part of it. "I learned that Valerie had been very much in love with someone before she met Rob and I was wondering if it was you." *And if it was you,* Lori thought silently, *you might have killed her for marrying Rob.*

"I'm flattered, but I'm not the guy."

Lori had no reason not to believe Jonathan and yet something bothered her. Maybe it was his rebuff. She hoped she wasn't that vain.

"Listen," Jonathan said, in a tone that made it clear the conversation was over. "I'll call you in a couple of months."

"In a couple of months." Lori said goodbye, thinking he was not the kind of man who accepted having his ego bruised. Jonathan would never call again. That thought didn't bother her at all.

CHAPTER 28

Rob was on the phone with a client when Lori slipped into his office. The room was one of those corner offices that young lawyers dream about as they sweat their eighty hours a week of grueling work. One wall held a row of windows facing east, overlooking the equally coveted corner offices of the surrounding skyscrapers and a jagged rectangle of sky. The other walls were covered with chrome bookshelves loaded with law books. These, Lori knew, were for show, as Rob hadn't cracked open a law book since he'd been moved up to this office. That was work for the peons.

Rob's hunched back was turned away from the door. He would have seen Lori walk in only if he had raised his head and caught her reflection in the window. Lori sat in one of the two chairs facing the desk, the one farthest from Rob, and waited for the phone call to end. She eyed the uneaten sandwich sitting in the center of the desk—a tuna melt by the look of it—and a sweating can of iced tea. At least that habit hadn't changed. It was lunchtime and Lori was hungry. To distract herself, she looked for changes in the room since her tenure as Rob's wife.

When Rob had been promoted to this office, she had offered to help him decorate, help that he refused. She would only make it look cozy, he claimed, when an office needed to express the seriousness and stature of its occupier. To her the result was cold and uninviting. A long glass and chrome table for a desk, a slightly smaller and lower twin for a coffee table. The sofa and two armchairs were upholstered in taut black leather that in the summer always stuck to her thighs. The phone was black, the pen and pencil holder was black, the halogen lamp was skinny, black, long-necked, and Italian. The wall-to-wall carpet was a rough, thick sisal that Lori was sure would scrape her knees if she ever fell on it. The chair she sat on was chrome and leather with no hind legs. It sank when she sat in it.

Rob hung up and turned around. When he saw Lori the expression on his face remained weary, lifeless. His jaunty defiance was gone. "Hi," he said.

"Hi, Rob." They stared at each other for a few seconds, Lori overwhelmed by a sense of futility. All those years together to end up staring, barely able to speak to each other.

"Kate sent your check this morning," Rob said.

"I didn't come for the check. I mean, not only for that." Looking at Rob's face, Lori was reminded of a deflated balloon, wrinkled and ready to be discarded. Was he overwhelmed by grief or fear? Both? "Do the police have any news?"

"I expect them to arrest me any minute."

"Because Valerie's death made you rich?"

Rob picked up his black pen, twirled it between his fingers, and said nothing.

"I know about Seth. Who else do you owe money to?"

"It doesn't matter."

Lori slammed her hand on the glass desk, rattling the plate the sandwich was on. "But it does! The people you owe money to could be suspects. Look, I'm trying to help. I know you didn't kill Valerie. Talk to me. Maybe together we can point the finger away from you."

Rob put the pen down, picked up a pencil.

"Please, Rob, for Jessica's sake, don't stonewall me."

His fingers now twirled the pencil. "What do you want to know?"

"About Waterside Properties. About being in debt and not paying back your investors. About claiming someone was trying to kill you and then denying it. About rushing to write a will."

Rob swiveled away from her and looked out of the window. Lori followed his gaze. In the office just opposite, a man was talking animatedly on the phone while trying to change into a clean shirt without losing his grip on the receiver. *Put the phone down and press the damn speaker button!* Lori wanted to shout at him. She turned back to Rob. "Please, Rob. Talk to me."

Rob kept looking at the man struggling with his shirt. Then he said, "Over lunch the day Val died, after we signed our wills, she told me she was in love with someone else. I had been begging her to help me out, and she told me about this other man, and that I had to get out of the mess I was in by myself. She didn't want to understand that I got into this mess because of her. The apartment, the car, the expensive restaurants, the engagement ring, the gifts she wanted. Everything had to be top of the line with her. She was convinced men wanted to marry her only for her money. I had to prove to her I was as rich as she was." Rob looked across at Lori with woeful eyes. "Val had terrible self-esteem."

Lori reached for a sandwich half and bit into it. She thought tuna melts were an insult to gastronomy, but she needed to stuff her mouth before she said something she'd regret.

Rob's eyes dropped to his hands splayed on the desk. "After she told me about having loved this man for years, the crazy thing is I should have walked out on her right then and there, but I couldn't. I didn't want to. I dragged Val out of that place and took her home and we made the best—"

Lori swallowed quickly. "I don't need details, Rob."

He was too lost in his own story to apologize or to realize she was eating his lunch. *He probably doesn't even realize he is talking to his ex-wife,* Lori thought, taking another bite. Instead of being hurt by his tactless confession, she found herself intrigued by his inability to accept defeat. She had, while married to him, never noticed the extent of his ego.

"I never thought of leaving Val," Rob said. "She assured me it was over between them even if she still loved him. I was going to make her love me. I knew I could do it."

His eagerness almost made Lori feel sorry for him. "I'm sure you would have." She put what was left of the sandwich down. "Did Valerie tell you who the man was?"

"I asked her not to. I didn't know she was going to get killed that night."

"I hope you told the police about this man."

"I got a skeptical grunt for an answer."

"Valerie's office manager confirmed your story." Rob's expression didn't relax. Maybe he was thinking the story would get to the papers and he would look like the fool he was. "Tell me what happened with Waterside Properties?"

"I committed to buying shares because Val was going to go in with me, plus Seth and two others you don't know. Then she backed off. I tried to scrounge up some more money but couldn't."

"What about the powerful clients you've helped through the years?"

"I stay away from former or possible future clients. Something goes wrong and that's the end of me as their lawyer."

"And something did go wrong."

Rob lowered his head in acknowledgment. "I used the money for Waterside Properties to pay off a loan. I thought I could stall for time, not let on that the deal wasn't going to happen, but the word leaked out anyway and my investors wanted their money back. The night the car almost ran me over, I thought Seth was giving me a warning. Pay back or else. I didn't think that for long, but I played it up for Val."

"So she'd worry about you and lend you money?"

Rob lowered his head in answer. "I insisted we write up our wills right away. No time to lose. I might get killed any moment." His voice held no emotion. "Val was okay with the wills and called the lawyer, Warren by the way."

"I know. My divorce lawyer. Funny choice."

"Her funny way of getting back at me for needing money. I was in too much of a hurry to object to Warren. After all that she still wouldn't lend me any money even though she knew I'd give her back every cent with interest." Rob leaned back, tilting his chair to the wall. Lori noticed the dark patch under his chin, where his razor had missed. "She was really fixated on money."

"Did you tell Seth the two of you were writing your wills?"

"He called me Monday morning while I was in a cab on my way to meet Val at Warren's office. I told him to get off my back. Val was going to give me the money I owed him any day now. I was still thinking she was going to come through."

"Did you mention you were on your way to rewrite your will?"

"Yes, I did. I don't know why." Rob picked up the half-eaten part of his sandwich and took a bite. "You think he killed her so I'd inherit and pay him back?"

"It's as a good a motive as any, but what the police think is what matters." Lori stood up and swept crumbs off her lap. If she was going to drive to Cape Cod, she had better get going. "Thanks for talking to me, Rob, and good luck."

Rob stood up. "I'm truly sorry about us." His face was stricken. Moved by the sincerity of this expression, Lori looked away at the building opposite. The man was still getting some urgent point across over the phone, but his transformation was now complete, the clean shirt neatly tucked in, buttoned. If only it were that easy.

"Us is in the past, Rob. Let's just worry about now. If you

have any news from the police, good or bad, please let me know."

As she walked to the door, he said, "When Jess comes home next week, is there a chance I could, you know . . ." He left the question in the air.

Lori turned around slowly. "You could what?"

"Spend some time at the house?"

How long was "some time," Lori wondered. Two days, a week? For good? She wasn't prepared to think about it now. "I don't think so, Rob."

"I didn't buy the Jaguar you saw. I only leased it."

As if that solved anything. Lori closed the door behind her.

With Streisand singing Sondheim in the CD player, an overnight bag in the backseat, an avocado and turkey wrap on her lap, and a full tank of gas, Lori headed for Cape Cod. She had refused to go along with her mother's request to call her every two hours, but she had given her and Beth Warren's Cape Cod address and phone number to stop them from worrying. During the hurried minutes she'd been home, Lori had called Jessica, who accepted her sudden upcoming visit with the usual teenage roller coaster of emotions, suspicion followed by elation, more suspicion, and closing with seeming indifference. Lori was looking forward to seeing Jessica, no matter what her welcome was.

Rob had to be missing her, too. "I'm so sorry about us," he had said with a stricken face. His first show of remorse. When he asked to come home for a few days, what had he been trying to tell her? Did he know what he wanted? Should she let him? Jessica would be ecstatic. Lori knew she didn't want Rob back in her home, not even for one day, but how could she explain that to her daughter? Lori imagined her reaction. "How could you, Mom? Don't you have a heart? What about me, Mom? What about how I feel?"

And if she did let Rob come home and sleep on the couch in the den? What would that change? He would still be the man who walked out, who had done irreparable damage to her and the daughter he claimed he adored, who was only back because his new wife was dead, who would surely walk away again as soon as he was healed. But with Daddy home, Jess would start hoping that maybe he was back for good. And if, by the slimmest chance, he did want to stay, Lori wouldn't, couldn't, have him. Not even for Jessica's sake. She loved her daughter more than she could say, but love for Rob was gone. Theirs would not be a family, only a cold, lifeless gathering of three unhappy individuals.

Once Lori hit Route 90, she punched the number Alec had given her. "I need cheering up," she said when he answered, not giving her name first, treating him like an old friend.

"Another picnic tonight, then?"

"I wish."

"Do you have a cold?"

"Sinus trouble."

"I'm sorry."

Lori could tell from the politeness in his voice that he didn't believe her. She was sorry she had lied to him now. She was sure he understood tears very well. She was also sure he would never pass judgment. How she knew this, she couldn't tell. Maybe the divorce had given her a sixth sense to recognize genuine goodness.

"Look, I'd love to try the gnocchi recipe you sent me," she said. "I bloom with optimism when I cook, and you're a great mood enhancer, I've discovered. That combination would really be great. Any chance you're free tomorrow night?"

"I would enjoy that very much, but first I should tell you that I'm not—"

Lori jumped in, her face suddenly hot. "I know. I think that's wonderful." What was she saying? "I mean, it's fine. Really. Seven thirty?" She thought she heard a chuckle at the other end.

"I'm glad you feel that way. Seven thirty it is. I'll bring the wine."

"Great." Lori said goodbye and punched the off button. He must have thought she was making a pass at him. Thank God, now the gay issue was out in the open. She turned up Streisand and took a large bite of her avocado and turkey wrap. She was feeling better, but Cape Cod and the town of Chatham were still a long way away.

Lori stepped out of the car into the white brilliance of what she called water light. She lifted her face to the sky, inhaled the salt air, and waited for the knots in her body to loosen, smooth out. Only then did Lori look at her surroundings. Warren's vacation home, bought when he was still married to Margot, surprised Lori. Knowing the Dixons' tendency to show off the money they had, she had expected a sumptuous ultramodern house with glass walls and impeccably kept grounds. Instead she was looking at the back of an old-fashioned, two-story beach house with cedar shingles that had aged to a soft pale gray. The small windows had white trim and peeling sky-blue shutters. At one side of the house, a narrow blue door, also peeling, probably led to the kitchen. The land the house sat on was a spontaneous mixture of wind-bent scrub oaks, weeds, sand, and tall grasses. Only its location, facing the beauty of a wide bay, spoke of money.

As Lori walked to the trunk of the car to get her overnight bag, a fanny-wagging black cocker spaniel hurled itself at her thighs, followed by a running Jessica, who flung her arms around her mother. "It's cool you're here, Mom."

"Thanks. That's a nice welcome." Lori gave Jessica a tight

squeeze while the dog wiggled itself between their legs, licking them to claim some attention.

"Stop it, Gertie," Jessica said. "That's icky."

Lori stepped back to enjoy the sight of her barefooted daughter, in frayed denim shorts and a moss green tank top, happily scratching the dog's ears. Her skin had turned to a warm walnut tan and her hair had bleached into a mass of pink-gold curls. "You look wonderful, sweetie."

Jessica blushed and pulled at the dog's collar.

"How's Deuce?"

"He left yesterday, but it's okay because I need my space, you know?" Jessica took Lori's overnight bag from her and they walked to the kitchen door with Gertie following. "I mean, I like him and all," she said while opening the screen door, "but why do guys have to take over?"

"Only some of them do," Lori said. Rob was in that category. Jonathan, too. "You have to stand your ground."

"That's what Angie said, but it's kind of hard when you want him to like you. You should do this. You should do that, like you don't have a brain of your own. It's so obnoxious. I finally told him to lay off and he left."

They walked into a large linoleum and Formica kitchen with yellow metal cabinets. Lori was reminded of the kitchen she grew up in until her mother, after a good year at the travel agency, went for granite and tile. "I'm sure he didn't leave because of what you said." Lori followed Jessica up a narrow back stairway to the second floor, wondering where Warren and Angie were.

"I knew he was leaving. That's why I told him. I want him to think about it." Jessica opened a door to a small, sparse room with striped cornflower blue and white wallpaper, a small bureau, a single bed covered with a yellow and white quilt, a child's rocking chair, a blue rag rug on the wide plank floor. A narrow window below a sloping ceiling overlooked the bay. Jessica sat on the bed cross-legged with Gertie pushing up against her.

Lori unpacked the few things in her bag. "You don't look unhappy," she said.

"Angie says I'll cry tomorrow, but I don't think so."

"Good for you." Her daughter had more gumption than she'd ever had. "You've made a friend," Lori said, watching Gertie stretch herself over Jessica's legs.

"Gertie's great. Can we get a dog now, Mom? Can we? I promise I'll take care of it. Walk it, feed it, everything. I promise."

A promise that might last at most until school started. Lori shifted her pajamas from one side of the drawer to the other. A big soft mutt who would fill the empty space in her bed and give her undying devotion. It was tempting. And it would keep Rob out of the house. He was allergic. "Let's talk about it when you come home, okay?" Lori turned to face Jessica and was met by wary eyes. "I'm not saying no, sweetie."

Jessica shrugged off her words. "Why did you come, Mom?"

How much more time would it take for Jess to trust her, Lori wondered, sitting down next to her. "I missed you and I needed to talk to Warren about a few things."

"Dad's okay?"

"I saw him this morning. I'd say he's as okay as he can be under the circumstances. It takes time to heal." Lori stopped herself from adding, "as you know."

Jessica pushed Gertie to one side, her expression still cautious. "You're not angry about my not telling you who called Valerie in the car that night?"

"I understand. You have to keep your promise to Angie." Anyway, she had a pretty good idea who the caller was.

"Thanks, Mom." Jessica stretched out her long legs to the floor. "We better go down. Warren's waiting for you to have cocktails on the beach. Come on, Gertie." She stood up and looked down at her mother's high-heeled sandals. Lori hadn't wanted to waste time changing to a more casual outfit. "Lose the shoes, Mom."

Warren, in a red bathing suit with florid stomach jutting out underneath an old yellowed polo shirt, stood up from his Adirondack chair as Jessica and Lori, now barefoot, approached. Behind his bulky frame a narrow path of sand cut through pale green grasses and led to the shimmering blue of the bay. To the right, a wooden sailboat rocked gently next to a short pier. Above, the paler blue of the sky held a low string of clouds that looked squirted from a pastry bag. Warren grinned. "Welcome to Margoland."

Angie, knee deep in the water, waved. Jessica and Gertie ran in after her.

"Thanks, Warren," Lori said, waving back to Angie. "What a beautiful spot."

Warren's eyes were focused beyond her shoulder, on the empty path leading back to the house.

"I'm sorry," Lori said, understanding. "I didn't reach Margot, but I left her a message."

"Thanks." His face didn't betray any disappointment as he reached for a glass pitcher filled with green leaves steeped in a cloudy liquid. He slipped dark sunglasses over his eyes. "A mojito to get you in the beach mood?"

Lori accepted half a glass and settled in the other Adirondack chair. They made small talk and munched on potato chips while watching the girls splashing in the water with the dog, whispering girl secrets in each other's ears, laughing. The sliding sun enveloped them with the soft light of late afternoon.

They are so happy together, Lori thought. *May it last forever.*

"You came up here for help," Warren said after Angie and

Jessica, with Gertie in tow, ran back to the house to change. "What can I do?" His jovial tone had turned somber.

"You wrote up Rob and Valerie's will."

"Yes, I did. Not my department usually, but they thought it was urgent so I complied. Good thing, too. Now that Rob inherits so much money, I think we should revisit your financial arrangement with him. It's worth a try. We can play on his guilt. No reason he should be the only one to benefit." Warren lifted the pitcher to refill Lori's glass.

"No more, thanks. That's not why I'm here, Warren."

He refilled his own glass. "I hope you aren't taking my helping Rob and Valerie personally."

"I didn't like it at first. I guess I felt you belonged to me, you were my lawyer, but I was being childish. Business is business."

Warren leaned forward, his big bear face now close enough for Lori to see his eyes behind the sunglasses. "I didn't stop to think how it would affect you. I'm not good in the sensitivity department, as Margot liked to remind me. Sometimes I think it's the secret of my success as a divorce lawyer, but it makes poor marriage and friendship material." His voice softened. "I'm sorry, Lori."

She wanted to believe him and yet she couldn't stop the questions. "I don't understand why Rob didn't use his own law firm for the will. He could have gotten some young lawyer to work over the weekend for him."

"It's good policy to keep your private business away from ambitious young lawyers in your own firm who might one day use it for their own advancement."

Lori hadn't thought of that. She never liked to focus on people's baser instincts. She took a stab in the dark. "You used to date Valerie before Margot came along."

Warren sat back and took a long sip of his drink. "That was a long time ago."

"She called you when she wanted a lawyer."

"What are you trying to get at?"

"Valerie received a phone call while she was driving the girls back to Margot's house the night she died. Angie made Jess promise not to tell anyone who it was. I can only suppose it was you Angie is trying to protect."

"Not Margot?"

"Why protect her? She had every reason to call, since Valerie was driving Angie home."

Warren's shoulders slumped. "Lori, what are you doing?"

"I'm trying to help Jess's father. Forgive me, Warren, I am turning into a woman I hardly recognize and don't like much, but I was looking at our two girls having a great time, and I want it to stay that way. Please tell me if you called Valerie that night?"

"Even if I did call Valerie, it doesn't make me her killer."

"I'm not saying it does. You called her and she told you she was driving the girls back."

"I had no reason to call her. The wills were signed. She left nothing in my office. Why would I call her?"

"Maybe because you were friends. Maybe because you are the man she was still in love with."

Warren chuckled. "Who fed you the fantasy that she was in love with anyone besides herself?"

"Her cousin Ruth." She wasn't going to tell him that Rob had confirmed it.

Warren slipped his sunglasses on the top of his head. "You believe her, but not me." He was looking at her kindly when Lori had expected him to erupt in anger. That disarmed her.

"I don't know," Lori confessed. "I'm so scared of what could happen that I clutch at anything that floats before my nose."

"I understand that, but you've got to admit you make a lousy sleuth. You expect everyone to tell you the truth. That's not the way it works with most people."

Rob used to remind her that she always saw the glass as three-quarters full, a viewpoint she had picked up from Papa and thought she had lost thanks to Rob. Maybe she hadn't yet. "Why would Ruth lie to me?"

"Ask yourself, instead, why would Ruth tell you the truth?"

"Because it's simpler."

"For you it is. For a lot of people, lies are easier. They make life livable. Ask your friend Margot."

"She had nothing to do with Valerie's death, so let's please keep her out of it. Are *you* lying to me?"

"You'll have to be the judge of that."

She felt manipulated. "Tell me about Waterside Properties."

"It's a good investment. I own a fourth of it."

"I know."

His eyes widened just enough to register mild surprise. "Your sleuthing isn't so lousy, then."

"Someone else found out. Why did you tell Margot not to invest?"

"Because I knew Rob would never pull it off."

"How did you know that?"

"Thanks to Valerie, he was spending way over his limit, and I sensed he was counting on her money to close the deal."

So he knew Valerie well enough to know she wouldn't deliver. "You could have let Margot invest with you, then," Lori said.

"Love and business are a lethal combination. Tell me this, why do you keep asking questions? If no evidence has turned up yet to implicate Rob, he's not going to get arrested."

Lori was surprised at how obtuse Warren was about being a parent. "If no murderer is found, Jess might look at her father and wonder. She already has to deal with the fact that he walked out on her—children always end up thinking it's their fault. That's enough of a burden for one lifetime. Don't you understand? I want to clear my daughter's head of any doubts about Rob and Valerie's death. If I can somehow uncover something that will help find the murderer . . ." Lori raised her arms in a gesture of helplessness.

"You think you can?"

Lori peered into Warren's face. He seemed genuinely curious. "I have to try, Warren. You would do the same for Angie. For Margot."

Warren looked down at his knees. "I love those two more than I thought a man could bear. Let's leave it at that." He lifted himself up from his chair like a man with a heavy weight on his shoulders. "The girls are coming back and it's time to get the grill going. I hope you like corn and shrimp."

"Love it," Lori said, not caring what she ate. She followed Warren's slow gait up the path, her feet sinking into the still-warm sand. She had come no nearer to knowing the truth of Valerie's death, but at least she had a better picture of Warren. He was an egocentric man, even an unpleasant one, but not mean or dangerous. Jess was safe. She had no reason to spoil her daughter's fun by making her come home.

Lori was about to fall asleep when she felt a sudden weight on the bed, followed by a wet tongue on her cheek. She pushed Gertie's face away and skated her hand down the dog's silky back. The only sound was Gertie's panting and the distant repeated ping of a line blowing against the mast of the sailboat. She didn't remember leaving the bedroom door open, but she must have. Lori pulled Gertie against her stomach. The dog was soft, pliable, sweet-smelling. Having a dog might be nice, she thought, as she found a fresh spot on the pillow and closed her eyes. Better than feeding raccoons.

"Mom?"

Startled, Lori sat up and turned on the lamp. "What's up,

honey? You can't sleep?"

"It's only eleven thirty!"

Jessica dropped down on the bed, lifted Gertie on her lap, and started rubbing her stomach, which made the dog throw back her head in contentment. Lori waited.

"Dad called," Jessica finally said. "He wants to come home."

How dare he use Jessica to get his way, Lori thought angrily. It was blackmail. "I know, Jess," she said.

"My heart started jumping, you know," Jessica said, the words coming out with unusual slowness. "I thought, wow, he wants us back. We're going to be a family again. And then I thought, Oh God, what if Mom doesn't want him back? I'll never forgive her."

"Jess, I—"

A flutter of hands interrupted Lori, followed by, "Let me finish, Mom."

"I'm sorry," Lori said meekly. Her own heart was pounding.

"I mean," Jessica continued, "this went through my head really fast. I know Dad was waiting for me to say how great that was. I thought it, but before I could say it something else popped in my head." Jessica leaned into the lamp light as she lowered Gertie to the floor.

Lori briefly caught her daughter's lovely profile and she felt her chest squeeze painfully tight. She would do anything for her. She really had no choice. "Hon, if you want—"

"I asked Dad what he meant about coming back. Like for how long?" She shifted her weight on the bed, coming closer to Lori. "Mom, you don't love Dad anymore, do you? You don't want him back, right?"

Lori reached out and placed a hand on Jessica's arm. It gave her courage. "This morning I told your father it was too late for him to come home. Please understand, it would only—"

"It's okay, Mom. I mean it. He would have just hurt us all

over again." Jessica leaned over and kissed Lori on the cheek. " 'Night, Mom."

Lori hugged her. "You are a very special girl, Jess. I'm so lucky to have you."

"Sure." Jessica stood up. *One day she'll take compliments in her stride,* Lori thought.

Jessica walked to the door. "I didn't mean that about not forgiving you," she said. "Dad just surprised me."

"What did he say when you asked him how long he wanted to stay with us?"

"Two or three days, that's all."

How could Rob be so insensitive? "I'm sorry, sweetie."

"I'm not." Jessica closed the door behind her, and Lori thought her daughter, their daughter, was brave, but she was going to hurt for years to come.

CHAPTER 29

"Hey, what got into you? I thought you were an early riser."

Lori felt sudden light trying to make its way through her eyelids. What time was it? And who was screeching at her?

"Come on, wake up. I've got to talk to you."

Lori opened her eyes. The window blinds were up and Margot looked down on her with glistening red lips, subtly shadowed eyes, and a mug of steaming coffee in her hand. "With half-and-half the way you like it," Margot said and twisted herself down on the bed with one sinewy motion. Lori glanced at the digital clock, the only touch of modernity in the room, sitting on the blue bureau. The red numbers read ten thirty-three. She had slept almost eleven hours, which didn't surprise her. Ever since she was small, she had buried raging emotions in the soft cotton of sleep.

"Good morning," Lori said, as she sat up and shook herself awake. She moved over to make more room for Margot, taking the coffee mug from her. Margot was wearing turquoise terry-cloth shorts that showed off her milky white long legs and a black strapless top that was sure to give Warren heart palpitations. "What time did you leave to get up here?"

"I couldn't sleep. And I'm here to see Angie and you."

Lori raised an eyebrow. "Just us?"

Margot managed to look annoyed.

"Well, I'm glad you're here," Lori said, "but you can see me anytime in Hawthorne Park. I'm going back as soon as I get myself out of bed and dressed. What do you need to talk to me about so urgently?"

"Oh." Margot blinked and turned her head away toward the door.

Lori took hold of Margot's arm. "Are you okay?"

Margot looked back at Lori with a toss of her hair. "I should ask you that. Do you need an aspirin or anything? You were sleeping so soundly I was sure Warren got you drunk last night. That Beethoven of yours has been ringing I don't know how many times since I got here." She handed Lori's cell phone over. It had been sitting on the table by the door. "The notes sounded urgent."

Lori flipped the phone open and checked the screen.

"Who called?" Margot asked, leaning over to see.

"Rob." Last night's dream came back to her: Detective Scardini reading Rob his rights while Detective Mitchell handcuffed him. Instead of being upset, she had felt vindicated. Maybe he had been arrested for real. "I'd better get this."

Margot didn't budge while Lori took a long gulp of her coffee and punched in Rob's cell phone number.

"Where are you?" Rob asked.

His impatient tone told her he hadn't been arrested, which was great, but she had a mind to tell him it was none of his business where she was. Since she had an audience, she chose politeness. Chewing him out for asking Jessica if he could come home was for another time. "I'm at Warren's in Cape Cod, visiting Jessica."

"She didn't tell me."

"Is there any news?" Lori now wondered why he had called.

"Yes. Thank you for setting my own daughter against me."

"Jess didn't consult me."

"You've set her against me."

Lori knew Rob was waiting for her to answer, but Margot

was still glued to the bed and, anyway, it was a waste of breath to argue with him.

"I hear you've been seeing Jonathan Ashe," Rob said in a sugar-coated voice. "I wouldn't put my eggs in that man's basket if I were you."

Lori felt her cheeks pulse with heat.

"If you're wondering how I know, someone in the firm saw you and him all goo-goo-eyed at some waterside restaurant. He's not too dependable with the ladies or his business partners. I tried to save his neck at the old law firm, but they kicked him out anyway for working with a client behind the firm's back. At least I stopped them from prosecuting."

"How kind of you," Lori said with as much sarcasm as she could muster.

"You're damn right. It would have looked bad for the firm. Funny thing is, his mother thinks I'm the one who got him fired. Sent me countless letters of venom. She'd drop dead if she knew he gave me a million dollars of her money for the Waterside Properties deal."

Lori clutched the top of her pajamas. The burn was turning into a clammy coldness. "Did you pay him back?"

"He can wait. Your new boyfriend owes me his reputation, and I told him that I don't appreciate him going out with my wife, even if she is an ex."

Lori shook her head in disgust. Rob was unrecognizable. He had turned petty and mean. Vengeful. She turned to Margot, who was looking supportive at the end of the bed. "Do you mind?" Lori asked, nodding her head toward the door.

Margot shot up. "Sorry. Of course not." Two long strides and she was closing the door firmly behind her.

Lori brought the cell phone back to her cheek. "What did you do, Rob? Threaten to tell his mother or refuse to pay him back?"

"You should be thanking me."

"This is absurd! What do you care who I go out with? What business is it of yours?"

"I don't want you to demean yourself with worthless men. It reflects badly on me. And I don't want him anywhere near Jessica. He's perfectly capable of seducing her."

Lori cringed as nausea edged up her throat. "Please stay out of my life," she said and flipped the phone shut. She felt seasick, with everything shifting and changing underneath her feet. Lori slipped down and pulled the covers over her head and, in the warm darkness, waited for the nausea to subside.

Maybe stress and grief were turning Rob into this awful person and soon, with the murderer found and time passing, he would turn back into the good father he had always been. She at least was well rid of him. The thought reassured Lori. She slipped out of bed and opened the bedroom door. Margot was sitting at the bottom of the stairs, carefully covering her legs with suntan lotion.

"I'll be right down," Lori called out.

Margot looked up at her. "You okay?"

"Yeah. He was just being obnoxious."

"Hurry on down. Warren is making French toast."

Lori began to dress. If what Rob had said about Jonathan was true, then Jonathan had consistently lied to her, about why he left the law firm, about not knowing Valerie, about not having enough money for Waterside Properties. What else had he lied about?

"Warren called me last night," Margot said, lowering the large brim of her straw hat over her eyes. "That's what brought me up here." Lori and Margot were alone, walking barefoot along the beach, Gertie panting behind them. A thick wall of clouds hid the sun and a strong sea breeze kept the air cool. After breakfast, which both Lori and Margot had barely touched, Warren had whisked the girls away to town to buy tickets for tonight's pop concert. Margot was going to stay over.

Lori rolled up her pant cuffs and splashed her feet in the water of the bay, which was surprisingly cold. She looked back at Margot, standing still, face hidden by her outsized hat, arms and legs shiny with suntan lotion. "He still loves you," Lori said, "and I think you're still in love with him, too. Am I wrong?"

Margot joined Lori and they started walking slowly, their feet dragging through the shallow water. "I've told so many lies to you, and Jan and Beth, some outright, some by omission. I don't know where to start."

Lori linked her arm in Margot's. "I'll make it easy for you. Beth sneaked a look at your driver's license once, so we know your real age. And we think you had work done on your face because you're too gorgeous and young-looking for words, and we're jealous."

Margot's body started shaking. Startled, Lori quickly peeked under Margot's hat to see that she was laughing without making sound. "What's so funny?"

"You are." Margot threw her arms around Lori. "You're wonderful and I don't deserve you."

This was a first. Lori didn't know what to make of it. "What's wrong?"

Margot kicked the water hard. Gertie ran to catch the arching splash. "I'm what is wrong. I've been such an idiot. Okay, let me explain. My divorce. Remember what I told you?"

Lori nodded. "That Warren bored you and you had met another man, and then it didn't work out."

"And you all felt sorry for me and were really sweet. And Callie stopped being nice to me because she thought I'd left a loving husband for no good reason. Well, she was wrong, but I couldn't even tell my best friends. I made up the story about the other man because I was too ashamed to tell you the truth."

Margot dropped down in the water, hitching her knees up to her chest. To keep her company, Lori joined her, trying not to gasp at the icy water seeping into her slacks.

"Warren never stopped seeing Valerie from the days they were dating," Margot said. "She had some kind of hold on him. It had to be more than sex because the two of us always set fireworks off in bed, and I don't know what more a man could want. And I thought we were really close. He kept telling me how much he loved me, but he couldn't stay away from her. When I found out, he was willing to give her up. He promised he'd never see her again, but I was too angry, humiliated, ashamed, I don't know what else. I wanted him to suffer as much as he had made me suffer. The humiliation was the worst. I couldn't face up to it. I know that doesn't say a lot about me, but I can't help it. I was so proud of being Warren's wife. Dumb me, whose only career is looking good, snagging this incredibly successful man who has a brain the size of Manhattan. Can you understand?"

"Now I do." Lori gave Margot a smile of reassurance. "I'm sorry I didn't before."

"Don't blame yourself. I'm a good actress."

Lori laughed. "That's the career you should have gone for." But as a good friend, she should have seen through Margot's bluster, the way she should have understood Beth's loneliness. Lori hugged her knees to her chest in imitation of Margot. "I think Warren was equally proud of having landed gorgeous, funny, generous, not in the least bit dumb you."

"Then why did he continue seeing her?"

"He wanted another feather in his cap? Having two women made him feel on top of the world? Who can figure what makes a man act like a jerk? Then once you left, I imagine he got very angry you wouldn't forgive him. And he's a proud man. He kept seeing Valerie to show you and maybe himself that he didn't need you."

"He wants us to get back together, but I'm not sure."

"Do you still love him?"

"I thought for a while I had stopped. I've been feeling young and excited again. Do you remember that feeling? Waking up in the morning, expecting something wonderful to happen, but not knowing what?" Margot had her head down, talking to her knees. "Then something not wonderful happened, and I felt like yesterday's trash, but now I think all I wanted to do with all my dating around was get back at Warren. He's the one I still love, but the problem with being cheated on, it shakes your belief in people. I don't know who to believe, who to trust. I'm always questioning what everyone says. It's awful. You know what I'm talking about."

"Unfortunately I do."

"If I go back to Warren, how do I know he won't cheat on me again?"

"I can't answer that. I doubt that Warren could." Lori didn't think much of Warren any more, but she told Margot that he did love her and Valerie could no longer do any harm. "It's up to you to take the risk. If you love him."

"I do."

"If you're sure, forgive him."

A gust of wind lifted Margot's hat off her head. She didn't seem to notice. "Warren did call Valerie when she was driving the girls back. He told me last night and that you'd asked him about it. You're not thinking he killed Valerie, are you?" There wasn't a speck of doubt in her eyes.

Lori shook her head. "I don't see motive." Unless Valerie was blackmailing Warren to stay with her. Unless killing her was the only way of ridding himself of her and getting Margot back. Yesterday she had thought Warren was not dangerous, but who knew? She was glad Margot was staying over with the girls.

Margot ran a hand through her hair and looked around for her hat. It was floating out with the ebb tide, Gertie swimming after it. "Good girl!" Margot called out. "Bring it home. Those two detectives, Scardini and Mitchell, found out about the affair, and they've been buzzing around Warren with their stingers out. They even asked me if I'd killed her to get my husband back. Thank God I have an alibi."

Lori remembered what Callie had told her. Margot had gone out shortly after the girls came home. "What is your alibi?"

"You're going to get angry."

Lori didn't think she had any anger left over. It was all aimed at Rob. "Margot, just tell me."

"I left the girls alone and drove to the Rye Hilton, which is in the other direction from where Valerie was killed. The bartender knows me and confirmed my story." Gertie dropped the hat in front of Margot, who gave her a quick pat on the head. "The girls are thirteen, they're fine by themselves. Please don't be upset with me."

So that was Margot's lie of omission, Lori thought as she grabbed the hat before it floated back out. She had left Jessica alone in the house at night a few times, but only to pick up a pizza or go to the store. Never more than thirty minutes. "Next time tell me beforehand, okay?"

Margot crinkled her eyes. "I'm sorry."

"Accepted. Does Warren have an alibi?"

"No. That's what I'm worried about. God, I'm completely soaked." Margot swung her knees down in the water and stood up. She held out a hand to help Lori up. "Let's go change."

"I have nothing to change into," Lori admitted. She was wearing yesterday's slacks with a clean shirt.

"I'll lend you something."

"I'll never get into it. I'll use your dryer."

As they walked back to the house, all three trailing water, Margot said, "The detectives wanted to know what Warren's phone call was about. He says he told Valerie that he wasn't going to see her again. Do you think that's true?"

What he had said to Valerie didn't matter anymore, Lori thought. Warren wanted his wife back and Margot wanted him back. Voicing her own doubts would accomplish nothing. She said, "Why should Warren lie at this point?"

Lori was back in Hawthorne Park by four thirty in the afternoon, after promising Jess and Margot that she'd be back on Saturday to celebrate the Fourth together. She headed straight for the supermarket to shop for tonight's gnocchi dinner with Alec. She looked forward to the evening. He would bring a welcome pause, a sense of peace. No, not peace. A sense of fun, Lori remembered, seeing him in her head again with the smile that was both quiet and mischievous. She found him sexy, despite his preference for men. Maybe because of it. "Nothing makes you drool like something out of reach," Ellie liked to say, but she was talking about the roasted peppers her aging stomach couldn't digest any more.

In the produce section, Beethoven's notes rang out. An older fellow shopper gave her a dirty look as Lori scrambled through her purse to find the loud phone. Lori had called Ellie on her drive down to say everything was fine. Beth she had saved for later, when she was home. It would be a long conversation and she wanted to concentrate on her driving.

"How did it go?" Beth didn't like to wait.

Keeping her voice low, Lori told Beth about her visit to Rob's office and her overnight stay with Warren and the girls. While she talked, phone clutched in one hand, she continued to shop with her free arm. A dangling microphone would have made life easier at this moment, but Lori refused to use one, convinced people talking into them looked like they had no one in the world except their crazy selves. Whatever happened to her, however real that image might become once Jessica left home, Lori did not want to look the part. She and Margot had a similar need to keep up a front. Maybe all single women did.

While Lori handpicked four large impeccable russet potatoes, she told Beth that she had resolved a few puzzles: Rob had admitted being in debt and hadn't paid back the people who had invested with him. In the pasta and sauces lane, she added that Jonathan was one of those investors. Rob owed him a million dollars of Mrs. Ashe's money and, if Rob was to be believed, had told her, Lori, a lot of lies. She hated to admit it, because Jonathan had been charming and fun in a smarmy way and she had almost gone to bed with him, in fact had wanted very much to go to bed with him, but, "We have to consider him a suspect now. He's got plenty of motive."

"The police haven't arrested him so he's got to have an alibi," Beth said, always ready to reason through things, an ability Lori knew she didn't always have. She took a carton of Pomi crushed tomatoes from the shelf and remembered Margot's alibi— drinking in the bar of the Rye Hilton where the bartender knew her well. Margot wasn't one to go to bars alone. Who was she drinking with that night? Not Warren. She had admitted he didn't have an alibi.

"Earth to Lori—come in, Lori?" Beth said.

"Sorry, I was thinking." Lori pushed her cart to the refrigerated cheese bin at the back of the store. She needed mascarpone—a thick, rich, soft cheese not unlike cream cheese—which was the one ingredient she hadn't guessed while eating gnocchi della regina in Rome. "I was thinking about Margot. She's been seeing someone. Do you think it could be Jonathan?"

Beth didn't answer right away. Lori pictured her frowning slightly while her brain received the question, spun the words around like Lotto numbers, then spit out the winning answer.

"You're not interested in Jonathan anymore?" Beth asked.

"You were right. I'm not interested in cheap fun."

"Margot dating Jonathan would explain her reaction in the coffee shop when you told us you'd gone out with him," she said.

"What reaction?" Lori hadn't noticed anything.

"She didn't like it. Then Margot got nasty with Jan. That was right after you told us. She left abruptly, too."

Lori remembered Margot's surprising tears crying in her kitchen last Saturday, while she was preparing for Mrs. Ashe's dinner. She had thought Margot was upset about telling the police she hadn't been able to reach Lori on her home phone when Valerie was murdered, but then Margot had talked about Jonathan. "Do you like him?" she had asked.

"Why didn't you say anything?" Lori now asked Beth.

"I didn't want to spoil your fun with Jonathan. I thought she was jealous that she hadn't gotten to him first."

"She's not that petty. You know she isn't."

"Petty has nothing to do with it. I was jealous of you when you were married, that your husband was still alive and mine was not. I'm sure you've been jealous of someone sometime or other."

Lori had to laugh. "Yes, of your strength."

"My strength? That's a good one. Anyway I've made my point. What else?"

"The night Valerie died," Lori said, "Margot left the girls at home alone and went to bar of the Rye Town Hilton. She could have had a date with Jonathan."

"Ask her."

"I will." She would call her after she'd gotten the sauce under way. Lori unearthed the mascarpone from under a pile of Brie and added it to her cart. She was done shopping. It was time to go home and cook. "I've got to go home. Alec's coming over for dinner."

"That's great," Beth said. "Listen, Lori, remember that Rob's a good liar so take what he tells you with a grain of salt."

"He told Jonathan to stop seeing me." She explained that was probably why Jonathan had planned to cancel the weekend getaway, except she had done it first.

"Rob's jealous now that he's wifeless. Give him a few days and he'll ask to come back home."

Lori didn't tell Beth he already had asked. Only for a few days, though. As if her home was a hotel he could come in and out of at will. It was too humiliating for Jess. For herself. Which reminded her of Margot's "lies." Walking to the car, she filled Beth in on what Margot had told her on the beach that morning. Beth's reaction was a low whistle, followed by silence and then, "What a mess we get ourselves into over men."

There was no answer at Warren's house. They were probably all in town having an early dinner before the concert. Lori left a message on Margot's cell. She remembered she still hadn't talked to Seth to get his version of what had happened between him and Rob the night of the murder. She punched in his number.

Janet answered and told her he wasn't home, that she didn't know where he could be reached. "I've told you everything that happened," she said in an angry tone. "He's not going to solve the murder for you. He didn't kill Valerie. Leave him alone. Please. We've had enough questioning from the police."

Lori stopped stirring the sauce. "Jan, please understand. Maybe there's something he knows without being aware of it. If he goes over it with me, maybe—"

"Maybe nothing. He's gone over it a thousand times. You can take his story, shake it to death, and all that's going to come out

is the same story. Please, Lori, just leave us alone for a while."
The anger in Janet's voice eased. "Seth and I have a lot of sort-
ing out to do between ourselves."

"Oh Janet, I didn't stop to think." Lori was chagrined. She
was being so self-involved that she hadn't thought about the
state of Janet's marriage. Seth taking his wife's inheritance
money on the sly was as bad as having an affair. Maybe. "I'm so
sorry you're going through this. Is there can anything I can
do?"

"I'm just so angry at him."

If their marriage broke up, they would both be devastated,
Lori was sure of it. "You are each other's backbone, try to
remember that."

"Backbones can break," Janet said. "I have to go."

"I'll see you at Callie's on Monday?"

"I don't know."

"Please try," Lori said, hoping she hadn't ruined a friendship.
"Good luck."

"Good luck to you, too." Janet hung up.

Lori put the potatoes to boil. She could understand Janet's
anger at Seth, at the murder, at the two years she had struggled
for money, at anything that had put her once well-ordered life
in jeopardy. Janet's anger at her, Lori—did it have anything to
do with being afraid of the questions she might ask Seth? Did
Janet have doubts about his story? Seth had reason to kill
Valerie. As did Ruth and Jonathan. But Seth had somehow
known about the will, and he had been the one to call Rob at
Pastis to make an appointment so that Valerie had to drive the
girls home. An appointment with Rob to which he had not
shown up. Did he instead follow Valerie?

CHAPTER 30

The sauce was gurgling on the stove, filling the kitchen with the sweet smell of tomatoes enhanced with onions, celery, carrots, and a hint of nutmeg. The basil, lemon zest, and mascarpone would be added just before serving, along with a few dollops of butter and some grated nutmeg. When the phone rang, Lori was bent over the kitchen counter. She had just finished kneading the mashed potatoes, eggs, and flour into a mound of firm, moist dough. Now she was dividing the dough into six equal pieces to then roll them out into long snakes, which she would cut into three-quarter-inch pieces. She would have more gnocchi than she needed for dinner, but she planned to freeze the rest for when Jessica came home. Across the room the phone kept ringing while Lori went to the sink to wash her hands. She heard the click of the answering machine pick up as she grabbed a towel and rushed to catch the call.

"Lori, Kate here. I'm so sorry, I—"

Rob's secretary. She sounded as if she'd been crying. Lori lifted the receiver so quickly it hit her ear. "Kate, I'm here. What's wrong?"

Kate inhaled loudly. "They arrested him."

Lori felt a suffocating weight move down her body, like concrete being poured into an empty shell. "Rob?" she managed to squeak.

"We were working late together and those two detectives came and they handcuffed him and read him his rights just like on TV. It was so familiar it didn't sink in. Not until Rob told me to call his lawyer. I'm so sorry."

"Give me the lawyer's name and phone number." She jotted them down, thanked Kate, and hung up. Slowly feeling began to pour back into her veins. From being cold and rigid she went to the opposite extreme, burning with a seething anger at police incompetence, at Rob's stupidity, at her own incapacity to help. She knew Rob was innocent. He was Jess's father. He had to be!

Lew Lichtman of Lichtman, Ferris, and Quintero had left for the day and his secretary wouldn't give Lori his cell phone number, but promised to tell him to call her. Lori called Ellie next and told her.

"Hon, maybe Rob's—"

Lori cut her off. "He's not. You've got to call Joey Pellegrino!" She tried to keep her voice at a reasonable volume. "Ask him why? What evidence do they have?"

"Joey's wife is back."

"Call him anyway."

"He's angry at me because I told him we couldn't go on."

"Mom, just call him! Please!"

"Let me finish, Loretta! This has to do with you. I'm not going to see him anymore because I've been thinking of you and what you went through with Rob, and here I was about to do the same thing to Joey's wife and I'm ashamed of myself."

"Oh, Mom, please don't be ashamed." Her mother's unexpected sweetness was too much right now. Lori couldn't make room for it in a head filled with thoughts of Rob arrested and Jess possibly losing a father. "I do need your help."

"I know. I know. I'll call him, even though it's going to kill me, but he's a cop so I wouldn't bet on him telling me anything that might help Rob. Besides, I hurt his pride."

"Thanks, Mom. I really appreciate it." Her mouth went dry.

"Now I have to call Jess."

"What for?"

"She needs to know."

"And what is Jess going to do with knowing tonight? Lie awake all night, crying her heart out, thinking her life is over? Is that what you want for her?"

"I'll drive up, stay with her."

"So both of you will be basket cases. Listen to me. Bad news should come in the morning when you can see the sun has come up anyway and birds are still flying. And you need to stay here and find out what's up first anyway. I'll call Joey now." Ellie hung up.

Lori went back to the kitchen counter and started to cut the gnocchi. Keeping her hands busy calmed her. Maybe Ellie was right. Tonight Jess was at a concert and would come home too late for the evening news. Lori needed to call Warren and leave him a message. She didn't want Jess to see the morning paper before she got up there. God, what if Jess came back from the concert and turned on a computer to read her e-mails. Would Rob's face appear in a little square on the AOL home page? "Lawyer Arrested in Second Wife's Murder. Millions at Stake."

On Warren's cell, Lori left a message. "Rob has been arrested. Please don't let Jess see the evening news, or tomorrow's paper, or turn on a computer. I want her to sleep tonight. I'm coming up early in the morning." She would set the alarm for four a.m. With no traffic on the road, she would be in Chatham by ten in the morning. Thank God Jess was a late sleeper.

Lori fished Detective Scardini's card from her purse and called his cell. There was no answer. She didn't leave a message.

She went back to cutting the snakes of dough, rolling each piece on the tines of a fork to give it a striped pattern. She kept cutting and rolling, her hands trembling occasionally, until there was no more dough left. She left the gnocchi for tonight's dinner on a spread-out kitchen towel and put the rest in the freezer. After putting the phone receiver in her apron pocket, she went out to the patio to set the table. Lori knew she needed to call Alec and cancel tonight's dinner. What kind of company was she going to be in her state of anger, confusion, fear? But the thought of being left alone, isolated, waiting for Rob's lawyer or Ellie to call, terrified her.

She cut what was left of the yellow cabbage roses and summer snow. Nothing else was flowering yet. Several times she checked the phone to make sure the dial tone was there. Back inside, she arranged the flowers in the blue ceramic pot that had come with Alec's flowers. Her flowers looked a little straggly in the large vase, but it didn't matter. Nothing mattered right now except clearing Rob. Lori took the phone out of her apron and punched Seth's number.

"No, he's not here," Janet said, barely holding back her impatience. "I'm giving the kids a bath. I have to go." The dial tone filled Lori's ear.

With the next call Lori got lucky. Jonathan answered his cell.

"You've been dating Margot, haven't you?" she asked after giving her name. She wasn't in the mood for the niceties of "Hi, how are you? Please forgive me but the reason I called is I needed to know if . . ."

Jonathan didn't answer.

"It's not an accusation, Jonathan. I don't mind if you are or were. I need to know, that's all. Actually all I want to know is if you were with Margot at the bar in the Rye Hilton the night Valerie was killed."

"What is this? Did the police hire you to check alibis? Are you suspecting Margot now?"

"I hired myself and no, I'm not suspecting Margot. I wanted to spare her the embarrassment of asking her directly. She might think I cared for you."

Another few seconds of silence. Then Jonathan said, "Yes, I've been dating her. Nothing serious. I didn't tell you because I didn't know where you and I were going yet. And yes, I was with her that night." He let out a small, timid laugh and said in a voice that brushed her ear like a feather, "You're angry at me so now that makes me a suspect?"

Looking back on the moment, Lori knew she should have calmly replaced the receiver in its cradle without uttering a word, but she was too enraged to hold back. "You owe your mother a million dollars and if word of that got out someone might look into why you left the law firm and then your mother would cut you out of her will and probably die of a heart attack and no one would close any deals with you. Yes, alibi or not, you're on the suspect list and no, I'm not angry at you!" He didn't matter enough to her.

The doorbell rang.

"Rob must have told you," Jonathan said. "He doesn't like sharing his ex-wife. I am sorry, Lori. About us, Margot, about my mother. I wanted to hit it big, you see. Prove my father wrong. He never thought I was worth much and I've only proved him right." His voice was raw, his usual bewitching tones gone. "I'm not happy about it. At least believe that."

"I do." She felt Jonathan meant it. He was a weak, insecure man who had had bad parenting, but somehow she couldn't feel sorry for him. The doorbell rang again. "Goodbye, Jonathan. Thank you for answering my question."

When she opened the front door, the pleasant sight of Alec with a wine bottle in one hand and a large bunch of daisies in the other filled her threshold. The smile on his face slowly disappeared as Lori moved aside to let him in. "Something bad has happened," he said.

Lori nodded, fighting tears. Still holding the wine and the daisies, Alec opened up his arms. She walked into them, felt them wrap around her, and felt like the girl she had been before her father died, safe, innocent, sure that life would only bring good things. She breathed in the clean starched smell of his cotton shirt and let herself cry. Alec rocked her gently, asked no questions and waited. Lori didn't know how long she stayed in his arms. Long enough to leave mascara stains on his white shirt. Long enough to need to blow her nose three times with his handkerchief. Long enough to feel embarrassed. Long enough to feel better.

"Thank you and I'm sorry," she said, pulling away.

"Don't be." Alec raised his arms. "I think a vase and two glasses are called for."

Lori walked with him to the kitchen, forgetting to close the front door. While she got glasses and a corkscrew and he arranged the daisies around her flowers, she told him about Rob's arrest, how she was waiting to find out what evidence the police had uncovered to incriminate him. "I'm sorry, I should have canceled tonight."

"I'm very glad you didn't." Alec looked at her with a gentle expression, full of concern. Lori felt embraced again.

"We're friends," he said.

"Yes, we are." Lori handed him the corkscrew and, embarrassed by the strength of her feeling, went to fill the pasta pot with water. While Alec uncorked the bottle, she placed the glasses on a wicker tray along with a bowl of olives and a wedge of Parmesan cheese.

The phone in her pocket rang just as they reached the patio. She had forgotten to take off her apron. Lew Lichtman, Rob's lawyer, introduced himself and told her not to worry. "There is no way the DA's going to put this case through. All they've got is a scrap of evidence that proves nothing. By tomorrow afternoon, Rob Staunton will be a free man again."

Lori felt her muscles relax at the good news. She held on to the table edge to steady herself. "What *is* the evidence?"

"An employee of Fast Rent-a-Car alleges that Rob came into his office around ten o'clock to rent a car the night Valerie Staunton was killed. That made the detectives very happy because, as you recall, Mrs. Staunton was driving Rob's car that night and the killer, whoever he or she is, needed a car to get to her."

Lori clutched Alec's hand. The olive he was about to pop in his mouth landed on his lap while Lori prepared herself for the worst. Rob indicted, Rob on trial. "Now there's no reason to push the panic button," Lichtman said in the hushed voice a doctor might use after he's delivered the bad news. "According to this man's testimony, Rob wanted to pay cash for the car. When this man explained company policy allowed payment only with a credit card, Rob walked out and supposedly drove off with one of the cars anyway."

Rob was going to be found guilty. He would get twenty-five to life. "How can you call that a scrap of evidence?" Lori asked, her voice a shrill complaint.

"Because the employee can't prove it. Rob categorically denies the allegations. He took a long walk on Fifth Avenue, along Central Park. He had a lot on his mind. He was upset about his debts, about having hurt the friends who had trusted him with their money, about his lovely young daughter who was suffering because of the divorce."

This is what he's going to say in the courtroom, Lori thought. *He's trying out his summation on me.*

"The employee can't even produce the car that Rob supposedly drove off with, claims he doesn't know which one it was. How can that be? Why did he wait so long to come forward? The case has been on television, in the papers. Why didn't he tell his superiors at the Fast Rent-a-Car agency that a car was stolen? And the man has a record, petty theft and extortion.

Someone put him up to this, I'm sure of it. As I said, the DA's going to dismiss the case. The police need to do a whole lot more legwork before they can pin this murder on your ex-husband." He hung up.

"Rob's lawyer says it's going to be all right," Lori said, relinquishing Alec's hand.

"Good." He cut a piece of Parmesan cheese. She looked down at his slacks and saw the oil stain the olive had left.

"I did that, didn't I?" Lori said.

Alec dropped the cheese into her mouth. "Now we're almost even." He waited for her to finish chewing to ask, "I'm here to listen all night if you want."

"Thanks, but I invited you to eat." She needed to insulate herself from reality for a while. Her heartbeat needed to slow down. "*Gnocchi della regina* coming up." She offered a smile and left him to go heat the sauce and throw the gnocchi into the boiling water. As she waited for the gnocchi to float back up to the surface—a matter of a few minutes—the stifling weight settled back on her chest. Could Rob be guilty? Had he been that desperate? She had to admit that during the arc of their marriage he had become a man who worried about appearances, who sought and thrived on power. Not raising enough money to close the Waterside Properties deal, having Valerie refuse to help him, and owing money must have been unbearably humiliating. Worst of all, his new wife told him she loved another man. For many men, that was enough to kill.

Lori looked into the pot. The gnocchi were floating, ready to get out. No, she had to trust her knowledge of Rob, gathered through the years of living together, sensing his disappointments, watching his reactions to the good and bad in their lives. He was not a murderer.

As Lori checked the boiling gnocchi, she heard footsteps and turned around with a welcome on her face for Alec. Seth, a scowl on his face, was standing by the refrigerator.

Startled, Lori dropped the skimmer in the water. "How did you get in?"

"The front door was open."

Lori wiped her hands on her apron even though they were clean. Now that he was here, looking at her fiercely, she wasn't sure how to start. And his timing couldn't have been worse. "They've arrested Rob," she finally said.

His shoulders sagged. "Shit!"

He's upset, Lori thought. *He can't be guilty, then.* "I need your help, Seth. You know Rob is innocent. Please tell me what happened that day? You called Rob when he was going to the lawyer that morning. Is that how you knew about the will? Did you tell anyone else?"

Seth straightened himself up again, the fierce scowl back on his face. "Look, I don't know anything and I don't appreciate you bugging us. I know what you're trying to do." His voice got louder as he got closer.

Lori stepped away from the boiling pot. "Seth, I'm not trying—"

"You'd like to pin the murder on me."

Lori shook her head but couldn't bring herself to deny it out loud.

"Let's get Seth hauled off to jail. That way Janet gets rid of a thief of a husband, Rob gets to keep his money, and one day Jess will be wallowing in dough."

"Everything okay?" Alec asked from the back door.

"We're fine," Lori said with a laugh and turned back to Seth, who looked as though he had just seen a rat cross his path. "Why don't you join us for dinner, Seth?" Alec's presence made her magnanimous. "The gnocchi are mush by now, but I've got more in the freezer and the sauce should be good."

"No."

"Well, then sit down and have a glass of wine. I don't want us to fight." Lori retrieved the skimmer from the boiling water and slipped the gnocchi into a colander. They didn't look too bad, she thought at the same time as she remembered something Seth had just said. When she turned around, Alec was gone and Seth was sitting at the kitchen table. He looked miserable and harmless. She picked up a few gnocchi with a spoon, dipped them in the sauce and held them out to Seth as a peace offering just as Alec came back from the patio with the white wine and the glasses, which he put on the table.

"I'll be on the patio," he said and slipped out the kitchen door.

Seth ate the gnocchi. "Good," he mumbled. His expression had softened, whether due to the gnocchi or Alec's absence, Lori couldn't tell.

"Want more?"

He shook his head and Lori sat down next to him. "What did you mean by Rob getting to keep his money if you were the murderer?"

"Not just me. Anyone but him. It's the Son of Sam law."

"What's that?"

"A New York State law that says a person convicted of a crime cannot profit from that crime. So if Rob's found guilty, he doesn't get Valerie's money, and I don't get my money back. I mean Janet's money." No wonder Rob's arrest upset him.

Lori filled Seth's glass with wine and poured herself the same large dose. She took a long sip. Jonathan had an alibi. He was with Margot at the Rye Hilton. Where had Seth been that night? Lori wanted to get up and check that Alec was still on the patio, not too far away, but she was afraid Seth would catch on and bolt. Instead she took another long sip and then watched Seth drink his glass dry.

"What prompted you to call Rob that night?" Lori asked.

"You had already spoken to him in the morning."

"I was furious. I couldn't hold back."

"So you made an appointment you didn't keep. Where?"

"I suggested Pat's Place, an Irish pub on Second Avenue. Shit, we used to go there a lot together. When we were friends. The bartender knows us. I thought it would keep me under control."

"But you didn't show up. And Rob didn't stay long enough to establish an alibi."

Seth looked up from his empty glass. "I was at Pat's. That's where I called him from. Then I had two or three shots and I got angrier and angrier. I wanted to break a bottle on Rob's face. That's when I decided to leave. I'd warned Jonathan I couldn't handle it."

Lori felt herself go quiet. "Jonathan?"

"Yeah. He's owed money, too. More than me, but he said Rob could make big trouble for him so he wanted me to confront Rob that night, scare him into paying us back."

Lori got up, the quiet replaced by a gale whirling inside her. She stumbled upstairs to her bedroom. She had to call Margot.

When Lori didn't come back down after ten minutes, Seth let himself out the front door, making sure it was firmly closed behind him. Out on the patio, Alec had listened to the steady murmur coming from the kitchen, ready to intervene if necessary. He finished the Parmesan and the olives and wished he'd kept a glass of wine for himself. When the silence from the kitchen grew suspicious, he tiptoed inside the house. Confronted by an empty kitchen, he called out Lori's name. He walked into the hall and called out again. Still no answer. He climbed the stairs. Lori's bedroom door was open. He could see the end of the bed, a pair of tan slippers upside down on the pale yellow carpet. He knocked on the doorjamb, called out a soft "Lori?"

An unintelligible murmur answered. She was sitting on the bed, legs dangling, her expression lax. "Hey, are you okay?"

Lori tried to smile, but didn't find the strength. She was tired. She wanted to tell Alec that it was over. Almost over. She patted a spot next to her on the bed, and when he sat down where she had indicated, she leaned her head on his shoulder. "I owe you a dinner."

He put his arm around her. "I expect a rain check."

"I called Detective Scardini," Lori said. "He was in the middle of dinner, but he listened. He's going to talk to Seth tonight. Margot's driving down with Angie and Jess. But he's not willing to let Rob go yet. He needs hard evidence." Lori was aware that Alec didn't know who all these people were, but she wanted to get the story off her chest. There was time later to explain. "He came late, you see. Margot waited a good half hour at the bar. He said he had a flat tire. He knew about Valerie driving the girls from Margot. The next morning I saw him at the car wash with Jan. They were both getting their cars cleaned. I didn't remember that, didn't make the connection. I thought he was sexy. I almost went to bed with him."

"Ah, Jonathan."

"Yes, him." She couldn't say his name. "It looks like he killed Valerie. It makes me sick to think of it."

Lori felt the weight of Alec's chin on top of her head. "I'm sorry," he said.

She was sorry, too, Lori realized hours later, while she sat downstairs in the kitchen, waiting for Jessica to come home. As the time passed, her heart swelled with regret and sadness. For Jess who only had a part-time father still in jail. For Rob, who was left with money but no wife. For Margot, who had let herself be fooled by Jonathan's charm. For proud Mrs. Ashe, who would not be able to live the shame down.

For Jonathan, she felt anger. For screwing up his privileged life. There were kids walking the city streets who grew up with poverty, with bad parents, if any, with bad schools and danger-ous so-called friends, and yet some—no, many—of them found the strength to fight for themselves, work hard, lead honest lives. Against all odds.

CHAPTER 31

Friday morning, thirty-six hours after Lori had called Detective Scardini from her bedroom, the usual breakfast group, expanded to include Ellie, Jessica, and Angie, met at Callie's. Callie, noticing that everyone's face was marked by more emotions than she could read, quickly sat them at a round table in the back of the diner, out of earshot of the other customers.

"They're releasing Dad today," Jessica blurted out to Callie as she sat down. Lori had told the others over the phone. It was the reason she had asked them to meet at Callie's—the place where they had shared so many details of their lives. The meeting would be a strange combination of celebration and regret.

Callie patted Lori's shoulder and grinned back at Jessica. "That good news deserves champagne, but you're underage and I don't have a liquor license. How about orange juice on the house?"

"And a slice of apple pie, please." Jessica grinned back, happy excitement glittering in her eyes.

Angie asked for the same. No one else felt like eating, and they ordered only coffee. Callie, who was known for loud rumblings if her customers didn't order enough to put some money in the cash register, said nothing and left.

"What hard evidence do the police have against Jonathan?" Beth asked Lori.

"His car gave him away. The forensic people found traces of Valerie's blood. The car wash people told Detective Scardini that Jonathan had his car washed four times in the four days following the murder, but it turns out they didn't wash the space underneath the accelerator. Jonathan's shoes must have gotten blood on them when he stuffed Valerie's body in the trunk of her car."

Janet shuddered. "To think I was with him the next morning," she said, "while our cars were getting washed, talking about Rob owing us money and he had already killed her."

"What about the car rental employee's story?" Beth asked.

"He was lying," Ellie said. "For two thousand dollars in cash that he tried to deposit yesterday."

Lori was surprised. "I didn't know that."

"Now you do."

"Joey Pellegrino?"

Ellie's flicker of annoyance was replaced by a stone face. "Valerie's cousin Ruth paid him. She'd inherit if Rob was found guilty of Valerie's murder."

Callie stepped forward with Angie and Jessica's orders on a tray, her forehead bunched into a formidable frown. "All right, girls, apple pie has to be eaten up in the first booth, otherwise it'll make you sick to your stomach." She gestured with her head toward the front of the diner.

Jessica groaned. "I want to hear all the details."

"Not in my diner, you don't. People fight to get in that booth. Come on. Up front you go." She walked away with a steep sway of her hips that brooked no argument. The apple pies and orange juices went with her.

"Go, honey," Lori said. "She's right."

Angie got up. "Jess, let's go. Everything is going to be on the Internet anyway. I'm hungry." She pulled Jessica up from her chair.

"But we watch *Criminal Minds*!" Jessica protested to Callie, letting herself be dragged by Angie.

"How did Jonathan know about the will?" Beth asked once the girls were gone.

"Seth says he didn't tell him," Janet said.

Lori looked down at the Formica table. She didn't know how to answer without being disloyal. "Maybe Rob told him." It was possible.

"I told him," Margot said, giving Lori a quick grateful smile. "I called Warren Monday morning about a tax-related issue, and he told me he couldn't talk right then because Rob and Valerie were in the waiting room. I asked why and he told me."

"Isn't that violating client confidentiality?" Beth asked.

Margot bristled. "Warren's always trusted me with information, but I wanted to be catty and make fun of Valerie's greed so I told Jonathan, you know, just a little piece of harmless gossip and then he went and—" Two forefingers flew to her eyes to stop tears from coming. She tried to laugh. "I won't cry. Too demeaning. Too much mascara."

Lori put her arm around Margot. She understood how betrayed she felt. First Warren, now Jonathan.

Janet offered a handkerchief. "It's really Beth's. She gave it to me last time we were in here. It's clean."

Margot's hands came down from her face. She batted tears from her eyelashes a couple of times. "I'm fine. Thanks."

"It's not your fault," Beth said. "Jonathan would have found out about the will sooner or later and then killed her. Come on, buck up, Margot. We love you."

"Thanks." She didn't look convinced.

"Believe Beth," Lori said. "We do."

Margot nodded.

Callie appeared with coffee for everyone. She gave Margot a quick look and handed out the cups. Her frown was gone.

"Jessica wouldn't stay home," Ellie said to her. "Lori's a good mother."

"Who said she wasn't?" Callie asked. "I just figured that having a double set of thirteen-year-old ears around would cramp your style." She walked away.

"That woman's always got an answer." Ellie sounded annoyed and admiring at the same time. She looked around the table. No one said anything. "Okay, I get it. The pot calling the kettle black."

"Oh, no," Janet said. "You've been awfully quiet this morning." She looked and sounded happier than she had in the past ten days.

Ellie shrugged. "It's not my show. All right, so where were we?"

"Cheering up Margot," Beth said, just as Callie's arm, from behind her, lowered a plate with a huge wedge of the famous apple pie on it in front of Margot.

"Don't go thinking anything," Callie said in her best gruff tone. "I had extra."

Margot opened her mouth in a perfect cartoon character O. "Now I'm really going to cry." Callie beat a hasty retreat.

"See?" Beth said. "You've even got friends in unexpected places."

Margot blinked. "I have to go hug that woman." She got up and went looking for Callie.

"She's probably hiding in the men's room," Lori said.

"How are you feeling?" Beth asked Lori. "You've been through the wringer."

"Relieved, sad, angry, exhausted." She spoke in shorthand because all her feelings were still too raw to examine, to make sense of.

"Sorry," Beth said, understanding as she always did. "Another time, another place, weeks from now." She turned to look at Janet. "How about you? You've had a tough time, too."

"It's over now." Janet gave one of her isn't-life-a-day-at-the-beach smiles, what Ellie called her Sandra Dee grimace. "Seth's a good guy and the best father and I do love him. He's got a good job now and Rob's going to pay us interest on the loan. I can sleep at night now."

"Lori's left something out of this early morning tale," Ellie said while the others sipped their coffee with the satisfied look of a job done and over with. It gave her the itch to shake things up.

"What have I left out?" Lori asked. She wanted to go home now with Jess. Take care of her garden, shop for food, start normal life again. She had no idea why Ellie was grinning. "What, Mom?"

Ellie dropped her elbows on the table with an attention-getting thud. "During this whole crazy murder case, my daughter's fallen in love. Did she tell you gals?"

Lori banged her coffee cup back in its saucer. "Ellie!"

"That's right," Janet said. "You dated Jonathan." The second the words were out, she covered her mouth with a hand. "Oh, Lori, that's so sad."

"No, no." Lori pulled herself back from the table. "I wasn't in love with Jonathan. Ellie's just kidding."

"Not Jonathan," Ellie said. "The gay guy."

Margot slipped back into her chair. "That's taking playing it safe to a different level." She filled her cheeks with apple pie and happily munched like a squirrel with a just-found stash of nuts. "I couldn't find Callie," she said, dropping another forkful into her mouth. "I used to dream about this pie."

Lori felt her cheeks get hot. "I am not, I go on record, in love with Alec. I like him, admire him, respect him, consider him a wonderful friend, but—"

Ellie interrupted with a coffee spoon pointed at Lori. "Loretta Corvino, your face has been a dead giveaway ever since you turned twelve and started growing breasts. For one thing, you break out. You've got two pimples on your chin."

Lori's fingers went to cover them. "That's stress."

"Then your cheeks get all splotchy like someone's been pinching them for hours. And you look prettier than ever. Look at yourself in the mirror if you don't believe me."

"You do look good, hon," Beth agreed. "And considering what you've just been through, that's a miracle."

"Very pretty," Janet agreed. "But Lori's always looked good."

"If you hear her start hiccupping out of the blue, then she's in love la-la land and we've lost her for good. So far, so good. No hiccups."

"None of this is true," Lori protested.

Margot looked up from her plate to peer at Lori. "Are you going to start hiccupping now?"

"No!" Lori glared at her mother. Why had she brought this up?

As mothers sometimes do, Ellie answered Lori's thought. "I want your friends to know because you're going to need them to help you pick up the pieces." Ellie looked back at the front of the room and beckoned with a wave of her arm. Alec stood up from the booth where Jessica and Angie were sitting, and walked down the narrow aisle between counter and booths.

Lori watched him approaching. She felt like a flock of blue jays had taken flight inside her. "Is this a surprise party or something?" she asked once Alec stood next to her.

"Hi, I heard about Jonathan," he said and acknowledged everyone with nods of his head. He stooped to kiss Lori's cheek. "How are you? Is there anything I can do to help?"

"Yes." Ellie got out of her chair. "Sit here, young man. I need to go up front to see that my Jess isn't poisoning herself with all this bad food." She gave her daughter a fast look. "Close your mouth, Loretta, the flies will get in." She hurried down the aisle before Lori could think of anything to yell at her.

Lori folded her arms across her chest to hold her heart in. She wished herself home, in bed, with the door locked, the shades pulled down. She was smashing her heart against a wall.

"Do sit down," Margot said, giving Alec the once-over and rewarding him with a smile that showed she was pleased by what she saw. She introduced herself and the other women. Still standing, Alec said his name and shook everyone's hand. With the introductions over, he sat down in Ellie's chair, opposite Lori. He looked uncomfortable and immediately Lori wanted to offer comfort.

"I'm all right," she said. "Jess is happy, so I am. Thanks," Lori said. "How did you know I was here?"

"Your mother called Mrs. Ashe last night."

Lori was getting tired of surprises. "My mother?"

"Yes. I went over to Mrs. Ashe when I heard the news. Your mother called, but Mrs. Ashe had taken a sleeping pill and so I answered. She wanted Mrs. Ashe to know how sorry she was and wish her strength. A mother-to-mother thing, she said." He turned to look down the length of the diner. Angie and Jessica were listening to something Ellie was saying. "I thought it was pretty great of her. They don't know each other."

No one said anything. Lori gave him a weak smile. He moved his chair closer to the table and caught her gaze. He didn't seem uncomfortable, Lori noticed. She was the self-conscious one. "How did you know—"

He knew what she was about to say. "She gave her name, Corvino, and I asked if she knew a Lori Corvino. We had a long chat after that. That's how I knew you'd be here. I came in, saw that you were all busy talking so I spotted your daughter up front—she looks just like you. I waited until your mother gave me the go-ahead. I think your daughter's pretty special, too."

"So is Lori," Beth said easily.

"That I know."

Lori studied the scratched Formica, desperate to sink her face in a bowl of ice.

"I'm sorry if I interrupted something." Alec stood up. "Very nice meeting all of you. Take good care of her." He walked around the table and squeezed Lori's shoulder. "I'll call you later."

Lori nodded. She felt stupid, unable to say anything, wanting him to stay, to leave, not to be gay, to be gay because then he couldn't hurt her. But his being gay did hurt her. She was making no sense. Beth reached out and held her hand under the table.

"You're a breath of fresh air," Beth said to Alec, "and you haven't interrupted anything. You presence has surprised us, that's all."

"A pleasant surprise," Janet said. "We're tired of talking about murder."

"Thanks," Alec said and turned his gaze to Lori. "Talking about surprises, I tried to tell you on the phone, but you wouldn't let me." His eyes had a wicked smile in them. "My brother's full name was Christopher Robin Winters. My mother was a Pooh fan."

"Chris?" Lori managed to say. Her mouth had turned into the Gobi desert. "Your brother?"

Alec grinned. "None other."

Lori's first hiccup was loud enough to bring Ellie and Jessica running.

"Are you all right, Mom?"

"I'll get her a glass of water," Beth said.

"Done," Alec said, as the hiccups continued. He put a glass down on the table. "You have to stand up and drink it from the other side."

Lori looked at the full glass. She looked at Ellie grinning, at her friends. At Alec hovering over her. Between hiccups, Lori told herself that she didn't believe in fairy tales anymore, in happy-ever-after endings. There was still a lot of shoring up to be done. For all of them. And although Alec was here now, he might not be tomorrow. Now was what counted, though. That much she'd learned.

"I've never felt better," Lori said and went right on hiccupping.

ABOUT THE AUTHOR

Born in Prague to an Italian diplomat father and an American mother, **Camilla Crespi** came to the United States when she was twelve and returned to Italy after she graduated from Barnard College. In Rome she worked in the movie industry as a dubbing producer\director. Back in New York City she got married, received an MFA in creative writing from Columbia University, and became an American citizen.

Camilla has published seven novels in "The Trouble With" mystery series, and several short stories in mystery anthologies. In 2007, Soho Press published *The Price of Silence*, written under Camilla Trinchieri, her real name. The paperback edition and the Italian edition came out in 2008. *Finding Alice* was published in Italy in 2010 by MarcosyMarcos. *Gathering Pieces* will be published in Italy in 2014.